BLACK HEART OF THE RAVEN

STACEY DIGHTON

First published by Stacey Dighton (2025)

ISBN: 978-1-0369-6476-4

Cover illustration by:

James Merner (Instagram @shipwreckedbones_)

To all my loyal readers. This one’s for you.

PROLOGUE

'Come on, it's time.'

He hears the voice through a crackle of static. Shuffling, slipping, a metallic scrape. There are images too, scrambled like a jigsaw. Hazy light and garbled interference turn everything into a kaleidoscope of faded colours and inky shadows. His mind organises the pictures into a mosaic of shapes. There's a dark figure standing over a half-hidden mass on some sort of table or platform, but he's not certain. Perhaps there's a hand holding a knife, but maybe it's not a knife at all. There's a weird soundtrack of percussive jangling and wet footsteps. He doesn't know where he is. He is a dream within a vision, a dim light in a well of claustrophobic blackness. He doesn't belong here. The gut-wrenching isolation is terrifying, the persistent, gnawing dread, crippling. All he knows is, this is bad. This is all bad.

'Come on,' she repeats, dragging him from his nightmare. The dream holds on like a spoilt child. 'Breakfast.'

'But I'm not hungry.'

'Don't give me that crap. You're always hungry.'

She pulls him up by his elbow. He goes willingly. He throws on his raincoat (it's hammering down outside) and gets into the car. She barely looks at him. Today, she's more distracted than usual. That's not good. If she's not in the present, she's thinking about things she shouldn't.

He holds a hand to his left temple. His headaches have been worse this week. Sometimes they get so bad, he can barely think straight. Not that his thoughts have been particularly structured since… since… no, it's no good. He still can't remember.

'You can't be sleeping at the table like that,' she says. 'Not by the window.'

'I didn't mean to fall asleep.'

'I know.'

'I was just watching the rain.'

'I know that too, but you have to realise somebody might see you and that would be bad.'

He knows she doesn't like it if he doesn't give some sort of indication that he's listening, so he nods.

'You understand why it would be bad, right?'

'Because we're not supposed to be in the cottage.'

'You got it in one. The owners never come here, but even so, people like the Cartwrights — people who have more money than sense — they get all shitty if they find out people like us have been living in their second home, rent free.'

He thinks about that. He can only remember this cottage, the stone walls, the neatly painted wood-frame windows and the secluded muddy track that stretches half a mile from the main road.

'Fuckers,' he says. She laughs.

'Right. Fucking inbreds.'

The village is a ten-minute drive away, less if she puts her foot down. Today she's too distracted to push it more than forty. That's fine by him. When she breaks the speed limit, she's rarely in control.

They pull up beside the SPAR convenience shop. There's free parking until mid-day. The rain's coming down so hard it's made two distinct rivers either side of the road. He gets out and pulls up his hood, bracing himself against the wind and freezing rain.

'Come on,' she yells. 'I'm drowning to death out here.'

He runs around the back of the vehicle, his headache kicking his brains in, and ducks under the café's awning. They come here every day, or at least every day he can recall. *Matilda's*. The owner makes pretty good coffee, and the queue is regularly ten deep for the Lincolnshire sausage and black pudding baguette.

'Morning Fran,' Matilda says from inside a cloud of hot grease. 'How's your brother doing today?'

'A little better I think,' Fran (not her real name) replies in the Glaswegian accent she never uses at home. 'Has his good days and bad, you know?'

'Och, the poor thing. I've got his food on the go. Shouldn't be too long.'

'Thanks, Matty. Sometimes I think breakfast at your place is the highlight of his day.'

'I'll take that as a complement.'

He sits at their usual table: at the back by the toilet. Fran-not-Fran doesn't like him sitting near the window here either. His stomach gurgles at the smell of bangers sizzling. He sizes up his paunch. He thinks he's put on weight but can't be sure. He feels heavier than usual. Fran-not-Fran says the extra meat looks good on him. Each time she says that, he wonders what she really means.

They sit in silence, watching the villagers come and go. Matilda's is the go-to place for the locals, not that there's a wealth of choice. The meagre high street is home to a café, the shop, a cluttered indoor market, and a pub. The pub always looks welcoming, but Fran-not-Fran says it's a 'shithole.'

The coffee arrives, followed shortly afterwards by his sandwich. It's the size of his forearm and just as thick. Fran-not Fran doesn't eat. She never does. She just sits there, sipping her coffee and watching. He tries to mask his thoughts but can't help thinking about the little yellow pills she gives him daily; the isolation up there in the hills; his nightmares.

'Your scar's looking better,' she says. 'You can barely see it now.'

He knows she's being kind. It's the one thing he notices when he stares in the mirror, the grotesque indentation in his forehead and the misshapen patch on the left side of his head where no hair ever grows.

'I'll be going out later,' she continues. 'Got some errands to run. You'll be okay at home by yourself, won't you?'

He nods, wiping grease from the corner of his mouth.

'You won't do anything you shouldn't?'

He shakes his head.

'And you know what to do if anyone comes snooping?'

'Hide in the basement. Lock the door.'

'That's right. And why is that?'

'Because people don't understand us. Because they'll try to take me away.'

She smiles. She thinks it makes him feel calm, but instead it makes him want to run and never look back.

'You know I'll always take care of you,' she says. 'I'll never let anybody hurt you.'

'Thank you.'

'You know, you were in a dark place before the event, a place where people were taking advantage of you. I put a stop to that.'

'I know.'

'One day, you'll come to realise how good this has been for you, this time away from everything.'

'It's helped me find myself.'

'Exactly. That's right. You were lost before me, but for some reason you couldn't see it.'

'I see it now.'

She reaches across the table and runs a finger down the uneven landscape of his scar. He fights the urge to pull his head away. Instead, he focusses on the mottled remains of the wound on the side of her face, the long crevice that runs down her right cheek.

She thinks it's invisible, but no scars are invisible, even the ones beneath the surface.

'I'm done,' he says, dabbing his lips with a napkin.

'Good boy. You ate it all up as always.'

She settles the bill, tipping well like she usually does, and they head back out into the rainstorm. It's even heavier now. The drive home is treacherous with visibility reduced to no more than fifteen feet. Fran-not-Fran's mood has improved at the wrong time, and she speeds along the narrow country lane as if the sun's out and the top's down (although there's no top to be down. Fran-not-Fran drives a hatchback).

Back in the relative safety of the cottage, she heads upstairs while he slumps on the sofa. His head is really pounding now. He closes his eyes and tries to shut out his thoughts. He's been having so many lately. There are the dreams that come to him in staccato form, as if he's viewing everything on an old analogue TV with a flaky signal. They're bad enough, but the visions that come to him through the day can be worse. There's the man with the grey beard; he hates him. Then there's the woman with red hair and a sharp voice; she means something to him but he's not sure what. Finally, there's the young boy: pink cheeks, blonde locks. When he thinks of him it's like his heart is being crushed.

He's in a light sleep within minutes, in a state of REM moments later. His dream comes at him through the darkness, like a carcass clawing its way from the grave. This time, he's looking down on the bare chest of what he's now sure is a dead body. The knife he wasn't sure was a knife is a scalpel. He wants to vomit. Through the haze, he hears himself retching. The scalpel prods at the flesh, tentatively at first. He notices the fingers holding the knife. The nails are painted black. The hand prods with the scalpel again, but now the movement is much more deliberate, forceful. Blood seeps from a small wound, tiny rivers of dark red. He tries to escape his nightmare, but the exit eludes him. The wound is elongated now, deeper too. He sees the layers of skin, the raw meat peeling away from grey bone. Something moves. Another hand grasps the knife, pushing it away. It isn't a dead body after all. Whoever's lying there, they're alive. A face comes into view, a young man. He's screaming. There's a bruise on his cheek and dried blood on his scalp. The wound in his chest is deep, too deep. Sticky red leeches from it like tar. The two fight, but the young man is weak and his attacker is armed. The scene becomes a tangled mess. Among the sea of blood covered skin and flailing limbs he catches a glimpse of the perpetrator but can only make out one thing: a tattoo on the upper shoulder; an inky depiction of a sea horse. The attacker reaches into the young man's body while the victim screams and thrashes. There's another struggle, this one even more violent. Eventually, the victim turns limp, his eyes rolling back into his head. The arm retracts, the hand holding something fleshy and pink. With a sickening revulsion he realises it's a heart, pulled from the body like fish guts. It beats within the tightly clenched fingers, blood oozing from torn arteries that hang flaccid and uneven. The killer turns to face him, but the reception falters and everything becomes a sea of hissing static once more.

*

He opens his eyes. Somehow, between the moment they returned from the café and the moment he awoke from his nightmare, he's made it to the cellar. There's a small window that used to be a coal chute, but now it's nothing but old green glass. The exterior of the window is covered in thick moss and dark smears. He can see just enough to know it's evening. There's barely any light in the cellar, and just enough air to breathe. The place stinks. He knows it's where she keeps all the meat. There's plenty. The freshest of it hangs from hooks that dangle from overhead joists, waiting to be butchered. The rest is in two deep freezers placed against the rear wall.

The dream is still with him, but now the boy with the blonde hair is in the cellar too. The kid tells him to sit down, so he does. In truth, he barely has the strength to stand. His head hurts so bad, he can't concentrate on anything else. The kid sits beside him but then he's gone, and then there's a guy with pale skin and dark eyes. His face looks like the surface of the moon with craters and deep crevices.

He shakes his head and the visions disappear. His head continues to pound. He peers into the gloom and senses something glaring back at him. There's a huffing snort like a bull, and something heavy hits the ground. He drifts away again, but not before she's with him, a ghost lady with short blonde hair. She reaches for him as she falls backward, tumbling down a set of stairs that don't exist in his reality. She lands at the bottom, her neck unnaturally twisted. She looks up at him, her lips covered in blood and spit bubbles. She laughs.

'I'm home,' Fran-not-Fran says. 'Time for bed.'

'I was asleep.'

'You can't sleep down here. It's not the place for that.'

He guesses it's late, or maybe it's very early, because there's even less light coming through the green window now.

'Where have you been?'

'Fewer questions, more action. Come on, I've still got a lot of work to get done. I can't do anything with you in the way.'

'I can help.'

'You can't help me in your condition. You're not strong enough.'

He climbs the stairs to the hallway. Fran-not-Fran barges past him into the kitchen.

'You want tea? Maybe that'll help you sleep.'

He declines. He still feels like he wants to throw up.

'Suit yourself. Now, if you wouldn't mind.' She eyes the staircase to the first floor. 'You know where your room is.'

He heads towards the foot of the stairs, but there's a tap on the door. He gasps. Fran-not-Fran jerks towards it. He watches her. She's anxious.

There's another tap, this one a little louder.

'Cellar,' she hisses. 'Now.'

He stands there, not knowing what to do. Nobody has ever come to the cottage before.

'*Get to the fucking cellar.*'

He backs away, slinking into the darkness of the doorway, but he doesn't pull it all the way closed. Fran-not-Fran wipes her small hands down her jeans and reaches for the handle. A crack of moonlight seeps in as she peers outside.

'Hello. Can I help you?'

She staggers back into the hallway as the door swings inwards. At first, he thinks there's nobody there, but then Fran-not-Fran steps to the side. The woman at the door is in a wheelchair. She has long dark hair and skin the colour of milk. He immediately recognises her but can't recall where from. He notices something else too, something missing. Her legs end at her thighs.

'How did you find me?' Fran-not-Fran asks.

'Not easily,' the woman replies. Her voice is calm.

'I didn't want to be found.'

'I'm afraid you gave up the right of anonymity when you killed all those people.'

Fran-not Fran doesn't reply.

'No-one deserves what you did to them.'

'I beg to differ.'

He listens from the doorway, trying to piece together what he's hearing. The woman he's been living with, the woman who everybody in the village believes to be his sister, is a murderer. How has he let that little bone-chilling fact pass him by?

The chairbound woman studies the inside of the cottage. 'Nice place. Is it yours?'

'Why the fuck are you here?'

'I came to put things right. I made this mess and it's only right that I clean it up.'

'Is that what I am to you? A mess?'

'You've become one, yes, but I still believe you can be saved.'

Another laugh. 'You've got some nerve coming all this way just to spout this crap. If anyone needs saving, it's you. You abandoned me.'

'I know, and I want to make it right?'

'By taking me to the police?'

'If I have to.'

'I won't come.'

'I'll make you.'

'And how are you going to do that? By dragging me behind your wheelchair?'

'I was hoping you'd come voluntarily.'

'You don't know me at all.'

'I'm only too aware of that, but I plan to. I want to find out everything about you, Molly.'

Something clicks in his head like a latch disengaging. Not Fran but Molly. Images come at him like bullets. The bodies in the cave, the creature beneath the mansion, the rain falling, the young woman with wild hair raising a handgun, pulling the trigger.

Her mother, Lorna (he now remembers her name) spies him over her daughter's shoulder, and recognition sparkles in her eyes. He holds a finger to his lips, but the action causes fresh pain in his temples. The memories have created a new headache, a tsunami of a skull cruncher. He holds his hand to the wall, stops himself from falling.

'You want to know what I've been up to while I've been hiding away?' Molly says. 'You really want to know how unredeemable your daughter is?'

Her mother's belligerent demeanour falters. 'If you feel like sharing.'

Molly heads outside, rushing past Lorna's chair while thumbing the key fob to her cherry-red VW Golf. He heads to the doorway, his legs like melted butter beneath him. He can barely keep his eyes open.

Molly opens the boot and reaches inside. She pulls out a black plastic sack and tosses it to the ground.

'You're sure about this?' she asks.

Her mother eyes the bulging bag. 'I said I want to know everything, so show me everything.'

'Okay, whatever. Don't say I didn't warn you.'

Molly opens the bag and pulls out an arm, severed at the shoulder. The sleeve of the victim's shirt still clings to the limb, as does a Fitbit watch and leather bracelet.

'Oh my God,' Lorna says.

'Oh wait, Mum, there's more.' Molly pulls out another bag, this one full of intestines, and tosses it at her. It lands on Lorna's lap, splitting open and spilling a stomach sac and lower colon all over her dress and jacket.

'Enough,' Lorna cries, heaving.

'Enough? Really? You don't want to see the head? Because I always keep those. The brain really is the best part. It's like a thick mousse but with a touch more bite.'

That's enough for her mum. The dry retch becomes a wet belch, and then whatever she ate for lunch comes up in one sloppy mess, spilling all over the chair and driveway.

'Oops,' Molly says. 'Too much? Did I over share?'

'I thought the time you'd had away would have given you some perspective,' Lorna says, another soggy heave threatening. 'Some time to realise what you'd done.'

'Nah,' Molly replies. 'Just gave me time to improve my methods.'

'And what about him?' Lorna asks, pointing towards the open door. He's exposed now and that terrifies him. He's been hidden for so long. 'What were your plans with him?'

'Wasn't sure,' Molly says. 'Thought about killing him too, but I kind of like having him around. When he didn't die from the bullet wound, I decided to keep him. He's a bit pathetic, but compliant, like a little doggy. Keeps me company.'

Lorna looks at him, and he knows then that she's lost all hope. The daughter she came to save is no longer there. The Molly she knew only as a toddler is now a fully grown woman, capable of doing things most normal people wouldn't ever contemplate.

'Go back in your hole, Raven,' Molly says. 'Go on, run away. Mummy and I have some serious talking to do.'

Raven. Another name that unlatches a lock. Luke Raven, that's who he once was. He used to be somebody. A police officer — no, a detective — but then something happened, something that sent the person he once was into a deep, dark hole.

'I'll think I'll stay right here,' he says, but the pain in his head is so bad now, he can barely see.

'Suit yourself,' Molly says and pulls a gun from the black sack. 'I guess this is where it all ends, Mum.'

'I guess it does,' Lorna replies. She's crying now, tears that trickle slowly.

'Don't do this, Molly,' Raven says. 'She's your mother.'

'I think we're beyond family loyalty now, don't you agree Mummy?'

Lorna wipes her eyes with the back of her hand. Raven feels a pang of tumbling emotions. Molly was never going to give up who she is, and that realisation is finally dawning on her mother.

'I'll take that as an agreement,' Molly says. 'Sometimes bad situations are just bad situations, and this is about as fucked up as they get.'

'We can make it right,' Raven offers. 'There's ways to solve this.'

'Doesn't need solving,' Molly hisses. 'It needs culling.'

She walks toward her mother, her gun aimed at her forehead.

'I'll kill her,' she continues. 'Then I'll kill you. Except this time, I'll do it properly.'

He staggers towards her, arms outstretched. 'You need help, Molly, and I can get it for you.'

'Really? You? Look at yourself, Raven. You can barely walk on your own two feet. You're not who you used to be. You're just a shadow these days, a faded water colour that people barely see. How do you think I've been able to keep you hidden for so long? Because nobody cares. Nobody gives two shits about a has-been, alcoholic ex-detective who can't think straight.'

There's another shard of pain that drives Raven to his knees. He grips the arm of Lorna's chair and tries to stand, but he falls down again, slumping onto his elbows while warm drool spills from his lips. He feels the muzzle of the gun pressed to the back of his head. She's right. This time she won't miss. She can't. A part of him wants it all to end.

'Looks like you jumped the queue,' Molly says, and he senses her finger slipping over the trigger. 'You can go first. Don't take it personally, Luke. It's been fun having you around.'

He braces himself for the bullet. This is it. No more nightmares, no more headaches.

There's a loud crack and a blinding pain that drives him to the ground. He lies there expecting everything to disappear — the visions, the debilitating pain, the fractured memories — but they're still there, scratching away at him like a family of mice.

He slowly raises his head, certain that he'll find his blood and skull fragments on the ground. There's a growing red puddle, but it's not coming from him. It's coming from Molly. She's lying on the gravel between her mother and the car, and she's not breathing. There's a hole in the upper right side of her chest the size of a tomato.

He smells the familiar scent of a discharged firearm and peers up at Lorna. The gun trembles in the pale woman's fingers, and she looks down in horror at the crumpled body of her daughter. Raven notices the hem of Lorna's dress raised where the gun was hidden.

'Molly,' she says as her voice breaks.

Raven tries to stand. 'I'm sorry. Sorry for your loss and sorry you had to do that.'

'I killed my little girl.'

'She left you no choice.'

Lorna doesn't hear him. She's still staring at the gradually growing pool of blood beneath Molly's corpse. Her lips tremble, her eyes glistening like tiny pools.

'Do you have a phone?' Raven asks. 'I need to call the police.'

Lorna reaches into the side pocket of her chair and pulls out an old Samsung. She unlocks it and tosses it to him. Raven holds it up to see if it has a signal — one bar, which he thinks should be enough. He tries to focus on the keypad which is a jumbled sea of shapeless digits.

'You say I had no choice, Raven,' Lorna whispers. 'But you're wrong. I had a choice more than twenty years ago when I decided to walk out on the one thing in my life I did right, and that single, heartbreaking decision is what led us all to this place, with my Molly lying in the dirt with all that blood pouring out of her.'

Raven hits dial and holds the phone to his ear, but before there's an answer, he lets it fall.

'Lorna, *no!*'

Molly's mother bites down on the muzzle of the gun and looks up at Raven, pupils like polished onyx. Her trembling finger hovers in mid-air for a fraction of a second more, and in that moment, he sees the resemblance with her daughter. He's barely made it three feet before Lorna Hanscombe, once cruelly dubbed Loony Lorna, closes her eyes and pulls the trigger.

The loud crack sends his senses reeling, and his mind becomes a white flare of blinding agony. He loses consciousness for a few minutes, maybe longer. When he looks up, Lorna is slumped forward, the rear of her head missing, blood, skull and brains on the headrest. He clambers towards her, grabs the wheel of the chair, but he knows it's a waste of time. Lorna is dead. Dead and gone, just like her daughter.

He turns to Molly's slowly decaying corpse, but only gore-soaked gravel remains. She's gone too. He looks for drag marks, signs a hungry animal may have taken her, but there's nothing. He wonders whether she was ever really there.

He forces himself to his feet and scours the ground for Lorna's phone. He needs to tell someone, anyone.

He's Luke Raven, detective with the West Hampshire Constabulary, and contrary to public perception, he's still very much alive.

PART 1: HOMECOMING

"Many a time have I pursued the phantom: never with this man's stride of mine to come up with it, never with these man's hands of mine to touch it, never more to this man's heart of mine to hold it in its purity."

Charles Dickens – The Haunted House

CHAPTER 1: SWEETHEART

'That'll be £44.50, sir,' Kaden Chapman says, handing over the Orca kiteboard fin and noticing how the middle-aged customer's tight-fitting wetsuit barely contains his overhanging paunch.

'Is that it?' the executive boardroom surfer replies, tapping his Mastercard. 'That's not bad. Cheaper than online.'

'Here at In Our Wake we pride ourselves on offering the best deals to all our customers, whether they're boarders, sailors or just ocean enthusiasts.'

'That sounds like a line you've used a lot.'

'I'm afraid so. Do you like it?'

The guy smiles. He has more teeth than a teasing comb but not as neatly spaced. 'Well, it worked on me. Next time I'm in town, I'll be back. In the meantime, sweetheart, have a great day.'

'Thank you so much,' Kaden replies. 'Have a great day yourself.'

He watches the customer depart with his new purchase tucked under his arm and wonders where the fuck the guy gets off calling him sweetheart. *Sweetheart*, as if he has a heart to be sweet on. Kaden thinks about going after him and smashing his head against the pavement repeatedly until the twat sees the error of his ways, but he knows it's pointless. Men like him have brains the size of edamame beans and dicks like rolled ham.

He checks himself in the mirror just to be sure. He's pulled his dark, blue-dipped hair back in a tight ponytail and slipped on a Saltrock vest that exposes his toned arms. The combat shorts he chose to complement the rest of the ensemble hang just above the knee, revealing his muscular calves and thick ankles. He's finished the ensemble off with cherry red Doc Marten boots. If the guy can't get his sexual denomination from all those clues, then he really is as blind as he is stupid.

'I'm clocking off in ten,' he yells, tidying a rack of men's swimming shorts while checking his reflection in the fitting room mirror. 'Remember? I have that thing tonight?'

His boss, Winston Carter, pokes his head through the narrow office doorway. 'The party? Yeah, I remember. Just make sure you're back in at 7.30 in the morning. No hangover, and definitely no throwing up.'

'When was the last time you saw me vomit?'

'Christmas 2023, just outside Gold Diggers nightclub, remember? I still have the photo on my phone.'

That ill-fated evening had been a mistake on Kaden's part, a night out he'd sworn never to repeat. 'I assume we have no Carl?'

'Nah, he's still suffering from man flu. Could be out for a while.'

No shit, Kaden thinks. *That lazy prick will string it out for as a long as possible.* 'No problem. I'll be here by 7.15, just to be sure.'

'That's what I like about you, Kaden. You're as reliable as a Rolex and just as easy on the eye.'

Kaden feigns embarrassment, hiding his face behind his hands. 'You know I don't like it when you say things like that.'

'I'm only speaking the truth. If that makes me a bad guy, so be it.'

As he disappears into the back office, Kaden stands there, air escaping through clenched teeth. He's worked for Winston for a little over eighteen months and hated him with a growing sense of spite for a little less. The guy is a misogynistic sexual predator who's in denial of his own sexuality. That in itself is bad enough, but what makes Kaden despise him even more — so much more than the customers who look at him like he's some kind of sideshow freak — is Winston's obvious sense of self-entitlement.

He thinks everybody is in awe of him and therefore obligated to put up with his sycophantic bullshit.

He takes a moment to compose himself before gathering his things, checking his hair in the mirror one more time before raising his middle finger at the back of his boss's head.

'I'll see you tomorrow.'

'You sure will,' Winston calls back. 'Just don't do anything I wouldn't do.'

I can't promise that, you fucking hypocrite, he thinks, allowing himself a satisfied smirk as he steps outside.

He stands with his backpack slung over his shoulder and looks out towards the ocean. The seafront is filled with holiday makers as far as the eye can see. That gives him tingles. It isn't even the height of the season yet. When the real summertime kicks in, the whole town will be filled shoulder to shoulder with tourists from all over the country, particularly with this being the two-hundred-year anniversary of the launching of the ill-fated Black Mare from the port of Fisherman's Catch. With the town set to have the biggest celebration in its history, every grain of sand will be covered bumper to bumper with beach towels, deckchairs and windbreaks, the whole beachfront buried beneath a sea of warm bodies from here to Annie's Cove. It's perfect for what he has planned, because when he's done with Westhampton, nobody will be in any doubt about who Kaden Chapman is ever again.

CHAPTER 2: HOW MANY BODIES?

Raven steps off the bus and retrieves his bag from the dilapidated vehicle's storage compartment. He stretches his back, looks up at the sky and breathes in the sea air. He hadn't realised how much he'd missed it.

The sky overhead is overcast, and the wind is buffeting, but that doesn't matter to him. What matters is he's home again, even if he doesn't know what sort of home Westhampton is to him anymore.

He walks towards town, marvelling at how little the place has changed. The train station is still covered in graffiti and used gum, the drive-thru MacDonalds still has a queue that stretches out onto the main road, causing traffic mayhem, and the local Wetherspoons still has the same old guys perched by the window, sipping breakfast beers and eating their body weight in fatty bacon and plasticised eggs.

He hasn't called ahead. He didn't think it was fair. As far as anybody that cares about him is concerned, he's been dead for almost four years. In that time, he would have been mourned, the grief would have subsided, and his memory would have been laid to rest. If he's going to have any sort of life with the people he's left behind, his son included, he will have to announce his continuing existence in person.

When the police had shown up at the cottage that night, he'd barely been conscious. The blood clot in his head had been slowly working its way toward his cerebral cortex. Another hour or so and there would have been two people lying there dead in the dirt, not one. What followed was a series of operations to stem the bleeding and relieve the pressure on his brain, and then an induced coma that lasted for almost a month. If the nightmares in the Scottish Highlands had been bad, the ones he had during those four weeks of enforced sleep were another level. He awoke thinking Molly Staker was right there, sitting on his chest, attempting to slice him up into thin cuts of beige steak. Two doctors and three nurses had held him down while they'd tried to get the sedatives into his veins.

It hadn't taken long for the detective in charge of the case, a stubby barrel of a man named McGoughlan, to identify Lorna Hanscombe, mother of Molly Staker, a.k.a. The Hawk. Once he'd made those connections, he'd turned up at Raven's bedside with a newspaper clipping in hand.

'This is you, isn't it?' he'd said, pointing at a picture of a police cordon around the driveway of a large house. The caption read, *Police Detective responsible for solving the Pale Faced Killer investigation missing after shooting at Staker Mansion.*

'I can't remember,' Raven replied, but in truth, things were coming back.

'It's you alright. I ran the facial recognition software on a photograph we took while you were under, and apart from that hole in your head, it came back a match. You're Luke Raven, former DI with the Westhampton police force.'

Raven shrugged. 'Well, if your machine says that's who I am, I guess it must be true.'

'You've been missing for a long time.'

'What's the date today?' he asked.

'Thursday 8th May.'

'What year?'

'2025.'

He noted the date at the top of the newspaper clipping. August 2021. A little under four years of his life stolen from him and he hadn't even noticed.

'Doctor says you're lucky to still be with us,' McGoughlan said. 'Said that blood clot has been in your brain ever since the shooting. Could have switched off your lights at any time.'

Maybe it would have done me a favour, Raven thought.

'He was also surprised how the girl, Staker, had kept the wound from becoming infected. Seems she knew what she was doing.'

'Yeah, she knew what she was doing alright,' Raven said, thinking about the drugs she'd been slipping him while convincing his ketamine sedated brain that he was her crippled brother.

'How many bodies?' he asked.

'Seven in total. Three men, four women. It's going to take a while to ID them all. There's a few bits… missing.'

Raven's stomach flipped. He thought about the meals he'd shared with Molly, the meat he'd consumed. He'd never questioned what she was serving or why the freezers had always been filled to bursting.

'Have you found her?'

'Who?'

'Molly. I told the dispatcher this when I made the call. She's still alive.'

'I'm aware, but from the dark blood on the driveway, her mother got her pretty good. We're looking for a body, but the landscape up there is vast and difficult to navigate. It could take us a few weeks.'

'You need to throw everyone you have at it, Detective. Molly Staker is dangerous. Smart, too.'

McGoughlan scribbled in his book and offered a barely comforting smile. 'Trust me, Raven. If she's alive, we'll find her. Now, about the small matter of your being in the land of the living. The office has made a list of all the people we need to inform about your whereabouts, starting with your next of kin: a woman named Lisa Clancy. Is that right?'

The name had been on the tip of Raven's tongue for months and in his mind for even longer. Red hair, tattoo on the side of a slim hand, pierced nose and lip. Every time he thinks about her it's like someone is punching him in the spleen. He knows he made a mess of things before he went away, a mess that he'd repeated too many times. He's been out of Lisa's life for almost half a decade, and perhaps that's a good thing. For her, anyway.

'No,' he replied. 'Don't tell anyone. I'd rather break the news myself.'

McGoughlan's brow hung heavy over his eyes. 'You know you could be in here for a few days yet. Surely you want the people you left behind to know you're safe and well.'

'I do, but not like this.'

What he'd really meant was that he didn't want to be the one to mess up whatever new life Lisa and their son had made for themselves, not until he had a chance to find out what had happened since he'd gone away. The last time he'd seen Lisa, Molly Staker had been standing there with their son in her arms and a gun at her head. He'd caused that. If he finds out that the life Lisa and Harry has now is a much safer, more secure existence, then he plans to walk away and never return, no matter how hard that will be.

He hitches his bag and pulls up his collar against the bracing wind, knowing that his whole future depends on what happens at his next stop, and thanks to Facebook and a little internet stalking, he knows exactly where that will be. He just hopes Billy West remembers his face.

CHAPTER 3: ANGELS

Lisa Clancy remembers the days and months after her partner's abduction with about the same clarity as the morning she'd woken with her head in the toilet, eyes bloodshot and mouth tasting like the inside of a rabbit hutch after she'd consumed three quarters of a bottle of Sambuca. To say it's a blur is like saying the works of Pablo Picasso are a little abstract.

She'd stood there in the rain on the driveway of the Staker house, watching that crazy bitch's white Corsa disappearing into the mist, not knowing whether the father of her child was alive or dead in the boot of that car. From that moment on, she became a spectator to the movie of her life, watching from someplace else as she was interviewed by the police, she and Harry were examined by the doctors, and the media descended on her home like a pack of hyenas.

As the days passed by in a mosaic of colours and fractured images, she'd heard people talking about the shootout at Bernie Staker's beachside property and the final confrontation in the mansion, along with the discovery of the bodies of Staker himself, his right-hand man, Robert Charon, and that psycho of a DCS, Christy Deveraux. Nobody could make sense of what had gone down, which is why everyone was so keen to talk to her. The DI, Randall Kipruto, fielded a lot of the questions, but it had been Lisa who had cornered Deveraux, forced her into taking her to Staker's home, and had watched while Molly had shot her own father point black in the face. She was the only one who had all the facts, and so she was the one who faced the desperate clamour for the bloody truth.

The local press seemed to want to take her apart piece by piece which she battled hard to prevent, but that didn't stop them from camping out on her doorstep, surrounding her as she tried to get to the shops, posting questions through her letterbox and constantly calling and texting.

All Lisa was interested in was where Luke was, but all the press seemed to want to know was what had happened during the final second of Bernie Staker's life, and what it was like to watch his brain explode like a roman candle of red meat and skull fragments.

Randall had led the search for Luke, and he kept her updated daily, but as the days turned into weeks, and the weeks turned into months, the regularity of his updates dwindled to once every fortnight and eventually stopped altogether. It wasn't his fault. Molly Staker was a smart young woman, and she'd covered her tracks like a highly trained mercenary.

While the DI's communications slowed down to a crawl, his partner and girlfriend, Ruby Cropper, was more stubborn in her approach. She came to Lisa's new flat weekly, to talk mostly, but sometimes to stay for dinner. Luke had been one of the team after all, and that meant something. Ruby was a good cook and brought pasta bakes, shepherd's pie, and even some pretty decent curries, but Lisa hadn't been the best friend to her. She resented everybody for their failure to find Luke, and eventually her lack of patience and ability to fire off snarky comments like bullets drove Ruby away.

On the first anniversary of Luke's disappearance, Lisa had taken Harry to his grandfather, Sam Raven's grave. Sam had been another victim of the beachside shootout, fighting off Bernie Staker and Robert Charon to help Lisa and Harry escape. It had been a selfless act of heroism that she would never forget. Sam had been a shit father to his son, but he'd helped her rescue Harry, and while that might never erase the years of hurt he'd imposed on his own child, she missed him.

She and Harry had stood at the graveside holding hands while the tears fell. Lisa felt so alone. Luke hadn't been the best boyfriend to her, but she'd never been able to shake her feelings for him. If it was true that love was blind, then their relationship was a desperate fumble in the dark. It was exciting but familiar. It was dangerous but it made her feel safe. Luke was all the things she didn't want but everything she needed. She wanted him back.

By the second anniversary of his disappearance, Lisa's waning hope was put to the test. Harry was at nursery by this time and Lisa had taken a full-time job at the café in town just to cover the increasing costs of looking after a growing son. There had been the occasional alleged sightings of Molly Staker in the Midlands and the North-West, but none of the leads had come to anything.

One day, DI Kipruto turned up at her flat to give her the news she'd been dreading. The police were standing down the team assigned to look for Luke. They weren't closing the case exactly, but the resources were being reallocated. Lisa had cried for two whole days: tears of remorse, but a lot of angry tears too. Every molecule in her body wanted to find Molly Staker and show her just how angry she was. That rage never went away, not really. It just covered her skin like eczema, treatable but never completely cured.

Months later when some true-crime crackpot bloke showed up at the café claiming to be her missing lover, Lisa lost her shit and attacked him with a pot of hot tea. She earned a charge of aggravated assault for her troubles and lost her job. She hadn't been surprised. It had been coming. The boss of the café was a stickler for timekeeping and not particularly tolerant of a single mother who sometimes got stuck in traffic while dropping her son off at school. The guy she attacked dropped the aggravated assault charge, but her landlord didn't drop the rent. After four months of no payments, she was kicked out. Broke and with nowhere to go, Lisa had been on the verge of falling on her hands and knees at the local homeless shelter and begging for food-bank handouts. They say angels come in all shapes and sizes, and the angel who had shown up at Lisa's door was somebody who owed Luke Raven her life, not once but twice — the former girlfriend of Tony Richards, a.k.a. The Pale Faced Killer, and a woman who had been kidnapped by Richard's psychotic father, Robert Charon, and left to rot in a cell beneath the maniac's so-called Church like a prisoner on death row.

Her name was Jane Butler.

CHAPTER 4: GHOSTS

Billy West stands at the window, thinking about the life choices he's made, wondering why it always rains when he has a day off. The dark clouds cast an inky shadow on everything that's been playing on his mind. Sally, his wife, has been going on at him about his non-existent retirement plan, and although he's starting to think that perhaps he should look into some sort of private pension, it's the memory of Luke Raven that keeps gnawing at him. It's true, the two men had never been good friends, not in the way Billy had been close to his old neighbour-cum-serial killer, Tony Richards, but during the build up to the Staker incident, he and Raven had formed a kind of dysfunctional bond. Even though the ex-copper had always been a closed book and hard to like, he hadn't deserved what had happened to him.

The whole thing was as fucked up as drinking vodka on ice during the daytime, but right now, that's exactly what Billy is doing, treating the gap in his usually hectic schedule as a pseudo cocktail hour, forcing the memories into the shadows like a vampire with social anxiety.

It's when he's standing there, feeling the burn of the cold alcohol as it slips down his gullet, that he sees the dead man come walking along the road with a sodden bag slung over one shoulder and a jacket that clearly isn't up to the job.

At first he thinks he's seeing things. As far as he knows, the guy is still missing, presumed murdered by the woman they called The Hawk. He approaches the window just to get a better look, but the rain is coming down so hard, he can barely see through the glass. He almost writes it off as a trick of the mind, some hallucination brought on by wilfully feeding his vices in the afternoon, but there's something about the way the guy is walking that triggers a memory. The slight shuffle with the right leg and the way the shoulders roll as he walks. The guy's face is different but the same: the determined glare, the half-snarl on his lips, the week-old black and grey beard.

He grabs his coat and heads out into the downpour, hardly feeling the rain as it soaks through his cargo shorts and socks. As he runs down the road, he thinks about that last night in the Staker mansion, the way the bullet from Molly's gun had whistled past his left ear. There were two things he had learned about himself that night. The first was that he had bravery in his makeup, even though Sally told him it was nothing more than inherent stupidity, and the other was that he was lighter on his feet than he gave himself credit for. If he'd been a fraction of a second slower, he would have wound up as dead as that girl's father, which was pretty fucking dead. He uses that lightness of foot now, covering the ground quickly, creating puddle tsunamis as he races to catch up with the man he thought had gone the way of Richey from the Manics.

He heads down the street, certain that the guy couldn't have made it more than a hundred yards, but even though he arrives at the corner of the road in less than a minute, he's nowhere to be seen.

He stands there, hands on his hips, blowing hard, before deciding to head up Harris Crescent, thinking he may have taken the cut-through toward Lisa's old place (how was the father of her child to know she'd moved?), but he can't see him. He tries the alleyway between the back gardens along Oak Road and Sycamore Lane, but there's no sign. He even heads across the playground, wondering if that's where he was headed after all, the old disused building that used to serve as Westhampton Police Station, but the place is deserted. By this time, his legs are shaking and his feet are about as wet as a fish in a synchronised swimming contest, so he heads back home.

Maybe he was wrong. Perhaps he'd been seeing things after all. Maybe he should give up the vodka and weed and switch to one of those new zero brands everyone's raving about (yeah, right) and a CBD vape (even less likely), but when he gets inside, his doubts evaporate.

The guy stands there in his kitchen, the rainwater pouring from his crumpled jacket like some internal pipe has burst. His salt and pepper hair is a little more salt than pepper these days, he's a bit thicker around the middle, but he has the same heavy brow and awkward smile.

It's Raven alright, alive and almost kicking, risen from the grave like Lazarus in faded jeans and old trainers. The only thing is, his head looks weird.

CHAPTER 5: PHALLUS

'You'd better wake up. Hey, you'd better get your arse out of bed before my girlfriend comes home.'

The voice is like crumpled paper, the smell like stale body odour mixed with too many fags. He tries to pull the covers up over his head to blot out the stench and nullify the paltry daylight, but his persistent intruder yanks them back, snatching the sheets from his hands and tossing them to the floor.

'I *said* you need to get out of here.'

Kaden sits up, taking in the sight of his latest mistake. Shaved head, piercing through his lower lip, ear stretchers like basketball hoops. The guy is wearing white boxers, sports socks and nothing else.

'Are you sure we spent the night together?' Kaden asks, wondering why he would go home with this skinny slip of bone and skin.

'Well you're in my bed, darling. You do the maths.'

'I'm nobody's darling, fuck face. Would you call one of your mates that?'

'You ain't a mate. You're just some bird.'

Kaden hisses at him. 'Well, fuck you very much. And, anyway, I'm not a bird.'

Skinny Ribs points to Kaden's crotch. 'That begs to differ.'

'A person's sex isn't governed by biology, arsehole. Haven't you read the news?'

Kaden gets up, grabs his underwear from the mess the guy calls his bedroom floor, and slips them over his slim buttocks. Beside the desk lies a bottle of cheap whiskey upended beside a packet of condoms that has seen better days. The top of the carton is ripped open, the box emptied.

'Look,' Skinny Ribs, real name Ollie, says. 'We had fun last night, a lot of fun, but I have a girlfriend, and she's due back from her nightshift in around fifteen minutes.'

'Don't worry,' Kaden replies churlishly. 'I won't tell if you won't.'

'Are you smiling? This isn't funny.'

'No, but that is.'

He points to the strap on dildo lying beside the guy's PC base-station.

'You say anything to anyone, you cunt, and I'll cut you.'

Kaden closes the distance between them in an instant, jabbing his recently adhered purple acrylic fingernails into the guy's throat, drawing a slim smear of blood. 'You could try, my little limp-dicked friend, but I don't fancy your chances.' He slips his other hand between the guy's legs, clamps his testicles, and squeezes. Ollie lets out a sharp squeal. 'You understand what I'm saying, right?'

'Right.'

'You were happy enough to let me shove that thing up your arse last night, weren't you?'

'I was.'

'So just because you've woken up with a bad dose of hetro-confusion, don't take it out on me.'

'Got it. I won't.'

Kaden releases his grip slowly, watching the guy's chewed up face relax like a squash ball regaining its shape. He likes it, relishes the control he has over this prick. People always take him for a pushover, just because he looks the way he does. It's their mistake, not his, a mistake he likes to exploit. People are arseholes. Most of them anyway. He's rarely surprised by his low expectations.

'We did have fun,' Kaden says, pulling on his jeans. 'But don't go getting any ideas. This was a one-time thing.'

'I just told you, I have a girlfriend.'

'And a lucky girl she is, too.'

He ties his boots, checks himself in the mirror and heads for the door.

'Nice flat,' he says sarcastically, looking around the little one bed, one bath, cobwebs dangling from the light fittings and dark grey mould growing on the wallpaper.

'Just go,' Ollie replies.

'Don't worry. I plan to.'

He's had enough of this little exchange, even if he is finding his one-night-stand's growing panic mildly amusing.

As his hand slips around the door handle, it jiggles in his grasp, and to his surprise, the door swung inwards, revealing a petite blonde with bangs, a tattoo of a hummingbird on her neck and a knee-length cardigan covering her slim frame.

'Who the fuck are you?'

'I'm just leaving,' Kaden says, trying desperately to hide a smirk of delight.

'Shen!' Ollie says, racing toward the girl. 'You're early.'

Shen steps into the apartment, slipping around Kaden. 'What the hell's going on, Ollie?'

'This is Kaden. She's a work colleague. We've been having some difficulties with one of the other guys on our shift, so she popped over to talk it through. Isn't that right, Kaden?'

'*He* popped over,' Kaden says, eyes flitting to the phallus lying beside Ollie's bare foot.

'Right,' Ollie says, noticing it too. He tries to kick it under the computer desk but misses, stubbing his toe on the metal leg. 'Ow. Shit.'

Shen's eyes snap to the floor, her face morphing into a knotted fist of revulsion.

'What the fuck have you been up to?'

'We had a little fun,' Kaden says, half-laughing. 'It seems your boyfriend has an experimental side to him.'

'Ollie?'

'Don't be too hard on him, sweetheart. From what I can remember, I was doing most of the work.'

Ollie pushes between them. 'Shen, I can explain.'

Kaden almost feels sorry for the tiny blonde. Her eyes are glistening with the swell of blossoming tears, and her bottom lip is trembling.

'Get away from me,' Shen says, slapping at his hands.

'Shen!' he cries. 'Look, this isn't what it looks like.'

'Don't lie to her, baby,' Kaden says. 'It's exactly what it looks like.'

'I…I'm going,' Shen says, grabbing her bag before turning to Kaden. 'And you, you…freak. I suggest you stay away from me from now on. If I see you, I'll…'

Kaden puckers his lips and leans forward. 'You'll give me a kiss, right?'

'I'll knock your fucking head off,' Shen hisses, flicking him the bird. 'I'll be seeing you around, dyke.'

'Shen, wait, please!' Ollie yells, shooting Kaden a seething glare before pounding down the stairs.

Kaden stands alone in the apartment, a glimmer of amusement kissing his dark eyes. He thinks about leaving, but something makes him stay. A thought. An idea. He remembers feeling Ollie's chest the night before, running his fingers through the thick hairs around his nipples, the thin membrane of skin covering his wiry frame. What he remembers mostly is the pounding inside the young man's chest, the rat-tat-tat of a heart on fire. He wonders what it looks like, the muscle and tissue, the blood-filled capsule keeping the guy breathing. It would be working so hard now, powering his thin legs as he chases after the little blonde with the plump lips. Even harder when he comes back up the stairs, his head filled with bad thoughts. High blood pressure damages the artery walls, turning the artistry of the aortic valve into a battered mess of blood cells and torn meat. Kaden can't bear to think of Ollie's perfect organ being put through unnecessary torture. It would be such a waste.

He looks down at the white ceramic bowl sitting beside the overspilling ashtray full of last night's blunts and spies a yellow smiley face emoji imprinted on a metal disc. Attached to the disc is a key. He curls his top lip, reaches down and plucks it from the bowl, slipping it into his pocket instinctively.

He makes his way to the lift, leaving the door to the flat open as he makes a decision. His next organ doner has fallen into his lap like a winning lottery ticket, and tonight, as a reward to himself for working so damn hard, he plans to make a withdrawal.

CHAPTER 6: NEAT EDGES

'How you doing, Billy?'

'I knew it was you. I bloody knew it.'

Raven stands there staring at his old friend. The memories peek through the thick gauze that separates his old life from whatever this new existence is, prodding at him with spindly fingers of fractious recollection.

Billy has put on a little weight and his hair has taken on the grey of someone approaching his late-thirties, but otherwise he looks the same as the faded image that is still imprinted on his car-crash of a memory.

'Where you been, Luke?'

That's a question Raven doesn't know if he can answer. Not right away. He's still processing everything, trying to put every tiny fragment of what happened since that fateful night in neat rows where the edges line up perfectly. He doubts whether he'll ever completely get there, but he knows he has to try. It's been four years, the longest four years of his life.

'I'll get into that later,' he offers. 'But right now I need to see Lisa and Harry.'

'Right.' Billy shuffles from side to side. 'When did you get back?'

'Just now.'

'Like, today?'

'Less than an hour ago.'

'Okay.' Billy heads towards the kitchen. 'Can I make you a coffee? You must be thirsty.'

'No, I'm fine.'

'Mind if I have one? I'm gasping.'

Raven stares at the half-drunk cup of tea on the coffee table beside the glass of vodka on ice. 'Didn't you just have that?'

'I did, but the milk was off.' Billy walks away, retreating.

'Look, Billy,' Raven says, keeping pace. 'I really just want to know where Lisa and my son are. I haven't seen either of them in four years.'

'I get it,' Billy says, his back turned. 'But, like you say, it's been a long time and things can happen.'

'Things? What things?'

Billy slips a mug under the Tassimo machine's spout and drops in a cappuccino pod. 'You know? Stuff.'

Raven raises a hand to the indentation in his skull and winces. A headache has been building all morning, darkening his mood.

'For God's sake, Billy, I came here to find out where they are, not solve a riddle. I've spent the last four years not knowing who I am or whether I'm going to live or die, wondering every day if my memory will ever return, or if the woman holding me captive will just put a gun to my head and put me out of my misery, but now I'm back, I want to see Lisa and my son. I don't have time for bullshit, so tell me? Do you know where they are or not?'

Billy nods. 'I do.'

'And?'

'I suggest you take a seat. You're not going to like it.'

CHAPTER 7: EXQUISITE HOMES

Lisa and Harry moved into the Butler residence at Jane and her mother Chelsea's insistence. Jane knew first-hand what being a victim felt like, and it seemed that in her eyes, Lisa and Harry were as much the victims as she was. What's more, she owed Luke Raven her life, a fact she repeated several times. Luke had stopped Tony Richards from killing anybody else in the most final way possible, and while Jane had escaped Tony's father's clutches on her own, it had been Luke who had rescued her from Molly Staker.

The year that followed them moving in with the Butlers was one of the best years of Lisa's life. Harry's too. She felt guilty about that, but she hid it as best she could. In any case, she was due a little good fortune, and if that good luck came from an unexpected source, so be it. Her responsibility was to her son, and the role of his protector was the one thing in her life she was determined to succeed at.

The Butler residence wasn't opulent, but it was certainly comfortable. Jane even moved out of her bedroom into a slightly smaller one to give Lisa and Harry more space. The room was large and well-furnished and included a luxurious en-suite half-bath. What's more, Chelsea, gave Lisa a job working for her slowly growing high-end property agency. It was only an administrative role, but that was fine by her. The hours were good, she could work from home when she needed to, and the pay was more than she'd ever brought home before.

It got a little weird towards the end of that year when Jane and her new partner (a barrister named Todd who worked in the city) moved into their own place, leaving Lisa and Harry living with

Jane's mother, but it actually worked out okay. Chelsea had grown to love little Harry like her own grandson — her words, not Lisa's — and Lisa actually began to look up to her like a pseudo mother figure. Not that Lisa had had one of those before; not a quality one anyway. She'd been pretty much left to fend for herself since the age of ten, so when Chelsea started to show her signs of familial affection, she grasped it with both hands.

Little by little, she started to forget Luke. She fought against the gradual fading of her memories and tried to cling onto his image for as long as possible, but the police had stood down almost all the resources, and she was getting less and less out of Kipruto and Ruby. As far as the state were concerned, Raven was dead, and while Molly remained a person of interest, her trail had grown cold. West Hampshire Constabulary seemed intent on washing away the stink of what had gone on during that fateful August bank holiday, leaving no trace of what had happened in the cave at Annie's Cove or in Staker's sprawling mansion. They'd even taken over the building and converted it into council premises, as if operating a more conventional operation from inside its bloody walls legitimised it in some way.

Harry started school at Cherry Park Academy, Lisa took on more responsibility at what was now called Exquisite Homes, and little by little their lives began to click into place.

She hadn't expected to meet Simon, a guy who bought one of the properties she had been itching to sell, earning herself a tidy commission in the process, and she certainly hadn't expected to fall in love. These things just happened, and they happened too fast for her to take stock and think. Before she knew it, she was engaged, and not long after that, she was married and living in the big house he'd bought from her.

Lisa Clancy was no more, and everything that had gone on before now seemed like a scene viewed through a smeared windscreen. From that moment on she was Lisa Draper, and all that mattered was the future she would build with her son and her new husband.

CHAPTER 8: AMANDA

Kaden opens the front door and steps inside. The house smells of piss and spoiled milk. He can't complaint about that. It's his own fault. He'd had hardly any time to spend at home yesterday, what with work, the party, and that thing with the boy and his angry pixie of a girlfriend.

He bends down and picks up the letters spilled like confetti on the floor, one of which he's sure is a final reminder for the electricity bill. He'll have to figure out a way of paying it soon before the energy company cuts off the supply. No power in the house would be bad. There are things there that have to be kept at a certain temperature.

The door to the front room is ajar to his right, and the kitchen door up ahead is wide open. He can see the remains of jam on toast on the tiny table, and a spilled cup of tea on the floor. Again, this is his fault. He's usually the one to fix the meals, make the hot drinks and tidy up the cups and plates.

He grabs a dishcloth and dabs at the spilled tea, throws the remains of the broken mug in the bin, and scoops up the crumbs from the table into the palm of his hand. With the room tidied as well as it can ever be (this isn't the Savoy after all), he heads upstairs.

'Amanda, is that you?'

He eyes the open bathroom door. The rim of the toilet is damp and the faded linoleum is covered in a yellow puddle.

'Can't even piss in a straight line,' he groans under his breath before grabbing the loo roll, unspooling a generous amount into a thick ball and soaking up the warm urine before flushing the wet tissue down the loo. With that done, he turns to the closed bedroom door.

'Is that you Amanda?' comes the voice again.

He opens the door and steps inside.

'I told you a million times, Uncle, it's Kaden.'

Again, his nostrils are assaulted with the smell of piss, mingled with sweat and lingering halitosis. His uncle lies on the bed, the sheets down to his waist. His grey skin is exposed like old paper and loose flesh hangs like an oversized suit. Faded green eyes peer up at him from beneath a mottled brown scalp covered with a few strands of lank, greasy hair. His lips are yellow and flaking.

'Your mother called you Amanda,' his uncle says, his voice a thin, scratchy wheeze. 'And so Amanda it will always be.'

You ignorant fuck, Kaden thinks. *What do you know about what my mother did or didn't do, and who I choose to be now?* He takes a breath to calm his pounding heart. His uncle always gets him this way, goading him, poking at him. That's why, recently, Kaden has taken to skipping the odd cleaning day. If the old man can't be polite, why should he give a shit about him? Except he promised his mother. A mother who is now nothing but dust and old bones.

'I see you made yourself some dinner yesterday.'

'No thanks to you.'

'Yeah, sorry. I got distracted.'

'Could have bloody starved.'

'Well, you didn't, so that's a blessing.'

'Your mother would have never forgotten to feed me.'

No, but she didn't do it for free, did she? he thinks, pulling up the sheets to cover his uncle's flaccid man boobs.

'Like I said. I didn't forget. I just have a lot going on.' *Like taking a guy from behind with a dildo big enough to beat you to death with.*

'There was a time when you did right by me,' his uncle says. 'But these days, seems like you only care about what's going on in your own little world. There's barely any time left for an old liability like your Uncle Dean.'

'If that were true, I wouldn't be here, would I?'

'Wasn't here yesterday.'

'And like I said, I'm sorry.'

His apology seems to placate the old man at the second time of asking, a little at least. Enough to stop his whining, anyway. Kaden grabs a Kleenex from the box by the bed and wipes the spit from the old boy's chin. His uncle smiles at him, his teeth like black peas.

'Now, have you had breakfast?' he asks.

'Not hungry.'

'Well, you have to have eat, whether you want to or not. How's your stomach been?'

'Feels like something's chewing me up from the inside?'

'Have you taken your pills?'

'Can't find them.'

'I told you where they are. They're in the bathroom cabinet, next to the toiletries.'

'I looked. I couldn't see them.'

Because you didn't look, did you? Kaden thinks. *Because you're too lazy to get your own pills or aim your skin tag of a penis at the bowl.*

'Don't worry, I'll get them for you. You want toast or cereal?'

'You choose. I don't care. Like I said, I'm not hungry.'

'Cereal it is,' Kaden says before turning to leave. He's half out the door when his uncle calls after him.

'Amanda?'

The name is like nails in his stomach. He wants to rip his uncle's tongue out and crush it beneath his boots. He wants to go back in there, plunge his purple manicured nails into the whingeing bastard's eye sockets and pluck out his eyeballs like winkles from a shell. He hasn't been Amanda for so long, and yet this old geezer refuses to give it up.

'Yes?'

'I… I need to shit.'

He takes a breath and holds it, counting backwards from ten with his eyes closed. Meanwhile, his rampaging pulse throbs in his neck.

This is okay, he tells himself. *This is just one of those blips. It's a test, just a stupid test you have to get through. Things are going to change, and real soon.*

And that's the blessing he has to savour. Things really are going to change, because he'll make them change. He isn't a passenger in this life. He steers the ship, and this ship is heading exactly where he wants it to go. Nobody can stop him. Not his uncle, not his boss, not the little bitch girl who flipped him the bird. He's Kaden Chapman, and he's creating a legacy. A legacy that people won't forget in a hurry.

CHAPTER 9: STILL BEATING

'I'm sorry mate,' Billy says. 'I really didn't want to be the one to tell you that.'

Raven sits there, looking at the coffee cup in the machine, the steam drifting upward like the ghost of his past. Married? Lisa? How could she?

'She thought you were dead, Luke. We all did. Even Sal, and she's an annoying optimist.'

Raven doesn't hear him. He just keeps thinking of Lisa and Harry, the two people he cares about the most, the first people he remembered properly once the drugs had worn off and the doctors had pieced his mangled brain back together. All that kept him going through the painful recovery and the endless therapy sessions was the thought of making it back to them, to maybe re-begin a life that his encounter with the Stakers had paused so suddenly. Now all that has to change. He can see Lisa from a distance, maybe look after Harry every other weekend? Is that what he wants? Is that what his son deserves?

'He's got money, too,' Billy continues. 'Simon Draper, I mean. Made his money buying shares in renewable energy companies just before the boom. I heard he has upwards of ten million in the bank, as well as another five to ten mil in stocks. And the place they all live in? That must be worth a —' He pauses, checks himself. 'Sorry mate. Again. Sally says I should know when to stop spilling my guts, and I think she's probably right.'

'It's not your fault, Billy. It's just a shock.'

'You could stay here for a while at least. Until you get yourself sorted.'

'No. Thanks. I'll be fine.'

'I hear there are flats going down by the waterfront. A bit pricey, and I reckon the parking's a nightmare, but they've got a great sea view.'

Raven stands, tries to shake off the impact. It doesn't work. He walks to the back window, places his hands on the sink and focusses on the garden. It's what his therapist calls grounding. Pick a spot, stare at it and think of nothing else. The problem is, the thing that draws his attention is the garden of the house next door, and that isn't a place filled with happy memories for anybody.

He grimaces, places a hand on his head. Something hot jabs at his temple so hard that there's a flash like lightning across his eyes. He shuts them, his teeth like blazing embers in his mouth.

'Luke, are you okay?'

His fingers clench the edge of the worktop, white knuckles exposed, while the hot poker bounces from temple to temple, his brain now like a bubbling pot of hot sauce.

'Luke! Mate! What's going on?'

He sees something, something horrific. A pair of yellow eyes lurch at him from within the darkness of his crippling pain, followed by a spitting snarl, and then he's in a room. There's a dim light coming from beneath a door that he can barely see. He's sitting in a corner on an old chair, upholstery pitted with cigarette burns. The room smells of weed and men's body spray. There's discarded clothing on the floor and a set of keys on the coffee table. In another room, perhaps in another house, the silhouette of a medium height, medium build individual stoops over a table, beyond which Raven can see a pair of legs thrashing and kicking. Blood is on the sheets and on the walls. There's a sound like a drill, followed by a sickening crunch and squelch. More blood sprays over the silhouette's shoulder and the legs kick and judder repeatedly until the drilling stops. Afterwards, the body lies motionless while the white sheets blossom crimson.

Raven tries to get up but his feet are frozen to the floor. He tries to call out, but the pain in his head is so fierce, he can barely move his lips. He watches in horror as the silhouette begins to turn, and in its hand it holds something wet and pulsing. As the figure approaches, Raven's fear rises in his throat like a jet of hot water, and he wants to stand and rip that grotesque thing from the killer's hands and put it back where it belongs. Then he's awake, and Billy West is standing over him and splashing cold water on his face.

'Oh, thank God,' Billy says. 'I thought you'd gone and died on me.'

Raven's in a chair facing the window, his face covered in hot sweat, the remains of his fingernails digging into the palms of his hands.

'I saw it again,' he says with a mumble, his tongue a ball of cotton in his mouth.

'Saw what?'

'I've seen it before, but only in flashes.'

'I think you passed out. You flopped onto this chair like a puppet whose strings have been cut.'

'Maybe it was because of the distance from the source, or maybe even the drugs she was giving me, but this time it was much clearer.'

'What was much clearer?'

Raven tries to get up. 'I have to do something.'

'I don't think you're in any fit state to do anything, Luke. Whatever Molly did to you, you've obviously not fully recovered. The hospital that treated you, they should never have released you like this. Like I said, you can stay here until you're fit and well, but you can't go anywhere. Not like this.'

'I need to get to Kipruto,' Raven says, pushing Billy's hand away.

'Kipruto?'

'Yes, DI Randall Kipruto. I assume he's still the one looking after my case?'

Billy shakes his head. 'Not anymore. He got promoted.'

'Promoted?' Raven takes a moment to think about that. 'Okay, that could be a good thing. Maybe. Either way, I need to speak to him.'

'What's the rush? Whatever's eating away at you, surely it can wait until you're well enough to do something about it.'

'I'm fine.'

'Look at you. You're a long way from fine.'

Raven wheels on him. 'I said I'm fine! Don't you see? It's just like last time, and if I don't do something about it right now, more people will die.'

'Die? What are you talking about?'

He's up now and grabbing his jacket from the coat hook by the front door. 'The signal's stronger here, which means this is where the killer does it.'

'Does what?'

Raven turns to face Billy, the shadows in the living room covering the mottled swell of the bullet wound he would never be able to fully escape. 'He rips out their hearts, Billy. He rips out their fucking hearts.'

CHAPTER 10: LINGERING SCAR

DCS Randall Kipruto stands in the briefing room and listens to the morning's update. The white board is peppered with images of three murder victims, each committed within a month of each other. The first is a blood-spattered gore fest, the second messy but nowhere near as chaotic, the third looks like a precision operation. The MO has been decided upon but improved. There can be no doubt. Every one of them bears the hallmark of the killer the press have dubbed The Heart Breaker.

His DI, a kid named Harvey Welling, is in over his head. Randall can see that. The transferee from Somerset Constab' has been thrown in the deep end with this one, and he's barely keeping afloat. Kipruto had known Welling was a little green around the gills even before he'd joined, but what were his choices? He's hardly been blessed with a wealth of resources. The West Hampshire Constabulary has been cut to the quick by the local hatchet man, Clarence Fitzwilliam, and as a result, the first job Kipruto was given after being promoted to DCS — a promotion he suspects was the result of some diversity and inclusion target Fitzwilliam was compelled to meet, and not because of his impeccable record — was to make a whole bunch of good people redundant. Because of that, he's now operating a skeleton crew who are working considerably more hours per week than is healthy and getting less than half the overtime they'd previously been entitled to. It sucks. It sucks hard.

He sighs. He's heard enough of the update. The blood samples from the latest victim, a twenty-three year old male named Charlie Rector, are being analysed by the lab and the crime scene report is still pending, but Kipruto already knows it will come back inconclusive. Their killer knows enough about DNA to ensure they've covered their tracks. There wasn't a shred of evidence at the first two murder scenes and there's no reason to suggest the third will be any different. This is now their third serial killer since 2019, which makes their little town number one in the country for sick psychopaths, a trend he intends to reverse as soon as he can get his head out of this latest clusterfuck. Westhampton is getting a name for itself, and for all the wrong reasons.

He retreats to his office and closes the door. Life had been different when he'd been out on the job. He'd felt more in control. Now he's nothing but a reluctant politician-cum-resource manager with a dozen spreadsheets to keep track of and a budget so small he can barely afford to keep the lights on. This hadn't been what he'd wanted when he'd signed up, and it certainly isn't something he's good at. He leans back and stares out the window, wondering where it all went wrong, and whether Ruby's right after all. Maybe he does need a change of career.

Of course, there's Luke Raven, alive and well and on his way back to Westhampton. Randall received the call yesterday, just after he and Ruby had put the twins to bed. It had been like a kick in the guts, not because he wasn't happy that the guy who had thwarted the town's last two murdering maniacs was still alive, but because Randall had been so convinced Raven was dead. Sure, he hadn't been the one to pull the resources from the case, but he'd gone along with it, and when all was said and done, he'd profited from his compliance, getting a promotion and a sizable salary increase to boot.

His phone rings in his pocket, and he looks to see who it is, suspecting yet another spreadsheet request or KPI report demand.

'Hi darling.'

'Have you called Lisa?' It's Ruby.

'Baby, we went over this. Inspector McGoughlan said that Raven wanted to deliver the news himself.'

'But Lisa and Harry deserve to know.'

'And they will, just as soon as he arrives in town.'

'Which will be?'

Randall shakes his head. 'Not sure. Last we knew, he got off the train in Euston yesterday afternoon from Glasgow, took the tube to Waterloo, then caught the next Southern Train to Southampton. From there, we sort of lost him.'

'Did you check the CCTV at the bus station? Or the local cabbies?'

'Ruby, you know as well as I do, I don't have the resources for that, and the Staker case is no longer an active investigation. Molly and her mother are dead.'

Randall still can't believe that. After four years and thousands of police hours costing hundreds of thousands, maybe even millions of pounds in the process, Molly's mother, Lorna, had achieved what the best detectives in the UK could not. She had found her daughter.

Finally, Ruby says what they've both been thinking.

'We could have prevented this. If only we'd kept looking, Lorna would still be alive, Molly would be getting the help she needed, and we wouldn't have the blood of at least seven more victims on our hands.'

'You can't know that, Rube.'

'I do, and so do you. In your heart you do. We could have done something. We could have tried harder, looked for longer, spent more money. We could have hired a PI. Anything.'

'They went completely off the radar. McGoughlan says the cottage they were squatting in had miniscule network coverage.'

'That's a bullshit answer.'

Randall chooses not to respond, knowing she's right. She's always right. Ever since they'd met on the Staker case, Ruby had shown herself to be razor sharp, with better intuition than some of the most successful detectives he'd ever worked with. That was why he'd fallen for her, and why less than a year later, he'd asked her to marry him. The moment she'd said yes, his life had irretrievably changed for the better. It was the happiest moment in his entire life, only to be matched eighteen months later when their twin girls, Grace and Charity, were born. Their lives are happy, really happy, but the Staker case is a lingering scar that just refuses to heal.

'You need to tell Lisa,' Ruby says, no longer willing to debate the point. 'And you need to tell her soon.'

CHAPTER 11: THE SOW

Kaden pushes through the group of customers perusing the 'For Sale' swimwear and tosses his bag behind the till, less than ten seconds before his boss emerges from the footwear section. Winston's face is scarlet, his upper lip twitching like a caterpillar in a footrace. He is pissed.

'Sorry I'm late,' Kaden says, wanting to laugh but knowing any sign of humour in a situation like this is a bad idea. 'I had a thing.'

'7.30, I said,' Winston replies. 'You said 7.15. Either would have been fine, but—' he checks his watch. '10.20? You rock in here at 10.20 like nothing has happened, and then try to fob me off with "I had a thing"? Do you think that's going to cut it, Kaden. You really think that's going to make everything okay?'

People are looking now. Staring. One of the younger boys points which makes Kaden feel one of those sharp emotional jabs he used to feel at school whenever the other kids made fun of the way he dressed. Mandy the Lezzy they used to call him. State school education at its finest. Mandy the fucking Lezzy; it didn't even rhyme.

'I said I'm sorry, Winston. What more do you want me to say? It's not like I do it all the time.'

There's muttering now. The group of four lads are talking and sniggering.

'I got a call from the area manager this morning,' Winston says, now standing so close to Kaden he can feel his rancid breath on his face. 'Do you know how often Jim calls me?'

'Once a week?'

'Try never.'

'He never calls you?'

'No. Only when he has bad news.'

'And today he had some bad news, right?'

'Of course he did. The store didn't open on time, and so somebody — God knows who — left us a bad review on Trustpilot. This… woman said she came out early on pay day to buy a hoodie for her son's birthday, which apparently is today, and guess what? Nobody was here to open the bloody door!'

'And Jim saw that and called you?'

'Jim watches those reviews like a hawk, Kaden. Like a fricking hawk.'

Kaden doesn't know what Winston wants him to say. So there's a disgruntled customer who couldn't be bothered to buy her son a birthday present until the morning of his actual, no kidding birthday, and a boss who is OCD about Trustpilot reviews, but he'd been less than three hours late. Three hours! It isn't like he'd called in sick like that layabout Carl. What's the big deal?

'Are you laughing?' Winston asks. 'Kaden, is that a smile on your face?'

Is it? Kaden thinks, realising that, yes, it really is. 'Sorry, it's just that—'

'You're actually finding this funny?'

'No, I just get this way when I—' A choked snigger sneaks out.

'I bet you wouldn't find it funny if Jim was on your back!'

The thought of Jim Douglas getting on Winston's back, like a bull mounting a reluctant cow, makes something flip in Kaden's brain, and he bends over double, tears streaming down his face.

'I won't stand for this, Kaden! I just won't.'

'Sorry, I—' It's no use, he can't help himself. He gives into his warped sense of humour and lets it all out, a cackle as loud as a police siren, causing the four guys standing there watching to break into hysterics.

'Whatever she's having, I'll have some of it too,' one of them says before digging his mate in the ribs. The fact the lad mistakes his sex doesn't bother Kaden this time. He's too busy laughing to give a shit.

'I suggest you get your things and go,' Winston says, the veins in his neck now pulsing so hard it looks like his head might explode.

'Okay,' Kaden replies, grabbing his bag and wiping tears from his cheeks. 'I get it.'

'And don't come back until you've learned how to behave.'

'I—' another snort of laughter. 'I won't. I promise.'

'Right now, you're about a micro-second away from being fired.'

Kaden walks past the four guys, barely able to see through his slowly drowning eyes, and heads for the exit.

'She got one over on you, mate,' one of them says to Winston. 'Made you look like an idiot.'

Kaden doesn't wait to hear her boss's response. It doesn't matter anyway. He'd already made his mind up long before this morning's little incident. If the skinny guy from last night is first on his shopping list, Winston isn't far behind, and if the guys standing by the cut-price shirts keep on mistaking him for a female, they'll find themselves up next.

The three losers who had already come up against him and lost would testify to that, if they could talk that was, which they couldn't. That's the thing about corpses. They keep themselves to themselves.

CHAPTER 12: INSULATION

Clarence Fitzwilliam steps out of the cab into a murky puddle that sloshes over his polished brogues and stifles a curse. He takes a look around. The sky is overcast, as grey as the filth that litters the streets, the walls around him smeared with scum and graffiti gang-signs. Westhampton. Fucking Westhampton. Like a boil that's impossible to lance, the pus inside toxic and grotesque. The place is an imperfection, a blemish on his otherwise rare Rembrandt of an existence, but no matter how hard he tries, he keeps landing back here in a Groundhog Day style nightmare.

'That'll be thirty-nine pounds, sir, if you wouldn't mind,' the cabbie says.

'Maybe next time use the country roads,' Fitzwilliam snipes. 'I'd really rather not spend the first hour of my day sitting motionless on the A35, watching some kid in the car beside us picking his nose and wiping it on the window.'

'Nothing I can do about that, I'm afraid,' the cab driver replies. 'Since the council decided to blitz the potholes in the middle of the day without any concern for the commuters, every journey's taking far longer than it used to. People call it progress. I just call it a giant pain in the arse.'

The council? Fitzwilliam thinks. *I'm a fucking Member of Parliament, and there's no use complaining about pot-hole repairs when not two months ago, the whole country was whining about the state of the nation's highways.*

'Cash or card?' the cabbie asks.

Fitzwilliam pulls a fifty from his wallet and tosses it through the window.

'Keep the change.'

'Thank you, sir. Very kind.'

'Not that you're worth my generosity.'

He looks up at the tatty council offices, soon to be vacated and turned into a homeless shelter for the town's several hundred waifs and strays. In his opinion, that's yet another waste of the council's meagre funds. It's the equivalent of handing out free alcohol at an AA meeting, hoping kindness will be rewarded with a change in behaviour. With so many woke, new-age hippy, social-media muck spreaders employed by the council, he's had no choice but to concede. It angers him, makes his blood simmer in his slowly hardening arteries, but if it means stopping his once-a-month trips to a place that has nearly ruined his career by not one, but two high profile serial killer sprees, then perhaps it's a frustration he can learn to live with.

There are, however, two remaining problems to solve, and both are nuclear missile sized ordnances that if detonated could fuck just about everything he's ever built. On one hand, there is yet another murderous psychopath on the rampage, a sicko with a fetish so disgusting it makes Fitzwilliam want to throw up his eggs royale lunch; and two, there is the rise from the dead of a guy who has been at the centre of the last two viral Tik Tok Westhampton catastrophes. Luke Raven. A nasty, barbed thorn that has been persistently stabbing Fitzwilliam in his rapidly diminishing testes for longer than is bearable.

Kipruto had been the one person brave enough to deliver Fitzwilliam the news, the guy he'd entrusted with running the West Hampshire Constabulary ever since that bitch Deveraux had let him down so badly, getting her head blown off by Staker's flesh-eater of a daughter in the process. The new DCS's number one objective is to keep the town out of the headlines, and so far, that task is slipping into the 'failed dismally' category of his end of year assessment.

Fitzwilliam hits dial on his phone as the lift doors open. 'I'm coming up,' he says. 'Get the coffee ready.'

He has a plan, one that he'd come up with while lying awake at 2AM that morning, his latest catwalk beauty lying naked across his chest. It was obvious really. Why risk being dragged down into the murky waters when he can step on the shoulders of a guy who has more baggage than a stag weekend in Ibiza. Kill three birds with one stone. Give the guy from the grave his DI badge back, task him with bringing down The Heart Breaker and watch as the stupid little fuck runs around like an AI powered robot chasing a ball. If he somehow succeeds, that's another sick fucker he can take the credit for putting behind bars. If he fails, Raven takes the blame, and Kipruto gets the heat.

Insulation is a blessing to a man in Fitzwilliam's position, and as it turns out, Luke Raven is now the best insulator in town.

CHAPTER 13: CRUMBS

Billy pulls the van up outside the police station as Raven grabs his things.

'Cheers for the lift,' Raven says. 'I'll catch a cab home.'

'I don't mind waiting.'

'It's okay. It might take a while. Kipruto and I have a lot of catching up to do.'

'Honestly, I can push a few jobs back, make up the time later in the week. It's no problem.'

'Billy, get back to that lovely wife of yours. I can take it from here.'

Raven opens the door and steps outside, peering up at the plush glass-fronted building of the West Hampshire Constabulary headquarters, remembering the battered old station house he'd once worked in. That building was left derelict in the name of efficiency, the government pulling every local force in the area into one central hub, laying off a third of the staff while expecting the people that were left to fill in the cracks. Deveraux had led the culling, slicing away at his old team like a cut of venison, leaving good cops on the slag heap, their pensions in tatters, careers in ruins. He had already been in the line of the white witch's fire at that time, so he'd had about as much influence as a comedian from the seventies at a feminism rally, but he'd tried to stop the maelstrom, raised his voice as loud as he could. The wheels of progress, however, were already rolling, and he was just a tiny speck in a much bigger picture.

He studies the modern design, the clever use of purposefully tarnished steel, juxtaposed against mirrored glass so expertly polished you would be forgiven for thinking you really were looking at yourself, not some smeared reflection. This is clearly what that money has been spent on. Bricks and mortar, not bobbies on the street, the people that make the police-force tick, or community initiatives that actually bring real people together.

He lets out a long sigh, the kind of sigh that used to mean he needed a drink — preferably a Rusty Nail with a double shot of Drambuie and a single cube of ice — and approaches the building. He thinks about what Billy has told him, the revelation that hit him like a short punch in the undercarriage. He needs to see Lisa and Harry more than anything, but the thought of meeting her husband, the guy that Harry now thinks of as his dad, makes him sick to his stomach. He can't face it. Not yet. The news is still sinking in. He knows that's crazy. What did he expect? He's been gone four years, and for all Lisa knew, he'd been killed that night at the Staker mansion, tossed into the back of a Corsa only to be thrown in the nearest lake. She couldn't wait forever. Nobody could. His head is filled with so many regrets, so many things he could have done differently. If only he hadn't trusted Molly. If only he'd taken the shot when he'd had a chance. If only he'd told Lisa how he really felt about her, rather than letting her think things were over between them. Everything could have been so different.

'Luke Raven,' he announces to the young, male PC at the desk. 'I'm here to see DCS Kipruto.'

'Do you have an appointment?'

'Not exactly, but he knows I'm coming.'

'The DCS is usually pretty blocked out, but I'll put a call through and see what I can do. Just fill in your details here.'

The call isn't necessary, because just before the pen touches paper, Kipruto comes through the door, wide eyed, his arms open. 'Luke Raven!' he cries. 'Man, I never thought I'd see this day.'

The two men hug.

'You're looking well,' the DCS adds. He's a tall man, black skin, well dressed, tightly clipped hair and neat goatee. He and Raven had been the ones to take Molly Staker down, but not before Kipruto had been shot. Raven still remembers his friend lying there with a bullet wound in his side, blood blossoming from the ten-pence-piece sized hole. 'You've lost some weight.'

'The food at the cottage wasn't so good,' Raven replies, only half-smiling.

Kipruto's mood changes. 'Yeah. Heard about that. It must have been hell. That woman, that crazed lunatic, she really did a number on you.'

'Not as bad as the number her mother did on her. I'm guessing you heard about that.'

'Yeah, Detective McGoughlan filled me in over the phone. They still haven't found Molly, I assume.'

Raven shakes his head.

'From what I understand, her mother got her pretty good, though. If she was still alive, they would have found her by now.'

'I hope you're right.'

Kipruto stands there, hands on hips, words eluding him. Finally, he says, 'Raven, I'm so sorry we let you down.'

'Forget about it. Molly did a pretty good job keeping us hidden, moving from place to place as soon as the heat was turned up. She had my head so screwed, I didn't even know where I was most of the time.'

'There's no excuses. We should have done better.'

'Randall, I've lost count how many times I've said that to relatives and friends of victims over the years. The fact is, sometimes the trail of breadcrumbs leads you to a dead end with no leads, no eyewitnesses and a bunch of information that doesn't make sense. It's just the way it goes.'

'Doesn't mean I have to feel good about it.'

'I'd be pretty pissed off if you did, but don't feel bad about it either. Be neutral. Neutrality is a prerequisite of being a copper. You'd do well to remember that.'

Kipruto allows himself a smile. 'You want coffee?'

'Sure, but first, I need to update you on what I know about this new sicko of yours.'

Kipruto glances at the young PC. 'Can you buzz Raven and I through to the conference room?'

There's a subtle click as a lock unlatches and the door to their right opens. Kipruto gestures for Raven to enter.

'You tell me what you know,' The DCS says, leaning against the door to close it. 'And I'll fill you in on what we have.'

Raven raises an eyebrow. 'Are you allowed to do that, what with me still serving my suspension?'

Randall smiles and pulls something from his pocket. 'I got the word from on high.'

'Fitzwilliam, I assume.'

'One and the same, plus whoever pulls his strings, but that doesn't matter. What does matter is that this is good news, Luke. Really good news.'

Raven eyes the laminated placard in Kipruto's hand and wonders what it is. His curiosity doesn't last for long because the DCS flips the badge open, and there, peering back at him, is his own image: younger, more meat in the face, eyes that still containing a hint of ambition. The faded words are readable, but only barely. It doesn't matter because he can recite them from memory.

'You're back on the team, Luke. Or should I say, Detective Inspector Raven?'

CHAPTER 14: SPITTING NOODLES

Kaden sits in his uncle's kitchen, smoking a cigarette and exhaling through his nose, watching the white haze drift to the ceiling like a ghost while picking at a bowl of Super Noodles. He reads about himself in the local Facebook gossip board, pausing occasionally to smirk or let out a groan of disapproval.

Garyxmykids: This bloke is one seriously sick fucker. Who cuts out another human's heart and keeps it for a souvenir?

CheryCook: If you ask me, it's the fault of Netflix and those other chanels. To many cereal killer documentaries. It's like a how–2–guide for creeps.

Bob_Dunning: It's channel and serial, thicko. Didn't you even go to school?

Jessloveshorror: Don't remember watching a documentary where the killer steals human hearts. Cool.

Rebaishot: I think he's cool, too, just leaving the bodies with the hearts missing. I wonder if he's HAF.

Dave.Bowyer: Probably just another immigrant who hates the English. Useless govt needs to sort those fucking boats out.

Kaden laughs out loud, spitting noodles all over the table, causing a severe coughing fit that has him retching and reaching for a glass of water. He glugs it down quickly, trying to wash away the shit he's inhaled, and takes in half a dozen deep breaths.

What do these people know about what he is trying to achieve? How dare they compare his actions with those of Geoffrey Dahmer, Ed Gein, or Fred fucking West? Those people couldn't control themselves, whereas he does everything as carefully as possible, adopting the precision of a top-class surgeon and the cleanliness of a clinical laboratory. Nothing is left to chance, no victims killed out of passion. He selects his subjects after a long process of studying, watching and collecting data. If the kill doesn't feel right, it doesn't happen. If the situation doesn't grab him, he moves on. If everything clicks into place, he acts with the pace of someone who knows their own mind and can control their desires. Seduce, coerce, nullify, execute, clean; a five-step process that has so far left the local police chasing their tales like overactive puppies.

'Amanda, is that you?' his uncle calls. 'Did I hear you honey?'

Shit, Kaden thinks. *My coughing fit's woken the leech. Maybe noodles for lunch wasn't the best idea.* He knows he'll have to go in there and change the old fart again. The thought repulses him. If it isn't for the excitement he's feeling, he might slump into one of his dark spells again, wallowing in hours of depression, thinking about cutting himself, obsessing about how fat he looks, or how nobody likes him, or how he's just a loser fuckwit who's bound to end up like his uncle, dying alone in a house that smells like vomit and piss.

He stands and looks at himself in the mirror. The fact is, he looks pretty hot today, and he feels hot, too. His high cheekbones stand out with the hint of blusher he applied earlier, and his skin, with the natural foundation he's dabbed on and brushed until it's smooth and even, makes him look like a supermodel. Maybe today he will be a female. Not Amanda. Never Amanda. Amanda is his dead name. Kaden is his chosen monicker, as in cool Kaden, chic Kaden, the sort of Kaden who would have been popular at school and probably would have got with one of the fit boys and then dumped him for one of his friends, causing the two BFFs to sort it out with a real passionate bout of bloodletting. Maybe one of them would have been hurt. Maybe one of them would have been killed.

The matter of his sexuality has been confused since birth. No, not confused exactly. Blurred. He has never strongly associated with male or female, but he isn't androgynous either. He feels things, urges, needs, but his preferences change with his mood.

When he was a child, it had been difficult. Too difficult. He'd had no idea how to articulate who or what he was. His mum didn't care because she didn't pay attention to anything other than herself, and although his dad did care, or at least he said he did, he couldn't handle it. He was barely home most days. Kaden always thought that was because of how he felt. Perhaps he was ashamed; ashamed of the little girl who sometimes dressed as a boy but would then put on a pretty pink dress and sing along to her father's David Bowie records. Kaden didn't conform. He couldn't conform. Didn't even know what conformity was.

The kids at school thought he was a freakshow, a deformity waiting to be fixed. He was the butt of cruel jokes, the victim of vicious bullying, and the brunt of so many social media posts, he could barely keep up. He cried himself to sleep most nights and dreamed about some grotesque, dystopian world where there was an angel of darkness with curved horns and thorny wings, and everybody who had ever laughed at him were just rats with human heads, the bodies split open, their guts spewing out as the creature crushed them one by one beneath enormous hooves.

The MeToo movement all happened too late for Kaden, and the advent of pronouns was just a thing he noticed but didn't pay attention to. He can't call himself a *they* any more than he can call himself *queer*. To him it's very simple. Some days he looks at himself and sees a boy, other days a girl. Anything else is just noise.

Today, the 24th of May, he will be Kaden the Woman, a female with enough sass to curdle milk. Kaden the Woman is so much better than Ollie's chavvie Sabrina Carpenter wannabe anyway, and if the young guy with the pencil dick can't see that, it's his problem, not hers.

She smiles, remembering the moment she realised she had a higher purpose, a purpose much more important than looking after her sickly uncle with wandering hands and drooling lips. It was when the older guy with the greying hair and dark eyes had noticed her for what she was. That was all the validation she needed. Kaden started to learn things about the version of the world she didn't pay attention to, the underbelly almost everybody ignored.

She'd clean up her uncle's shit, take a shower, change her clothes and get on with her work. The excitement raced through her like the strongest MDMA. Tonight, she would take a step toward the retribution her saviour had promised her, and pretty soon she would be standing at the precipice of immortality, with her allies among the Legion standing by her side, welcoming the arrival of the one true deity.

There would be retribution for the whole world, the kind of retribution that only those in the inner circle would survive.

CHAPTER 15: SINGLE MALT

Raven sits in the meeting room, everything he knows spilled onto the table like vomit. He'd told Kipruto about the dark room, the tall silhouette, the bloodied knife in an anonymous hand, the still beating heart of the victim as it was torn from the gorged body. He'd told him how the visions had been flitting and distorted when he had been held captive in the Highlands but had become much clearer the closer he'd got to Westhampton. He'd suggested it was possible these visions had been brought on by the drugs he'd been given to nullify his senses, but he suspected not. After all, they were no different to the nightmares he'd endured when Tony Richards had gone on his killing spree, and when Molly had followed soon after. When he was done, he slumped forward, head in his hands, the world's worst headache building behind his eyes.

'Look, Randall,' he says. 'I know this sounds bat-shit crazy, but I was in that room with whoever did this, and I saw exactly what he saw.'

Randall eyes him over the rim of his glasses, pen tapping against his teeth. 'I understand.'

'It was a damp, dark space, possibly a basement, maybe an attic. Way too small to be a warehouse.'

'Got it.'

'My guess is it's a residential property, just like Richard's MO, but rather than draining the victims' blood, this guy is taking their hearts.'

'As a memento.'

'Maybe. You know as well as I do that killers like this keep all kinds of shit, often so that they can relive whatever sordid thrill they get from committing such violent, sadistic acts.'

'So you don't think the hearts mean anything?'

'I didn't say that. I'm saying I don't know, but what I do know is we need to narrow the search to homes with basements, attics, garages or outhouses, of say, no more than three metres by three metres.'

'That's a lot of properties.'

'Then I suggest we get started right away.'

Randall leans back in his chair, arms folded, lips clamped together and forming a thin, pink line beneath his moustache.

'As I said,' Raven conceded, 'I know it sounds crazy, but I was given all this information before, and I was too slow to act. I even took it to Deveraux, thinking she might do something with it. I'm not going to make the same mistake again. You've given me my DI badge back, and I appreciate it, I really do, but what good is it if I can't follow my hunches?'

'This isn't a hunch, Raven. This intel is based on something you dreamt. My superiors will never go for that.'

'Then don't tell them,' Raven says, voice raised. 'Make something up, tell them you have a source, somebody who thinks they know the killer, whatever. We just need the manpower.'

Kipruto shakes his head. 'I don't know if you've heard, but that kind of resource is in short supply these days.'

'Just a few guys, Randall, four, maybe five. Police officers with enough street sense to know what they're looking for.' Raven leans forward, eyes wide. 'We can get this guy, I know we can.'

Kipruto stands, walks to the window facing the foyer and places one hand on the glass. He doesn't speak for a couple of minutes, but Raven lets him have his time. He knows he's asking a lot, particularly when this is his first day on the job, but this case is all he has. He's been given something to focus his attention on, something to distract him from the life that has been taken away from him.

'Have you spoken to Lisa?' Kipruto asks without turning.

The question kicks Raven in the guts. 'Not yet.'

'Ruby has been on my back about telling her you're alive, but I wanted to speak to you first.'

'I appreciate that.'

'I'm telling you because I can't put it off much longer, not if I want to stay married.'

'I know. I'll go see her, I promise. I just need to get my head in the right place.'

Randall returns to the table, takes a seat. 'This whole thing is fucked up,' he says, and this time it's the DCS's turn to look distressed.

'I'm guessing we're no longer talking about The Heart Breaker.'

Randall shakes his head. 'You know, when I got this job, I thought I'd be happy. It was what I'd been aiming for, after all, ever since I signed up to become a PC. I wanted to make my parents proud, but more than that, I wanted to prove to myself that I could do it, the black kid from working class London. The odds were stacked against me, but I always believed.'

'I'm guessing Fitzwilliam hasn't been as supportive as you expected.'

'I think if I walked out that door and never returned, he wouldn't think twice about replacing me. I'm a number on a quota, Raven, just a DEI statistic he can wave around at management meetings to prove he's signed up to the new way of thinking.'

'You're a good copper, Randall, don't forget that. Whatever reason Fitzwilliam had for putting you in this position, it doesn't change that fact.'

Randall crushes his empty coffee cop and tosses it in the bin, clipping the edge on the way in.

'I'm going to give you what you want,' he says, 'but it has to be on my terms.'

Raven suppresses a smug grin. 'You won't regret it.'

'No drinking,' Randall adds, brow furrowed.

'You got it.'

'I mean it. Like, totally none. You have even a nip and I'll know it.'

'Randall, I haven't had a drink in four years,' Raven lies, relishing the taste of single malt on his lips. 'Getting kidnapped by a flesh-eating sociopath is sort of the best way to get clean.'

Randall's eyes narrow. 'No pissing off the bosses. You play nice, even if you think the people we have to deal with around here are morons.'

'Morons are my kind of people,' Raven replies. 'The more moronic, the better.'

'And you go and see Lisa and Harry.' This last request hurts a lot more.

'Okay.'

'And you do it tonight.'

Raven nods, knowing coming clean with his family is the one thing he has to get past more than anything, but it's also the thing that terrifies him the most.

CHAPTER 16: TRANNY

Night is drawing in. Things are getting moving. Westhampton settles down into a familiar rhythm: beach goers heading to the bars and restaurants, bass laden pop music booming from high powered speakers, kids with plastic glasses filled with premium lager (Spanish, the latest trend) talking in loud voices, singing, chanting, often yelling. Kaden is uncomfortable in this setting — it heightens her already crippling social anxiety — but it's her hunting ground, her plain of the Serengeti.

She is dressed in tight black jeans, a figure-hugging black top and four-inch, black heels. She has a skull ring on the middle finger of her right hand and an angel ring on the middle finger of her left. Her lips are dark red, so dark they're almost grey, her eyeshadow sage. She's applied just enough blusher to her cheeks to heighten her impressive jawline. Her hair is high and tight, exposing her long neck and broad shoulders. She feels so feminine she can barely remember Kaden the boy, although she knows that can change in an instant. Tonight, she hunts as a woman, but her thoughts are filled with testosterone.

'How you doing sweetheart?' a young guy in a white polo and skinny jeans demands. 'You want a cocktail?'

She walks past without making eye contact, happy in the knowledge her appearance gets the guy's attention.

'Hey, I'm talking to you!' the kid hollers. 'No need to be so fucking rude.'

She keeps walking, smirking, enjoying the laughter and mock jeering.

'Fuck you. You look like a tranny anyway.'

The comment stops her dead in her tracks. What was that he said?

'Ooh, look at the tranny in her stupid fucking clothes,' the guy continues. 'Hey tranny! RuPaul just called. He wants his fake tits back.'

Kaden turns, her blood racing. How dare this guy she's never even met turn on her like that, just because she wouldn't accept a fucking cocktail. How dare he shatter her thin layer of confidence, destroying what little self-love she'd managed to scrape together while applying her makeup and anxiously checking her appearance?

'What the fuck did you say?'

White Polo eyes her arms, which she's worked on a lot, and her shoulders, which she's deliberately bulked up. His pals laugh at him, poking him, asking him if he's going to let some blokey bird talk to him like that.

'I said you look like a tranny,' White Polo replies, his fake bravado like a panto costume.

'Take that back,' Kaden says.

'Or what? You gonna beat me up, tranny? You gonna kick my arse?'

'She's gonna get all AJ on you, Row,' one of the friends says.

'Doesn't bother me,' White Polo replies. 'AJ ain't got it no more anyway.'

'Dubois then. Yeah, she's gonna knock you out like Dubois did to AJ.'

Row, which she presumes is short for Rowan, turns to her, right hand clenched into a fist, the other hooked into the pocket of his way-too-tight jeans. 'Are you, tranny? You gonna knock me out?'

Kaden thinks about it. She thinks about punching this guy so hard he chokes on his own teeth, possibly swallowing his tongue in the process, and then stamping on his head until his skull cracks and the jelly stuff that masquerades as brains comes oozing out all over the pavement. She thinks about that long and hard, her anger so palpable she can barely breathe, But then she realises that would only validate the insult. The fact that today she is a female would not even register with these neanderthal, lager-inhaling, illiterate halfwits. News of her conquest would spread across the town like a new strain of COVID, and before she knew it, she'd forever be Kaden the Tranny, just another comic book epitaph on the gravestone of her life.

'Go fuck yourself,' she says, turning and walking away.

'Yeah, walk away bitch,' Rowan calls after her. He sounds happy with himself, his reputation once more intact. Kaden swallows her pride and keeps pacing, safe in the knowledge that if she'd wanted to, she could have ground the little limp-dick into the dirt faster than he could say 'beaten up by a girl.'

'Thought you weren't coming,' her date says as she enters the café.

'Had a little trouble on the way here,' Kaden says.

'What kind of trouble?'

'Chav trouble,' she replies. 'Don't worry, I'm used to it.'

'The town's full of them,' her date replies, half-laughing. 'Sometimes I think the whole place is going to the dogs. Westhampton used to be a nice town, but these days, it feels like a slum.'

'And that's putting it mildly. Anyway, I'm not really in the mood for small talk anymore.' She traces a finger down his arm, her freshly applied plastic nails leaving a groove in his flesh. 'Shall we just cut out the bull and head back to my place.'

Winston's eyes come alive. His lips move like slugs climbing a leaf. 'Woah, that's kind of sudden.'

'You want this or not?' she asks, becoming frustrated. 'I mean, after the way you treated me today, I should be giving you the cold shoulder, not inviting you back to my home.'

'Yeah, yeah,' he replies, sensing he's fucked up. 'Of course I want this. Ever since that night—'

'At Gold Diggers.'

'That's right. Ever since then, this is all I can think about. *You're* all I can think about. Personally speaking I mean, because professionally, you're—'

'—difficult to deal with?'

'To say the least, but that doesn't matter. I can get past that, but this? I can't get this out of my head.'

Kaden studies his arms, his chest, the way his rotund belly pokes out from beneath his too short button-down. His physique isn't ideal, his personality is less than appealing, but she can't forget the way he made her feel today, and she can't forgive the way he spoke to her. Winston has jumped the queue, which means he gets the golden ticket. She wants his heart, physically, not metaphorically or in some other puke-inducing way. She wants to feel its gelatinous bulk pulsing between her fingers and its dark blood slipping down her wrists. Just the thought of it makes her horny, like some sort of acid induced aphrodisiac. She grabs his hand and pulls him along, just a little too hard.

'I can't wait any more,' she says. 'We're leaving.'

CHAPTER 17: DIRTY LONDONERS

Raven stands outside The Golden Swan, looking up at the faded sign, the queen's favourite bird dappled in gleaming gold leaf. Overhead, the sky is dark, tiny specks of shimmering light just penetrating the hazy cloud cover, the moon a milky phantom hanging above the bright yellow streetlights. He used to love this place. It held so many memories for him, most of them bad, many of them fractured glimpses within a sea of nothingness. He'd punched the landlord once for laying hands on the girl he'd been seeing behind his actual girlfriend, Lisa's, back. Daisy had been an addiction he'd always struggled to shake, the forbidden one, the poison he just couldn't resist. She had haunted his nightmares while he'd been holed up in Scotland, her death like indelible blood on his sub-conscious. She had been the heart and soul of this pub, the scowling, foul-mouthed barmaid who had always known what the punters wanted, even if they hadn't known it themselves.

The Golden Swan had lost its way after her death, and the locals had gradually moved on, looking for cheaper thrills from places that served shitty food for less than the price of a packet of cigarettes and employed kids who didn't give two shits about whether the place survived or died. Perhaps that was why it now lies in the centre of town, windows boarded like scabs, old posters stuck to the walls, peeling and faded. Barely readable graffiti tells the residents of Westhampton that 'Kai sucks for free,' (good for you, Kai), and 'Dan Saunders fucked your mum,' although the question of whose mum got laid is left tantalisingly unanswered.

Despite what Kipruto demanded, Raven wants a drink. He wants a drink like a heroin addict wants a needle. He craves whiskey like somebody suffering from chronic pain craves morphine. He is so tethered to this burgeoning, desperate desire that the nettles lining its crazed, winding path are constantly stinging his insides and poisoning his thoughts. He doesn't understand how it can be that way, this senseless, pointless collection of withdrawal symptoms. He hadn't lied to Kipruto, at least not completely. When he'd been under Molly Staker's supervision, he hadn't touched a drop of Satan's deadly serum. He'd been clean for four years and not once had he craved alcohol. Not once. Maybe that had been the drugs, or perhaps his head wound had robbed him of all pointless obsessions. The fact remained, as soon as those shots were fired by both Molly's mother Lorna and Molly herself, the addiction had come rushing back, as if an ulcer had burst, toxic pus rushing through his veins, contaminating his body.

During his stay in the hospital, he'd made friends with one of the other patients, an Indian guy named Ravindra whose family ran a restaurant in Glasgow. He'd bribed him with what little possessions he'd had with him — a watch, a slim gold chain, even a pair of good socks — convincing him to smuggle in the odd miniature: twelve-year-old scotch, spiced rum, even a nip of vodka. He'd added them to his tea while the orderlies weren't watching and then swilled mouth wash repeatedly to get rid of the reek of it on his breath. That first hit had been like a lorry load of bricks being tipped onto his chest. It had taken his breath away. He knew it was wrong, knew that he was undoing the only good thing that had come out of his forced incarceration, but that thought never stopped him. It only proved to him that some things couldn't be washed away, that rehab didn't work, and that some people were born alcoholics.

Kipruto was pretty insistent though. Alcohol was a no-no. If Raven wants to keep his badge, he has to stay away from the good stuff. He can do it. He's sure he can. Pretty sure. He came to the pub just for old time's sake, not to buy anything. That's what he tells himself. The fact it's now closed is just fate confirming his already under-lined, written in red ink set of rules. No arguments, no booze, talk to Lisa.

That thought brings him to his next stop. Lisa's place. The house she shares with her new husband, Simon fucking Draper. It's a thirty-minute walk from the centre of town, most of it uphill. He's okay with that. It gives him time to think and some much-needed exercise. The years locked away have reduced his cardio to that of a man in his eighties. It was never great — of that he is under no illusion — but it used to be better. If he's to stand any chance in his newly reinstated role as DI and the man in charge of catching the nefarious Heart Breaker, he at least has to be able to walk up a flight of stairs without getting so out of breath he wants to puke.

He runs the events of his first day back over in his mind. It's been one to remember: welcomed back into the arms of the local constabulary; introduced to the man he'd be taking charge of, a kid who looks like he's just finished his college degree; given a team of fresh-faced PCs who'll do the door-to-door legwork. He was even re-introduced to two faces he knew well: the newly trim detective Allison Bailey, and the ever reliable DI Ray 'Lola' Davis. They would be his eyes and ears, his reconnection to a force he had once known inside and out. It had all panned out in a way he couldn't have foreseen, and something about that sat wrong with him. It wasn't that he didn't trust Kipruto, he just didn't trust authority, and with Kipruto's strings being tugged by Fitzwilliam and the faceless bureaucrats who ran the county's law enforcement operation, he suspected something else was at play. He'd get to the bottom of that, just like he planned to get to the bottom of the case, but he'd stick to his promise. No face-to-face square ups, no public challenging of his orders. He'd be discrete but he wouldn't be compliant. Compliance was a trait he'd never possessed, and he didn't plan on changing.

He passes the terraced houses, the dusty streets of the working class, the inevitable Co-Op convenience store where kids congregate on battery powered scooters (when had that become a thing?), glaring threateningly at the old guy with the oddly shaped head pacing past. He passes the comprehensive where he'd once barely studied, ducking out for smoke breaks in the middle of dysfunctional classes or copping off with one of the girls behind the school-farm's storage shed. He walks past Lisa's old flat, third floor, second window from the left. It's the one where he'd regularly shown up late, sometimes by hours, often by days. The one where they'd made love for the first time, where their once notorious rows had started, where Lisa had thrown things at him, called him every curse word in the English dictionary (and many that were not), and where they'd made up time and time again, because they were kindred spirits, because their upbringings had both been national level catastrophes, and because they owned their many flaws, all of them. They were as tied to the relationship as their names and their bodies. He and Lisa had been conjoined at the soul level, beyond emotions and physical attraction. He didn't believe in the afterlife, but if he did, he would argue that Lisa was his fallen angel, and he her unrepentant demon. He had a devil on his tail, after all, and maybe that was fate once more coming calling.

He keeps walking until the houses get a little bigger and the on-road parking morphs into long driveways and double garages, no doubt housing top-down Porsches and battery powered coupés. These houses are newer, built on green fields that had once grown corn and potatoes, sold to big city board members at inflated price tags because they're the only people who can put up the capital. He suspects Lisa is in the minority around here, a born and bred local who actually knows something about the town's history and the people that live within it. He knows she would hate that. She was never one for snobbery, and she distrusted anybody who didn't have at least a sniff of the southern county twang. Dirty Londoners she would call them, even if they came from further afield. It didn't matter. They were all city dwellers to her.

Lisa Draper. Draper, not Clancy, and definitely not Raven. No, that name would have been way down the list. It begs the question, what about Harry, his son, the only thing he'd ever made perfectly? He would be nearing five now, his birthday just a couple of months away. Raven had missed four of those years, some of the most important years of his life, formative and lasting. Did the kid even remember him, or were the memories of the times they'd spent together now so diminished by time that only a fraction of them remained? Did they talk about him, Lisa and Harry? Did Simon — a name he couldn't bring himself to speak out loud — allow talk of Harry's father in the house? Was he a banned topic, like Brexit or the rise of the Reform party? Had he been erased?

He's there now. Lymington Crescent, number eight. It's an impressive place. Two storeys, four upstairs windows overlooking a deep, perfectly green front lawn. Wide driveway, two garages, a BMW parked out front, a Mini Cooper beside it, both shiny and relatively new by the looks of them. The Mini Cooper's personalised number plate is LS4 DRP. The sight of it makes him sick. He wants to rip it off, stamp on it, put it through a metal crusher and then take a dump on it. How dare Lisa move on so quickly? How dare she rubber stamp this farce of a relationship with a 'middle-class, two-thousand-pound excuse for a penis extension' personalised number plate; her words, not his? How dare she abandon his memory like this? Was he nothing to her? Was their time together just a lie, a fairy story, her way of treading water until something better came along? Was she happy he'd managed to get himself shot and kidnapped? Did it suit her twisted agenda?

He's getting angry now, his stomach so tied up in knots he can barely breathe. If he wanted a drink before, now his insides are demanding it. A Rusty Nail, double, one ice cube, vigorously stirred, and put a chaser beside it, same again. He can taste it, feel it, cherishes the way it makes his insides burn and his head spin. More quenching than water, more delicious than an aged red wine. If there was a keg of it right then on the lawn, he'd lie beneath the tap, open his mouth and let it fill his body until his liver explodes.

He slaps himself in the face and pushes the ridiculous notion away. Lisa lives here because she met somebody better, and she has a nice car with a personalised number plate because she can. Doesn't she deserve this? Hasn't she earned true happiness? She was almost killed. *Harry* was almost killed. Neither of those things would have happened if she had met Simon earlier and if she had never bumped into him. Everything bad she'd ever had to deal with since they'd met had been his fault. All of it. Every last ounce.

There's a silhouette at the downstairs window. Slim frame, hair down to the shoulders, female. His heart stops, mouth as dry as leather. He feels a flutter of anxiety, as nervous as the day they'd first met when he'd barely had the courage to talk to this new beautiful, punky redhead serving cigarettes and milk at his local shop. The blinds are closed, but it doesn't matter. It's Lisa. He would never forget her body or the way she stands, as if she's ready to take on the world at the drop of a hat.

He steps into the light, his face illuminated by the yellow glow of the streetlamp, and he cries. He actually cries. Not fake tears, not the kind of tears that spoilt kids shed when they can't get their own way; these are real tears, real salty drops of sadness, and he has no idea where they're coming from. He hasn't cried since he was a boy, not even at his father's fake funeral when he and his mother buried an empty coffin. He'd had this, all of it. Not just a small piece, but the whole package.

A blind twitches, and suddenly it's her face peering into the gloom. He moves back into the shadows and wipes away the damp from his cheeks. She hasn't aged a minute. Not one second. She looks just the way he remembers her. Slim nose, high cheekbones, dark eyes, as beautiful as the day they first met. She stands with one hand on the glass, the other in the pocket of her black jeans. She's scanning the front lawn, the driveway, the spot beneath the streetlamp where he'd just been standing. She senses something, perhaps him. He holds her glare, his gaze locked with her own, and for a moment he thinks she sees him, but he's not sure. Then there's somebody standing beside her: small person, shaggy blonde, round face, blue eyes. She slips her hand from her jeans and reaches out to clutch this newcomer's small one, peering down at him, smiling. The boy is Harry, his son. He's taller and he's grown into his body, but there's no mistaking his cheeky smile and sparkling eyes. Raven almost breaks his cover, but he somehow manages to stay put, despite every ounce of his being demanding that he goes to them. Harry says something to his mother, and she replies, pointing to the street. They both stand there looking, and Raven suddenly feels exposed. What if they think he's an intruder? What if they've been told he's coming, and they don't want him anywhere near them? He pushes the negativity away. Of course they want him. He's as much a part of their family as they are to each other.

He doesn't know what he's waiting for. This is the moment he's dreamed about, the reconciliation he's craved. He has so much so to catch up on. He wants to know everything: how they've been, how Harry is doing at school, how Lisa's new job is going. Did they miss him, do they still talk about him? He edges closer, his foot on the cusp of slipping into the light. One tap on the door, that's all it would take. One 'Hi, it's me,' or, 'Remember me? I'm alive,' and then the healing process can start.

Then there's another movement, this time a man. He appears at the window. Short, dark hair, the hint of a moustache, blue sweater, dark-grey trousers. He looks like an estate agent masquerading as a solicitor. It's Simon Draper, Lisa's new husband. He hands her a cup of something warm, probably sweet, and he kisses her forehead. She gives the street one last longing glance before the blinds close, and then she and Harry disappear from view.

The pain he feels is unbearable. The burgeoning need for whiskey is like a rope around his neck. He leans against the lamppost and draws a breath. The oxygen entering his lungs is hot and sharp. He can't go to the door now, not after seeing that. He can't predict what he'll do if he comes face to face with her new man. He hates the guy. He has a violent dislike for him.

He gives the house one more glance before he turns and walks away, tripping over his own feet and almost going down. He needs to get out of there. He needs to put distance between himself and number 8, Lymington Crescent. The sterile feel of the crisp lawns and neatly arranged petunias makes him want to throw up. He needs dirt, he needs grime, blood, fumes, cigarette smoke, the smell of spilt beer and broken glass. These streets aren't meant to be there, they don't fit in. These people, these new Westhamptonites, they don't belong. Lisa isn't this. She hates this. If she's living here with him, then she's changed. He has to escape. If he stays here any longer the sterility will infect him, rob him of his edge. He has a killer to catch, and the only way he can do that is to be him, to feel what he feels, understand what he's thinking. Yes, that's it. He isn't running from Lisa, he's running to do the thing he came back to do, the one thing that can make the past four years make sense.

He has to stop The Heart Breaker.

CHAPTER 18: SEAHORSES

Winston Carter has never been one to be pushed around. At school he had gotten into countless quarrels, and not ones he was ever likely to win. He was never much of a fighter, but he couldn't down from an argument, no matter the consequences. He had been a small kid — big head, short arms, stubby legs — but he had a big mouth and a short fuse. Later on, people would dub his personality as a bad case of 'small-man-syndrome', but back when he was a kid, people just saw him as an angry know-it-all. Things changed as he got older. His arms got longer, his torso stretched and he put on a few extra pounds, but that angry know-it-all demeanour only grew stronger. When he'd been promoted to store manager at 'In Our Wake', his true self had really come to the fore, and he'd gone through shop assistants quicker than an alcoholic gets through a six pack of Tennant's Extra.

That had all changed when Kaden Chapman had started, because even though Kaden had an unconventional look and an even more unconventional personality, he had been drawn to her. Or him. Or whatever personality Kaden chose to don on any particular day. He liked that about her. Loved it. It turned him on, even though he would never admit that to himself. The moment they had shared at Gold Diggers, that one tantalising glimpse of lust that had flitted like a firefly between them, had never left his mind. If anything, it had intensified, making the few seconds of interchange seem like much more than it actually had been, but now that Kaden has him by the arm and is dragging him toward her house like a dog on a lead, the feeling has concentrated to mind-melting levels. He can feel it in his body, his mind, his gradually hardening penis.

'Come on,' Kaden says, pulling him up the three narrow steps to the front door. 'Before I change my mind.'

He doesn't want her to do that, so he runs after her, almost tripping over the threshold as he steps inside. He's immediately assaulted by the smell of piss.

'What's that?'

'Dog,' Kaden says. 'Bloody thing needs to be toilet trained.'

Winston doesn't stop to wonder where the pissy dog is or why there's no sign of dog treats or a bowl. He just keeps moving, stepping around a rubbish bag that's just lying in the hallway, flies buzzing around its festering contents. There's a door up ahead, but they go past that and keep going beyond a darkened living room and a dining area with a tiny, grime covered plastic patio table and two white, plastic chairs. The staircase is up ahead, and Kaden heads towards it, turning around to beckon Winston to follow.

'My room's just up here,' she says.

Winston's desire burns like a towering flame in his lungs. He can barely compose himself. He doesn't pay any attention to the peeling wallpaper, flaking paint and the yellow, dripping nicotine stains on the ceiling and woodwork. These things are immaterial to him. He keeps thinking about Kaden, her tall frame, toned body, the swell of her breasts and her well-proportioned arse.

They enter the landing and turn left, past the bathroom that reeks of damp and mould, and the first bedroom where the smell of piss is now so strong it hits the back of his throat like a shot of absinthe.

There's one more door on the left, but Kaden pulls him past that and heads to the bare wall at the end of the landing. It's covered in blue wallpaper depicting all sorts of ocean creatures: clownfish, dolphins, angelfish, seahorses.

'What's going on?' Winston asks. 'I thought we were—'

'Shut up,' Kaden hisses, and it's the first time he notices a subtle shift in her demeanour.

She reaches into her pocket, pulls out a key and pushes it into a lock that's hidden behind a loose piece of skirting board. She stands, slides one long nail into a crack in the corner of the wall, and suddenly the ocean is moving towards them, swinging to the left and revealing a dark doorway.

'Kaden, what is this?' he asks, but then he's being pulled again, and he gets caught up in the excitement of it. A secret room, some sort of kinky sex chamber, maybe. He's down with that. Fetish is his thing, after all. If Kaden wants to play that game, so be it.

Kaden reaches behind them and closes the door, latching it from the inside. The room is completely black now, a darkness so thick it almost chokes him. For a second, panic threatens to overcome him, but then there's a movement, followed by a soft click, and a dull light comes on, revealing a twelve-feet by seven-feet room, a single, metal-framed bed, a wooden chest of drawers, and a large fish tank filled with a collection of some sort of sea animal.

'This is nice,' he says. 'I dig it. You don't want people to see what you get up to.'

'They wouldn't understand,' Kaden says, turning and cupping Winston's testicles in her hand.

'Woah, you don't waste any time.'

'Why wait when I can take what I want, whenever I want to.'

'You're a woman after my own heart.'

'And you're the only man I need right now.'

She turns them around and pushes him onto the bed. They kiss, slowly at first, but then harder, more passionately. Kaden's tongue slips into his open mouth, and he returns the gesture, relishing the apple sour taste of her lips and the bubble-gum spit in her mouth. Something hits the back of his throat, and he starts to cough, but then whatever it is slips down his gullet.

'Acid?' he asks, now more turned on than ever.

Kaden doesn't reply, she just stands, walks to the chest and opens the top drawer.

Winston can't take his eyes off her. He wonders what she looks like beneath the fitted top and skin-tight jeans. The anticipation is killing him, but he doesn't want to rush. He wants this night to last forever.

He begins to feel lightheaded, which he guesses is the tab she's just slipped into his mouth. That's cool. He's not naïve. He knows how drugs can heighten the sexual experience. He's done drugs before. Marijuana mostly, but a little MDMA too.

He's getting high now. He can feel it. His body is becoming numb, his fingertips like little plasticine people attached to his hands, his toes like blocks of wood. He looks at the ceiling and sees an odd pattern on the yellow plaster. Spots of darkness, the opposite of stars, more like an artist has taken a pot of paint and flicked it from the end of a brush. He gazes at the tiled floor and sees clear patches where it's been scrubbed, maybe to remove stains or mould. He then turns his attention to the fish tank and stares at the oddly shaped sea creatures or tropical plants. They're thick and round with little tube-like protrusions. They just float in the water, which is a little yellow.

Next to him, Kaden turns. She's holding something, but now the acid goes to his vision and everything becomes a little swimmy, like somebody has adjusted the tuning on the TV set. The thing in her hand reflects the light, so he guesses it's made of metal or glass.

'Are you going to handcuff me?' he thinks he says, but in reality, he's just making garbled sounds that make no sense.

Kaden doesn't reply, but that's okay. They're in the middle of the game, and she's playing the part of the dominatrix. That's cool too, because that's exactly what he's into. He wants to be dominated. He wants Kaden to show him what a bad boy he's been. He wants to know how much he upset her when he shouted at her in the shop in front of all those boys. He wants to be punished for being such a dick. He wants to be taught a lesson he'll never forget.

He looks up and she's there, and now he can see her again: green eye shadow, dark red lips, the tattoo on her shoulder of some sort of seahorse with glowering eyes and a knowing smile. He sees the black latex gloves she's now wearing, and the curved blade of the bone saw. Something's not right. This isn't a game anymore.

'Kaden,' he tries to say. 'Whatever the safe word is, I'm saying it. I've changed my mind. I don't want to be here.'

Her expression remains impassive, as if she isn't really there.

She places a gloved hand on his chest and tears his shirt open, revealing auburn curls surrounding his left nipple. She sets the saw aside and takes a marker pen from a bowl beside the bed. Sharpee. Black. She removes the lid and presses the nib against his sternum, moving it to her right around his left breast and bringing it back to just left of centre. The nib of the pen is cold, but he barely feels it. He can barely feel anything.

'This is fucked up!' he yells. 'Kaden, whatever you're doing, stop!'

She collects something else from the bowl, and as soon as he sees it, he starts to scream. It's a scalpel, surgical, the steel glistening under the glare of the overhead light.

'Get away from me!' he screams in his garbled, saliva-soaked way. 'Get that thing away from me!'

She doesn't listen, pressing the tip of the knife against his pert nipple and slicing into the skin. This time he does feel it, and he screams again.

'Fuck you, bitch! Fuck you!'

She keeps cutting, pushing the knife beneath the erect teat until its completely severed from the flesh beneath. Blood is pouring down his chest now, soaking his white and pale-blue button-down. He tries to kick his legs, thrash his arms, but he has barely any control of them. He manages to move his hands, but they just look like upturned crabs, his fingers tensing, clawing at the air.

'Please stop! Please! It hurts so bad!'

She holds the nipple up to study it, rotates it so he can see it too, and then licks it. Winston's stomach lurches as Kaden wraps her tongue around the severed flesh, caressing it and dripping blood and saliva all over his upturned face. He retches, choking on his own vomit, but she drops the chunk of meat into a clear plastic bowl and lifts up his head, clearing his airway.

'Don't die on me, sweetie,' she says. 'We still have so much work to do.'

He sees the knife coming and can do nothing about it. Tears ooze from his right eye, then the left. He's terrified, but he's angry too. How dare she do this to him? How fucking dare she? She draws the blade along the black line from left to right. The pain is unbearable, like a hot brand being held against his flesh. This time he finds feeling in his legs, and he kicks out, striking Kaden in the thigh.

She extracts the knife and jabs it into his calf, and there's an explosion of agony. He screams again, louder this time.

'Keep still,' she says. 'This won't take long.'

'Just let me go. Whatever you're planning, do it to someone else. I won't say anything. I swear. I won't say a thing.'

She goes back to her work, drawing the knife along the line, peeling skin from flesh, blood pouring from the long, precise incision. He thinks he's going to pass out from the pain, but he remains conscious and feels every movement of the keen blade. The warmth of his blood coats his chest, his stomach, his spine.

He's lying in his own essence. He can't be sure if it's all blood or if his bladder has let go. When the cutting stops, it's a blessed relief, but he knows it won't be for long. He still hasn't forgotten about that bone saw.

A deep, sickening dread settles into the pit of his stomach. Despite the pain in his chest and leg, and the high dose of morphine she obviously slipped him, he can still think straight. He's read about this in online. The new sicko in town. As Kaden turns to fetch the next blade, he spins his head to the fish tank, and now he sees it for what it really is. It isn't a fish tank at all. It's a preservation container, and those aren't sea creatures or some sort of coral. They're hearts. Three of them. Brown meat dissected by thick veins and large, organic tubes that protrude like hollow fingers. They're bobbing in yellow liquid, bouncing against each other before rolling away. Vomit rises in his throat like hydrochloric acid, and he turns to one side, spilling three beers and a half-eaten burger all over the pillow and mattress.

'Oh dear,' Kaden says. 'Is Winston feeling a little under the weather.'

'You're a fucking psycho,' he spits through a mouthful of his own sick.

'What was that? You want me to get it over and done with? There's no need to be impatient, dear. I'm going as fast as I can.'

His cheek sticks to the vomit. The sensation causes more retching, and even more of his dinner comes up. Now he's practically drowning in his own puke.

The bone saw whirs, and he looks up to see Kaden bearing down on him, her eyes so dark he can barely see her pupils. One side of her mouth is drawn upward, exposing her teeth, incisors biting, jaw clenched. 'No!' he screams, but the saw strikes bone, and there's a shower of crimson and grey. As the agony threatens to blot out his conscious thought, he realises what the dark marks are on the ceiling. It's not paint after all. The others were killed here, too. There's a sensation like the snip of a barber's scissors, and then she's rummaging inside him, fishing around in his chest like she's looking for an old pair of socks. There's a squelching, sucking sound, and more blood sprays as the crescendo of agony reaches atomic levels. Everything begins to slip away, but not before he sees his own heart gripped in the killer's raised hand, the valves still frantically pumping, ejecting crimson spatters over Kaden Chapman's beaming smile.

CHAPTER 19: THUMP

Raven is drunk. He knows he is because he remembers being in the local Wetherspoon's, The Pride of the Solent, sinking more Rusty Nails than he could count, and staggering out into the street on legs that felt like Playdough. He even remembers convincing the lady behind the desk at the Travelodge to give him a room, even though he could barely string three words together. He doesn't know where he is now, though, because this isn't a room in a hotel. Not any hotel he's ever stayed in anyway.

He's sitting downstairs in what appears to be a house. It's dark outside, and the only thing lighting the room is the hazy glow of a streetlamp outside. He can't move because something is binding him to the chair. He looks down at the ground, but the floor is covered in what appears to be some sort of thick skin which covers his feet. There's a shadow in the corner of the room that stands six feet tall. It's darker than the other shadows, an impenetrable black hole in a sea of grey.

There's a thumping sound from upstairs, like somebody is slamming their hands on the floor. He looks up at the yellow ceiling, but dust particles hit his eyes, and he's temporarily blinded. He closes them, using his tears to wash the crap away, and when he opens them again, the shadow has moved closer. It's now standing by the fireplace, less than six feet from where he's seated.

There's a gentle tapping on the window, but when he turns to the sound, there's nobody there. The thumping stops for a moment, throwing the room into an eery quiet. Something moves beyond the glass, a body, a person. A hand touches the windowpane, the palm caked in dried blood. Raven tries to inch the chair closer, but his feet are trapped beneath the skin membrane and the chair stays put. Another hand reaches for the glass, and this one holds a knife. A scalpel. As the hands slide away, they leave a smear of blood.

Raven turns back to the shadow, and sure enough, it's moved again, this time to the wall to his right. It's only three feet away now. Whatever it is, he's terrified of it. He doesn't want to be in this house, he doesn't want to be in this room.

Somebody screams in a room upstairs.

'I don't want this! I don't want this!'

He turns his attention to the staircase. There's a person standing there, a silhouette in the darkness, its hand gripping the handrail. It slides towards him, a lock of hair slipping from behind an ear.

'Who are you?' he asks, but then the thumping starts again, and this time it's so loud, he can barely think straight.

'I need to pee!' somebody yells, the words in time with the thumping. 'I need to pee!'

The black shadow to his right lurches forward, and now he can smell it. It reeks of sulphur. There's a stream of hot air too, as if somebody has left a hairdryer on.

'I need to pee!'

THUMP

'I need to pee!'

THUMP

There's another scream, as though somebody is in the throes of some horrendous torture. He tries to place it. It appears to be coming from a room on the first floor, toward the right-hand side of the house.

'I need to pee!'

THUMP

'I need to pee!'

THUMP

The shadow surrounds him now, as if a thick blanket has been thrown over him. He feels what it feels, senses what it senses. It's angry, snarling, spitting. It wants him, every part of him. It has been searching for him for so long. A debt needs to be repaid. He was taken from it, stolen away at the precise moment it intended to feast. He's back now, which is good. When the time is right, it will return, and then there will be no escape.

'I need to pee!'

THUMP

'I need to pee!'

THUMP

Another scream, a gurgling, blood filled shout, and when the shadow disappears, the skin at his feet has been torn in two and beneath him is a bubbling, spitting pit of lava and flames, and within the flames is the snarling face of something he has faced many times before but has somehow managed to keep two steps ahead of.

He turns to the silhouette on the stairs, and it holds out its hand. The streetlamp flickers a little brighter outside, its yellow glare reaching the downstairs hallway, and now he can see what the dark figure is holding. It's red and beating, blood oozing from severed arteries, slick liquid coating the grimy floor in a crimson gloss. This is the place where it happens. This is the house where those people were killed. He tries to take a mental image, attempts to recall everything he has seen, but just as he begins to take an inventory, the floor collapses and he's sent tumbling into the infernal abyss.

CHAPTER 20: OUROBOROS

There's a loud ring followed by a rumbling vibration, and he sits up, causing a blinding pain to shoot between his temples. He grasps for his mobile phone, but it tumbles to the floor, flipping on its front and throwing the room back into darkness. He reaches for the table lamp, fumbles for the on-switch, but only succeeds in knocking over a plastic cup of water he must have very responsibly placed beside the bed before crashing out. The water spills all over the bedside cabinet, soaking the base of the lamp and the floor.

'Fuck,' he says. 'Fuck, fuck, *fuck.*'

He swings out of bed, tosses the duvet and gropes around on the carpet, searching for the vibrating phone. He finds it, flips it on its back and sees Kipruto's name glaring back at him from the screen. His stomach lurches and he heads for the bathroom, throwing the toilet seat up just in time to eject enough whiskey and Drambuie to put a horse to sleep. Everything comes out: the booze; the meat and chips he'd devoured on his way to the hotel; the Snickers bar he'd managed to extract from the vending machine as he made his way up the stairs to his room. The stench is enough to make him want to vomit again, but he holds it in, collapsing against the bathtub, bile and leftover doner meat smeared down his chest.

'Not a good look,' he says, peering down at himself.

The phone has stopped ringing, which is both a good and a bad thing. He knows Kipruto will be calling about the case, and he is literally one day into the job. The least his new boss can expect is that his DI will pick up the phone at—he checks his watch—5.10 in the morning? He wipes sleep from his eyes and checks again.

5.10 a.m.? It's early, even for a relatively new DCS, and way too early for Raven to have sobered up yet.

He remembers Lisa and Harry staring out the window, the new guy in her life handing her a cup of tea. He remembers feeling like his life has been wrenched from his guts and stomped all over the tarmac. Then he remembers the dream: the thing in the shadows; the skin-carpet keeping his feet glued to the floor. He recalls the repeated thumping and the figure on the staircase holding the fleshy, oozing heart. He knows he's too late, that the killer has struck again. He thinks of the bottle of booze he'd drowned himself in, and the time he'd wasted on his own self-pity. It's the same old mistakes, the same old frailties. Molly couldn't cure him of those, any more than she could cure her own sickness.

He splashes cold water on his face, glares at the ugly scar on the side of his head and grabs his phone.

'Kipruto, it's me. Sorry I missed your call.'

'Not a problem. It's a little earlier than I'd usually contact you, but there's been a development.'

'A development?'

There's a moment of silence.

'It's probably best you head over, see for yourself.'

Raven grabs a pen and a notepad from beside the kettle. 'Address?'

'You're not going to believe it, but it's your old stomping ground.'

Raven knows what Kipruto is about to say before he says anything, because the world is a funny place. It works with a strange sort of symmetry, a cycle on repeat like one of those oriental dragons that eats its own tail.

'Westhampton Common,' Kipruto says. 'The body's at Westhampton Common.'

CHAPTER 21: ACRYLIC

He's on the scene in less than twenty minutes, showering, throwing on a crumpled shirt, creased trousers and jacket while crunching on a packet of extra strong mints, also obtained via the hotel's well stocked vending machine. He walks a mile to the common, stopping only to grab a Maccy Dee's americano and sausage and egg McMuffin combo. He knows it's not healthy, but he's survived a bullet to the head, so he figures he's got credits to spare.

Bailey is the first to greet him. She's dress in a pale blue suit and white shirt. She looks great, and although her usually beaming smile is kept well hidden, it feels good to see her.

'Raven, you made it.'

'Wouldn't miss this for the world,' he replies.

'I'm warning you, it's not good.'

'What are the low points?'

'Victim is one Winston Carter, thirty-three years old, manages the surf shop by the beach front.'

'In Our Wake,' he says.

'What's that?'

'The shop. It's called In Our Wake. I guess it's what you might call a pun. That place has been there longer than I've been alive.'

'Right,' Bailey replies. 'I'll look into that. Anyway, Carter was last seen leaving the shop at around 6 p.m. last night. After that, we don't know.'

'You have somebody checking the CCTV across town?'

Bailey nods. 'Davis is seeing to that now.'

Raven sips his coffee. Bitter, just like his mood. He still can't shake the image of Lisa at the window, that fucker handing her a mug like he owned her.

'Well, let's get this over with,' he says, passing Bailey his cup. 'Finish that if you like. Black, no sugar.'

She turns her nose up. 'I prefer a cappuccino, two sweeteners.'

'Good for you, now where's the victim?'

They walk past two uniforms who are making sure the area is secure, crouch beneath the cordon tape, and descend into a copse of trees separated by a small area of bare earth. In the middle of this patch of ground is Winston Carter, naked, butt unceremoniously pointing towards the sky. He's face down, head cocked to the right, eyes open. His arms are spread out in front of him, his legs bent beneath his body.

'Any significance of the pose?' Raven asks as he walks around him, recalling the splayed body of the Pale Faced killer's first victim, Tracey Webb. She had been positioned just across the common, less than a quarter of a mile from this exact spot.

Bailey shrugs. 'Not that we can think of. Maybe to hide the cause of death.'

'Which was?'

Bailey drops to her knees and points to the right side of Carter's chest. 'Heart cut out, same as the others.'

Raven recalls the figure on the staircase again, the blood oozing from the still pulsing organ.

'We follow protocol,' Raven says. 'Get the crime scene investigators in, then get the body off to the pathologist. We didn't want another victim, but we've got one, and that means there has to be clues.'

'There weren't any the last three times,' Bailey replies, arms folded. 'And we looked really hard.'

'Doesn't matter. Serial killers get lazy sometimes, comfortable, maybe even a little arrogant. This guy last killed less than a month ago, right?'

Bailey nods. 'Three weeks and four days.'

'And the time before that was two months? Maybe three?'

'Seven weeks and two days.'

'Right, so he's speeding up. That means he's taking risks. That's the kind of thing we need to exploit.'

He stands, wipes the back of his hand across his mouth. Bailey eyes him with suspicion. He wonders if his breath reeks of whiskey.

'How are we doing on those house calls?' he asks, popping another mint in his mouth.

'They're starting this morning,' she says. 'Kicking off on the east side, working their way past the university district and then up into the Palisades.'

'Keep to the working-class areas,' Raven says. 'Places that look like the owners haven't been keeping up with the maintenance.'

'Why?' Bailey asks. 'Middle class people are equally as likely to do something like this.'

'I know, but you're going to have to trust me on this. I have a hunch.' *It's more than a hunch*, he thinks. *I saw it, or at least I heard it. I was right there.*

Bailey shrugs and lets out a long breath, reaching into her bag to extract her notebook

'Something wrong?' he asks.

'Wrong?'

'You look pissed off.'

She shakes her head. 'Not pissed off exactly. Just worried.'

His eyes narrow. 'Worried? About what?

'About this case. About you.'

'We can handle this,' he replies. 'We have a good team, and with Kipruto's backing, we have the resources.'

'That's not what I mean. Look, boss, I've worked with you a long time, right? Longer than most of the people here have been with the force.'

She was right on that score. Bailey had been a PC when Raven had been coming through the ranks. Over the years they'd worked on drugs busts, domestic abuse cases, armed robbery and murder investigations together. She'd been promoted to detective shortly after he'd been suspended for drunken battery.

'What's your point?' he asks.

'My point is, I know you. I know how you act. Turning up in a crumpled shirt like the one you're wearing, smelling like you've just walked out of a distillery? Those are the kinds of things that got you into a mess in the first place.'

He feigns shock. 'I haven't touched a drink since before I was kidnapped.'

'Lying is another one of those things.' She pushes her notebook into her pocket. 'Boss, I'm one of the people who searched for you, we searched all over. I was driving around the country for weeks, chasing down every potential sighting, sleeping in cheap hotels, interviewing hundreds of people. I was as distraught as anybody when they shut the case down, so when the DCS told us you were alive and coming back, I cried my eyes out.'

'Happy tears, I hope.'

She smiles. 'Of course they were happy tears, but this case, boss, this case is important.'

'I know that.'

'No, you don't. You can't, because from the smell of you, you stayed out all night, drinking more alcohol than your body can handle, and came straight here from a hotel room. I'm guessing the Travelodge in town.'

He's impressed with her instincts, but only for a second. The crime scene team are walking their way, which means he has less than a minute to extract himself from this conversation.

'Lisa's married,' he says. 'I went there last night to see her.'

'I know. I'm so sorry.'

'Couldn't go in. Just stood there on the street like some kind of creepy stalker. I saw Harry. Saw her new husband too. From a distance I mean. I never actually had the courage to knock on the door.'

'Did she see you?'

He thinks about that. Did she? Did either of them? 'I don't think so. I hope not. I don't think I would have given a good impression of myself.'

She places her hand on his arm. 'Does she know you're alive?'

He shakes his head. 'Not yet. I want to be the one to tell her.'

'Then you have to do that before she finds out from someone else.'

'I'm working up to it,' he smiles. 'Really, I am. I just need a little more time.'

Two crime scene guys step into the clearing, but he holds up a hand. 'One minute,' he says.

'Sure thing.'

'I know how much you'll be hurting,' Bailey says. 'I know it from personal experience, believe me, but the sauce isn't going to make what you have to do any easier. In fact, it'll make it a hundred times more difficult.'

'Don't tell Kipruto,' he says. 'I promised him I'd stay off the booze, so please, don't tell him.'

She shakes her head. 'If he asks, I'm not going to lie.'

'I'm not asking you to lie, I'm just asking you to have my back.'

She chews her lower lip, shakes her head again.

'For old time's sake,' he pleads. 'For all those times I covered for you when you were off shagging the guy from accounts.'

'Boss!' she cries. 'Is that really how you're going to play this?'

'Just for me, then,' he says. 'And I'll do a good job, I will. We'll catch this guy, Alli, I promise. We'll have this guy behind bars before he kills again.'

She thinks about it, exhaling through her nose before leaning forward and whispering in his ear. 'Okay, but don't make me regret this, Luke. I mean it. Don't make me hate you.'

'You won't,' he says, spying something odd on the ground. He drops to his knees. 'You might want to bag this.'

'What is it?' she asks.

He reaches up, takes one of her hands in his and points at the long red nail at the tip of her index finger.

'Acrylic would be my guess,' he says, eyeing the purple fingernail embedded in the mulch. Bailey's mouth falls open. 'Looks like our killer made her first big mistake.'

CHAPTER 22: DOPAMINE

Lisa Draper wakes up at 5.45 that morning, just as the man she conceived her son with is picking an acrylic fingernail from the dirt in Westhampton Common. She hasn't slept well. She hasn't really been sleeping well for a couple of weeks. Something is on her mind, but she can't put her finger on it. She wakes up with a sense of dread, but no matter how hard she tries, she can't figure out why. She should be happy. She is living in an expensive home, married to a guy who loves her, and rather handily, has more money than sense, and her son is becoming a well-mannered, extremely handsome boy. The people she grew up with would kill for a life like hers, one where she doesn't want for anything, she has a job she loves, and a man who would do absolutely anything for her.

She gets up, heads to the kitchen — which is bigger than her first flat — and makes a coffee. The house is huge. Four bedrooms, two bathrooms, a dressing room, two offices, a large living room, games room and a kitchen diner that stretches right across the rear of the property. When she sold it to the man who would become her husband, it had been the biggest single sale Exquisite Homes had ever made. Almost a million pounds, enough to bring in a commission that cleared all her debts, put Harry in a good school and left her with a sizeable nest egg. Her husband earns more money than she could even begin to comprehend, but she isn't a kept woman. She would never be that. It isn't in her nature.

She sits at the table, gazes out the bi-fold doors at the wide lawn, the two-tier pond, and the planted flowerbeds, and yawns.

She wonders how she can be so tired yet barely able to get any sleep.

Her husband is already at work. He leaves at the crack of dawn to beat his employees into the office. He works hard for his money, of which there is a lot, but he never complains. He's different to her old flame, Luke Raven, in many ways. He doesn't drink, he doesn't go around punching people just because they've looked at her the wrong way, and he never lets her down. Raven, on the other hand, could go absent for days at a time, only to turn up at her flat, off his face on whiskey and as horny as a rabbit in season. She misses Luke, she misses what they had, but she cherishes Simon. He's given her son the life he deserves, and for that, she will always be grateful.

Her phone pings. It's Ruby. She doesn't sleep well either. The kids won't let her.

Morning beautiful. You sleep as much as I did?

Lisa types a reply, pausing only to laugh at her own attempt at humour.

If you mean, did I manage to close my eyes for longer than the time it takes for my husband to start snoring, then yep. I guess I did.

Ruby sends her a laughing face emoji, followed by,

I've been thinking about Raven recently.

Her comment is so out of the blue, Lisa almost spills her coffee. Ruby hardly ever mentions Luke anymore, not since the case was put on long-term hiatus. She wonders why she brings him up now. Has she been reading her mind, somehow reaching across the distance between them and rummaging around in her head? She considers her response, and after a moment to consider, decides that honesty is the best approach.

I've been thinking about him too.

She hits send and immediately feels like she's betraying Simon. Somebody could read that message and think that if she's been thinking about Luke, she hasn't been thinking about her husband, but that isn't true. She thinks about Simon all the time, mainly because he's there most of the time. That thought shocks her too. That isn't the only reason she thinks about him. She loves him, of course she does. If she didn't, she wouldn't have married him, would she? *Would she?*

Has anybody spoken to you about him recently?

Another bolt out of the blue from Ruby.

You mean, like a therapist?

She had seen a therapist not long after Luke's disappearance, but that was only because Ruby had forced one upon her. Lisa has never been good at opening up to people, especially not strangers, and even though Doctor Lambert had her best interests at heart, Lisa abandoned the sessions after just two weeks. Luke Raven is her own emotional trauma to nurture. She doesn't need somebody else prodding at him.

Not exactly. I mean anyone. Like anybody at all?

Now Lisa is really intrigued because it's obvious Ruby has something to say. She thinks about hitting dial and actually speaking to her friend, but she doubts Ruby would pick up. This seems like a conversation she wants to have behind the comfort of her phone screen. She bats the question back like a skilled tennis pro.

Who else would want to talk to me about Luke? A police officer? The press?

There's another long pause and for a moment Lisa thinks the chat is over. Perhaps Ruby has interpreted that last message as an angry reaction. Perhaps it was. Why bring Luke up now? Especially after the way Lisa had felt last night, standing at that window, looking into the darkness. She had never felt so close to Luke as she had at that precise moment, as if he was somehow right in front of her, staring into her eyes the way he used to, holding her glare, daring her to leave him, knowing she couldn't. The tension between them had always been so… intense, so exciting. Like a dopamine hit. He'd been bad for her, but he'd been good for her too. When he wasn't there, she missed him. When he was there, she hated him, but she wanted him too. She pushed him away, but she always pulled him back. He would upset her, make her so angry, but he would also make her laugh like nobody else ever could. Love, hate, anger, joy, desperation, adulation. She had felt all those emotions last night, as if she was reliving their whole time together in a few short minutes. It was like he'd never really been taken, which of course was ludicrous. She'd watched it happen, felt her heart be torn from her body and then suffered the loss over and over again as the search went on and on for years and years.

Randall has new information. I was hoping he'd already been over to see you. I asked him to.

She read and re-read that message several times. New information? What did that mean? She'd had enough new information to fill an encyclopaedia, and none of it had amounted to anything. Sightings all over the country, witnesses claiming to have had long conversations with Luke, conspiracy theorists throwing around wild theories about Clarence Fitzwilliam wanting his old DI out of the picture and that Staker's weird, cultish organisation, The Legion, had conspired with the politician to have him murdered.

The only new information that would mean anything to me is if Luke was to show up at my door. Unfortunately, that's not likely to happen any time soon.

She swigs the remains of her coffee, rinses the cup out and places it in the dishwasher. Although she likes Ruby, their conversation is going nowhere. Time is ticking, and pretty soon she will have to wake Harry up, get him ready for school, drop him off, and then head over to her boss, Chelsea Butler's house for a breakfast meeting. They'd just secured a client who wanted to sell three of their properties, which meant a lot of hours going through paperwork and liaising with solicitors. She loves the job but it's full on, and she's still only a novice dealing with imposter syndrome. She finds the only way she can cope with the burgeoning workload is to stay ahead of it, and that means not getting caught up in pointless WhatsApp chats about a topic that has been dragging on for almost as long as Harry has been alive.

She heads upstairs, leaving her phone on the breakfast table with the new message from Ruby staring at the ceiling, pleading with somebody to read it.

That's just it, Lis. That's what I wanted Randall to tell you. Luke's alive.

CHAPTER 23: KILL THEM ONCE

Kaden Chapman sits in her room and stares at the preservation tank. She's humming a song she used to sing a lot when she was a kid. Tainted Love, the Soft Cell version. She stares at Winston's bloated heart. It's bigger than she thought it would be. Healthier too. It looks strange against the others in her collection, which now seem a little meek and withered by comparison. Four hearts aren't enough. They're not even close to being enough. She has to keep going. She has to fill the tank. There is so much work to do.

She knows they're watching. The people that matter. The task has changed. At first it was for her, only for her, but now it's for them. Her too, but not in the same way. She once worked in an office, selling garden furniture for a home improvement company. She wasn't very good at it, and after a few months, her manager offered to mentor her. She had declined, of course, suspecting that the guy who was old enough to be her granddad just wanted to have some alone time with the girl with the weird hair. She'd quit right there on the spot, calling him a sick paedo pervert, and had received a letter of apology from him shortly afterwards which had clearly been written by a lawyer. She's being mentored now, but the man who runs the organisation she's collecting hearts for isn't like the guy from the home improvement company. He mentors her in a different way. All he wants is for her to inflict as much pain on the people of Westhampton as possible, because that's in the best interest of the cause they both share. The righteous cause.

She puts her mouth to the glass of the tank, leaving lipstick residue in a round welt. She can almost taste the muscle tissue and the congealed blood. She shakes the container, watching as the organs crash together like bumper cars, thinking how similar they are to sexual swingers, four hearts in an enclosed space, naked, rubbing against each other. She senses the friction, feels the heat, and that makes her horny.

She has scrubbed the room clean, changed the bed sheets and thrown the plastic covering in the firepit where its charred remains still smoulder. Sometimes she gets complaints about that, but not often. People tend to avoid her because they don't understand her. Ignorance, she finds, is the best disguise there is. She even disposed of Winston's severed nipple, but only after she'd given the flaccid teat a little bite. She wonders if in some parallel dimension a version of Winston felt her teeth on him, and the sensation of her got him off. She holds onto that thought because having a link with her victims after death has always been a kink of hers. Kill them once, control them forever.

The excitement of the kill has left her feeling masculine again, so today she's decided she will be Kaden the boy. She has removed her tight-fitting jeans, skinny top and eyeshadow, replacing her womanly clothes with black combat trousers and a Blink 182 T-Shirt. She no longer wears high heels. Instead, she's donning well-worn Doc Marten boots.

She exits the room, locks the door and replaces the piece of skirting board. She slips the key into her pocket and goes for a piss. She listens to the urine splashing into the water and thinks about the gore gushing from Winston's butchered chest. She wipes, flushes and stands in front of the mirror, washing the piss from her hands and the blood from beneath her fingernails.

That's when she notices one is missing. One purple acrylic nail. The tip of her index finger is as bare as a baby's bald head. She lifts her hands, checks every finger and thumb. She doesn't panic because panic is for the unintelligent. Instead, she finds her key, pulls the piece of skirting board up and heads back into her secret room. She finds her phone, flips it to torch mode and scours the floor. It's just been cleaned so there's nothing there, just a house spider making a new web in one corner. She crushes the plump arachnid between her fingers and flicks its oozing carcass across the room.

She checks her cabinet, the drawer where she keeps her tools, feeling sure the nail must have been dislodged there. It wasn't.

She goes to the tank, puts on a pair of gloves, reaches inside and pulls out Winston's heart. She checks the severed arteries, the ventricles, the left atrium. She thinks it might have gotten jammed in the soft tissue like a tiny sword, but the flesh is intact, the arteries unclogged. She drops the heart back into the fluid and closes the lid, tossing her gloves onto the bed.

It's not here. The nail isn't here. That can only mean one thing. She must have left it where she disposed of Winston's pathetic, flabby excuse for a body. It's somewhere out there in the woods and by now the scene will be filled with coppers and forensic experts. They'll find the nail, take it back to the labs and extract the wealth of DNA adhered to it.

'Amanda? Amanda? Is that you?'

The sound of her uncle's voice is enough to incite something inside her. Fury. Animalistic rage. She's had enough of him, the useless bag of piss and shit she's had to wait on hand and foot every single day since her mother died. The elderly relative who used to fiddle with her breasts and slip his hand beneath her skirt, pretending he'd lost his cigarette lighter, as if it had somehow made its way into her knickers. The man who'd slipped his tongue into her mouth when she'd been asleep and then proceeded to expose his penis, only for her mother to come in and accuse her own daughter of trying to seduce her uncle.

She heads back into the bathroom, scrapes away the remains of her makeup, takes a pair of scissors from the mould-stained bathroom cabinet and hacks at her long hair, pulling it away in thick clumps, hacking and chopping. She goes at it like some sort of crazed gardener. After a frantic minute, she's left with an uneven, shaggy clump of black, her fringe snipped in a straight line across her forehead. She looks untidy, unkempt, but she doesn't care. She is Kaden the boy today, and Kaden the boy is angry. In fact, he's fucking spitting blood.

'Amanda, I need to pee!'

He glares at the scissors, pushes one finger against the tip until it draws blood and turns to her uncle's bedroom.

'I'm coming, Uncle,' he says, his left fist clenched, right hand clutching the blades. 'I'm coming right now.'

CHAPTER 24: QUESTIONS?

Raven isn't thinking about Lisa or Harry anymore. There's no room in his head for anything other than the case. He has the proverbial bit between his teeth. He hasn't felt like this since the Staker thing. The thrill of the chase, the excitement of new evidence being uncovered. Things are already starting to snowball, and when they do, it's important to keep the momentum going.

He's only twenty-four hours in but that's immaterial. He's been dreaming about the murders for months. He knows more about The Heart Breaker than anybody on the task force. He's seen how he does what he does, he's experienced the pain his victims feel, and more importantly, he's seen where he commits the brutal slayings. Nobody else has that intel. Nobody else can get into the killer's head like he can. It's taken him six years to come to terms with his unexplained talents, but right now he's embracing them, knowing they're key to stopping yet another homicidal maniac.

'Coffee?' Bailey asks, filling her cup from the steaming pot.

'Please,' he replies. 'Any news on the fingernail?'

'No, not yet.'

'Do we think our killer's female?'

'Maybe,' Bailey says. 'Maybe not. Could be a guy who likes to wear acrylics. There's plenty that do.'

Raven stares at his own hands. 'We need to get something from the labs ASAP. That evidence is key to our investigation.'

'It's literally just made it to the lab. It could be another three or four days before we get anything back, and that's only if the stars align and the wind blows the right way.'

'Well, hurry them up,' he says. 'I don't want anybody thinking this can wait. We pick up DNA from that, and my guess is we'll get a match with somebody on the PND. If we do, boom, this case is put to bed and nobody else gets murdered on our watch.'

'I know, but they've had it less than three hours.'

'That's three hours too long.'

Bailey huffs as she heads back to her desk, her feet hitting the floor harder than necessary.

Raven pours his own cup, takes a sip and smiles at the lukewarm bitterness of the stale coffee. Despite his extended absence, it appears some things in the police force don't change.

He turns and bumps into a kid in a sky-blue jacket, matching trousers, and white shirt. He has auburn hair that's combed and waxed to the left, and the sides of his head are shaved to stubble. It's ironic, because the kid's attempt at a goatee is limited to a few strands of bumfluff on the end of a narrow chin.

'Sorry,' Raven says, and then realises who the kid is. 'It's Harvey, right?'

'DI Harvey Welling, Somerset Police.'

'And the lead investigator on this case until yesterday.'

The kid's eyes twitch. 'When you showed up.'

'Yeah, sorry about that.'

'Never had my own case before. I was as shocked as anybody when they asked me to transfer. Thought I was doing okay though.'

'That's what I heard,' Raven lies. 'I guess the people in charge just wanted to go another way. These things happen, kid. The trick is not to take it too personally.' There's something about the young detective he likes, a rough around the edges brashness. His ex-partner had been like that. Damian Barber. He'd lost his life too soon, but his memory is something Raven still cherishes.

Welling puffs out his cheeks. 'To tell you the truth, when Randall told me you were taking over, it was kind of a relief. We were getting nowhere fast. The perp seems to have all the bases covered. No fingerprints, no DNA and only a few seconds of Ring Camera footage.'

'First of all, we don't call them perps in real life. Nobody does, unless you count TV cops and newbies like you. And second of all, you have CCTV footage?'

'A few seconds, yeah.'

'I didn't see that in the summary report.'

'Because it was nothing to shout about.'

'When you say shout, what kind of shouting are you talking about?'

'Just a few seconds of the first victim, Cane Nicoll, walking toward the petrol station on East Berkley Street.'

'The night he was killed?'

Welling nods.

'I need to see this,' Raven says, tipping his coffee and dragging the kid to his office. 'It's somewhere in this thing, right?' He points to his laptop which he's yet to log into.

'I don't think it's been uploaded yet.'

'Then who has it?'

Welling pinches one eye closed. 'I do?'

'Is that a question or an answer?'

'An answer?'

Raven's eyes become lost in his furrowed brow. 'Are you going to end everything you say with a question mark? Because if you are, I might have to kill you.'

'Bailey said you could be a little hard to take.'

'Oh, you have no idea, kid,' Raven replies, heading towards the door. 'Now which one of these desks is yours.'

'Well, I was sitting in this office, but they moved me out into the pen last night. Right now, I'm hot desking over by the toilets.'

Raven heads to the standing-height table, pausing to let a female PC exit the lady's room.

'I'll get you a better desk if you get this video loaded in the next five seconds,' Raven says.

'It's just here in my downloads,' Welling replies, opening the folder and finding the only mp4 file marked Heart Ripper. Raven frowns. 'I thought it was a better name,' Welling offers. 'More likely to catch on.'

Raven scowls. 'You want a better desk or not?'

The media player opens, and at first, they're staring at a dark screen, but then a car drives past, then another, and pretty soon a man comes into view. Dark jeans, red hoodie, hands shoved deep into his pockets as if he's protecting them from the cold.

'That's East Berkley Street,' Welling says, 'and to the left of the screen, just a little further up the hill, is the petrol station. It's an Esso, I think, or a Jet. I can get one of the officers on the team to check.'

'Why are you so sure he was heading there?'

'Because it's the only thing of significance on that road.'

Raven flips open his phone and pulls up a map of the area.

'How far along East Berkley is this?'

'We got the footage from flat 6a,' Welling replies. 'A young woman in her twenties, art student. Says she only recently had it installed.'

'So it's maybe a hundred metres to the petrol station from here.'

'Something like that.'

Raven stares at the map. It's pretty sparse. Most of the properties at that end of the street have been demolished, pending the development of a new affordable homes complex. Suddenly his eye is drawn to something.

'Is that building site completely closed off to the public?'

'Most of it, yeah.'

'Most of it?'

'Well, there's a cut through walkway that takes you from Berkley to Horsemonger's Lane, but nobody uses it.'

'Why's that?'

'Because it's full of homeless people and drug users, and because Horsemonger's is a—'

'Shit hole,' Raven interjects, remembering the rundown terraced house where he'd cornered his first bust, a lowlife pimp named Charlie Garner.

'Exactly.'

'So Cane Nicoll could have taken the cut through.'

Welling cocks his head. 'Nicoll came from a good family and was a manager at an outsourcing specialist. Why would somebody like that visit Horsemonger's Lane? And even if he did, why take that route?'

'Because people do unexpected things, Welling,' Raven replies. 'And because we're not here to direct the leads. Just follow them.'

Bailey appears from the lady's room behind them, furiously rubbing moisturiser into her hands.

'I made the call,' she says. 'The lab didn't appreciate being pushed on it, but they said they might be able to get us something useable in two days.'

'That's good,' Raven replies. 'One day would be better, but I can make my peace with two.'

'You're such a saint.'

She goes to leave, but Raven heads after her. 'I'm going to send Welling to Horsemonger's Lane to check on a hunch I have,' he says. 'You think he's up to it?'

Webber eyes the young DI who's still hunched over his screen. 'That boy was pulled out of the training pool and thrown into the ocean, and for a while there, he was actually swimming. I think he'll be fine.'

'Good,' Raven replies. 'Because you and I are going for a little swim ourselves.'

'Are you joking?' she asks, eyes wider than sink holes. 'Tell me you're joking.'

Raven grabs his coat. 'You said Carter was manager down at the surf shop, so I think it's about time we had a little chat with his staff.'

CHAPTER 25: LONE ISLET

The clean-up had been difficult, bloody and widespread, tissue and organs splattered over the floor and furniture like somebody had put a firecracker inside a dead rabbit and tossed it into the bedroom. He'd acted recklessly, letting his emotions get the better of him. It was so unlike him. The missing nail had pushed him over the edge, but he should have never been standing so close in the first place. Deep down, he knew his first mistake had been moving his boss up the kill list ahead of the skinny guy just because he'd embarrassed him in front of those boys in the shop. Ollie would have been the right call. He'd worked on him, checked out where he lived and even had a set of his house keys in his bag. Winston on the other hand was the equivalent of a turd on his doorstop, and he'd stepped right in it.

The look on his uncle's face, though, had been priceless. When he'd rammed the scissor blades into his abdomen, he'd thought the old guy was about to spontaneously combust. Then the profanity had come.

'I always thought you were a messed up little cunt,' he'd said, blood streaming from the corner of his pink slip of a mouth. 'Always complaining when I laid a hand on your filthy little tits.'

'You abused me,' she said, jamming the blades home again.

'Your mother said you needed to grow up a bit, so I helped you grow up. You were always such a baby, always whining, so I tried to make you happy.'

'You fucked up my life.'

'You fucked it up yourself. Just look at you with your man clothes, more muscles than a dockworker, those awful tattoos and that stupid haircut. You think that looks nice? You think any decent man would ever want to be with you when you look like that? You think you're ever going to find someone to love you, *Amanda*?'

'My name's not Amanda.'

'Oh yes, that's right. It's Kaden. So very original.'

She pulled the blades out and stabbed him in his thigh.

He cried out, eyes tightly closed, but then he opened one, and the defiance returned to his glare. 'You think that hurts? Try harder.'

She did the same again but in the other leg. By now, the sheets were soaked and the floor was covered in a growing pool of crimson.

'I think I just shit myself,' he sneered. 'You want to clean that up, Kaden, before the whole place starts to smell like a sewage works?' He laughed at him, teeth coated in gore, pink spittle on his lips. 'Your mother always said you were a dirty bitch. And your dad? He ran away just to get away from the stink of you. Filthy fucking Amanda, they called you. That filthy, fucking, hateful child!'

Kaden stabbed him again and again, slamming the rusted tip of the scissor blades into his torso, puncturing his ribs, his lungs, his liver. Blood spattered his body and face, but he kept going, raising the makeshift weapon above his head and bringing it down over and over again until his uncle was nothing but a bloodied slab of meat and the walls dripped with red.

'I hate you,' Kaden spat. 'I hate you.'

He'd thought about cutting out the old man's heart, but he didn't want to keep a piece of him any more than he wanted to clean up the shit and piss he'd evacuated during his final moments. He'd bagged up the body, thrown it in his kill room for disposal later, and got to work with the clean-up. He could still smell the reek of him, the essence of a man who had been slowly capitulating to the gradual advance of death while continuing to torture his only remaining relative, one agonising day at a time.

With the job completed, he tosses his clothes, showers, and gets ready for work. He's now the de-facto man in charge after all, even if the owner of the store doesn't know it yet.

As he heads out, he feels lighter than he's ever felt. A burden has been lifted, a burden so great he hadn't even been aware he'd been carrying it. His uncle had been a tumour on his life, so sneaky and devious that he'd managed to dig his deadly entrails into his organs, creating a bond so unbreakable that only surgery could remove him.

'I am the surgeon,' he whispers, so happy he feels like breaking into song. Instead, he laughs, a rip-roaring guffaw so loud and so long that the two guys on the other side of the street turn to see who the crazy guy is.

'What's so funny, love?' one of them asks, digging his friend in the ribs.

Kaden doesn't answer. He can't. He can barely breathe. He pauses, rests his head against a wall and waits until the tremors subside. He wipes tears from his cheeks as an old man comes to check on him.

'Are you okay?' the geezer says. 'Do you need me to call anybody? Your mum or dad, perhaps?'

The suggestion that anybody in his family would give a shit about him brings about another fit of the giggles, and this time it's more than his body can bear. He slumps to the ground, his head between his knees, and he laughs until he thinks he's going to puke. Eventually the laughter becomes something else, and he starts to cry, and now he's so sad he can't even think straight. He's killed his uncle, the one person his mum asked him to take care of. He's failed her, just like he failed his dad. His uncle had been right. None of them ever wanted him. He's been a disappointment from birth, a tiny bundle of nothingness. He isn't Amanda or

Kaden or anybody else. He's barely air. Now his uncle's gone, and that leaves him with no tether to his bloodline. He's cut loose in an ocean of uncertainty. He can't be a lone islet in the bloody water. He can't be invisible anymore. He has to finish what he's started. He has to make the people at the head of The Legion see him for what he truly is. They have promised him so much.

He pulls himself to his feet, shakes off the emotional baggage and walks along the seafront, chin jutting forward. The shop is just up ahead. He has to focus on that for today. Normality has to resume at least for a little while. Appearances have to be maintained.

He slots the key into the lock, opens the door and breathes in the scent of Winston Carter, now deceased. *Good riddance to bad news*, he thinks. *It has no place in my life.*

'Amanda Chapman?' a woman asks, her Anglo-Caribbean rasp coming at him from the direction of the street.

'It's Kaden,' he replies, turning to face a broad-shouldered black lady and a middle-aged guy with an ugly scar on the side of his head.

'We wanted to ask you some questions about your boss, Mr. Carter,' the man says, holding up his ID. 'My name is Luke Raven, and I'm a Detective Inspector with the West Hampshire Police Force.'

PART 2: ASSASSIN

"My dreams were terrifically disturbed by visions of the Angel of the Odd. Methought he stood at the foot of the couch, drew aside the curtains, and, in the hollow, detestable tones of a rum puncheon, menaced me with the bitterest vengeance for the contempt with which I had treated him."

Edgar Allan Poe – The Angel of the Odd

CHAPTER 26: OINK, OINK

He sits behind his desk, large knuckles resting on a polished mahogany surface, the gold band of a heavy sovereign ring tapping against the hard wood. Tap-tap-tap.

He's waiting. Waiting patiently, which really isn't his style. He used to go mackerel fishing with his old man off Fisherman's Catch. They'd get up at the crack of dawn, so early he could barely keep his eyes open, and jump in the back of his dad's Ford Cortina, racing to get to the water before the tide went out. They'd set up at the end of that long spit of sand and shingle, cast their rods, and pull their coats up high around their ears to keep the bracing wind from cutting their heads in two. Sometimes they'd sit like that for hours, just watching the lines, waiting for something to happen. He'd never told his dad, but he'd hated it: hated the monotony; hated the slow tick of his watch; hated the dependency on luck to put food on their table. He swore that when he grew up, he would make his own luck, grow his own food if he needed to and take whatever the hell he needed whenever the hell he wanted. He wouldn't wait, because waiting was what poor people did. He wouldn't be poor. He would be filthy rich.

Not that the way ahead has been smooth sailing. Lots of things have happened along the road, his personal journey has become sidetracked several times, and often he's got distracted by the sparkle of something shiny or the flash of a long leg. He's only human after all. His last venture ended catastrophically, and for a couple of years he's had to lie low. All that changed when he saw the opportunity, the seat at the head of a global enterprise that lay vacant, just waiting for the right leader to come along.

He knew about The Legion. Of course he did. You couldn't be involved in underground business dealings on the south coast without running into them from time to time. He'd known Sam Raven quite well when Sam was a senior member of the organisation, the so-called Curator. He greased the wheels for the guy they called The Cardinal, Bernie Staker, and because of that, he was a powerful man to stay on the right side of. When Sam was killed for gunning down Robert Charon, Staker's right-hand man and father of Tony Richards — the Pale Faced Killer — and Staker himself was blown away by his own daughter, things came to a head. However, he only learned of the events of that fateful day when he came out of hiding, and when he did, the whole criminal business scene in Westhampton had changed considerably. No Staker meant no Legion, and no Legion meant a vacuum had formed, one that was waiting to be filled by someone with enough conviction and determination to pick up the pieces. He's never been one to back away from a challenge, and so he took up the reins, breaking bread with the largest local gang — The Medics — before approaching members of the council who he knew had been affiliated with Staker and his corrupt practices.

It turned out there were several high-profile people in Staker's pocket, many of whom he'd known for decades, and all of them had been quaking in their soft leather boots ever since the police had taken control of the mansion. All he'd had to do was suggest he would be willing to reinstate proceedings and keep their names out of the headlines for a very reasonable annual salary, and suddenly he had more votes supporting his appointment than Donald Trump in a Republican leadership contest. He had the contacts, he had the muscle (by this time The Medics had agreed to toe the line), and he had the balls. It turned out that was all he really needed.

Staker had no surviving relatives, so when the police released his assets, the people in power saw to it that everything was signed over to him with one caveat; he had to further the interests of The Legion in the county and see to it that its influence and reach were re-established. That seemed like a small price to pay, and so he spent the next few weeks locked away in a sizeable property the higher-ups had generously given him, reading the texts, understanding the history, and becoming increasingly amazed at the atrocities The Legion had committed in the name of their one true deity.

He has never been a religious man. Even his mum, who had died not twelve months ago at the tender age of 92, had never really been a churchgoer. She thought vicars and priests were nothing but kiddie fiddling sycophants who would try to convince you the sky was purple if it lined their pockets. These people from The Legion, however, are so in tune with their faith, they put even the most devout Catholics to shame.

The books he read spoke of Angra Mainyu, an evil spirit who, according to the Zoroastrian faith, ruled the earth when mankind had been in its infancy. They also spoke about Shaitan from the Islamic faith, Mara from the Buddhist faith, Pazazu from Mesopotamia, and every other version of Satan depicted by the world's many religious texts. The details blew his mind. There was too much to take in. He doesn't believe in God and so how can he believe in the devil?

What he couldn't shift, and still can't, are the things that happen in the house. It's a sizeable cottage on the edge of the New Forest, far enough away from town to keep it discreet, but close enough for The Legion's many members to stop by whenever they feel like it. He tries to stay out of what they get up to, but he can't help but notice things that go on. It's like the house is alive.

Not three months ago he'd just held a meeting with the heads of three of the largest distribution companies in the county, and was sitting in the study, sipping a whiskey and wondering how he'd managed to land on his feet again, when one of the windows slammed shut at the top of the stairway. Swearing blind he'd locked it, he ran to the landing, peering into the shadows, looking for an intruder. He scoured every room, opened every wardrobe door, looked under every bed. There was no-one, but the sensation remained. Somebody was in the house. He continued his search, even going into the attic and rummaging through boxes and boxes of books, historic artefacts and old maps. He'd slumped into a chair, thinking he was too old to be running around in a big house like that, chasing shadows just because he'd been scared by a bump in the night. That was when he saw what he saw.

He thinks about it now. He can't describe it, even to himself, but he's seen it several times since. He's felt it too. The dread. The despair. He's always been an optimist, convinced that things will always come good if you give them enough time, but this thing, it brought out the darkness in him. It has never left. He can even see it in his own ageing face when he looks in the mirror. It's in the lines of his skin, the curve of his jaw, the way he stoops ever so slightly. He sees it in the shadows behind his eyes and dreams of it at night.

His position of Cardinal of The Legion comes with some symptoms that were never described in the contract, but that's okay because it also comes with some benefits. He gets told about planning applications before they make it to the council approval committee, he knows about the imminent arrival of high-profile visitors before the trips are planned, and he gets intel on police investigations in real time, meaning he can put contingency plans in place before any heat makes it to the people he's protecting.

He was informed that Raven had been discovered alive, way before Fitzwilliam or the DCS in charge had been told, and even though his personal preference was to meet the ex-Detective

Inspector on the way into town and run the bus carrying him off the road, he'd decided that a better plan was to let Raven build his own gallows and tie his own noose. What he hadn't expected was for his contact to call him and tell him that Raven had not only found telling evidence at a murder scene, but that he was now questioning the person his organisation had sponsored to do their bidding. That could not be allowed to stand.

He has options, some of them subtle, others more nuclear. He taps his sovereign ring against the desk again, mulling them over. Raven has been an enormous dick up his arse for too long to think about. It's time for that dick to be castrated, cut into tiny pieces and fed to the pigs. He flips a coin, and it lands tails side up. He grins at the irony. A curly tail for a dirty swine.

'Oink, oink,' he says, forgetting he's placed a call.

'What's that?'

'The new DI has to go.'

There's a pause. 'I see. Any preference?'

'Painful, bloody. Make a scene of it.'

'Location?'

He thinks about that. Raven has no fixed abode, and the intel he received suggests he doesn't appear to be too keen on heading back to his ex. That leaves only one option.

'He'll be going straight back to West's house tonight. Let's do it there.'

'What about collateral?'

Ronnie Valentine recalls the moment Raven and Billy West turned against him during the Greenbaum heist, and he doesn't hesitate.

'Collateral is good,' he says. 'If that fat fuck and his pretty little wife get in your way, show them what we do with little piggy traitors.'

CHAPTER 27: NAKED

'Is this going to take long?' Chapman asks. 'Only, I really ought to be opening up. Winston hates tardiness.'

'It's just a few questions,' Bailey says. 'Shouldn't take too long at all.'

Chapman glances at Raven, and he spots something in her eyes that makes him pause.

'I suggest we go inside,' Bailey says, gesturing to the door.

'Of course,' Chapman replies, and she pushes it open, turning on the lights as she heads towards the office. 'Would either of you like a tea? Coffee?'

'No thanks,' Raven says before Bailey can answer. 'As my colleague said, we don't plan on being here long.'

'But a cup of tea always gets the day off to a good start, don't you think?'

'I've always been more of a coffee drinker,' Bailey replies.

'Then coffee it is, detective. Milk? Sugar?'

'Both,' Bailey says, shrugging at Raven. 'A little of the former, two of the latter.'

'A woman after my own heart,' comes the voice from the office.

Raven is pacing the store, browsing the Salt Rock T-Shirts, Fat Face hoodies, and Billabong shorts. Surfboards fly close to the ceiling overhead and wetsuits hang like seal skin on the far wall. He's visited places like this a thousand times, but never during a case.

'How long have you worked for Mr. Carter?' he asks.

'Winston? About eighteen months. He was already a manager here when I started.'

'Are you friends?'

'Friends? Hardly. We've been out for a couple of work's night's out, but they're rare. No, it's a pretty standard manager-employee relationship.'

There's the angry hiss of a kettle boiling, followed by the jingle-jangle of cups clinking.

'When did you last see Mr. Carter?' Bailey asks.

'Let me see. Yesterday morning if my memory serves me correctly.'

'What time would you say that was?'

The jingling stops and Chapman's head appears from behind the door, eyebrows raised. 'Can I ask what this is about?'

'We're currently conducting an investigation into Mr. Carter's whereabouts yesterday,' Bailey replies. 'Any information you can provide would be most helpful.'

'Is he in trouble?'

'Unfortunately, we're unable to comment at this stage.'

'Is he dead?'

'Why would you say that?' Raven asks.

Chapman shrugs. 'He's either in trouble or he's dead. They're the only possible explanations for the two of you showing up here so early on a Saturday morning.'

Chapman hands Bailey her cup of coffee and perches on a high stool behind the till. She takes a sip of her drink, eyeing them over the rim of the cup, and sets it down beside the payment machine.

'To tell you the truth, I only saw Winston for a little while yesterday. I'd had a heavy night and woke up with a terrible hangover, so I was late opening up. One of the managers got a call from a trouble-making bitch of a customer, and that manager called Winston and gave him an earful down the phone. He then comes steaming in here, balls me out in front of the customers and sends me home with my tail between my legs.'

'He suspended you?' Bailey asks.

'Not as such. Winston and I have a mutual respect for each other. He can be honest with me when I fuck up, and he lets me defend myself if he's in the wrong.'

'And was he?'

'Was he what?'

'In the wrong?'

'To yell at me in front of those teenage boys like that? Of course he was, and he knew it, too.'

'But he still sent you home,' Raven says. 'Which suggests he was pretty pissed off.'

'He has a temper, that's true, but I've learned if you give him some time, eventually it all just peters out to nothing. He's just a cuddly bear, really.'

'Did his temper ever make him do things that went too far?' Bailey asks.

'Such as?'

'Did he ever hit you?' Raven interjects.

'Hit me? Never.'

'Did you ever feel like he might?'

'No. I've never felt physically threatened by him.'

Raven approaches the till, places his hand on the counter. 'How about verbally? Did he verbally threaten you?'

'He verbally threatened to sack me, so I guess the answer is yes.'

'My colleague is talking more about mental abuse,' Bailey says. 'Did it ever get to a point where your mental health suffered because of something Mr. Carter said or did? Maybe you became stressed or your anxiety was heightened? Perhaps your home life suffered.'

Raven notices a twitch in Chapman's right eye as if something has tugged a nerve.

'My mental health is just fine, thanks. I get my fair share of abuse from the world, looking the way I do, but I have a pretty thick skin so most of it bounces right off.'

'Most of it?'

'I'm not a machine. Some of it gets through, but when it does, I take a moment to remind myself how fabulous I really am.'

'May I ask how you identify?' Bailey asks, and this time, that little twitch pinches one eye closed.

'I identify as Kaden Chapman.'

'I mean your sex. Do you have any particular pronouns you prefer? For our records I mean?'

'I don't conform to titles, Detective Bailey, just as I don't subscribe to any particular sexual denomination. My belief is that a person can be whatever or whomever they please, regardless of so-called social norms. Today I choose to be a male, but tomorrow, I may make a different choice.'

If Bailey is taken aback, she doesn't show it. 'Well, may I say, you make a very dashing man, Mr. Chapman, and if tomorrow you make that different choice, I'm sure you will also be a very beautiful woman.'

Chapman clearly considers the conversation over because he gets up from his stool. 'While that's very nice of you to say, Detective, it still doesn't change the fact that I have to open the shop.'

He heads for the door, pulling it open as he ushers them outside. 'Of course, if you have any other questions, please don't hesitate to call.'

'We'll do that,' Raven says, glancing at Chapman's hand. The fingernails are clear and bitten down to the quick, but he spies something else, too. A white smear on one of the nails. It's subtle but visible, easy to miss if someone is trying to give the impression they've not being wearing fake nails. Perhaps acrylic, maybe purple.

'We'll be in touch,' he says, handing Chapman a slip of paper. 'In the meantime, if you think of anything, there's my number. Call me anytime, day or night.'

'Oh, I will,' Chapman replies, a broad smile on naked lips. 'I promise.'

CHAPTER 28: MISSING PIECE

Lisa sits in the meeting room of Exquisite Homes, listening to her boss extol the virtues of their fast-growing enterprise to the multinational property developer, but she barely hears a word. It's as if everything is happening around her, as though she's watching proceedings through the smeared lens of a movie camera and the sound is coming at her through a muffler, smothered and inaudible.

She can't get that morning's WhatsApp conversation with Ruby out of her head. It was the one piece of news she'd been praying to hear for so long, but seeing it written down like that made it seem unreal, made up. Luke has been missing for four years. He's been a memory to her, one that slowly fades with every passing day. She's tried to hold onto him, to cling to him like a precious piece of jewellery, but little by little his features have become indistinct and blurred. Now he's back and she doesn't know how she feels. She's happy, of course she is, so happy she wants to scream, but then there are the complications. Harry, Simon, her new life. Luke had been a puzzle piece that had gone missing, and rather than find that piece, she'd thrown the puzzle away and bought a new one. Now there was no hole for him to fit in. She'd effectively made him obsolete, and the thought of that made her want to throw up. Looking at it through the lens of that WhatsApp message made her appear cruel and impatient. Luke had been her one. Her one and only.

'Lisa?' Chelsea says, glancing anxiously at their client. 'Did you want to step in here?'

'Of course,' Lisa replies, shuffling papers as if she knows what she's looking for.

'I was just telling Stefan how our knowledge of the local community puts us in prime position to sell his properties for the highest price.'

'That's right,' Lisa replies, but she's playing catch up. 'For example, we have some very good contacts in the Palisades who, erm, let me see—'

She shuffles more papers, looks for the data she'd so meticulously pulled together the night before.

'—contacts in the Palisades who were looking for homes for their wealthy city dwelling friends. In fact, only recently I sold…' There's more shuffling, 'I have it right here, if you'll just give me a second to—'

'What she's trying to say,' Chelsea interjects, 'is that she fulfilled the demands of two London based clients for properties in the north of the town that sold for six figures.'

'Very good,' Stefan says. 'Those kinds of prices are what we are looking for.'

He picks up a slim blue folder and nods to his partner, a tall man with the face of an undertaker.

'Jared and I will mull over our discussion, study your portfolio, and get back to you by the end of next week.'

'That sounds perfect,' Chelsea replies, standing and shaking Stefan's hand. 'And if you have any questions, any questions at all, please don't hesitate to call us.'

Stefan glances at Lisa who is yet to stand, and offers a curt smile. 'We'll be in touch,' he says, but Lisa can tell her lack of accuracy has left a mark.

Chelsea escorts the two men to the door, but not before shooting Lisa a worried glance over her shoulder.

She sits in the room alone, her head all over the place, her mouth as dry as a packet of digestive biscuits. She's not even thinking about Exquisite Homes or the meeting she's just slammed a wrecking ball into. She's thinking about Luke. She's wondering why he hasn't been to see them. She's hoping he's okay. She's trying to decide whether to tell Simon, or whether this is a path she has to navigate alone. At the end of all that, she thinks of Harry. His father, his *real* father, is alive, and he has to be told.

'Okay, so that didn't go so well,' Chelsea says, fixing herself a Cappuccino from the machine. 'You want to tell me what's on your mind?'

'I'm sorry,' Lisa replies, realising she may have just cost the company enough commission to keep them afloat for at least a year, maybe two. 'I should have been all over that. I had everything I needed right here.'

'It's okay,' Chelsea says, perching on the edge of the table. 'I didn't like the guy anyway.'

'He was a little slimy,' Lisa replies. 'And what was with his partner?'

'Looked like an extra from the Addams Family,' Chelsea laughs. 'Still, the revenue would have been nice.'

'I can go see them, convince them we're the right company to put their faith in.'

'No offense, Lis, but on the evidence of that performance, I'd rather you didn't.'

Lisa takes the blow. She deserves it.

Chelsea hands her the cup and slips another one beneath the steaming dispenser. 'You want to tell me what's going on?'

Lisa bites on her lip. The truth is hard to share. She should have gone to the station to find Luke as soon as Ruby had dropped her bombshell, but she hadn't, and even now, she doesn't know why.

'It's okay,' Chelsea says, touching her arm. 'Whatever it is, if it's too painful, you can tell me when you're ready.'

'Luke's alive,' she blurts out, catching herself off guard.

Coffee slips over the edge of Chelsea's fresh cup.

'Say that again?'

'I know, it's crazy isn't it.'

'But… how?'

'I've been asking myself the same thing.'

'The police. They looked everywhere. Jane and I, we scoured the internet, we made calls, we paid for a private investigator. We even visited some of the places people claimed to have seen him. There was nothing, not one shred of evidence. We would have done anything to find him, anything. He saved my Jane's life, not once, but twice.'

'I know you did all that,' Lisa replied. 'I know how hard you worked. I know that was why you invited me into your home, why you did what you did for Harry and me, and I appreciate it, I really do.'

'No thanks required. Luke put himself in the firing line to bring Jane home. He loved you and he loved Harry, and as far as I'm concerned, that makes us family.' Chelsea takes a seat beside her. 'This is good news, Lisa, no matter how unbelievable it seems.'

'I know that.'

'If it wasn't for that awful woman, Harry would have been raised by both his mother and father these past four years, and you and Luke would have been together.'

'I know that, too.'

'You have to go and see him, wherever he is.'

'Well, that's just it. He's not far. He's not far at all.'

'Then take the day off, jump on a train and show him how much you've missed him.'

'I won't need the train because he's right here in town.'

Chelsea coughs in her cup. 'In Westhampton?'

Lisa nods almost apologetically.

'For how long?'

'Since yesterday.'

'And he hasn't been to see you?'

Lisa shrugs. 'Maybe. I don't know. I know it sounds strange, but last night, I had this feeling, like somebody was standing outside our house.'

'A feeling?'

'Yeah, like a sensation, you know? Like old memories were coming back to me but all in one go.'

'You think he was out there?'

'I don't know. Perhaps. I could smell the scent of him. I even had that same tumbling feeling in the pit of my stomach that I used to get whenever he'd drop by.'

'Did you go out there?'

Lisa shakes her head.

'You were scared?'

'No, it wasn't that. Well, maybe a little, but not of him.'

Chelsea turns to her and takes her hands. 'It's okay to worry about the impact this will have on your marriage, Lis,' she says. 'It's also okay to be concerned about what this might mean for your new life with Simon and with this company, because your new life is pretty damn good compared to your old one.'

'Doesn't that make me seem like a selfish bitch?'

'Maybe,' Chelsea smiles, 'but aren't we all a little bit like that, even if some of us hide it better than others.'

'It's not that I don't want him back, of course I do,' Lisa says. 'But I know that when I meet him, everything will change. *Everything*. The way I am with Simon, the way Simon is with me, Harry's relationship with his stepfather. I can't just walk out on the man I married just because the man I used to love has returned from the grave. Does that even make sense?'

'It makes imperfect sense, because the situation you find yourself in is imperfect. You're finding it difficult to rationalise because the whole thing is irrational. Raven was dead, everybody thought so, especially the police, even if they didn't come out and say it to your face, so you did what any sane person would do, and you moved on. It's not your fault that the person you met is such a great guy, and it's not your fault that you and Harry have landed on your feet in the most spectacular way possible. It could have easily gone the other way, and that wouldn't have been your fault either. The fact remains, Luke is back, he's right here in town, and you do have to see him. You just do, for your sake, but especially for Harry's.'

Lisa nods. Chelsea's right. Of course she's right. She's just putting off the inevitable, chasing the consequences of what that might mean from her thoughts, because those consequences are just little ripples on a big lake, and she can't even begin to comprehend how big those ripples might become when they reach the shore of that lake, but she's pretty sure they'll be big. Very big.

'Sorry about what happened in the meeting,' she says. 'I really should have been on my game.'

'Fuck the meeting, and fuck those Jeff Bezos wannabes,' Chelsea replies. 'You've got more important things to think about.'

Lisa smiles. She has landed on her feet, and the person who should take the credit for that is sitting right in front of her.

'I love you Chelsea,' she says.

'I love you too, Lis, but right now, you're annoying me. Take the rest of the day off, go tell your husband this big news, and find Luke Raven.'

CHAPTER 29: ISOLATION

'So what do you think?' Raven asks Bailey. They're eating lunch in her car because he still hasn't been given the all-clear to drive. He's devouring a cheeseburger, she's taking polite bites from a prawn salad sandwich.

'I don't know. My gut tells me he was a pretty genuine guy.'

'Because?'

'Because he seemed to be speaking from the heart.'

'You didn't catch the little tic in his eye, especially when you asked him about his sexuality.'

Bailey swallows her last bite. 'Just because somebody is sensitive about something that's probably made them the butt of a thousand and one jokes since they were at primary school, that doesn't make them a suspect, Raven.'

'It wasn't just that. It also happened when I asked about his state of mind.'

'Another topic that triggers more people than you can ever begin to imagine.'

He backs off, sensing he's standing in a minefield with absolutely no idea where the explosives are buried.

'No fingernails to speak of,' he says, changing tack. 'But I'm pretty sure he wears them. I spotted a white smear on his fingernail. Could be glue.'

Bailey pushes the empty sandwich box into the side pocket of the car door and turns to him, a dab of Marie Rose sauce on her chin. 'You don't really believe that Kaden Chapman is our killer do you?'

Raven shrugs. 'Stranger things have happened.'

'But you heard him. He hadn't seen Carter since yesterday morning, and that was right in the middle of the shop with a lot of witnesses.'

'Then we track the witnesses down and we corroborate his story. Either way, I still have this feeling.'

'That the transgender killed the big blokey boss?'

'You say that like Chapman's choice of sexuality is prejudicing my opinion.'

'I'm just stating a fact,' she says. 'You like Chapman for it, and because of that, you're going after his story.'

Raven bites his lip and holds out his hand. 'As I'm such a neanderthal who has no idea how Gen Zs think or feel, I'll go and throw that sandwich box in the bin along with the bag my big greasy burger came in, shall I?'

'I never said you were a neanderthal.'

'You didn't have to. Look, I don't care who Chapman is, what he wears, or how he chooses to express himself. What I do care about is that there are now four dead bodies with their hearts ripped out, and that means there are four families who no longer have somebody they love in their lives. Until I can prove otherwise — and the proof has to be pretty damn fucking convincing — everybody they came into contact with is a suspect.'

He gets out of the car and tosses the food containers, closing his eyes as a whiskey fuelled pang hits his abdomen. If ever he needed a drink, it's right now. He's never felt so out of place, so isolated in a world full of loners and the socially anxious. The world has changed since he's been away, and right now he feels like he's having to run a personal best just to stand still.

There's something about the shop worker he can't get out of his head. Something familiar. He runs his appearance over in his mind: the naked face, hair that looks like it's recently been hacked with a set of garden shears, thick arms, muscular thighs. He recalls the image of a bloodied knife being held. It's so stark it almost blinds him. Could Kaden Chapman's hand and the one in his vision be one and the same?

'I don't know,' he whispers. 'But it could be. It really could.'

'Let's head over to Horsemonger's,' he says, getting back into the car. 'I want to see how Welling and the others are doing.'

'Welling's about as green as a tin of peas.'

He nods. She isn't wrong, but something in his head is linking Chapman with that road. And besides, the kid is keen.

'He just needs a bit of guidance,' he says.

'Then give him a Sat Nav and tell him which way is north. Ever since he was shipped down from Somerset, I've been holding his hand, making sure he knows when it's safe to cross the road. I don't get paid to be a baby-sitter.'

'You sound bitter.'

'Like John Smiths,' she replies, 'only I cost more.'

He laughs and she laughs with him. It lightens the mood.

'Horsemonger's is a dive, Raven, you know that, right?'

'I do,' he says, glaring at the fuzzy haired troll keyring dangling from the ignition. 'Which means it's exactly the kind of place we need to be looking.'

She raises one eyebrow. 'Not at In Our Wake?'

Raven pulls on his seatbelt. 'Time will tell,' he says. 'Sometimes the thing you don't expect is the one thing that squares the circle.'

CHAPTER 30: GHOSTS

Kaden is panicking now. He's so discombobulated, he can't even organise his own thoughts. He doesn't like the way it feels. He doesn't like being out of control like this, like a windsurfer without a sail. His ex-boss has been dead less than one day and already the filth has come knocking. The lady detective looked like she believed his story, but the old guy with the ugly scar? He definitely hadn't.

And then there's the nail. The fake fucking nail. Have they already found it? Is it already with the lab? Is some white coated geek in a white mask and hair net currently leaning over it, plucking loose skin from flaking glue, swabbing the tiny sample for DNA, amplifying it, creating a profile they can check against the millions of records they hold in their database? Does the mutilated guy, Raven, already know the results? Is that why they showed up this morning? Were they baiting him?

He thinks about going back to the common again, but he's sure that would be like putting his hand in a box filled with scorpions. He thinks about getting out of town, heading for somewhere they'd never look, but he's hardly inconspicuous. The blokey looking bird with the hack-job hair. People remember him for all the wrong reasons, another thing he'd had to take on the chin since he was a kid. He thinks about going home, emptying his kill-room and disposing of his heart collection. The thought of doing that hits him the hardest. He's worked so hard, toiled for so long. He's become attached to the tragic beauty of them, the natural, unexplainable artistry. It's such a magical thing, a living organism with an electrical impulse all its own. That's why it can continue pumping long after it has been removed from the body. It just needs oxygen to breath. The energy it creates in a single day is enough to power a large truck for over twenty miles. It beats almost three billion times during an average lifetime, pulsing automatically, responding to signals from the brain, and it has tiny cells that help maintain rhythm. It's a marvel of biomechanical engineering, an organically derived masterpiece of intelligent design. He cannot dispose of those four aortic cores any more than he can dispose of his own limbs.

He checks his armpits and realises he's sweating. Damp patches are forming on his shirt. He goes to the bathroom, splashes cold water on his face and breathes. He tries to inhale slowly but he's gasping for air, his chest rapidly rising and falling. He grabs the basin with both hands and lowers his head, his eyes tightly closed. He tries to picture somewhere calm and tranquil, but he's never known calm. He's never had the sensation of tranquillity.

His uncle's face appears, grey and drooling. Kaden opens his eyes, but the old man's still there, a shadowy reflection in the mirror, colourless eyes peering over his shoulder.

'Get lost,' Kaden says. 'You're dead. I killed you. Now fuck off!'

His uncle doesn't move, doesn't speak, just stares.

'I mean it, Uncle. I don't want to have to kill you twice.'

Kaden shakes his head and tries to clear his thoughts of the insanity of it, but his uncle is still there, still staring. A hand slips beneath Kaden's arm, decaying meat on matchstick bones, and grasps for his breast. Kaden tries to slap it away, but his own hand moves through empty air, and he hits himself on the tit.

'You were scum when you were alive and you're still scum in death,' he says. 'I wish I'd tortured you. I wish I'd taken my time.' He starts to cry. 'You've been abusing me since I was a child, since I was born. You and mom, you were sick, both of you. You were fucking sick!'

A hand appears on the other side of him, but this one moves south across his abdomen towards his crotch. Kaden tries to grab it with both hands, but his tight fists are empty, his fingers clawing at his own palms. The old man's fingertips snake away past his naval and work their way into his jeans. The first button pops open and then the next and the next, and now his boxers are visible, and his uncle's fingers have slipped inside. Frothy saliva drips from the old man's lips and falls onto Kaden's T-shirt, creating a dark circle just above his nipple, but still those hands keep moving until he can feel them in his pubes and tracing a line around his vulva. He wants to scream, he wants to fight and kick and punch and claw, but he's frozen like a slab of ice, unable to move or think or breathe.

Bzzz.

The vibration in his pocket is like an elastic band snapping in his brain, and when he looks up, his uncle has gone.

Bzzz.

It takes him a second to figure out what's going on, but then he remembers his phone, and he rummages for it, finding it in his back pocket where he'd shoved it during his interrogation by the two police scum.

Bzzz.

It's an unknown number and he thinks about ignoring it, but then he realises who calls him on an unknown number. Of course he does. Untraceable.

'Hello?' He jumps at the sound of his own voice. He sounds weak, like a tiny mouse.

'You've fucked up.'

It's him, the man who's been directing him.

'I have. I'm sorry. I should have done what I said I was going to do and stuck with the plan.'

'Horse, stable door, bolted,' the man replies. 'We're going to have to clean up for you.'

'Can you do that?'

'We can do anything. Comes with a price though.'

'Anything, I'll pay anything.' He doesn't have any money and has no idea if he still has a job, but he'll find a way. Whatever it takes, he'll find a way.

'What did you tell them?'

Kaden thinks about that. What did he say? Did he give anything away? 'Nothing. I told them nothing.'

'You must have said something.'

'Only that I last saw Winston yesterday morning.'

'Did they believe you?'

'I think she did, the female detective. Not so sure about the guy with the scar.'

'Raven.'

'Yeah, that was his name.'

There's the sound of breathing down the line, and then the clink of a glass.

'Here's what you're gonna do.'

'Okay.'

'You open the shop again, you act like nothing's happened, and you say nothing that might incriminate you.'

'Got it.'

'Later, you'll go home, you'll have dinner with your uncle, and you'll watch TV.'

Kaden tries to swallow, but every ounce of saliva in his mouth has evaporated. 'Okay,' he lies. 'No problem.'

'Tomorrow, when you wake up, your problem will have been dealt with, and you'll be in even more debt to us. You understand?'

'I understand. And thank you.'

'Don't thank me. Just don't fuck up again. Too much is at stake here.'

'Praise be the one true deity,' he says, but his voice is trembling like a plucked string.

'Don't praise *Him*. Honour *Him*. Do something to make *Him* proud.'

There's a faint click as the line disengages, and he's left staring at his reflection again, knowing that the real fuck up is the bagged-up body in his kill room, and the empty bed in a house full of ghosts.

CHAPTER 31: ELEPHANT ON ACID

She taps on the door, expecting nobody to be home, but to her surprise, Billy answers. He's dressed in a pair of combat shorts, flip flops and nothing else. He's drinking a cocktail — something colourful — but when he sees her, the straw flops out of his mouth and his jaw falls open. He stands there, gums flapping, looking like he's in the middle of a stroke.

'Lisa. How… how you doing?'

'Depends on what you tell me, Billy West,' she says, peering over his shoulder. 'Can I come in?'

He looks shocked. 'Of course you can. Yeah, just come on in. You want me to fix you a drink?'

'Billy, it's three o' clock in the afternoon.'

'And?' he asks. 'Three's pretty close to five, and as I understand it, five is the internationally recognised time for bottle tops to be unscrewed.'

'Except it's three, and your breath smells like you're that number of margaritas in.'

'It's two actually,' he says, sticking out his bottom lip. 'This is my third.'

She follows him into the kitchen. It's a tidy house, well kept. Not flamboyant, practical and homely.

'Sally not home?'

'She's having a shower,' he says, nodding to the staircase. 'She's got a work thing tonight. Some posh dinner followed by some guy in a suit singing swing numbers. Apparently there's only one invite, which suits me right down to the ground. I'm having a horror-thon in the den later if you're at a loose end. The whole Saw series back-to-back. I've already done the first three, so we'll be kicking off at number four, which, if my memory serves me well, is pretty fucking disturbing.'

'No, you're alright,' she says. 'I have a husband, remember, and a child. They kind of expect me to be around.'

'Right,' he replies. 'Yeah, responsibilities. They can be a bitch.'

She eyes the room. There's a photograph of Billy and Sally on the wall. They're on a beach somewhere, a sea of sunbeds and parasols behind them. Billy is dressed in pretty much the same clothes, but Sally looks gorgeous in a black swimsuit and her hair tied back. They're both smiling, and their smiles are real, not Tik Tok fake. Lisa has always found their relationship interesting, as endearing as it is enviable. The two of them shouldn't work. Billy is about as subtle as an elephant on acid, and Lisa is classy and elegant. Luke used to say that whatever Billy was paying, it was worth it, but Lisa never thought that. There was real love there, the kind of love you couldn't fabricate.

'Luke's alive,' she says, deciding that beating around the bush is just going to waste time.

'Really?' he asks, but the way he draws the word out tells her everything she needs to know.

'Where is he?'

'How would I know that? I thought Luke was dead, just like the pol—'

'Don't bullshit me, Billy. I want to know where he is right now. I need to see him.'

Billy leans against one of the solid wood worktops. 'He hasn't been to see you?' he asks.

Lisa shakes her head, arms folded.

'I told him he needed to.'

'And yet he hasn't.' She bites her lip and tries to stop her rapidly increasing anger spilling out.

'I think he knows about you and your new husband,' he says, giving her a patronising look that makes her blood spit and boil.

'Why would you think that?'

'He just gave me that impression.'

'You told him, didn't you?'

Billy's face turns white as he fumbles for an answer. She's on the verge of blowing her top when Sally emerges.

'Oh, hi Lis,' she says, brushing Lisa's arm with her fingers as she heads towards the kettle. 'I didn't know you were here. Has my thick lump of a husband offered you a tea or coffee?'

'No,' she replies. 'But it's okay. I'm not thirsty.'

'Well, I'm having one if you don't mind. I've been on conference calls all morning and my throat is as dry as an old rag.'

'Go ahead,' Lisa says, but she's so strung out, she can barely hold herself back. 'Luke's alive, Sally. Did you know?'

Sally turns round, eyes wide. 'Alive?'

Lisa throws a hammer down. 'Didn't Billy tell you?'

'You knew?' Sally asks, whirling to her husband.

Billy forces a nod, but Lisa can see he's looking for a way out. 'He came by yesterday. I was going to tell you, but—'

'But what? It slipped your mind?'

'You've been busy.'

'Oh, for fuck's sake,' Sally says. 'I'm so sorry, Lis. If I'd have known, I'd have called. The important question is, how is he?'

'I don't know,' Lisa says. 'I haven't seen him. I only found out he was alive earlier this morning when Ruby messaged me.'

Sally's eyes open even wider. They look like two saucers embedded in her skull. She turns to her husband. 'So Lisa didn't know her missing husband was in town, but you did. Did you not think to let her know?'

'I didn't think it was my news to tell,' he says, but the pitch of his voice has increased considerably. 'I just told Lisa that I tried to convince Raven to go to her.'

'But then you told me why he might not have, right?' Lisa says. 'Because of something you said?'

'What did you say?' Sally growls. 'Billy Arthur West, what did you say to that poor man that would make him not want to go straight to his partner and child and tell them that he was still living and breathing?'

Billy is trying to inch closer to the back door but Sally cuts off his path, and now he really is cornered with his back to the refrigerator and the other way out blocked by the breakfast bar. 'I told him Lisa was married.'

Sally doesn't answer, she just does a little shimmy on the spot while her hands open and close.

'It's okay,' Lisa says, suddenly feeling like she's caught in the middle. 'Sally, it's fine. He was going to find out at some point anyway.'

'But not from my husband. I'm so sorry, Lisa. Sometimes Billy thinks with his mouth, and that's not a good thing when you've got a brain the size of a peanut.'

'I'm sorry, Lis,' Billy repeats. 'I am. It's just that, I was so shocked to see him, and he was so desperate to see you. He came here to find out where you lived.'

Those words hit her the hardest. Luke's first thought was to come and find her and Harry, and if she hadn't gotten herself caught up in her new life and agreed to marry the first guy who'd really shown her any interest since his disappearance, he'd have come straight to her door, and the life they'd been building, the one that was difficult and complicated but also exciting and heart pounding, it could have carried on building, and everything would have been so much easier.

'Where did he go?' she asks.

'Where did he go? Billy asks in return.

'Don't be thick, Billy,' Sally says. 'It's not a complicated question. Just answer it.

'I dropped him at West Hampshire police HQ,' he says. 'He'd been having some sort of premonition. He didn't tell me what, but he wanted to see Kipruto.'

Lisa chews the inside of her cheek. Kipruto, Ruby's husband, the guy who should have told her about Luke the moment he'd found out. Now Luke was with him, and she was chasing her tail, trying to find out what the hell was going on.

'Drop her there,' Sally says.

'What?' Billy replies. 'I've been drinking.'

'Those margaritas you make are about as strong as a glass of lemonade, Billy. Now get your keys and take Lisa to the police station. It's the least you can do.'

Billy folds in on himself, and for a microsecond, Lisa feels sorry for him. It's not his fault that Luke was taken, and it's certainly not his fault that she'd gone and got married. It is his fault, however, that Luke has been in town for almost forty-eight hours, seemingly working a case while she's been sitting at home, ignorant to the fact that the man she once loved, possibly still does, is just a short drive from her door.

'You ready?' he asks, ignoring the fact that Sally is hugging her goodbye.

'You'll find him,' Sally says. 'And everything will be fine. I promise.'

Lisa hugs her back and then walks after her reluctant chauffeur, knowing that even if she does find Luke, it's only the start of a treacherous journey.

CHAPTER 32: MOSS BROS.

Horesemonger's Lane is in a part of town that not even the police go unless they're called. It's the kind of place that's been in existence since the end of the industrial revolution, properties crammed in side by side like factory chickens, their rendered exteriors grey from exhaust fumes and pollution. Front doors open onto narrow paths that in turn lead to a busy road. Ageing cars line either side of the bustling street while haphazard graffiti decorates the walls and fences with illegible slogans and badly spelled taglines. Drains lie clogged with rizla wrappers, condom wrappers and crushed cans, while cracked paving slabs jut from the walkway like broken teeth.

Bailey steers her Vauxhall Insignia into the last empty slot, crammed between a Fiat Panda and a two-tone Maestro. Welling appears from an open front door, his notebook tucked into his top pocket. The young detective is talking to an older guy with gaunt cheeks and thinning hair. Beside him is an even younger male PC, his cheeks decorated with bright pink pimples like popping candy. Further along, two more PCs are tapping on another front door with a sign taped just above the letterbox that reads, "Cold Callers will be Shot."

Welling spots the Insignia and finishes up, calling over one of the other PCs to take the guy's details. A kid pokes his head through a gap in a gate and yells something offensive. Welling turns to him angrily, but another kid in a Superdry jacket appears and whips out his middle finger, firing a perfectly spherical blob of phlegm more than four feet and landing it on Welling's polished, Italian leather brogues.

Raven comes to his rescue. 'Piss off, the lot of you,' he says. 'And if I catch you bothering my officers again, I'll arrest you for being nasty little shites.'

'Nah, bruh,' Superdry kid replies. 'We ain't going nowhere. Fams come round here, tapping on doors and aksing bare questions, disrespecting the community like we ain't nuttin.'

Raven turns to him and takes in the kid's dark eyes, freshly tanned skin and designer haircut. He knows the boy. 'Well if it isn't little Alfie Chambers,' he says. 'A little older than when I last busted your granddad for selling stolen flat screen TVs down at the indoor market, but there's no mistaking that Chambers arrogance.'

Alfie's eyes flit to Raven. 'My dad would beat you down, fam, if he heard you dissing my family like dat.'

Raven laughs. 'I'm sure he would, but you see, I know you, and I know who you are. You talk like you're from some street gang, but your mum and dad live over in the Palisades, your dad brings home more money than all the people on this street put together, and you have a trust fund so big, you'll probably never have to work a day your whole life; unless you choose to, of course, which I doubt, because you look like the kind of lazy, self-entitled mummy's boy who'd be quite happy living on handouts, playing video games, and eating your body weight in fourteen inch Meat Feasts, loaded fries, and chilli cheese bites until your arteries harden and your body literally explodes. You're only down here hanging around with this dipshit because you think he makes you look cool.'

Alfie glances at his shaven headed friend before puffing out his chest like a peacock fanning its feathers. 'Better watch your mouth, fuzz. Fam's got bare friends.'

Raven pokes him in the shoulder a little harder than he intended, but it gets the desired effect. 'Then why not go fetch your *bare* friends and bring them back here. I'd love to introduce myself.'

Alfie stands there, eyes flitting back and forth, weighing up his options, before turning to his pal. 'C'mon fam. Ain't in the mood for chatting with the fuzz. Cop looks like he's been hit with the ugly stick.' The boys laugh and run off, but not before giving them one last middle finger and a shake of a loose fist. 'Wankers!'

Bailey opens the car door. 'I see you haven't lost your way with the youth, boss,' she says. 'Those boys seemed to take a real shine to you.'

'They put a real shine on Welling's shoes, too,' he replies, peering down at the glob of phlegm on the younger DI's foot.

'Bastard thing's cost me over a hundred quid,' Welling says, grabbing a folded handkerchief from his pocket and wiping the offending material from the brogue. 'Knowing my luck, that little shit's gob will stain the leather.'

'If you're stupid enough to walk the beat in a place like Horsemonger's in a pair of hundred-quid shoes then you deserve everything you get,' Raven replies. 'Now you want to tell us what you've found? Or should we just stand here and talk about mouthy little crackheads all day?'

Welling deflates, his shoulders sag. 'Not much. I personally questioned a couple of families who agreed to come to the door. Neither of those houses had basements, and although one family let us come in and take a look around, the other family were less cooperative.'

'They told the detective that just because he dresses in a Moss Brothers suit, doesn't make him any less filth than the rest of us,' one of the PCs says, grinning as she walks past.

'Keep the family who refused to let you look around on record,' Raven says. 'Take a look into their history. See if there's anything worth poking around in.'

'Just because they wouldn't let us come in without a warrant?' Bailey asks. 'Seems a bit over the top, boss.'

'Being over the top is the way we're going to catch this creep. If anybody tells you anything else, they're talking rubbish.' Raven turns to Welling. 'How many houses have you checked?'

'Not sure. Let me check.' Welling rifles through his notebook. 'There's twenty-four houses in all. I've checked seven of them, PC Chadwick has checked eight, and PC Kaur has checked six.'

'Which leaves three houses unchecked,' Bailey says. 'Any reason for that?'

'Only the obvious one,' Welling replies, raising his eyebrows sarcastically.

'So, nobody was home,' Bailey says.

'You've got it in one.'

'Which numbers?' Raven asks, ignoring the jibe.

'Seven, thirteen, and twenty-two.'

Bailey folds her arms. 'You checked the gardens?'

'First thing we did. The houses are all locked up.'

'What about the occupants?'

Welling checks his notes again. 'Number seven is occupied by a single father, Mister Rowley, who works nights at the supermarket warehouse just off the A35. A young family, the Ladipos, live in number thirteen, but according to their neighbours, they've been away on holiday all week. The owner of number twenty-two is a retired guy who's lived on the street for longer than most of the other residents. A Mister Dean Eccles. Next-door neighbour says he rarely leaves the house.'

'Why's that?' Bailey asks.

'No idea,' Welling replies, shooting her a frustrated glance. 'Maybe he doesn't like being bothered by people who ask too many questions.'

'Asking questions is what we do,' Bailey shoots back. 'Failing to ask them is just laziness in my book.'

'Meaning?'

'Meaning just that.'

'So you're insinuating I'm lazy.'

'If the boot fits.'

'Okay, okay,' Raven says, stepping in. 'Arguing amongst ourselves isn't going to get us anywhere.' He eyes Bailey. 'I'm not sure what's going on here, but we're a team, and a team can only function if everybody in it pulls in the same direction.'

Bailey holds his stare. 'I was just making the point that—'

'I know what point you were making, but criticising another officer's ability is not helpful. We all learn on this job, and we learn together.' He turns to Welling. 'Hang back here, wait for Mister Rowley to get home from work and see if you can't spot Mister Eccles at the window, convince him we're not here to spy on him or whatever else he might be thinking. I'd like to at least tick those two properties off our list before the Ladipos return home from holiday.'

'And if they don't?'

'Don't what?'

'Return home from holiday.'

'A good point, and one that even I hadn't thought of,' Raven says, shooting a smug grin at Bailey. He turns back to Welling. 'Make a few calls, find out where they've gone, and see if this story they've told their neighbours checks out.'

'Will do.'

Raven heads back to the car with Bailey in tow. He looks up at the second floor of the Ladipo property. The windows are smeared with dust and grime, the flaking external render in need of urgent repair, plus a paint job that might cover up the soot and black splatters. He has a hunch that something bad happened here, but he's been away from the job for so long, he has no idea if his internal bad-guy GPS is as accurate as it used to be. He only knows about the room from his dream, and that room could be in any one of these houses or even in an entirely different street.

'Where to now, boss?' Bailey asks, unlocking the car.

'We shake the tree,' Raven says, opening the passenger door.

'Which means?'

He gets inside, pulls the door closed behind him and opens the window. 'If anyone's going to know anything about these killings, it's going to be someone on the wrong side of the law, someone who mixes in the same kind of circles as a sicko with a heart fetish and asks the sort of questions that could give us the break we're looking for.'

Bailey shrugs. 'You want to fill me in? Because I have absolutely no idea where you're headed with this.'

'The Medics,' Raven replies, watching as a black Carrion Crow swoops by on the slip stream. 'We go knock on the door of the leader of the biggest drugs and extortion gang in the south of England.'

CHAPTER 33: EMPTY BIBLE

Lisa turns to Billy as he swings the car into a tight parking space between two squad cars.

'Thanks,' she says. 'For dropping me here. I appreciate it, but you don't have to wait. I can make my own way home.'

'Bugger that,' Billy says, opening the car door. 'That's what your other half said and look what trouble that got me into with the missus.'

Lisa concedes the point and steps outside, pushing the van door closed as she heads towards the entrance. She doesn't get far before the automatic glass doors open and a tall, smartly dressed black man emerges. He's holding a clipboard and walking beside another smartly dressed white man in a tweed jacket and light grey chinos.

'Randall,' she calls out, raising a hand to get the newly appointed DCS's attention.

'Lisa?' he says, glancing at the officious looking guy beside him. 'What... what are you doing here?'

His dispassionate question shocks her, and she reacts accordingly. 'I'm here to find out why you've been keeping Luke's return from me.'

Kipruto's mouth opens and closes like a mackerel clamouring for oxygen, while the guy beside him thrusts out a hand.

'Fitzwilliam,' he says. 'Clarence. And you must be...'

'Lisa Draper,' she replies, ignoring his gesture. 'Luke Raven is... *was* my partner, and he also happens to be my son's father.'

If Fitzwilliam is offended, his expression doesn't betray it. 'Of course you are.' He turns to Billy. 'And you are?'

'West,' Billy says, offering his own hand. 'Billy West. I'm a friend of the family.'

'Ah, the electrician,' Fitzwilliam replies. 'You almost took a bullet for our new DI, did you not?'

Billy shrugs. 'Anybody would have done the same thing.'

'I'm not sure that's true,' Fitzwilliam says, clasping Billy's hand in his own. 'But I admire your humility.'

'I was going to tell you,' Kipruto says to Lisa. 'But Luke wanted to do it himself.'

'Just a call' she replies. 'Just a heads up. That's all I wanted. That's all I've ever wanted.'

Kipruto takes a deep breath. 'I understand. It was wrong of me to keep it from you like that.'

You're damn right it was, she thinks, but she tries to keep it together. All that matters now is that she finds Luke.

'Is he here?'

Kipruto shakes his head. 'He went out with another of our DIs.'

'So you've got him working a case already?'

'It's what he wanted. He came here looking for me. He told me he had information on something we've been working on.'

'Sounds like Luke,' Lisa says. 'But that doesn't mean it's okay to put a guy who's been held prisoner by some freak, sicko for the past four years back out on the streets to chase down yet another crazy.'

'It was my idea,' Fitzwilliam says, holding up his hands. 'If anyone needs shooting, I'm afraid it's me.'

'And why would you get involved?' Lisa asks, feeling her anger escalating. 'You're just an MP, right? Why would you care who's working a case down here in Westhampton?'

'It's a big case,' Kipruto says. 'And Raven is more experienced than anybody on my team.'

'He's right,' Fitzwilliam adds. 'You see, the town is getting quite a bad name for itself, what with all the murders that have taken place over the past five or six years, and with Raven returning from the dead with most of his faculties still intact—'

'Most of his faculties?' Lisa interjects, glaring at Kipruto. 'What does he mean by most of his faculties?'

Kipruto tries to avert her gaze.

'Look at me, Randall,' she says. 'What does this guy mean when he says—'

'He has a pretty nasty head wound,' Kipruto says. 'From the gunshot. Molly dressed it and kept him on painkillers, but the damage was pretty severe. The doctors said if he'd been out there any longer, he could have—'

'—died? Are you telling me Luke could have died?'

Randall nods. 'Or been permanently brain damaged.'

'For fuck's sake,' Lisa whispers, tears building in her eyes. 'That bitch. She's been torturing him all this time, allowing him to suffer, and for what? To punish him? To punish me?' She turns to Kipruto. 'And you? You give up on him, you pull every resource from the case, practically admitting he's dead, but then when he shows up on your doorstep with his head in a mess, you send him back out there to catch some sick fuck because your whole team has been decimated and anybody with an ounce of experience has been let go in the name of progress. Do you see how fucked up that is, Randall? Do you see how that might really piss me off?'

'Lisa, I do, but—'

'Once again, that was me,' Fitzwilliam says. 'You mustn't blame DCS Kipruto. I felt, and DCS Kipruto agreed, that if anyone can catch The Heart Breaker, your partner is the prime candidate.'

'The Heart Breaker!' Billy cries, immediately becoming animated. 'Have you heard about this, Lis? The guy that's been killing people and cutting out their hearts for keepsakes? It's been all over the news.'

'Of course it has,' Lisa hisses. 'Which is exactly why Luke's on the case.'

'What do you mean?' Kipruto asks.

'You know exactly what I mean, Randall. We've seen it all before. The mayor tried to throw Luke under the bus when he was on the trail of Tony Richards, and that bitch Deveraux tossed him out into the cold, even though he told her he knew how to catch Molly Staker. This is no different.'

'No,' Kipruto objects. 'I wouldn't do that. I'd never use Luke as some sort of human shield. He's here through merit, nothing more.'

'That's bullshit!' she cries, pointing at Fitzwilliam. 'He's already said it was his idea to put Luke on the case, and the only reason somebody from Westminster would be involved in the choice of DCS on a murder case like is for political points scoring. If Luke succeeds, you all get the credit, but if he fails, he'll be thrown into the media pit as the feeding frenzy begins.'

'Now, now,' Fitzwilliam interjects. 'You seem to be jumping to all sorts of wild conclusions, none of which are—'

'You saw an opportunity, didn't you!' she says, glaring at him. 'You found out Luke was coming home and you decided what better person to throw into the lion's den than a damaged DI with a track record as blemished as a badly bruised apple.'

'Mrs. Draper, I wholeheartedly refute such allegations and am offended that you would think a man of my standing would stoop to something so disingenuous as to promote a long-standing detective in this constabulary for such nefarious reasons.'

'That's a lot of long words to describe stabbing someone in the back!' Lisa yells. 'But that's exactly what you're doing. The both of you.'

Kipruto looks crestfallen, the clipboard hanging from his hand like an empty bible. Behind him, the door opens and detective Ray Davis steps outside. He spies Kipruto and Fitzwilliam, sees Lisa standing there with her fists clenched and Billy looking like he's caught in the middle of a crossfire, and he backs away, palms held out defensively.

'Good to see you, Lis,' he calls out. 'Hope you and Harry are okay. I'll catch you when you finish up with the DCS.'

'Oh, I'm finished,' Lisa says, grabbing Billy by the arm and dragging him back to the car. 'I'm so finished.'

CHAPTER 34: SINK THE PINK

Raven and Bailey cross the street and walk past a group of kids puffing on disposable vapes and rolling spit-soaked fags. Behind them are the washed out remains of what was once a greasy spoon café and the boarded-up exterior of a once renowned local fish and chip shop. The kids stop spitting rhymes at each other long enough to glare at the two detectives. One of them rolls his eyes, another says something funny to a girl with a tattoo of a Pokémon character on her neck. On the opposite side of the street, an old drunk yells, 'I used to be a king!' before collapsing in a heap in the doorway of a cluttered newsagent.

'Where did you say this guy hangs out?' Bailey asks, watching as one of the kids picks his nose and wipes it on the shirt of the boy next to him.

'At the snooker hall,' Raven replies. 'Sink The Pink. It's been the HQ of The Medics since I was walking the beat.'

'I'd always heard of the place, when I was a PC I mean, but I've never actually been there.'

'Most of the coppers steer clear of it. It's not exactly police friendly.'

'Name me a place that is,' Bailey says, grinning. 'I've gotten used to being a scab around town these days. In fact, I've grown to like it.'

'Makes you wonder whether these people really believe they'd be better off without us.'

'I don't wonder that at all,' Bailey says. 'I know that's exactly what they think.'

Sink The Pink sits above an old department store that's been closed for over a decade. Dark windows face out to the street, while a slim blue door is hidden in a deep recess with a single bell connected to the property upstairs. There's a pink painted logo above the entrance and a poster to the right advertising the venue's nineties house music night. Raven notices the poster is about three years out of date. The recess smells of piss and weed, but none of the town's homeless dare sleep in this black hollow. It's protected ground.

'You ready?' Raven asks, his finger hovering just above the doorbell.

'Of course,' she says. 'How can I go wrong with you as my guardian angel.'

Raven presses the button and waits for someone to answer. They stand there for almost thirty seconds before they hear the soft click of the lock disengaging.

'Come on up,' a mysterious voice says. 'I'll put the kettle on.'

Raven nods to Bailey and they enter, climbing a steep set of stairs, the carpet covered in dark marks and sticky patches. There's only one point of illumination on the staircase, a single spotlight set into a mould-covered ceiling. The bulb blinks on and off like a warning beacon. The walls run with remains of liquid nicotine, yellow streaked memories from when smoking inside public spaces was still legal. Overhead, the ceiling is criss-crossed with deep cracks in the plaster, as if some sort of seismic shift has occurred on the second floor.

They reach the landing and turn left towards a wooden door with a single glass pane revealing a wide bar, two pool tables, a slot machine and another doorway to the snooker hall. Raven glances at Bailey.

'This is it,' he says. 'Brace yourself.'

'Detective Luke Raven as he lives and breathes,' a guy behind the bar declares. He's got a thick crop of tangerine-coloured hair, a ginger moustache and narrow, blue eyes that peer out from beneath a heavy brow.

'Hello Shane,' Raven says. 'Long time, no see.'

'What the fuck happened to your head, man,' the guy, Shane, replies. He has a Southern Irish accent laced with a New Forest twang. 'Looks like some eejit took a baseball bat to your skull.'

'You should see the other guy,' Raven says, approaching the bar. He can already taste the peat in the whiskey and feel the beautiful numbness of the alcohol as it slips down his throat. He shoots a guilty glance at Bailey, but she's distracted by an old-fashioned vinyl jukebox.

'Word on the street was that you were dead, man. You crawl out of your own grave just to come down here and see me?'

'Trust me, if I had risen from the dead, the last place I'd come would be here.'

'I see you haven't lost your wit, Raven. That was always a thing with you.' Shane gestures to the array of bottles behind him. 'Now, can I get you a drink? It's on me.'

Those six words are like bullets from a semi-automatic weapon. They penetrate Raven's skull with malicious intent. His brain fires off dozens of electrical impulses that fizz around his body at a speed his mind can't comprehend. He wants to say yes; he needs to say yes. Everything about him is desperately pleading for him to accept the offer, to take a glass in his hand and throw back the distilled liquid as if it were oxygen.

'I'm fine, thanks,' he says, his voice coming from a different reality.

'Really? I've never known you to turn down a glass of twelve-year-old Jamesons before.'

'I'm… working,' he says, forcing the words out one at a time. 'And in any case, I've been dry for four years.'

'Good for you, man. That's what I like to hear. A copper who looks after his health and is dedicated to his profession.'

'Enough with the platitudes, Shane. Where's your boss?'

A wry smile spreads across Shane's thin lips. 'If you mean Conor, he's not here.'

'When will he be back?'

Shane shrugs. 'What am I? His personal assistant?'

'More like hired muscle.'

'I hope you can back up that accusation, because saying unsubstantiated things like that could get you in hot water with your superiors.'

'Do I look like the kind of copper who gives a shit about that?'

Raven senses Bailey flinching beside him.

'Who's she?' Shane asks, cocking his head towards his partner.

'*She* is Detective Allison Bailey,' Bailey chimes in. 'And if you think Raven can be a hard ass, you're in for a nice surprise.'

'Is that how you breed them these days, Detective?' Shane says without shifting his gaze. 'All lit up and full of spunk.'

'If you're talking about me, sir,' Bailey interjects. 'Then I'd appreciate it if you would address me personally.'

'As I said,' Shane continues. 'Conor isn't here, and I've no idea when he'll be back. He tends to do what the fuck he pleases, does Conor. Sometimes we don't see him for weeks.'

Raven snorts his disbelief. Conor Byrne has been a boil on the arse of Westhampton for decades, and his father had been an even bigger blemish on an otherwise idyllic landscape for years prior to that. The minder, Shane Byrne, is a pain, but he's nothing compared to his ruthless cousin.

'We're looking for information regarding a series of violent crimes that have taken place over the past year,' Raven says. 'I'm hoping that your organisation can shed some light on who might be perpetrating them.'

'Even if Conor knew anything, why would he want to tell you?' Shane asks. 'He's not the kind of guy who likes to liaise with coppers. You know that just as much as I do.'

'Because there's heat on The Medics, and giving us something helpful could just turn the temperature down.'

Bailey flinches again, and this time Shane notices.

'I don't think your partner likes you offering to help a few Irish rogues like us,' Shane says. 'You sure you want to barter with the Byrnes?'

'I can take care of any fallout,' Raven says. 'I just need information.'

Shane pours himself a whiskey and knocks it back.

'I assume you're talking about this crazy lunatic ripping out people's internal organs,' Shane replies. 'If you are, you must know that kind of violence really isn't our thing.'

'No, you're more the nail gun and Colombian necktie types,' Bailey says, turning up her nose.

'Calm your Rottweiler down,' Shane says. 'Accusations like that are likely to make Conor nervous.'

'The offer's there,' Raven replies. 'Information. *Good* information. Something that'll help us bring this nutjob in. You give us that, and I'll do what I can to redirect the DCS's attention.'

Shane pours two whiskeys and sets one down in front of Raven. He inches it forward, making sure Raven gets a hit of its enticing scent.

'I'll pass the message on,' he says. 'But only if you have a drink with me.'

Raven shakes his head. 'I told you, I don't drink.'

'Then we don't talk. Where we come from, you want to make a trade, you drink to seal the deal.'

Raven glares at the amber liquid. It swirls inside the glass like a cyclone, the vortex threatening to pull him in. He's still reeling from his prior infraction. One more drink could push him over the edge.

'Come on, Detective. The Luke Raven I know would have thrown that back already and demanded a top up.'

Raven eyes the whiskey. It's tempting. More than tempting, it's irresistible. He can feel Bailey's eyes on him and hear Kipruto's words in his ears, but he doesn't care. All he can think about is the alcohol in his gut, the anaesthetising sensation in his body, the fluid rapidity of his blood. He wants the drink, but more than that, he wants the fucking bottle. He wants everything behind the bar. He wants to drink it up, suck it in, inhale it like smoke. He wants to lick the place clean, crawl out the door and find somewhere else to carry the session on. He wants to drink and drink and drink until his body is so chemically altered that it ceases to think or feel or regret. He wants to throw up, drink some more and throw up again. He wants to pull himself into a protective little ball and pretend he doesn't exist, because existing means he has to face up to some home truths, some gut-wrenching, mind-shattering realities he can't even begin to confront. He wants to fight and punch and kick. He wants to smash this fucking snooker hall into the ground.

'Drink it, Raven. Drink the fucking whiskey.'

He edges closer, fingers opening and closing, clutching at air. He feels Bailey's hand on his arm, but he shrugs it away like filth. He doesn't want proximity, doesn't want lucidity. He places his palms on the bar and raises his eyes to the barman's penetrating stare. He wraps his fingers around the glass and relishes the coolness of it. He swills the liquid, feels it sloshing against the smooth surface. He opens his mouth, lets the air in and lifts the tumbler. The weight of it is comforting, like an old blanket. Shane grins, a smile so wide it threatens to tear his face in two. The barman lifts his own glass, and now the pair of them are a mirror image, two old foes just about to drink to their health when health is the last thing on their minds.

'Bottoms up,' Shane says, but Raven is seething. He's so angry, he wants to rip the guy's throat out.

'Fuck you!' he hisses and tosses the glass at the bottles on the wall, smashing a twenty-year-old cognac and a slim bottle of Sambuca. They're showered in liquid and glass. Shane dives to his left but Raven lets the booze douse his jacket and shirt.

'You fucking lunatic!' Shane hollers. 'Look what ya done. Ya could have just said no.'

Raven grabs his collar and hoists him across the bar. They're so close now, Raven can smell the cheap aftershave and whiskey buzz. 'Tell Conor about the deal,' he says. 'Tell him it has a short shelf-life. Twenty-four hours or it's off.'

He pushes the barman back and heads to the door, not pausing to see if he's regained Bailey's approval. He's down the stairs before he realises it, rushing out into the street, his chest heaving. He can barely breathe. His head is pounding. He can feel the bullet that barely missed his cerebral cortex and can see the girl, Molly, leaning over him, telling him to *'relax, it'll be fine, everything will be fine.'*

It's not. Nothing is fine. Nothing will be fine ever again.

CHAPTER 35: BACTERIA

Kaden heads to the seafront. It's a nice evening. The bars are full, the arcades are rammed. There's still a smattering of people on the beach and even some random, die-hard swimmers in the water. She can't go home. She can't go back to the house. Her uncle is still there, even though he isn't. She knows as soon as she walks through the front door, he'll start calling out her name. Her dead name. She can't face that. Things have gotten out of hand which means she's out of control. An out-of-control Kaden is dangerous, she knows that, but right now, she relishes the danger.

She feels feminine again. Perhaps it's the thrill of the police interview, or maybe it's the conversation she had with The Cardinal. He's made her feel special, invincible. She can do anything, be anything, *say* anything. The Legion is her crutch, her stabiliser. It's the perfect accompaniment for everything she has planned. Her hearts are in a good place. They can never be found. Her uncle is keeping them safe, after all. He would never let her down, even though she used him as a pin cushion. Family is family. They look after each other.

'Later, you'll go home, you'll have dinner with your uncle and you'll watch TV.'

That's what The Cardinal had said to her, but how was he to know that having dinner with her uncle meant a meal for one? She wasn't about to sit there in that shitty little living room, watching a crappy CRT TV while slopping microwaved noodles into her pretty mouth. She had a much more exciting thing planned.

She passes a young couple who are carefully examining the insides of their mouths with their twisting, bacteria infested tongues. She walks past a married woman who looks like she's waiting for her extra-marital pastime to show up; her made up face, too young skirt, and look of hopeless desperation give her away. She bumps into some letch of a guy in a Next sweatshirt and ASDA George jeans who says something unintelligible and creepy. She helps an old man pick up his walking stick and receives the most beautiful smile of thanks in return.

She's not a bad person. She doesn't think evil thoughts just for the sake of it. The people she hurts are the people that hurt her. She collects the organs of the sick, the weak, the grotesque. The display she is planning has a theme, and the theme is darkness. All humans harbour it, some more than others. Her hearts will reveal that blackened rottenness in all its sordid, fetid glory.

She passes her gym and raises a hand to her personal trainer, a muscular transgender who can deadlift 300 kilos without breaking a sweat. She continues on, turning right up Rosetta Hill, past the corner shop where kids used to yell insults at her as if they were aeroplanes made from paper and card. She narrowly avoids a voluminous pile of dogshit before taking a right down Bracken Drive. The keys jangle in her pocket. She touches them and a sharp bolt of electrical excitement travels up her arm and rattles her jaw. This is where she should have headed in the first place, not to the meet up with the boss she knew would have done anything to get inside her boxers.

She traces her finger along the black railing and whistles an old eighties tune. She's always loved the eighties, even though they occurred almost a decade before she was born. Perhaps it's because, back then, she hadn't been a lost little imp of a thing, and her mother and uncle hadn't gotten their sharp, hooked talons into her yet. Maybe it's because, back before she was born, she hadn't been so confused, so out of place, so broken. Maybe it's simpler than that. Maybe it's that the music was better and there were no mobile phones and social media accounts to pummel every ounce of individuality and morsel of confidence into a pestle, compounding it with hatred and loathing.

The song's by The Human League, a band who knows what it's like to be unique, to have an image that is contrary to societal norms. She likes that about them. She's even been to see them a couple of times at the International Centre in Bournemouth, standing at the back on her own, singing every line, screaming every lyric. When the singer, Phil Oakey, joined forces with Georgio Moroder and sung about Electric Dreams, that had spoken to her in a way no other song could. Every dream she's ever had since then has been electric. Her whole life has been powered with that dark, unstoppable energy. Right now, it's what's keeping her moving forward in the face of so much negativity. It doesn't matter. The Cardinal is going to deal with the detective with the lying eyes and disfigured skull, and then everything is going to get back on track. In the unlikely event that it doesn't, she has to make sure the job gets done. That means picking up the pace. Fortunately, she already has a backlog of ideal candidates, and she plans to go through them like a virus through a cruise ship.

She looks up at the black door and fingers the keys in her pocket. She climbs the three steps, slips the largest of the two into the lock, watching as the smiley face emoji swings back and forth, and turns it. The latch disengages and now she's inside, peering up the stairs at flat number two, the one she had exited less than forty-eight hours earlier.

'Hello, Ollie,' she says, her expression betraying her escalating emotions. 'Time to finish what we started.'

CHAPTER 36: LINGER

It's late. Raven is exhausted. He keeps forgetting that he's been cooped up in a series of off-grid properties, and then in a Glasgow hospital, for almost as long as a US president's first term in office. He hasn't exercised for so long, his body is resisting prolonged motion. His headache has worsened, as has his thirst for substances contrary to the furtherance of his rejuvenated career. He has to get himself back on the straight and narrow. For Lisa. For Harry. How can he see them when he doesn't even know if he can stay sober for another day?

He doesn't have anywhere to stay, and he can't trust himself alone in the hotel. He needs company, but that company can't be Lisa and her new husband. Being there will push him over the edge, he knows it. He isn't used to the idea yet. Perhaps he never will be.

He thinks about bunking down with Bailey, but her place is on the other side of town, and he reasons that turning up on her doorstep with nothing but a holdall and a forced smile would be wholly inappropriate. She'd seen what he'd almost become today, and she hadn't liked it.

He thinks about Randall and Ruby, and although he'd love to see the young PC and her new twins, Randall is his boss, and he suspects every moment he spends there, he'll be constantly under the microscope.

He thinks of his old chief, Dave Simmonds and his partner Stuart, but since their connection to The Legion had been discovered during the last case, they'd picked up sticks and moved north to avoid the media attention. He's never suspected

Simmonds of any wrongdoing, but mud can get sticky, and when it does, it's impossible to shift.

That only leaves one option, and although he'll be imposing on two people who owe him nothing, it's the only place he'll feel protected. From himself. Right now, he's his own worst enemy, a bad one at that.

'Hey, Sal,' he says, and instantly her eyes light up. He hasn't seen her that way before, and before he knows it, she's wrapped him in her arms.

'Hello you,' she says. 'It's so good to see you. So good to have you home.'

'I didn't know you cared,' he smiles with her hair in his mouth, his chin buried in the crook of her neck.

She releases him and holds him at arm's length, eyes narrow, lip chewed. 'You're kidding, right?'

He waits a moment before answering just to hang out the suspense. When his face breaks into an impish grin, she actually slaps his arm gently, but he feels it.

'You know I could have you arrested for assault.'

'So arrest me,' she says, her mouth turning into an oval shape when she sees his scar. 'It looks like someone else should be arrested for assault. What the hell did she do to you?'

'She shot me, Sal,' he says, turning his head away. 'Like, a real bullet.'

'Come in,' she says, tugging on his arm. 'I'll make you a tea.'

He follows her. This isn't the welcome he'd been expecting, but he savours it. He hasn't felt this wanted since his son was born. His son. His Harry. He misses him, every tiny piece of him. He wants him now, wants him beside him. He's missed out on so much.

'Is Billy home?' he asks.

'I sent him out,' she scowls. 'Told him not to come home unless he's got pizza.'

'You've rowed.'

'Not rowed. He pissed me off. It's okay. I'll forgive him eventually. Just, right now, I can't face him.'

He takes a seat at the kitchen table and sets his holdall down by the refrigerator. If she sees it, she doesn't mention it.

'Care to share?' he asks.

She shakes her head and waits for the kettle to boil. He doesn't mind the silence. It's comforting. This is what he needs. Normality. He's forgotten what it's like, if he ever even had it at all.

'Oh my God,' she says, pouring hot water into two cups. 'I just realised. Your mum? Does she know you're—'

'Alive?'

'Yes, exactly. Have you told her?'

Raven thinks about that. The truth is, he hasn't thought about her at all. Ever since Detective McGoughlan informed him of his father's passing — the second one, since his father had faked his own death years earlier — Raven had put all thoughts of his childhood out of his head. It was Lisa that mattered. Lisa and Harry. Everything else was just noise.

'I haven't told her.'

'Luke, you should. She's your mother.'

He shakes the idea away. 'Sal, I need to ask you something.'

'Not until you call your mum.' She tosses him the landline. 'Don't make a second mistake since you came back. You'll regret it, I promise.'

He glares at the handset. It looks so strange to him, like an alien lifeform. Can he remember the number? Does he even know what his mother's voice sounds like?

'This seems like a ransom demand,' he says. 'Is it?'

'If you want to stay here tonight, and I know you do,' Sally replies. 'Well, let's just say this call is a prerequisite, as is another call you know you have to make, and one you should have made as soon as you woke up in that hospital.'

He hits the numbers. They come back to him like confetti. He reasons it's the fear of having to call Lisa that's prompted his fractured memory to pluck the digits from some obscure place. The call's answered on the second ring.

'Hello?'

His mum sounds different, older. He doesn't know why he's surprised. She's in her sixties now, or maybe her seventies. He's ashamed that he can't remember.

'Mum, it's me.'

The silence is so long and complete that for a second he thinks the call has been cut off.

'Luke?'

'Yeah, surprise.' It's all he can think of to say.

'You're alive?'

'The doctor says I am, so I guess I must be.'

There's a wet, snotty sound, and he realises his mum is crying. It shocks him.

'Mum, I'm okay. Just a little tired.'

'The police told me you were probably dead. They said that girl had killed you.'

'You know me, I'm like a cat. It takes more than a bullet and a truckload of drugs to take me down.'

'Where are you? Are you near the house?'

He doesn't know how to respond to that. Of course he is. He's less than five miles away, but his family home hadn't even figured on his potential list of possible places to crash. He doesn't have time to rationalise that, just to accept it.

'Not really, but I'll be home soon. I promise.'

He hates that he's lying, but he doesn't want his mum to feel any worse than he's already made her feel. If facing Lisa is going to be tough, facing his mum will be even harder. The memory of his dad still lingers in that house, as does all the shit he put them through.

'I miss you, Luke. I can't put into words how much.'

That hurts. Those words hurt a lot. He loves his mum. Her only crime was putting up with a man who didn't love her and who barely noticed his kid. The problem wasn't her. It was the association. She had been tarnished with those memories, and like blood, it was almost impossible to wash off.

'I've got to go,' he lies. 'But I'll call again just as soon as I can.'

'I'm so happy, I really am,' she says, but her voice betrays her tears. 'Promise me you won't get hurt again.'

He ends the call, leaving the request unanswered. Sally's standing by the window, arms folded, her small frame enveloped by the darkness seeping through the kitchen window.

'See, that wasn't so hard, was it?' she says. 'You ready to make call number two?'

The phone slips through his fingers and clatters to the floor, sending batteries spinning like tumbleweed across the linoleum. He stoops down to collect them, chasing them across the floor like a drug addict hoovering up spilled charlie.

'Jesus, Luke,' Sally says. 'Seems like you'll do anything to get out of talking to the one person you should be talking to.'

'Sorry, it was an accident,' he says, but then there's a crash like a car hitting the back door and a window shatters. He gets up, the phone hanging from his fingers like a gun, and sees two masked men in the back garden slamming a police battering ram against the UPVC frame.

'Run,' he says to Sally, her face whiter than a chef's hat. 'Sally, get the fuck out of here.'

He pushes her into the front room and turns to face his attackers, knowing that the odds aren't good. When he takes the kitchen knife from the magnetic rail, the door crashes inward and two men enter. One of them raises a gun.

'Top of the day to you, Raven,' he says. 'We have a message from The Cardinal.'

CHAPTER 37: SPARE KEYS

Kaden sits in the darkness. She's on the bed, legs crossed, a Rizla paper on the bedsheets, strands of tobacco clenched between two freshly manicured fingers. Ollie doesn't have any weed, which is a shame. She really wants to get high. Instead, she'll have to settle for a smoke. She licks the paper, rolls the cigarette and places it between her dark red lips. When she lights up, she inhales deeply and blows smoke all around the room. She wants him to know she's there, even before he sees her. Fear is born out of anticipation, and Ollie needs to be afraid. He needs to piss his pants. Tonight, his heart is hers, and if the bitch-blonde gets in the way, she'll get a blade in the throat for her troubles. Chav organs aren't her thing, so she won't cut them out, but she'll make sure the bleached blonde bimbo knows who's slicing her up. She'd insulted her and that can't go unpunished.

She thinks about the lost fingernail and the two coppers who'd showed up at the shop. Right now, one of them is getting a right pasting. The thought excites her. The stark image of the detective being beaten into a smashed mess of blood and meat sends her mind racing. The pain he would be feeling, the terror. He will fight back — he looks the type — but he will lose. The Legion never lets a live one get away.

She should have asked The Cardinal for the heart. It would be a good one, as black as an infected wound. It would sit nicely with the others. She thinks about making the call, of asking him to set it aside for her, but she changes her mind. There'll be plenty of time for that after. After she's harvested Skinny Ribs. His body is so thin, the cut won't even need to be that deep. Just enough to get past the sternum and the upper ribs.

There's a sound from below, a door opening and closing. Her own heart skips. She holds her breath, listening for footsteps. There aren't any. She relaxes, takes another drag. It's probably someone from the flats downstairs. Maybe the lady with the shaky leg. The old bag walks around like she's Elvis, thigh trembling, hips gyrating. Kaden almost laughs out loud, but then she hears laughter, followed by muffled voices. It's him, she knows it is, even before the third step lets out its familiar groan.

She gets up and moves behind the door. The adrenalin soars through her body causing her hands to tremble. This is so exciting. She's never killed outside her own home before. The spontaneity is exhilarating, the element of risk like an aphrodisiac. She's so horny, so jacked up on endorphins she can barely stand it.

When the key clinks against the lock, she readies herself. This is it. This is her fifth heart. Her maker will be pleased. She will be well rewarded.

*

'Has someone been smoking in here?' Shen asks.

'Not me,' Ollie answers, trying to remember whether he'd had a crafty one before he went out.

'You know I don't like the smell of it,' Shen says, nose wrinkled like a pinched cherry. 'For once, could you just do as I ask and smoke outside.'

'I just said it wasn't me,' Ollie replies. 'I don't like the flat smelling like an ashtray either.'

He turns the key, but something about the smell is bothering him. It isn't just the odour of smoke and nicotine. There's another scent. A pleasant one. One that tweaks his memory, but not enough to connect the dots.

He pushes the door open and does the gentlemanly thing, letting Shen enter first. It's the one thing that saves his life. He doesn't even realise what's happening at first, just that there's a shuffling noise, followed by a gargled, bubbling sound. When Shen hits the floor, he thinks she's tripped over.

'Shen, are you okay?'

He fumbles for the light switch, but he slips in what he presumes is water and then trips over his girlfriend's crumpled body.

'Let me help you up,' he says, but it's only when his finger touches the blood on her chest that he realises she'll never be getting up again.

'What the fuck?'

His brain hasn't put the pieces together yet. He's still tugging Shen's arm to help her to her feet when a shadow moves in the darkness. He looks up and takes a punch in the face for his troubles. He flails around on the floor, slipping in the sticky puddle while more blood gushes from his broken nose.

'If you want money, I'll get it for you. Just don't hurt me. Please don't hurt me.'

The shadow doesn't answer. It just punches him again, this time knocking him out cold.

When he comes to, he's on the bed and there are ropes around his wrists and feet.

'Hey,' he says. 'Hey, whoever you are. Please don't do this. Please. Whatever I've done, I'm sorry. I didn't mean it, I swear. I can pay you. I can give you whatever you want.'

A cloth is pressed to his face. There's a strong, sweet smell of alcohol, and then he loses consciousness again.

This time when he comes round, there's a rag tied around his mouth. He can barely breathe. His shirt has been removed, exposing his chest and stomach. His attacker's shadow looms over him. He turns his head and in the dim light he sees Shen's body. It's now surrounded by a dark puddle. He sees the deep slash around her throat.

He looks up and the moonlight catches his captor's face. He recognises her instantly. He tries to say Kaden, but all that comes out of his mouth is a muffled grunt.

She peers down at him, her face expressionless. Her eyes are dark, emotionless. He wonders if she's really there, or if her body is just a drone being controlled by some other force. He pulls at his binds, but they're tied so tight, the coarse rope cuts into his skin. Kaden bends down and grips his cheeks. Her long fingernails dig into his face, drawing blood.

He tries to scream, 'Get off me, you bitch!' but his words are unintelligible. Kaden doesn't react. She doesn't say anything. She traces a finger down his chest, around his nipples and across his abdomen to his naval. It's the exact same move she played out when they were in entirely different circumstances. Then it felt erotic, but now it terrifies him. What is she planning? What's on this evil bitch's mind. She's already killed Shen, which can only mean one thing. If he doesn't get off this bed, he's dead too. His body reacts, tugging at the ropes, jerking upwards. She slaps his face so hard he sees little shimmering stars.

He can't die here. He won't die here, just because he once let this psycho monster into his home. He's done nothing wrong. Shen had done nothing wrong. He had a life. He has things he wants to do. This can't be the end.

Kaden disappears, which is even worse than her standing over him. Not knowing what she's doing is the worst part. He scans the flat, but he can't see her. His eyes scour the bedside cabinet for something that could help him. There's an ashtray with a crushed roach still smouldering, a Bic lighter propped against it. Sorrow grips him like a tight fist. If only he'd listened to Shen she'd still be alive and he wouldn't be tied to this fucking bed. Kaden had been in here all long, helping herself to his tobacco and deliberately sending him a warning. She'd known he wouldn't heed it, just like she'd known he'd send Shen in first.

The only question is, how the hell did she get in? The door hadn't been forced. Then he remembers rushing out for his dinner date and seeing the empty tray by the door. It hadn't registered then, but the pieces click together now. His spare key had been missing. The bitch must have slipped it in her pocket before she'd left the previous day. His stomach flips. She'd been planning it all along. He'd signed his own death warrant the moment he'd asked her up for coffee. Shen had forgiven him and that had been her biggest mistake. If she'd done what she should have done and dumped him right there and then, her throat would still be intact and her future would still be something she could look forward to.

He tries to scream, but the sound is just a muffled groan.

Kaden returns. She has something in her hands. She holds it up so he can see. He tries to scream again, but his throat is so dry he starts to choke. He wants to throw up, but he knows if he does, he'll drown in his own vomit. Not that it matters. Kaden means to kill him. She presses a button and the little circular saw whirs into life.

'Nnng!' he cries. 'Nnng, heese nnng!'

A car drives past outside and the headlights throw a beam of yellow across Kaden's emotionless face. Her eyes don't dilate. They're just glassy marbles, black as coal. She's getting high on the experience, soaking it up like a sponge. He can't believe she's doing this. He's done nothing to make her want to kill him.

The saw spins and spins like a Catherine Wheel, and that's when he knows there's no getting away. No more beers with his mates, no more sneaky joints while his girlfriend's not watching. No more Chinese takeaways, no more five-a-side football, no more crafty wanks while watching home-made, three-way porn.

When Kaden moves the saw towards his chest, she's grinning, but it's not a happy face. It's a crazed, maniacal expression, ghostly and vapid. He tries to press himself into the bed, to pull himself away, but it's no use. The blade hits flesh, spraying his face with blood and tissue, and the pain is so horrific, it blinds him. He cries out, screaming with every ounce of strength he has, but nobody will hear him. Kaden presses down and the bone gives way. He feels his ribs separating, his sternum collapsing.

Before he loses consciousness, he says a prayer, but he's never been to Church. He hopes that if there is a God, he forgives him. He hopes Shen forgives him too.

CHAPTER 38: DOCS

There's something they don't tell you about getting shot. It's an odd thing, something you wouldn't expect. They say the average bullet travels at 1,700 miles per hour. Even the fastest brain impulse is less than a sixth of that, but when you've been shot before, your body anticipates the bullet even before it leaves the gun. When the guy in the black hoodie and dark jeans pulls the trigger, Raven is already diving to the floor, and the bullet misses him by a hair. A mug shatters into a thousand pieces, spraying ceramic shards all over the counter and floor, but Raven doesn't hang about. He grips the knife, runs at his attacker, and drives the weapon home, pushing it into the man's stomach with enough force to drive it in, handle deep. The guy goes down with a grunt, dropping the gun, but there's still another intruder to take care of.

The weapon goes skittering across the linoleum and comes to rest beneath the breakfast table. Raven dives for it but takes a kick to the head, sending him flying. He tastes salty blood and tries to get to his feet, but the guy punches him again, cracking his jaw. He figures his attacker's wearing a knuckle duster, because the punch causes too much damage to be just skin and bone. Raven's barely conscious, but he knows he has to keep the guy occupied. He has to give Sally enough time to get away.

'You're not walking away this time,' the guy says, but Raven still tries to get to his feet. 'Oh, no you don't.'

He takes another punch to the chin, and this one sends him smashing into the range oven, cracking the glass. He tries to stand again, but his legs won't comply. Blood pours from his mouth and nose. He leans over and spits out a tooth.

'Didn't hurt,' he says, blood coating his teeth and tongue. 'You punch like a two-year-old.'

The guy is tall, thick set, heavy beard. His fists are like battering rams, both of them clad in blood-stained metal. Raven tries to take in his attacker's appearance, hoping he'll live to make use of the memory, but his priority is to protect the woman who opened the door to him. She doesn't deserve any of this.

'I'm going to enjoy this,' the guy says. 'You might have got the jump on Hugo, but I'm not as slow as that thick bastard.'

'You're fucking ugly though,' Raven replies, spitting more blood.

The guy throws two hooks, one that strikes him in the temple, the other in the neck. Raven's head slams against the floor and he fights to remain conscious. He's determined not to give the guy the satisfaction of beating him to death without a fight.

'Ish that it?' he grunts. 'Ish that all you got?'

He pushes himself up on weak hands, palms slipping in blood and drool. He can see a blurred image of the gun, but now it seems too far away.

'You won't get to that,' the thug says, studying Raven's pulped face. 'And I won't be using it, either. You're not worth the bullet.'

He aims a kick at Raven's lower abdomen. The pain is so excruciating, he throws up.

The guy laughs. 'Fuck me, Raven. You puked on my new boots.' The thug grabs a tea-towel from a rail above the oven and tosses it at him. 'Clean' em,' he says. 'Clean your disgusting vom' off my new Docs before it stains.'

'Fugg you,' Raven replies.

'That's not very nice, is it? I was told you were a decent bloke.'

There's another kick, this one to his ribs. Raven feels a snap as something gives way. He cries out but bites down on his tongue, trying to stifle it.

'That's another goal to me,' the guy sneers. 'Come on, Lukey boy. Play the game. At least make a fist of it. This is too easy.'

Raven turns onto his side and pulls up his knees, attempting to protect himself from another strike. It doesn't help because the guy kicks him in the head.

He lands back in the cottage, crouched in the cellar where the bodies of unknown victims hang from rusted hooks. The smell of meat is overpowering, as is the taste of blood. A door opens and Molly is standing there, a bag of meat and tissue dangling from her closed fist. Behind her, something growls, something unseen. He knows that snarl, recognises the scent of sulphur and the sour smell of smouldering ash. The creature from the darkest pit has been following him for years, tracing his scent. It wants him. One day it will get him. He wonders if that day is today. He isn't stupid. He can't deny the inevitable.

'I'm not afraid of you,' he says, but Molly doesn't respond. She just holds up the bag and looks at it. She sees something that amuses her, and she smiles. Something moves within the translucent plastic. At first, he thinks it's some sort of animal, a rat maybe, but it's the wrong shape, and there's something oozing from within. Then he hears the sound, the steady repetitive beat. He knows instantly what it is. It's a heart. A black heart. He feels a warm, damp sensation on his chest and looks down to see a gaping hole where his own heart should be.

Molly turns and nods at the thing standing behind her, and she says something he can't hear. He tries to crawl towards her, but something is holding him back, and he realises the guy with the knuckle dusters is gripping his legs. He comes back to his senses and tries to take in his surroundings. He's still in the kitchen, but something's different. His attacker must have gone outside to get something because now the table's been moved and there's a sheet of plastic beneath him. It covers the entire kitchen floor. The big guy holds up the object he'd gone to collect. A chainsaw. Raven starts to panic. He's going to cut him up into tiny pieces to make it easier for him to dispose of his body.

'I'll get to you in a minute,' he says. 'But first, I need to take care of this dead muppet.'

Raven watches in horror as he fires up the chainsaw and slices off the arm of the bloke he'd stabbed to death earlier in the exchange. The limb comes away as easily as a chicken leg from a Sunday roast. The guy cuts off the other arm, then both legs. The place is covered in blood. The plastic obviously isn't there to hide evidence, it's just to wrap the body parts. The butcher doesn't care about DNA and mess. This is all about convenience.

'Sorry Hugo,' he says before taking the saw to the bloke's neck, cutting through meat, sinew and bone. The head rolls across the floor and comes to rest beside Raven's bloodied face. The vacant eyes glare at him and Raven sees his own reflection in the lifeless pupils. He barely recognises himself. Everything is swollen, bloated.

'Never liked the fucker anyway,' the guy says. 'He was so full of himself, like he was God's gift or something. No idea why Conor agreed to take him on, the ignorant twat.'

Raven takes in the mention of Conor Byrne's name. He'd already guessed The Medics had something to do with this. He'd obviously rattled them more than was healthy, but killing a police detective? That would seem to be a massive over-reaction. What would it even achieve, unless the attack had nothing to do with his impromptu visit to the snooker club? He tried to think. He'd felt the collar of a few of the Byrnes before, but he'd never been able to get anything to stick. At best, he'd been a nuisance to them. Sending two guys to take him out was a nuclear option with massive ramifications. Even if the thug with the chainsaw did succeed in disposing of his butchered body, there was still more than enough DNA in this kitchen to build a solid case. Why go to all that trouble for a few casual threats and some minor damage to their bar?

'Your turn, Raven,' the goon says, his face dripping with blood.

'You can't get away with thish, you know that, right?'

'If you say so. Not bothered. I get paid either way.'

'You'll spend the resht of your life in prison.'

The guy laughs. 'You've been away too long, buddy. Conor has friends in high places now. Nobody can touch us.'

The reply confuses Raven. Even if what the guy says is true, avoiding the rap for the murder of a serving police officer would be almost impossible. Almost.

'Friendsh? What kind of friendsh?'

'I think you're confused, Raven. This isn't a Bond movie. I'm not going to stand here and tell you the bad guys' secrets while you figure out a way to escape. Conor's paying me to cut you up, and that's what I'm gonna do.'

The chainsaw roars into life once more, chattering metallic teeth sprinting around an elongated bar, spitting the remains of the recently decapitated Hugo. Raven tries to push back, but he's so heavily concussed, he can barely move. He can still see Molly standing in the doorway. She bends down to pick something up, but this time he can't make it out.

The guy steps toward him and lowers the chainsaw. Now it's inches from his right arm.

'Let's get rid of this piece first,' the guys says, yelling above the noise. 'You know the old joke? How do you cure a copper of being a wanker? Chop off both his arms.'

Neither of them laugh. It isn't funny. The teeth still chatter. The deafening roar continues. Fleshy remains spatter Raven's face. He spits out skin and gristle, but he barely notices. He can't take his eyes off the whirring blade. There's no way out of this. If he can't move, he can't fight, and if he can't fight, he can't escape. It all seems so pointless. The kidnap, the journey home, Lisa, Harry, the unexplained visions, his return to the force. All meaningless. He'll never see his son grow up, never get to talk to Lisa about how he feels about her.

The spinning chain inches closer, nicks the sleeve of his shirt, and then there's a loud crack as if the ceiling has caved in, and the chainsaw goes spinning away from him, striking the leg of a breakfast bar stool, severing it at the knee. Raven shields his eyes from dust and splinters, and then he notices the hole in the big guy's abdomen and watches him fall slowly to the ground, his head striking the kitchen worktop, knocking him out cold.

He turns to the kitchen door, and there's Billy West, gun held in trembling hands, smoke streaming from the hot muzzle. The image takes a moment to register, but then he figures it out. It hadn't been Molly Staker bending down to collect something unseen from the ground after all. It had been Billy.

'Sally said you needed help,' Billy says, his eyes never leaving the guy bleeding out on the linoleum. 'I saw the gun, so—'

Raven starts to laugh, and Billy looks at him as if he's gone crazy. Raven finds the stunned look on his friend's face hilarious, and now he's laughing so hard his ribs hurt. The pain it causes is unbearable, but he can't stop. At this moment, it seems like the funniest thing in his whole life, in the whole world.

'I'm calling Randall,' Billy says, stepping over him. 'This whole thing is FUBAR. It's fucking FUBAR.'

CHAPTER 39: TWENTY-FOUR HOURS

Kipruto stands in the kitchen of 39 Warwick Avenue and peruses the carnage. The walls and ceiling are dripping with gore. Body parts litter the ground. A severed head peers up at him, two startled eyes set within the brow of a bearded, blood-stained face. A chainsaw lies discarded. Petrol dribbles from beneath an askew fuel cap. A stool lies on its side, one leg cut away like sliced meat. A handgun is on the ground. Glock 17, 9mm. The back door has been forcefully breached and the garden gate swings back and forth, slamming repeatedly against the concrete fence post.

He turns and heads to the front of the house. This is a mess he is struggling to come to terms with. Raven has been back less than forty-eight hours, and already the body count has risen by two. That's five and counting. Billy West sits on the sofa, his wife beside him. The big guy looks like he's been hit by a truck. Sally doesn't look much better. They've both been very lucky to get out of this situation with their lives. Whoever had authorised the hit, they'd meant business.

He nods to Billy who's reciting a statement to the attending officer. He'll be taken to the station shortly. There's no getting around that. He's shot a man and that can't be taken lightly, no matter what the circumstances are.

The front room is painted with blue and red spinning lights. There are two police cars out front and two ambulances. A dozen or more neighbours stand outside the cordoned off area, looking like extras from some horror B-movie. A woman in the front is dressed in a peach towelling gown, cup of tea gripped between narrow fingers. A middle-aged couple stand beside her. They're whispering excitedly to each other as if they're witnessing the unravelling of some sort of state secret. A kid on a BMX bike races up and down the road, pointing an imaginary gun at the house and making machine gun noises.

'How are you feeling?' he asks Raven who's lying on a stretcher, his face as swollen as a cabbage patch doll.

'I could have taken him,' he replies out of one side of his broken mouth. 'I wash jush getting warmed up.'

'This isn't a joke, Luke. Somebody wanted you dead. Badly.'

'Onor Hyrne,' he says, and at first Kipruto's brain can't translate.

'Wait. Did you say Conor Byrne?'

Raven nods.

'As in, the head of The Medics, Conor Byrne?'

'One and the thame.'

'Why would Conor Byrne order a hit on you? And even if he did, why make such a public display of it?'

Raven doesn't answer, which either means he doesn't know or he plans to take care of things himself. Either version isn't good. He makes a decision.

'I'm going to take you off the case.'

'You can't do that.'

'I can, and I am. You're in no fit state to continue the investigation, and I can't have my lead detective mixed up in some sort of crazy underworld vendetta while there's some nutter out there slicing people open for fun.'

'Thatsh the reashon you need to keep me on the cash, Randall. Don't you shee?'

Kipruto shakes his head and turns to walk away.

'They came after me after Bailey and I showed up at their HQ and began ashking questions.'

Kipruto doesn't want to hear it. He doesn't want to know about Raven's methods. He's studied all his cases, read his notes and dug into all his unofficial contacts and below the radar informants. This is the kind of thing that can derail a case, and Fitzwilliam isn't the kind of guy to champion flaky, tangential thinking. He wants a clean case, a solid outcome, and more importantly, a psychopath behind bars. What he doesn't want is the town's preeminent criminal organisation waging war against the local police.

'You're putting two and two together and coming up with an answer that fits your narrative,' Kipruto says, hating how pompous he sounds. 'Why would The Medics be protecting a guy with a severed heart fetish?'

Again, Raven doesn't answer, and again, Kipruto is left with the distinct impression his DI is keeping something from him.

'I have a hunch,' Raven says. 'Let me follow it. Pleash.'

Kipruto glares at the other ambulance. Inside is a man in a coma. The chainsaw wielding maniac has been identified via their database as one Nico Kuznecova, a private security goon who's got a record as long as a Tesco's till receipt. The decapitated guy with the recently removed limbs has been identified as Hugo Morrison, ex-British Special Forces and known associate of the now deceased Bernie Staker and his band of merry followers. Kipruto isn't ignoring the connection to Raven's previous case, but it's possible it's just a coincidence.

Kuznecova has lost a lot of blood, and he also has a blunt force head wound that the attending paramedics suspect has led to a bleed on his brain. They're feverishly working on him in the back of the meat wagon, but the outlook doesn't look good. Kipruto wants Kuznecova to pull through, because a dead suspect is no good to anybody. He wants the injured security guy to confirm Raven's story because he wants to believe it. Right now, he just doesn't know that he can.

'I'll give you twenty-four hours,' he says, hearing his wife, Ruby telling him that he still owes Raven his life, and he also owes him an apology. 'One day is all I can afford on a pressure cooker case like this.'

'It'sh all I'll need.'

He looks down at his battered colleague, and despite his beleaguered condition, Raven glares back at him. Something clicks between them. An understanding. Raven isn't going down without a fight, and if that means knocking heads together and digging up bodies to uncover the truth, then that's what he'll do. Kipruto only hopes that it doesn't cost him his own career.

His phone vibrates in his pocket, and he turns to take the call.

'It's me, boss,' the inspector, Ray Davis, says. 'I've got some bad news.'

Kipruto's jaw clenches. He knows what's coming. It's the same news he's been receiving on a semi-regular basis ever since this whole nightmare began. He takes a breath and tries to sound composed.

'Go ahead.'

'Two more bodies have been discovered.'

He sucks in air. Two more bodies in addition to the mutilated corpse and critically wounded man lying in the house behind him? Can his evening get any worse?

'Where?'

'On an area of wasteland between All Saints Road and James Street. If memory serves me correctly, it's the same place Raven encountered that maniac, Richards, just after he'd dumped the body of Trudy Yates.' Trudy Yates had been the third and most viciously beaten victim of the Pale Faced Killer. Kipruto couldn't let that influence his thinking. He has to keep a cool head.

'Cause of death?'

'The first victim, a young female in her twenties I'd say, her throat has been cut. The second victim is male, and you won't be surprised to hear that his heart has been—'

'—ripped from his chest.'

'You got it, boss.'

He grips the phone, wanting to crush it and let it crumble between his fingers. Two more victims, one with the same MO, the other with a very different one. It doesn't make sense. None of it makes sense. Raven begins to move, unstrapping himself from the stretcher with one hand while painfully pushing himself up with the other.

'I'll call you back,' Kipruto says, before turning to his DI. 'Where the hell do you think you're going?'

'Thish is my case. I need to be there.'

'You've got two cracked ribs, a broken nose, and a suspected fractured cheek bone.'

'I've had worsh.'

'Luke, you need to go to the hospital. You've suffered a concussion. There's no way I can let you drive in this condition.'

Raven holds up his phone and points to the screen. A Facetime image of Detective Inspector Allison Bailey peers back at him.

'Sh'okay. Don't need to. My chauffeur'sh on her way over.'

CHAPTER 40: HELLES

He's eating rib-eye steak and sipping a perfectly good lager when the phone rings. He checks the clock. 9.45 p.m. It's a little later than expected but that's okay. If a job's worth doing, it's worth doing properly. He hopes they took their time. He hopes Raven suffered. The fucker deserves it.

'I'm listening.'

'I thought you said you'd take care of this.'

It's not who he expected. In fact, it's the one person he absolutely did not expect.

'If you're talking about our little piggy problem, it's being handled as we speak.'

'Yes, that's exactly what I mean, and no, it's not being handled. It's being fucking mis-handled.'

The tone of the guy's voice is beginning to irritate him. Just because he holds a position of some importance, doesn't mean he gets to shoot profanities down the phone at him like bullets from a BB gun.

'I have to confess, you have me at a disadvantage. You see, I'm sitting here after a long day eating a very late dinner and enjoying the best Helles the Germans have to offer.'

'Then stop eating and fucking listen to me. I just took a call from the Hampshire Police Commissioner. It seems two men turned up at a property in Westhampton and tried to take a chainsaw to Detective Inspector Luke Raven, only one of them wound up being chopped up into beef cutlets, while the other is in intensive care with a bullet in his lower intestines and a severe bleed on the brain.'

He grips his fork and forms a fist.

'And Luke Raven?' the caller continues. 'He's a bit battered, has a few broken bones, but otherwise he's fine.'

The fist is now so tight, he can barely feel his knuckles. The fork, on the other hand, has taken the brunt of his frustration. It's now bent in half, the tines pointing down toward the bloodied rib-eye.

'That is unfortunate.'

'Unfortunate? Unfortunate? It's a fucking catastrophe is what it is. Not only is Luke Raven still on the case, but the police now have the identify of both the men you sent to kill him, and one of them's still breathing.'

He ends the call and tosses the phone at the wall, smashing it into a dozen pieces. His actions will annoy his superiors, but he'd rather that than listen to the idiot on the other end of the line open his kimono and tell whoever is listening that he's been involved in the attempted assassination of a senior detective.

That word. *Attempted.* It gives him heart palpitations, and that's the last thing he needs in his condition. He takes more blood pressure tablets and statins than a junkie snorts smack. Byrne had guaranteed him this operation could not fail. Maximum damage for minimum pain. Sure, there was always going to be wastage, but you don't go knuckle to knuckle with the authorities and come out without at least a bloody nose. The two guys committing the crimes would go down for what they did, but they'd be paid well, and a few years in, several grand would make its way to a senior parole board member's charitable fund, and the killers would be out after serving less than a quarter of their time. Raven would be history, and nobody would connect anything to The Medics or The Legion. Simples. Except it clearly hadn't been simple enough.

He takes a moment to calm down. His new wife is upstairs and she's sleeping. If he lets his anger get the better of him, he'll wake her up, and that wouldn't be fair on her. She puts up with enough of his shit as it is. She doesn't need to know how bad this day just got. He'll deal with it, because he deals with everything. That's how he got the job in the first place, and it's how he intends to keep it. As his old man used to say, 'In a world full of luxuries, be the loo roll, because people will always need paper to wipe their arses with.'

He opens a draw and pulls out a burner, dialling the number he needs from memory. Conor Byrne picks up on the second ring.

'I know what you're gonna say, and I can only offer my deepest apologies,' Byrne says. 'Those two scuts came highly recommended.'

'I'm not interested in apologies, Byrne. You gave me your word.'

'I hear West was the one who pulled the trigger. We hadn't anticipated him being home.'

'I don't pay you to anticipate. I pay you to make fucking sure.'

'Yeah, I understand. In hindsight, it was a mistake. A big one.'

'The people who matter are not happy, and that makes me very unhappy. You know what happens when I'm unhappy?'

There's a pause in the conversation before Byrne says, 'We can still get to Raven. From what I hear, he took a pretty heavy beating before West came in and put a stop to it. If you want, I can send out one of my own guys to finish the—'

'*No*, I don't want you to go after Raven!' he yells, causing yet more palpitations. He hears movement from his wife in the master bedroom and lowers his voice. 'What I want you to do is make sure the guy you hired, the one who fucked it all up, does not open his mouth and tell our little African friend that you, and ultimately I, paid him to do it.'

There's another pause, this one more notable. 'That's gonna be tough. The ward is surrounded by coppers.'

'Tell somebody who gives a shit,' he replies. 'This is your mess, you clean it up.'

He ends the call and tosses the phone back into the drawer. He glares at his beer, but he knows the hoppy lager won't even touch the sides. What he needs is a scotch. In fact, he needs several.

'You okay, my darling,' his wife says, running her delicate fingers through what remains of his hair. He hadn't even heard her come downstairs.

'Trouble in the office,' he replies.

She eyes the smashed telephone lying in pieces on the Persian rug. 'I see,' she says, moving her hand down his cheeks, his neck, his chest, and then traces a line across his abdomen to a much lower destination. 'Is there anything I can do to help?'

Suddenly, Scotch is the last thing on his mind, as is the guy lying in an ICU bed in Lymington hospital. Byrne will take care of the shitstorm, and if he doesn't, he has another call to make, and that one will most definitely put the proverbial pussy among London's flying vermin.

'I think you know exactly what you can do,' he says, taking her hand and following her back upstairs. Raven can wait. It's already been four long years. One more day won't kill him.

CHAPTER 41: ALL GUNS

Lisa takes the call. It's Sally. She tells her about the two masked men who smashed their way into her home and tried to kill Luke. The strength goes from Lisa's legs and she slumps into an armchair. Harry looks up from his iPad but doesn't study her for long. He's too engrossed in a streaming program about friendly dragons. Sally continues, while Lisa struggles to process everything that's happening. She explains how she made it out the front door with her phone in her hand, but accidentally bumped into Billy who'd made it back with a fourteen-inch spicy barbecue chicken and a nine-inch vegetarian thin crust. Inexplicably, Billy had gone inside, managed to get hold of a gun and shot one of the attackers. If Lisa could have crawled down the phone line and found the big lump of gristle, she'd have hugged him until he couldn't breathe.

'Where's Luke now?' she asks, trying but failing to keep her voice low key.

'We thought he was being taken to Lymington,' Sally replies, 'But Randall just told us he's refused medical aid and headed off to another crime scene?'

Lisa can't believe what she's hearing. 'Another crime scene? You mean somewhere other than your house?'

'I know it sounds crazy, but you know what he's like. Randall said he tried to stop him—'

'—but he didn't, just like he didn't tell me Luke was alive and on his way home!' She's spitting feathers, so angry she can barely control herself. Harry looks up again and this time he doesn't get distracted. 'It's okay, baby,' she says. 'Mummy's just a little cross.'

'Do you want a juice?' he asks, setting down the tablet and getting up.

'That would be lovely,' she replies, trying to hide the tremble in her voice.

'Apple and blackcurrant?'

'My favourite.'

He heads towards the kitchen and she watches him leave, the fury building in her belly.

'Did he say where?' she asks.

'He didn't, but I overheard one of the other PCs. It sounds like two bodies have been found on that patch of barren land near All Saints Road.'

Lisa is up before Sally's words have come out. She knows the place because Luke had taken her there. He had a habit of doing that, taking her to crime scenes long after the case was solved just to get some sort of closure. She wasn't sure whether this new Luke was the same, but then she realises she doesn't really know this new Luke at all.

'I'm so sorry about your home,' she says. 'Whatever the damage is, we'll pay.'

'Right at this moment, Lis, I'm not sure if I can live here anymore.'

'A new house then. If that's what you need, Simon will make it happen.'

Sally doesn't answer, and Lisa realises she's overstepped the mark. This isn't the time to flaunt her new-found wealth.

'Sending you big hugs,' she says, trying to paper over the cracks. 'And tell that husband of yours he's now at the top of my all-star favourites list.'

'He'll like that,' Sally laughs. After a moment, her tone changes. 'He's not like he was, Lis. Luke, I mean. This thing with the Staker girl, it's affected him. I'm not saying you need to treat him with kid gloves, but… don't go in all guns blazing.'

That triggers something in Lisa. 'I know how to treat the father of my child, Sal. Luke and I have a history. A long one.'

'Of course. I'm not trying to tell you how to act. It's just—'

'Then don't.'

Lisa ends the call. She glares at the phone. She's angry. Not at Sally. Not for what she said — she didn't say anything that wasn't true. She's angry at herself. She's let this go on for too long. She should have found Luke already. Maybe if she had, he wouldn't have been at Sal's and Billy's house. He wouldn't have been beaten almost to death.

'I'm going out, Simon,' she yells towards the home office. 'Can you watch Harry?'

Harry emerges from the kitchen, two plastic beakers of OJ in his hands.

'Sure,' Simon calls back. 'Just plonk him in front of the TV. I'll be finishing up in a bit. Where you going?'

'To the shop. I need some chocolate.'

'We have some in the fridge. Green & Black's. Your favourite.'

'I'm having a retro day where only Cadbury's Fruit and Nut will do.'

Simon laughs which makes her feel guilty. She hates lying to him.

'You can take the girl out of Brownside—'

'—but you can't take Brownside out of the girl. Haha, very funny. We didn't all get the luxury of a private education and a trust fund, you know.'

She slips on her trainers, takes the beaker from Harry's hands and kisses him on the forehead.

'Simon will be out in a minute to put you to bed,' she says. 'Make sure you do as he asks.'

Harry takes her hand. 'Can't you read me a story before you go?'

His plea breaks her heart. She doesn't want to leave him. She doesn't want to put anything between herself and his future. He's been the only thing that's been important to her for so long, and that's been fine, but now Luke is back and he's hurt, and he's doing what he always does and risking his own life for people he's never even met, and for what? For some sort of personal redemption? To prove he still has it in him? What about her? What about his son?

'Sorry, baby,' she says, grabbing her car keys. 'Not tonight. But I will, I promise. Tomorrow, I'll read you all the stories you want, and even some you don't.'

'Funnybones?' he asks, his face turning into a bright beam of a smile. 'Will you read me Funnybones?'

'Again?'

'Yep. You said you'd read me anything.'

She ruffles his hair. 'Then Funnybones it is.'

She takes a mental snapshot of him, savours it. He's the embodiment of everything she once was and everything she now is. Nothing else even comes close. She steps outside, pulls the door closed behind her and hits the key fob. Tonight, she finds Luke, and they get everything out on the table. There's a lot to unpack.

CHAPTER 42: HERRING

Raven sits beside Bailey, his head pounding like a ticking bomb. His face is swollen, his lips like sausages, but at least the blood has been cleaned away. His partner even brought him a change of clothes. He looks like a well-dressed zombie. Everything hurts, but his head is the killer. The area around his scar is on fire, but he doesn't let that distract him. He came here to do a job, and he intends on seeing it through, no matter what The Medics want to do to him or what Kipruto says. He now has twenty-three hours and he'll make them count.

'You know this is lunacy, right?' Bailey says. 'You being out here, I mean. Just look at you. You're a mess.'

'I'll take that as a complement.'

Luckily the anti-inflammatories are helping, and he no longer sounds like he's talking through a mouthful of cotton wool.

'Don't, because it's not. You making me come with you like this, it's not fair. I feel like I'm an accessory to insanity.'

'Insanity or lunacy? Because they're quite different.'

'Both, times two. If you die on me, Raven, I'll never forgive you.'

He doesn't answer that. He can't give her any guarantees. The demon has already caught up with him once. Next time, he doubts it'll let him go so easily.

'So tell me about the crime scene,' he says. 'What do we have?'

'Davis has managed to run ID on the two victims. The girl is Shen Milton, twenty-four years old, works at Perfectly You, the beauty salon in town.'

'Shit, twenty-four. She's barely out of school.'

Bailey sighs. 'It happens more often than you think.'

'And the male?'

'Oliver Shepherd, Ollie for short. Twenty-eight years old, works at the auto car wash. The one by the Morrison's supermarket. You know it?'

Raven nods. He does know it, and he also knew Ollie Shepherd. He'd questioned him six years earlier over a bag of pills he'd confiscated from a little runaround dealer in town, and all routes led back to Ollie. He'd avoided the rap, but there was no doubt Shepherd had been into the distribution of some less than legal substances.

'And Shepherd is the one who's heart has been… removed?'

'That's right.'

He rubs his hand through his beard. This wasn't a gangland thing, any more than the attempt on his own life had been retribution for his little visit to the snooker club. This was The Heart Breaker.

'Why the girl?' he asks.

'Maybe she was collateral damage.'

'But that's inconsistent with the other murders. Our guy has been methodical. He hasn't taken any risks. If he really wanted Ollie Shepherd's heart, he could have waited until he was alone. He wouldn't have risked someone walking in on them.'

'A spite killing then. Maybe Shen Milton said something that offended the killer.'

'Were there any links between Shepherd and Milton?'

'Davis is checking, but at least one family member has suggested the two of them had a casual thing going on.'

'So they were an item.'

'It seems that way.'

Bailey pulls the Insignia up behind a squad car. Raven waits until they're stationary and opens the door. It's beginning to rain which is fine by him. The cold spatters feel good on his inflamed wounds. Right now, he needs all the soothing he can get.

The area of wasteland beyond All Saints Road is cordoned off with yellow and black tape. Beyond it, a white crime scene tent sits among a tangled collection of brambles and nettles. The ground around it is littered with cigarette butts, plastic bags, crushed cans and crisp packet wrappers. This used to be home to a chemical warehouse way back in the eighties, but after its demolition, the place has been left to mother nature and the many waifs and strays that wander the back alleys and footpaths. The last time Raven was here, he was being outrun by a homicidal maniac with a penchant for female blood.

Davis is the first to meet them. He's a sight for sore eyes. Raven and he go way back. Davis had been the first guy he'd been buddied with when he'd passed his detective exams. A lot of water has flowed under a hundred bridges since then.

'You look like you had an argument with a rhino and came out on the losing side,' Davis says.

'This is nothing,' Raven replies, pointing to his backside. 'You should see where it shoved its horn.'

Davis shoots him a wry grin. 'You probably enjoyed it.'

They head to the tent and Raven takes a look inside. Both victims are naked. Shepherd is lying on his back, eyes wide, his chest cavity splayed apart like something has torn him open from the inside. Milton is on her side, hands between her legs, a long slash across her throat. Her head rests on Shepherd's crotch, her mouth open, his flaccid penis between her lifeless lips.

'Artistic isn't it,' Davis says.

'It's gross,' Bailey replies.

'At least this answers our question,' Raven offers.

'Shepherd and Milton were an item,' Bailey answers, 'And our killer was the third piece of the triangle.'

Raven nods. 'Exactly. The way he's positioned his victims is a statement. If they want each other, they can have each other, but only in death.'

'You want me to a run a check on who either of these two might have been seeing on the side?' Davis asks.

Raven nods. 'And as quickly as you can. It seems to me our killer is getting more and more careless. We find out who Shepherd or Milton were seeing—'

'Or even Shepherd *and* Milton,' Bailey adds.

'Very true,' Raven agrees, realising the world is a different place these days. 'We find out who they were screwing, and we'll find our killer.'

He waits until Davis leaves and turns to Bailey. 'Any news on the fingernail?'

'Not yet,' she replies. 'With any luck, we'll have something back in the morning.'

Raven touches his inflamed scar. It's eased a little, but not a lot. The sensation is not dissimilar from when the bullet penetrated his skull, like a hot skewer being pushed through his eyeball. He doesn't know what damage the guy with the heavy boots caused when he kicked him in the head, but he guesses the prognosis isn't good. He only hopes he has enough time to nail this fucker before the ball of jellied meat in his skull ruptures and everything gets scrambled indefinitely.

'You still with us, Raven?' Bailey asks.

Her voice snaps him back into focus. 'Yeah, I was just thinking.'

'About what?'

'About where we go next.'

As if by magic, his phone springs to life. It's Welling.

'This is Raven.'

'Hi boss. Are you okay? I heard you took one for the team.'

'I'm fine,' Raven replies. 'Nothing a couple of paracetamols won't cure. Now, if you've got something to tell me, spit it out.'

He doesn't like the tone of his own voice, but the clock is ticking. He now has only twenty-two hours before he's taken off the case.

'Maybe,' Welling replies. 'I think so. We did what you asked and waited for Rowley to return home from work. He arrived about an hour ago. I spent some time with him. Nice guy.'

Raven shakes his head. A nice guy hadn't ripped out Shepherd's heart and shoved the guy's cock in his dead girlfriend's mouth. 'Did you check his cellar?'

'We did. Checked every room, including the loft. There was nothing, just a few boxes and some old paintings. The place was very clean, very organised.'

'So Rowley's not out guy.'

'Not unless he redecorates his house every time he kills somebody.'

Raven thinks that's a possibility but not likely.

'What about the Ladipo family?'

'Story checks out,' Welling says. 'They're currently in the Canary Islands, no doubt sipping cocktails and lapping up the sunshine.'

'And who confirmed this?'

'The travel agency they booked the holiday with. Gone For The Summer? I even had the office run their passports. They've been out of the country since last Tuesday.'

Raven's headache intensifies. With Rowley and the Ladipos out of the picture, that only leaves the old boy at number twenty-two, and the fact is, a guy in his eighties is unlikely to have the strength to overpower a twenty-eight year old man and his twenty-three year old girlfriend. He asks the question anyway.

'And the old boy?'

'No luck,' Welling says. 'He hasn't come to the window, and no matter how many times I knock the door, there's no answer.'

So Horsemonger's Lane was a red herring, Raven thinks. *Another impotent hunch*. He begins to wonder whether he's lost the knack.

'But here's the interesting thing. I ran some background checks on Dean Eccles, and it seems he had a sister, Belinda, who lived with her brother before she died of cancer seven years ago.'

'Go on.'

'Belinda used to live with her factory worker lover, but he ran out on her after she found out about his affair with her best friend, Beth Rivers, who also happened to work in the office of the same company who employed her boyfriend. That was over seventeen years ago.'

'It's a nice romantic tale,' Raven says. 'I assume this is going somewhere.'

'You'll like the ending,' Welling replies, now sounding amped. 'The guy's name was Chapman — Doug Chapman — and he and Belinda Eccles conceived a child twenty-seven years ago, a daughter. By all accounts, Doug loved the little girl, but couldn't stand Belinda's brother, Dean, who he felt his girlfriend was unreasonably close to. A few years after he ran off with Beth, the daughter moved in with her infirm uncle at the request of her dying mother, and she's been living at Horsemonger's Lane and taking care of him ever since. Do you want to know the child's name.'

Raven already knows the answer, but he lets Welling say it all the same. He needs it spoken out loud.

'Her name was Amanda,' Welling says. 'Although she now calls herself Kaden.'

An image of a seahorse tattoo comes back to Raven, the one he'd seen in his dreams when he'd been shut away in the basement of the cottage in the Highlands. His brain now connects it with his visit to the surf shop earlier that day. Kaden Chapman had that same tattoo, he'd just not made the connection. Now there are two more victims, murders that he could have prevented.

'Make the call. Get the warrant,' Raven says. 'We'll be there in ten.'

He turns to Bailey and gestures towards the car. 'We've got her,' he says.

'Chapman?'

Raven smiles, but there's no happiness there. The old version of him would have seen what he now sees as soon as he'd walked into the shop. Molly Staker might not have killed him, but she's taken the one thing he was good at. Maybe that was her parting shot, to rid the world of the version of him who could actually make a difference.

As they get into the car and Bailey pulls away, Raven doesn't see the brand-new Mini Cooper turn left onto James Street, or notice the single occupant with red hair, nose ring and dragon tattoo on the side of her hand exit the vehicle. If he'd seen her, he would have recognised her, because Lisa Clancy, now Draper, was once the love of his life, and right now, she's the only person who can save him from himself.

CHAPTER 43: KUZ BROS.

The hospital is alive with activity. Orderlies push trolleys past a sea of bodies loitering on plastic chairs, cardboard coffee cups gripped between tired fingers, dark eyes hovering behind steadily drifting steam, while cigarette smoke and cold air wafts in from the pavement through slide doors that seem to be constantly in motion. A mother hugs her child into her breasts, another man sits beside her with a haphazardly tied, blood-stained bandage over what appears to be a deep gash in his cheek. An old lady sits with a leg up on a stool, a crutch balanced against a vending machine that's being assaulted by a steady queue of sick and wounded, each desperate for diabetes inducing sugar fixes before being diagnosed by semi-comatose nurses who walk around on shuffling, unsteady feet. A trainee female doctor emerges from behind a swing door, clipboard in tiny hands. Everybody looks up, eyes snapping open with misguided hope, eager to be the next one (oh, to be the next one), but when the young woman calls out a barely audible name, only one person stands, and a sea of heads drop like tumbling dice, the air filled with grumbles and barely hidden curses.

Shane Byrne stands in the doorway, his nose turned up at the stench of sickness. He hates hospitals. The last time he'd hurt himself, almost slicing off his thumb during a pub fight, he'd taken care of his own wound, sticking himself back together with super glue and Steri Strips from his mam's emergency box and pouring disinfectant into the gash while biting down on a handkerchief. He doesn't trust doctors, and he hates sick people.

He heads through a sea of unsightly faces and stands with his feet pressed against the enquiries desk.

'I'm looking for a Mr. Kuznecova,' he says. 'First name, Nico.'

'And you are?' the old, black guy behind the counter asks. He doesn't look up. He's barely awake. Byrne eyes his nametag. Gabriel Nevis.

'Brother. Younger by three years,' Byrne says, holding up a driving license he's had fast-tracked through a printing company The Medics have on payroll.

Nevis taps on his keyboard, seems to find what he's looking for, and then bites the end of his pen.

'Says here Mr. Kuznecova is under police guard. No visitors allowed.'

'That's because he was attacked by a member of a street gang,' Byrne replies. 'The guard is something our mother asked for, and the police, god bless their good Catholic souls, did as she asked.'

'You have an Irish accent. Kuznecova doesn't seem like an Irish name.'

'My parents emigrated to Dublin from Romania,' Byrne replies. 'We moved to England three years ago to look for work. My brother and I have our own company. We lay driveways. Block paving. If you have your own parking space and ever fancy giving it a makeover, look us up. You'll find us under The Kuz Brothers. We do a nice little discount for front-line workers like yourself.'

Nevis's expression is unmoved. He barely even looks at the license. 'The message on the machine is quite clear. No visitors, family or otherwise.'

Byrne can see he isn't going to get anywhere with this half-wit, so he pulls out his wallet, thumbs out six fifty-pound notes and slides them across the counter.

'Does this make things any easier?'

Nevis eyes the money, glances up at the queue forming behind Byrne, and utters two words. 'Four more.'

Byrne slips out four more fifties, adds them to the neat little stack he's already deposited, and presses his finger on top of them.

'Now, I want the ward and the bed number, and no fucking with me or I'll be back down here to collect my money, and I'll take your shrivelled little testicles as interest.'

'Excuse me,' a woman says, tapping Byrne on the shoulder. 'Will you be much longer, only my daughter has—'

'I'll be as long as this fucking takes,' Byrne replies, giving the woman the kind of stare he usually saves for blokes who get on the wrong side of The Medics, just before he gives them a good shellacking. The woman shrinks and pulls her daughter close.

'Penguin Ward,' Nevin replies, his stubbornness evaporated. 'Bed 17B, private room.'

Byrne leans in close. 'Then the cash is yours, my friend, and let's hope, for your sake, that we don't get to see each other again any time soon.'

CHAPTER 44: CUCKOO

They head to the house, Bailey driving as fast as the traffic will allow. She has the blue light on, but even so, the streets are so crammed, it's almost impossible to manoeuvre the vehicle past the creeping traffic, even at this time of night. Raven checks his watch. Another hour has passed. If he's made a mistake—if Welling's intel is inaccurate—the whole case is blown. Chapman has to be the killer. There's no other answer that makes sense.

'It would be quicker to take the bypass,' Raven says. 'Too many tourists take this road.'

'You stick to figuring out next steps, boss,' Bailey says. 'Let me do the driving.'

Raven's head is pounding and the bruising just beneath is right eye is so tender, it hurts to blink.

'We're running out of time,' he says.

'We don't even know Kaden Chapman is there.'

'She's there.'

Bailey weaves between a bus and a sea of taxis, driving so close the wing mirrors very nearly clatter together. A group of well-dressed boys stagger out of a bar, pushing and slamming into each other, oblivious to the vehicles crammed together like sardines. A pair of girls in crop tops and tight skirts, walking on heels so high they can barely stay upright, spy the boys and click-clack towards them, and now they're all standing in front of the car, laughing, hugging and high-fiving.

'If you don't want to spend the night in a police cell, I suggest you get out the way!' Bailey hollers.

'Ooh, check out the big, black copper,' one of the boys replies, reaching for his phone. 'You gonna arrest us?'

'If you don't move, yes. That's exactly what I'm going to do.'

One of the girls steps up. 'On what charge, love? Having a good time?'

'Obstructing a police vehicle, which, by the way, carries up to a 51-week prison term.'

There's an eruption of laughter, followed by half a dozen middle fingers.

Raven's had enough. He leaps out of the car, grabs the boy closest to him and spins him onto the bonnet. He has the kid's wrist in his hand in an instant, yanking his arm up his back hard enough to make the joints crack.

More phones come out, all of them pointed in his direction.

'That's police brutality,' one of the other boys says. 'We could have you sacked for that.'

Raven whirls on him. 'Oh, trust me, at this point, the last thing on my mind is worrying about a bunch of too skinny, jacked up, hair preening, Joey Essex wannabes running to my boss and telling tales because I dared to show them that acting like dicks just makes them look like actual dicks. Now, if you don't want to end up with your shoulder dislocated like your little friend here, I suggest you step back onto the pavement and let me and my partner do our jobs.'

The boy sticks out his chest, but when Raven steps into the light, his expression changes.

'Woah, your face,' one of the girls says. 'Brah, do you see his face?'

The boy closest to her, a kid with his hair combed so close to his head it looks like it's been painted on, nods and sneers. 'Let's head to Glitz's,' he says, his eyes flitting between the disfigured copper and the pretty blonde. 'It's boring here anyway.'

Raven releases his grip on the kid and watches as the boy staggers away while rubbing his pained shoulder and glancing anxiously behind him. He gets back in the car and tries to ignore Bailey's accusing glare.

'I had that under control,' she says. 'I didn't need you to go in there like a frikking battering ram. I can take care of myself.'

'Let's talk about the rights and wrongs of male chivalry later,' he replies, pointing at the long length of open road ahead of them. 'Right now, we have somewhere we need to be.'

Bailey guns the accelerator, and in less than ten minutes they're at Horsemonger's Lane. Welling meets them as they pull up and leans into Raven's open window.

'Shit,' he says. 'You look like you've been—'

'Save it,' Raven interjects. 'Did you get the warrant?'

'Just came through. We're free to go in.'

Raven checks his watch. It's 2.30 a.m. With a little luck, they'll have Kaden Chapman in custody in the next thirty minutes, leaving him with a little over nineteen hours to get something to stick.

'Then let's go knock on the door,' he says.

Beside Bailey's vehicle, there's Welling's Mazda and two squad cars parked discreetly up the road so as not to arouse suspicion. Two officers stand beside the doorway to number twenty-two, an Enforcer battering ram standing upright between them.

'You ready?' he asks the first officer. The young PC nods. 'Then let's go.'

They swing the long, red cylinder at the lock, causing the wooden door to shake in the frame, and with one more swing, the timber splinters and the deadbolt sheers away from the cavity. Six officers run into the building, heavy boots slamming on threadbare carpet and creaking stairs.

Raven stands in the open doorway, waiting for the all-clear, but even out there in the street, the stench of death is overwhelming.

'You're going to want to see this, boss,' the lead officer says, standing aside so Raven can enter. He looks around him. The place is a slum, nicotine-stained wallpaper peeling away from mould infested plaster, a sofa so worn and faded it looks like it's barely there. He sees the fireplace, the old hatstand, and he's back in his nightmare. He glances at the window, half-expecting to see a blood-stained hand pressed against it, but the glass is so dirty, it's impossible to see outside. There's an old cuckoo clock on the wall, the hands stopped at 09.43. The cuckoo hangs from its open mouth like a mutilated tongue. Antique cigarette butts spill from an overloaded ash tray onto a scarred coffee table. There's a lamp on the rug, the bulb smashed, a twisted cord hanging from a blackened socket.

He approaches the stairs and holds the back of his hand to his nose. The smell is now so strong it infects his throat like a bad dose of the flu. You never get used to the vomit-inducing stench of a decaying corpse, no matter how many times your senses are assaulted by it. Every step creaks beneath his shoes, as if the whole staircase is about to collapse beneath him. He reaches the top, and by now he's fighting his gag reflex.

The master bedroom door is to his right. Two officers are standing inside, one of them looking at the ceiling. Raven eyes the room. It's as dank as the rest of the house, black and green patches of damp, fungus growing like cancer. The carpet is bare in places, see-through in others. An old wardrobe stands with its contents spilled out, doors hanging from barely attached hinges. A chest of drawers sits beside the bed, cigarette burns in the pale wood, a white stain down one side. The bed is freshly made, but the sheets are covered with light-brown marks, as if somebody has spilt tea all over them. The bed itself is metal-framed, almost completely covered in rust that's eaten into some of the supports. The window is obscured by dark brown curtains that shut out most of the light.

'What am I looking at?' he asks.

The officer points to the ceiling. 'That.'

Raven looks up. At first, he doesn't see anything, but then he spots them: three little dots of dark red, easy to miss if you're in a hurry.

'Body?' he asks.

'Still looking,' the officer replies. 'We're in the cellar now, then we'll check the loft.'

Raven recalls his dream. It was quite clear: a single room, no daylight, just an overhead bulb, a bed and a metal cabinet filled with tools and surgical implements.

'It has to be somewhere here,' he says.

Bailey enters, a pale blue handkerchief pressed to her nose.

'Anything?' she asks.

Raven looks up at the ceiling and she follows his gaze. 'Body's been moved,' she says. He nods his reply, but he's barely listening. He follows the stench, stepping out of the bedroom into the hallway.

'The body won't be in the basement because the smell is stronger on the first floor than downstairs,' he says.

There's a narrow hatch in the ceiling above the head of the stairs. It's barely big enough for a single person to fit through. He watches as one of the officers unfolds a step ladder and pushes the hatch open. There's a cool breeze like the opening of a refrigerator, and Raven steps away. There won't be a body up there either. The breeze brings fresh air, not toxicity.

He walks past the bathroom and the much smaller second bedroom. Both are in equally bad states of disrepair. He steps into the bedroom and peers up at the posters on the wall: Slipknot, Bring Me the Horizon and Parkway Drive. Raven knows the bands, although he's a little out of touch. There's some framed artwork depicting fantasy creatures in various mysterious places. A centaur in hell, a minotaur in a labyrinth. Clothes hang from a rail, long dresses, black skirts, dark jeans, T-shirts, hoodies. The bed is freshly made and clean. The room doesn't look like the lair of a serial killer.

He steps back outside, hands on hips, and glances down the landing at Bailey who's diligently making notes. Something is off, he just can't put his finger on it. He looks at Bailey again, then at the wall to his right, the end of the hallway. He goes to the stairs, leans over the banister and looks into the front room. It could just be perspective, but he doesn't think so. He descends, stands against the wall, drawing odd looks from the officers coming up from the cellar, and paces to the other side of the house, taking care to make sure his steps are even. By his reckoning, the distance from one wall to the other is around eighteen feet. He turns and goes back up to the first-floor landing.

'Would you mind standing back?' he says to Bailey. 'Just for a minute.'

'What are you up to?' she asks, reluctantly shuffling out the way.

He does the same thing, counting his steps, being as precise as he can. Eleven feet, seven feet short. He walks back to Bailey, once again counting every pace, and he comes to the same conclusion.

He heads to the end of the hallway and glares at the assorted sea-life depicted on the wallpaper. The pattern doesn't match the rest of the house. He looks down and spies a section of skirting board that looks like it's been recently added. He drops to his haunches, grabs the piece of white wood and pulls. Sure enough, it slips away, revealing a keyhole. He's found it. A false wall. It stetches from the front of the house to the rear, plenty big enough for someone to hide something.

'I need this door breached!' he hollers. 'Now!'

Two officers appear, bright red Enforcer in hand. 'What door?' the female officer asks.

'The lock's here,' Raven says, pointing to the keyhole. 'But I suspect there's at least three deadbolts holding this thing in place.'

'Got it,' the officer replies, the realisation dawning on her. She and her colleague work in unison, slamming the battering ram into the edge of the wall-cum-door, smashing through it in less than a minute.

Raven pulls it open, and now the stench is so strong, he has to turn away. When he turns back, it's like stepping into his own head. The bed is pushed against the far wall, running lengthways from the front of the house. The cabinet is beside it, sharp implements laid out neatly in a row. The electric saw is still plugged into the wall socket. There's a package on the floor, a big one, a malformed object wrapped in clear plastic. Dark liquid oozes from it and runs across the lino. He turns on the light, and the scene becomes even more stark. There's a fish tank toward the rear of the room, and inside are dark, fleshy objects, tubes protruding from meaty parcels.

'Jesus bloody Christ,' Bailey says, peering over his shoulder, her voice coming in thick whoops as she tries to hold in the contents of her stomach. 'You found it, Raven. You bloody found it.'

His headache returns, and this time it's so painful he can barely stand. He grips the edge of the wall, trying with all his remaining strength to hold himself upright, but there's something about the scene, something about what he is sure is a slowly liquifying body wrapped in plastic sheeting and the collection of severed hearts floating in a thick, slightly yellow liquid, that's sending his mind into a tailspin. He doesn't hear Bailey's phone ringing or her answering it almost immediately, turning her head away as the person on the other end relays the information to her. He doesn't hear the front door open or the babble of raised voices as whoever has stepped inside decides they no longer want to be there.

'It was her!' Welling yells to the coppers downstairs. 'You bloody idiots. Why didn't you grab her?'

Raven stumbles along the hallway as bright stars dance across his vision. He trips over his own feet, almost falling headlong down the stairs, but regains his balance in time to see Welling beneath him, pointing furiously to the door.

'Get after her!' he screams at the nearest PC. 'Don't let her get away!'

'Who was it?' Raven asks, the voice in his head drenched in thick reverb.

'It was Chapman,' Welling replies. 'That was Kaden Chapman.'

CHAPTER 45: WATERMELON

What an idiot. What a complete twat. She'd walked straight into a house full of coppers without noticing the two police cars at the end of the road and the two obviously unmarked vehicles closer to home. The place had been swarming with them, and that meant they had to have something on her. The fingernail. If she had to bet on anything, it would be the fingernail. That detective, Raven, she hadn't seen him there, but he had something to do with it. His eyes had been all over her at the shop as if she had some sort of stink on her. The Cardinal said he'd take care of him, but maybe he'd been too late. Maybe the damage had already been done.

She takes a left down the alleyway, but not before a stream of PCs come running from the house. She slips into the darkness, but a young detective sees her before she disappears, a guy with short, auburn hair and a ridiculous sky-blue suit.

She heads towards the building site, pushing herself through a wire fence and catching her jeans on a loose nail, ripping a slit along her thigh and tearing her skin.

'For fuck's sake,' she hisses, but she keeps moving, ignoring the sharp sting.

The sun's starting to come up, casting a hazy light over everything. She can just make out a deep trench to her right and the beginnings of a wall to her left. Ahead, there's the beginnings of a block of flats with stairs leading to a first-floor set of apartments that are currently empty shells. She takes the steps which are bare concrete while the detective comes through the fence, his suit jacket snaring on the same nail.

She makes it to the open hallway and runs towards the far wall, all the while desperately looking for another set of stairs. She finds them and hastily climbs to the top, but to her dismay, the floor above is incomplete. She finds herself out in the open with nowhere to hide. She turns to head back down, but the detective has already spotted her.

'Get down,' he yells, pulling his Taser. 'Get the fuck down, now!'

She backs away, eyes scanning her surrounding for a way out.

'Get down on the ground!' he repeats, but she can hear the uncertainty in his voice. She's bigger than he is, stronger too. If she can just get the jump on him without getting tazed, perhaps she can neutralise the little prick.

'I'm not doing anything you ask,' she says. 'So don't waste your breath. I'm done with having blokes boss me around. This is my time, my life.'

She continues inching towards the edge of the building, but the detective follows her, Taser gripped in both hands. 'I'm warning you,' he says, voice hesitant. 'You either do as I ask, or I'm putting a hundred thousand volts in you.'

'Tell that to someone who gives a shit,' she replies, goading him. 'I'm getting out of here, and there's fuck all you can do about it.'

To her surprise, the young guy presses the trigger, almost catching her off guard, but she instinctively moves to her right, allowing the cartridge to zip past as it clatters to the ground.

'Stupid dick,' she says, rushing him, throwing an elbow at his throat before shoving him to the concrete. The Taser is sent skittering across the floor. She grabs his head in both hands, lifts it towards her, smirking as the dumb guy's eyes widen at the realisation, and slams his skull against the floor three times, the last of which sounds like a watermelon cracking open. Blood pools beneath his head and trickles towards her knees like spilt juice. She sits on his chest, her hand hovering just above his mouth. There's a faint wisp of breath, but only just.

'Okay, that's enough.'

She turns to see the older detective appear from the stairwell, and the black lady, Bailey, accompanied by another officer, arriving from the other side of the unfinished platform. She's pretty much surrounded.

'He tried to shoot me,' she says, not sounding as helpless as she had hoped.

'We found your uncle,' Raven says, glancing anxiously at the unconscious Welling. 'We know you killed him.'

'I didn't do it,' she replies. What she really wants to scream is, *That fucker deserved everything he got!*

The female approaches, while the other PC grabs her hands and cuffs her. She doesn't resist. What's the point? This is all part of The Cardinal's plan.

'Amanda Chapman,' the female detective says. 'I'm arresting you on suspicion of the murder of Dean Eccles. You do not have to say anything, but it may harm your defence if you do not mention when questioned something which you later rely on in court. Anything you do say may be given in evidence.'

She looks up at Raven and smiles, because smiling is all she has left. She can hear his heart, the soft putt-puttering of it, and the sound excites her. It will be the last of her collection, the crowning glory of it, and the best thing is, Raven doesn't even know it yet.

But he will. Some day soon he will be left in no doubt.

PART 3: BLACK HEART

"Over the rocks, in the crevice of which the candle burned, there was thrust out an evil yellow face, a terrible animal face, all seamed and scored with vile passions. Foul with mire, with a bristling beard, and hung with matted hair..."

Arthur Conan Doyle – The Hound of the Baskervilles

CHAPTER 46: APPROPRIATE ADULT

It's been a long night. Perhaps the longest of his life. Raven is exhausted and in acute, unconscionable pain, but his job isn't done yet. Far from it. They have a suspect in custody, but putting someone in a cell isn't enough to convince Kipruto the case is a done deal. Raven's DCS is demanding a confession, or rather, Fitzwilliam is, and at that moment, Chapman isn't talking except for repeating her right to an appropriate adult. She isn't stupid. That's the kind of thing that takes time, and time is the one thing he doesn't have.

'Coffee?' Bailey asks, handing him a steaming mug.

'Have you got something strong to go with it?' he asks.

She raises an eyebrow and ignores the request. 'The lawyer's here.'

Raven shakes his head. That's all he needs. 'Who'd she get?'

'Kai Maynard.'

'Haven't heard of her.'

'She's new, wants to prove herself. She'll be all over us like a bad case of the measles.'

'We've played this by the book. There's nothing to pick holes in.'

Bailey raises an eyebrow. 'You haven't met Kai Maynard yet. You'll see.'

Raven necks the coffee, washes it down with a gingernut biscuit, and heads to the interview room. They're in 3C, a bright green space with a lime plastic table, four cushioned chairs, and a water dispenser. He marvels at the luxury of it. Back in his day, you were lucky if you had anywhere to sit.

Chapman sits on the far right-hand side, while Maynard sits to her left. The lawyer is dressed in maroon trousers and a pale maroon blouse. Her dark hair is pulled back into a tight ponytail, a single strand of hair hanging down her left cheek. She has sharp eyes and a tight mouth.

'Detective Raven,' she says, standing. 'I understand you are the officer in charge of this operation.'

'That's right,' he replies.

'Then you will know my client suffers from acute asperges, and under the home office guidelines she is asserting her right to an appropriate adult.'

'I heard.'

'Do you consent to this request?'

'Of course,' he replies. 'And I'm reliably informed that someone is on their way.'

Maynard folds her arms and leans back in her chair. 'Then you will also know that no questioning can begin until such an individual has presented themselves and has been allowed to consult with my client.'

'I wouldn't have it any other way.'

Raven shoots a glance at Chapman. She's staring straight at him, dark beady eyes, a mouth that twitches in one corner.

'You have something to say to me?' he asks.

'Only that I've been thinking about you a lot since you visited me in the shop.'

Maynard touches her arm. 'As your counsel, I would suggest you don't say anything until the interview has commenced.'

'What have you been thinking about?' Raven asks. 'How I was going to catch up with you eventually?'

Chapman shakes her head. 'Nothing like that. I'm a fatalist, detective. I truly believe that what will be will be.'

'I wonder if your victims would agree with you,' Raven replies, prompting a sharp elbow in the ribs from Bailey.

'I was thinking more about your heart,' Chapman says. 'How big it is. You do have a big heart, Detective Raven, don't you?'

She's glaring at his chest. Suddenly he feels clammy, as if he needs a shower. Something's creeping beneath his shirt, like a giant spider but with fingernails instead of hairy legs. It slips over his abdomen, moves towards his sternum and rakes his skin.

'Is that what you look for?' he asks, attempting to shake the sensation. 'Big hearts? Only the best for your collection?'

'Perhaps.'

Maynard whispers in Chapman's ear and the suspect adjusts her stance.

'No comment,' she adds, a smile like dead leeches.

'You know, it really is quite the display,' Raven continues. 'The attending police officers were pretty shocked. A fish tank filled with the hearts of your victims, preserved in formaldehyde for good measure. Did looking at that grotesque ensemble get you horny? Is that what this is all about? To feed some sort of sycophantic sex fetish?'

'May I remind you that my client awaits her appropriate adult,' Maynard says, tapping the table with her ballpoint.

'What gets you horny, Detective Raven?' Chapman asks, leaning forward. 'Does death get you horny? Or the thrill of the chase? Perhaps my gender fluidity gets you hard? Is that the kind of thing you like, something you can't understand or control?'

Raven glances at Bailey who's watching his every move. He needs a drink, something to stabilise himself. His head is a mess, the pain in his skull now akin to somebody pushing a hammer-drill into his frontal lobe.

'When is she getting here?' he asks Bailey, checking his watch, but Chapman doesn't let up.

'I bet you wonder what I look like down there,' she says, looking down at her crotch. 'You want to know if I have girly parts between my legs or a big fat dick, don't you? I bet you're wondering whether I'm clean shaven, or whether I grow it long like a bird's nest. I bet you're so curious, you'd give anything to take a sneak peek.'

'I'll be back when your chaperone arrives,' he says, backing towards the door. 'Until then, if you have something useful to say to me, your lawyer knows where I am.'

He heads into the corridor, too backfooted to breathe. He still has that feeling in his chest, as if something is scratching around in there, and his brain feels like it's about to erupt.

'You okay?' Bailey asks.

'I'm fine.'

'She really got to you, didn't she.'

'I said I'm fine,' he snaps.

He heads to the kitchen, pours himself a large glass of water and gulps it down, slipping two Co-Codamol for good measure. His body is covered in sweat and his temperature is soaring. He has no idea why he let the suspect get to him like that, but she did. She really did. It's as if all his years of interview training never happened. He needs to lie down, but there's no time.

A door opens and a woman walks in. She's dressed in a black hoody and blue jeans and has mousy, curly hair and thick glasses.

'That's the appropriate adult,' Bailey says.

'About time,' he replies, torn between wanting to get on with it and taking an extended time out.

'I'll go and introduce myself to her,' Bailey says, but then her pocket pings and she pulls out her phone. 'I need to take this.'

Raven shakes his head in frustration and walks past her, holding out a hand to the new arrival who looks like she wants to be anywhere but here.

'Detective Raven,' he says. 'I'll be leading the interview.'

'Rebecca Tawdry,' the woman replies, shaking his hand. 'Is it true? Do you really have The Heart Breaker?'

'We're talking to Amanda Chapman about her uncle's murder as well as the murders of six other victims, including the man she worked for.'

'I've never been asked to sit in on an interview like this before,' she says. 'I'm not sure I'm the right person for it.'

'You'll be fine,' he says, directing her to the interview room. 'It'll be like every other case you've attended, only with a lot more media attention.'

Tawdry shudders, but he's not letting her off the hook. Chapman wanted an appropriate adult, so that's what she's got.

'Go in and introduce yourself,' Raven says, nodding to the window. 'My partner and I will be in shortly.'

Tawdry opens the door and slips inside, like a lamb being led to the slaughter, and as the door closes, Bailey grabs Raven's arm.

'That was the lab,' she says.

Raven's too caught up in his own thoughts to piece together what Bailey just said. 'Okay,' he mutters.

'They have a result. On the acrylic. You know? The one we found at the murder scene?'

His mind snaps back into focus. 'And?'

'They have a match. It's a slam dunk. The fingernail definitely belongs to Amanda Chapman. I think we've got her, Luke. I think we've really got her.'

CHAPTER 47: CHRISTMAS TURKEY

Mason takes a right along the edge of the common, keeping the road to his left and the wide-open grassland to his right. He's been jogging now for a little over three months, and everybody says how much weight he's lost. He needed to. At the height of his morbid obesity (his doctor's words, not his), the digital scales had clocked him at just under nineteen stone. That's 120 kilograms in new money. For a man of diminutive height, that's a lot. He's never tried to kid himself about that. He could devour a bargain bucket on his own and still have room for ice cream. When the stark warning came, initiated by a period of light headedness that had resulted in a highly embarrassing fainting episode in the supermarket (something that was witnessed by his next-door neighbour, a racist homophobe who he despises), he'd decided things needed to change.

What came next was a period of near starvation that his body had fought against like a screaming adolescent. It had been tough. There had been times where he'd wanted nothing more than to devour a box of Dairy Milk on his own, or head to the local pizza place and order as many stuffed crust pepperonis as he could afford, but in those moments when his stomach was growling its vehement disapproval, all he had to do was take a look at the letter from his last hospital appointment. *At greater than 70% risk of pulmonary heart disease before the age of forty*, it said. *Acutely escalated blood pressure. Cholesterol abnormally high.*

For a long period he had blamed his mother. She had always been the one to bake him a cake when he was low, or serve him something fatty when he'd done something worth praising. One time when he was at primary school, he'd slipped down some icy steps and badly grazed his back. When his mum had shown up to collect him, she'd taken her sobbing son home, cleaned his wounds, and drove him straight to Burger King where they'd both had a bacon double cheese XL meal, extra fries, and a side order of cheese bites. She wasn't a bad person, she was a carer, and her way of caring was through food. When she died at fifty-four years of age, weighing twenty-four stone and with arteries hard enough to underpin a house, he'd cried for a month.

After a few months of wallowing in self-pity and wondering why his life was such a mess, he'd slowly began to realise his issues with food were his own to bear. His mother hadn't shoved the food into his mouth, and she certainly hadn't stopped him from exercising. It was time to do something about it.

He's vegan now, or at least he tries to be, and he exercises daily. He's joined a running club, goes to the gym, and is preparing for his first half-marathon. In a little over two years, he's transformed himself, and while he will never be rake-thin, he's happy in his own skin. His mum would be proud. He only wishes she could be there to see it.

He takes a right onto a path that leads through the thickets and laughs to himself as a squirrel runs out into the open, stops to take a look at him, then disappears up the nearest sycamore. He's always been a nature buff. Animals don't judge. They don't even pay attention.

He takes a left down a dip that disappears beneath a canopy of overhanging branches, and then a right alongside the kids' play area which includes tyre swings, an extremely tall slide, a rocking horse and a set of jungle bars he fell from when he was kid.

He keeps going, heading deeper and deeper into the woodland, down a steep drop and past the place where a girl had been found dead six year's prior.

He thinks about the dinner date he's going on later that day, a trip to his friend's house for a vegan banquet with a few pals from work. He might even allow himself a glass of red. Maybe even two. He has a lot to celebrate. Life is surprisingly going in the right direction for once, and he intends to ride the wave of euphoria until he makes himself sick.

When the blow comes, he goes tumbling onto the hard gravel, scraping the skin from his right cheek and left elbow. He cries out, more in shock than in pain. For a minute he thinks he's tripped over his own feet — his mum always said he was a clumsy lummox — but then he feels the blood leaking down the back of his neck and presses a hand to an extremely painful divot in his skull.

'What the hell?' he cries, but then somebody is standing over him, obscuring the meagre light that penetrates the canopy. He holds up a hand, but a knife pierces his palm and comes right out the other side. Blood splatters on his face and neck.

He screams, but it's short lived, because his attacker brings a boot down on his jaw. He hears a crunch, feels the pain, and then the lights go out.

*

A whirring sound. An electrical hiss. The chatter of gears.

He tries to open his eyes, but he's still in a daze.

His attempts to push himself up are futile because his arms are restrained. His tongue tastes like copper. The side of his face hurts like a bitch. He thinks his jaw is broken because he can't open his mouth. Instead, he groans and growls, but the sounds he makes are nonsensical and pointless.

He feels the bed beneath him. It's covered in plastic sheeting. He's watched enough crime films to know that's not good. Panic sets in. He connects the dots between what's happening to him and the thing he's read about in the news. The Heart Breaker. The acid in his belly forces a belch from his trembling lips.

There's more high-speed whirring, and now he knows what it is. A saw. He manages to prise one eye open, and instantly his suspicions are confirmed. Someone is standing over him, face covered in a surgical mask. They're wearing a T shirt that says, "Smile and the world smiles with you."

He struggles against his restraints again, but he's bound as tightly as a Christmas turkey. He groans louder, tries to plead for his life. Why would someone want to kill him? He's done nothing wrong. He's turned his life around, runs races for charity and even helps old people across the street.

There's blood on his shirt from his wounded jaw and split skull. At first, he wonders how he's going to get the stain out, but then he realises the shirt is ripped open and there's a square drawn in the centre of his chest. He starts to cry. He weeps for his life; he weeps for the mum who's not there to save him. He sobs for the friends he'll no longer see and the half-marathon he'll never be able to run.

When the saw comes down, he bites his lip and braces himself, but nothing can prepare him for the pain of a hundred tiny teeth chewing through skin, tissue and bone. Before he blacks out, he sees the eyes of his murderer, but there's nothing behind them. Only death.

CHAPTER 48: BOBBY PIN

Lisa arrives home after a long night. Since chasing Luke to the murder scene, she'd headed to the station, only to be told he wasn't there. She'd hung around outside, smoking countless cigarettes (a habit she'd never quite been able to quit, despite keeping it from her new husband), and mentally beating her ex-boyfriend over the head for making her feel this way. She wants to see him. She has to see him. There has to be some closure to this never-ending nightmare.

It's still early-ish, 9.30 a.m., and her phone is filled with countless WhatsApp messages.

'Lisa, where are you?'

'It's two in the morning and still no sign of you. I'm worried.'

'If you don't answer me soon, I'm calling the police.'

'I'm taking Harry to school then heading to work. Please message me back.'

She doesn't know why she didn't answer Simon. Sending him a little note to say she was out with friends would have been simple enough. Sure, he would have had questions, but they would have been easy to answer. She suspects there's something deeper than that, something more subconscious. Raven was her first big love, and while she's moved to a different place, on paper at least, her emotions are still unresolved. Getting back to her husband would have meant she was validating it in some way, while leaving him hanging kept everything on an even keel. If Raven isn't the man she remembers, then perhaps she can pretend he never came home. If, however, he's still the guy she's loved, hated and fought passionately with for most of her adult life, then who knows? She'll have a choice to make, a tough one. She has no idea how that will play out, but she at least deserves to own that problem.

She tosses her keys on the side, flicks the kettle on and collapses onto the sofa. She's exhausted. Raven is exhausting her. Again. Why not come straight to her house? Why not come and see his son? Harry deserves to know who his father is. After enduring a childhood where his dad was never there, she would have thought Luke would understand that being missing from his child's formative years would affect his son forever.

She watches the steam rise through the open doorway to the kitchen and pictures Luke being there with her, sharing her family home, taking their son to school, being the partner she had always wanted him to be. Is that even a realistic scenario? Is Luke that kind of guy? The picture flicks in and out of focus, as if her mind is struggling to solidify it. Luke Raven, dad, husband, responsible adult. Would she even fancy him if he became those things? Wasn't their relationship built on volatility, passion, arguments that could only be resolved by long-nights of make-up sex and mornings where he would disappear before she'd even opened her eyes?

There's a light tapping on the front door which startles her out of her thoughts. It's Simon. He's come home to see if she's there. She thinks about hiding but wonders why? Simon's her husband, for God's sake. Why would she want to hide from her husband?

She realises she can check who it is without even leaving her seat. She reaches for her phone, opens the Ring Doorbell app and takes a look. She sees her driveway, the shrubs that line the path and an empty street. She puts her phone back on the coffee table. Perhaps she's hearing things.

She remembers the boiling kettle and heads to the kitchen, plopping a decaf tea bag into a mug, filling it with water and topping it off with skimmed milk. Despite her secret smoking habit, the rest of her life is one big health kick. She forgets about the tap on the door that never happened and focusses on what to do next. She could go back to the station, of course, see if Luke has returned, or she could call Sally and find out how they're doing. Somebody tried to kill Luke, and the Wests were caught in the crossfire. While other people might find that terrifying, her ex-boyfriend has had more death threats than a Chinese takeaway has fortune cookies. This attack was so brazen, however, so ruthless, that she can't push it from her mind. Something has happened since Luke has returned from Scotland. She has to find out what it is.

There's another tap, this one so loud it makes her jump. She sits forward in her chair and listens. There's nothing. She checks the Ring Doorbell app again, but once more the street appears deserted.

She gets angry. Somebody is obviously fucking with her. Now isn't the time for hesitation. She goes straight to the front door and throws it open, ready and more than willing for a fight. Nobody's there. There's no sign that anybody has been. She steps outside, fists clenched, teeth gnawing anxiously at her bottom lip.

'If you're there, show yourself,' she says, but her voice is no more than a whisper. Her neighbours haven't witnessed her violent temper just yet, and she's not ready to let Angry Lisa out into the open unless she absolutely has to.

She wonders if it's Luke. Is he knocking on the door to get her attention but isn't brave enough to show himself? Why would he do that? What would he get out of it?

She has a thought and goes back inside. She opens her phone again and scans through the doorbell app, specifically the night when she'd been sure somebody was standing on the street and looking in her front room window. She doesn't spot it at first — she's scrolling too fast to see anything — but then she notices the shadow just beyond the streetlamp: medium height man, average build, dark eyes, unshaven face. She's not sure, so she zooms in, and even then, she can't make out any features. Suddenly the unseen watcher steps into the light, and it's as if she's been taken back to a time over four years ago when the man was a constant presence in her life and an irritation in her side she could never quite scratch.

'Luke,' she says without realising she's crying. 'Why didn't you come home?'

Someone's in the open doorway. She doesn't see them. She just notices the light dimming and hears a shuffling of feet. She looks up, but by the time she's moved her head, the presence has disappeared. She spots a shadow running past the front room window. She goes to chase after it but stops abruptly when she sees something sitting on her doorstep like an Amazon parcel with a difference. There's a red river that slips from the concrete onto the block paving, filling the gaps, creating a maze of crimson. She can barely breathe. The flesh is grey, the meat spongy and pungent. Someone's left a liver at her front door, and it's big enough to be human. She sees the note sticking out of it, a bobby pin that spears a piece of card before disappearing into the gelatinous lump. She doesn't want to bend down and touch it, but she stoops involuntarily, hands moving in slow motion as if the whole world is now slipping past at a crawl.

Get him to stop, the note says in a neatly scrawled script. *Or Harry will be next.*

CHAPTER 49: KET

Raven is going to take great pleasure in what he plans to do next. The DNA on the fingernail is irrefutable. Add to that the discovery of the uncle's body with over fifty stab wounds found in a hidden room in the house he once shared with his niece, and you have something close to a guaranteed conviction. Dead uncle, dead boss, and a serious assault on a serving detective, one who's fortunate to still be alive. While none of that necessarily links Chapman to the other victims, it's a bloody good start.

He peers through the window at the suspect. She's sitting arms crossed like a sulky teenager, crammed between her lawyer and the increasingly uncomfortable Ms. Tawdry. He wants to know what's going through Chapman's mind. Does she really think she's getting away with this? Does she truly believe there's some loophole she can squeeze through?

He checks his watch. He still has plenty of time. Just under twelve hours. Even if Chapman does put up a fight, she'll be charged and held pending a court hearing. If Kipruto is forced to take him off the case, it won't matter. Chapman won't be able to hurt anybody from inside a cell, and that's good enough for him. Maybe the nightmares will stop. Maybe he's head will return to the way it was before the fucking premonitions began. He can't take any more. His skull feels like it's filled with nails.

'Ready?' Bailey asks, notebook tucked beneath her arm.

'Are you kidding?' he replies. 'I can't wait.'

Raven opens the door. Three heads snap up, each of them bearing entirely different expressions. Maynard looks like she's chewing a brick, while Tawdry appears to be sitting on pins. Between them, Chapman is straight backed, eyebrows raised, head nodding slowly. She chews the inside of her mouth and squeezes her fists together, knuckles like ball bearings.

'About fucking time,' she says.

'Sorry about that,' Raven apologises. 'We had some new information to go through.'

'If it pertains to my client, I demand to see it,' Maynard snipes.

'We'll get to that in a little while,' Raven says, enjoying the sport. 'Firstly, I have some questions to ask Ms. Chapman.'

'I trust you've had a chance to speak with your appropriate adult,' Bailey adds.

'For what it was worth,' Chapman replies.

'And you, Ms. Tawdry? Are you comfortable that Ms. Chapman understands your role in these proceedings?'

'I am,' Tawdry says. 'Although, I'm not really sure why I'm needed.'

'I have to inform you, Ms Chapman, that this interview will be recorded for our records,' Bailey says, ignoring Tawdry's anxious fidgeting. 'Are you happy to proceed on that basis?'

'If it means I'll get out of here, then yes,' Chapman replies. 'I've got nothing to hide.'

Bailey hits the necessary buttons and states the time.

'When was the last time you saw your uncle, Mr. Dean Eccles?' Raven asks.

'I try to ignore the old fuck,' Chapman spits. 'Have you smelt that house? It's like a waste recycling centre.'

'Just answer the question to the best of your ability,' Bailey insists.

Chapman chews on a hangnail. 'Yesterday morning,' she says. 'Made him a cup of tea.'

'And he was in good health?' Raven asks.

'Good health? You've gotta be kidding. He barely gets out of bed, and he never takes himself to the toilet. I've been cleaning the shit off his sheets for years now.'

'What can you tell us about the room hidden behind the wall of the first-floor landing?' Raven asks.

'Hidden room? In that house? I'm sorry. You've got me there,' Chapman replies. Her shock is almost believable.

'Who do you think would have created such a room?'

'Must have been my uncle.'

'The man who could barely get out of bed?'

'Maybe it's been there longer than I have.'

'And you never noticed it?'

'I thought you said it was hidden,' Chapman smirks. 'How could I notice something I can't see?'

'You didn't see anybody coming and going from that room?' Bailey asks. 'Not in the nearly twelve years you've lived there?'

'As I said, I tried to stay out of the old boy's way. Most of the time I was working, or if not, I was out with friends.'

'How close were you with Winston Carter?' Raven asks, switching tack.

'Not close at all.'

'And yet your co-worker, Mr. Carl Hayes, suggested you and Mr. Carter had gotten close during a work's night out.'

Chapman's face screws into a tight ball. 'I wouldn't believe a word that comes out of that lazy fucker's mouth.'

'His story was corroborated by another of your colleagues, a Ms. Kerry Staines.'

'Another lazy cunt.' Chapman sneers. 'Are these serious questions?'

Maynard leans across the table. 'Do you actually have any evidence that my client was involved in any of the crimes you are accusing her of, or is this some sort of fishing expedition?'

'As I said, we'll come to that,' Raven replies. 'For now, we want to know exactly what Ms. Chapman knows.'

'Which is nothing,' Chapman replies.

'Perhaps if you just relax a little,' Tawdry says to her. 'Try not to get yourself so worked up.'

Chapman whirls on the little mouse. 'Why don't you stay the fuck out of this!'

'May I remind you that you asked for an appropriate adult to be present,' Bailey says. 'Ms. Tawdry is simply doing her job.'

'A pretty crap one at that,' Chapman replies. 'As I said, I don't really hang out with Winston. He's a rubbish boss, he has an attitude I don't like, and as far as I'm concerned, I run that shop, not him.'

'You are aware he's dead,' Raven says. 'You do know that, right?'

'Of course,' Chapman replies. 'And I'm very sorry about that, but that doesn't make him a good person.'

Raven slips a photograph from a file and slides it across the table. It shows a grainy image of Kaden Chapman standing next to Winston Carter at a beachside bar.

'Do you recall meeting with Mr Carter on the night of his death?'

If Chapman's shocked, she doesn't show it. 'Of course. He wanted to talk to me about my behaviour at work, so I agreed to meet him for a drink.'

'And yet you claim to not be close with him.'

'Meeting for an after-work drink doesn't exactly make us best buds.'

'But it suggests you have a relationship beyond just boss and employee.'

'Oh, come on!' Maynard cries. 'You're making one hell of a leap.'

'Rather than arguing the point, just jump with me,' Raven replies. 'The fact is, Ms. Chapman here was out with the deceased mere hours before his body was found on Westhampton Common. Couple that with the fact that her uncle's body was found in her house the very next day, and we have a series of events that incontrovertibly connect your client to a double murder.'

Tawdry lets out a soft groan and shuffles in her chair.

'The link is unfortunate,' Maynard replies. 'But you know as well as I do, without hard evidence, what you have is circumstantial at best. From what I can see, Ms. Chapman has been the victim of two unconnected, and highly coincidental, tragedies. Tragedies that are clearly very upsetting to her.'

Raven eyes Bailey. He thinks about unloading his big reveal but decides against it. Not yet. He wants more from Chapman. He needs to link her to all the killings. Two isn't enough.

'Tell us about Oliver Shepherd and Sabrina Carpenter,' he says.

'Who?' Chapman replies.

'Come on, Kaden,' Bailey says. 'We have an eyewitness placing you at Oliver Carpenter's flat one day before his murder.'

'Never heard of the guy.'

'So why were you at his flat?'

'I wasn't.'

'So the eyewitness is lying?'

'Or they're mistaken. I've got quite a common face. People claim to see me all the time.'

'On the contrary,' Bailey says. 'It seems to me you do everything you can to stand out.'

'What the hell does that mean?'

'Would you say you are sexually fluid?' the detective asks.

'So what if I am?'

'The eyewitness was quite specific. She described a female with no makeup in men's clothing who had broad shoulders.'

'Maybe what she saw was a man,' Chapman says, her expression monotone.

'Did you also know the bodies of Oliver Chapman and Sabrina Carpenter were found on wasteland off All Saints Road last night?' Raven says.

'What's that got to do with my client?' Maynard asks.

'Another coincidence?' Bailey asks. 'Or just another link in the chain.'

'What I don't get,' Raven says, 'is why the hearts? Why go to the bother of cutting the bodies open and collecting their internal organs? What do you gain from that?'

'I have no idea what you're talking about.'

'We found a fish tank filled with preserved human hearts, Ms. Chapman. Those hearts are in the lab as we speak. While we don't have confirmation just yet, we expect to have it confirmed shortly that those organs belong to Winson Carter, Oliver Carpenter and each of the other three victims discovered in and around Westhampton in the past six months. Would you like to hazard a guess where we found that tank?'

'Not really, but I'm guessing you're going to tell me anyway.'

'At number twenty-two Horsemonger's Lane, the house that you share with your uncle.'

It's the first time there's a flicker of doubt in Maynard's stoic expression. Raven has the lawyer on the ropes, and it feels good.

'As I said, I've never been in that secret room.'

'Who said anything about the hearts being in the secret room?' Bailey asks.

There's a slight tic in Chapman's rigid stare. 'I assume that's where you found them, considering if they were anywhere else in that house, I would have noticed them. They're not the kind of thing you miss now, are they?'

Raven's had enough. Chapman isn't going to fold, and he's sowed enough doubt in the lawyer's mind to go for goal. He has nothing to lose, and the clock is ticking. He reaches into his folder and pulls out the lab report. It contains an image of the purple fingernail found by Winston Carter's body, and confirmation that the DNA is a match to Kaden Chapman. He slides the report across the table to Maynard.

'This copy's for you,' he says.

'What is it?' Maynard asks.

'It's a report from our forensic team.'

'Disclosing what?'

'I can see you wear acrylic nails, Ms. Chapman,' Raven says. 'Do you wear them often?'

'Depends what mood I'm in,' she spits back, but he can see she knows where this is leading.

'Do you ever wear purple acrylics?'

'I can't remember.'

'Do you remember wearing purple acrylic nails like the one in that photograph?'

'No comment.'

'Ms. Chapman, were you on Westhampton Common on the morning of 24th May 2025?'

'I never go there. It's full of drug addicts and rapists.'

'Were you there with Winston Carter?'

'I just told you, I never go there.'

'Were you there to dispose of Winston Carter's body?'

'Are you deaf? I already told you, I didn't kill that fat fuck and I was never at Westhampton Common.'

Raven opens his own copy of the report. 'There's a problem with that, Kaden. May I call you Kaden?'

Chapman doesn't answer.

'Maybe you remember 3rd September 2021?'

'How the hell would I remember a date almost four years ago?'

'You don't remember being arrested for being caught in possession of a baggy of ketamine?'

'I don't do that shit anymore.'

'But you recall being arrested?'

Again, Chapman remains silent.

'What's this got to do with these latest charges?' Maynard snipes.

'Do you remember being swabbed?' Raven asks Chapman, ignoring her lawyer.

'No comment.'

'That swab was to collect your DNA, Kaden, and the results of that swab have been stored in our database ever since. You're not stupid. I know you're an intelligent individual, and I know I don't have to state the obvious here. You're looking at that report like it contains your last rites, which tells me one thing; that you know what we found. You knew you lost that nail, you knew you made a mistake, and ever since you've been panicking because you do remember your prior arrest, and you're clever enough to realise we collected your DNA, and you would have figured out that the tests our team ran on that acrylic nail came back with a match.'

Chapman turns her head away, a little innocuous motion that is worth more than a thousand words.

'I need to talk to my lawyer,' she says. 'Alone.'

Raven suppresses a smirk and is about to put the icing on the cake when the door opens. It's Kipruto, and he doesn't look happy.

'Raven, Bailey, can I have a word?'

'Interview paused at 11.44 a.m.' Bailey says. 'We'll be outside, so please feel free to confer with your counsel.'

Raven tries to read Kipruto's expression, but the DCS has a pretty good poker face. He heads into the corridor while Bailey pulls the door closed behind them.

'We have a problem,' Kipruto says.

'What problem?' Raven asks. 'We have the kill room, we have the severed hearts, and we have DNA evidence linking Chapman to the murder of Carter.'

'There's been another killing.'

His words throw Raven off.

'Another killing?'

'Same M.O.,' Kipruto adds. 'Mutilated body left naked on wasteland, heart removed.'

'That's impossible,' Bailey says.

'How fresh?' Raven asks.

'Sorry?'

'How fresh was the body? It's possible Chapman committed the murder before we brought her in.'

Kipruto shakes his head. 'The pathologist puts this one at around 5.30 a.m. this morning.'

'Six hours after we arrested Chapman,' Raven says, barely able to believe what he's hearing.

Kipruto's expression is grim. 'We have the wrong suspect.'

'No,' Raven replies. 'It's her. It has to be her. We have her DNA at the scene.'

'You have a fingernail that could have been dropped there at any time.'

'It contains trace DNA of Winston Carter.'

'She worked with the guy, Luke. She could have touched his arm or picked up his jacket. You know as well as I do that with this new murder, we have to cut Chapman loose.'

'We both know she did it, Randall.'

'No, we don't. Not anymore.'

'Maybe there's more than one killer.'

'Now you really are leaping.'

A bolt of pain shoots across Raven's eyes, forcing him to steady himself against the wall.

'Are you okay? Kipruto asks.

'I'm fine.'

'After everything that happened to you last night, nobody would blame you for taking a couple of days.'

'I said I'm fine.'

'Then you know what you have to do,' Kipruto says. 'I'm sorry, Luke, but if you don't draw this to a close in the next eleven hours, I'm going to have to re-assign the case.'

'I'll solve it,' Raven replies, but his head is swimming. All of a sudden, he can see two of everything, and the pain in his head is so bad, he can barely stand.

'Raven!' Bailey calls out from somewhere in the distance. 'Luke! Are you okay?'

Raven picks up the muffled sound of Ray Davis telling Kipruto that Kuznecova has been found dead in his hospital bed with his throat cut, but everything is falling away from him, as if he's on a bungee cord, tumbling and spinning into a deep valley. As the darkness welcomes him, his legs give way and he collapses in a heap.

As he lies there flitting in and out of consciousness, the killer appears like a faded video reel and starts to laugh. He laughs with her, because what else is there to do?

CHAPTER 50: COMA

When he comes round, he's in an uncomfortable bed with tubes protruding from his nostrils and forearm. He can barely feel his head, and his mouth is so dry, it's like he's been fed a diet of ash. He's alone, but not for long, because the machine next to him is beeping so loud that a nurse appears in the doorway to see what all the fuss is about.

'You're awake,' she says while scribbling on her clipboard. 'That's good.'

'Orta,' he says.

'You want a drink?'

'Irsty as uck.'

'Now, now, Detective. No need for that language. I'm only here to help.'

She pours water into a plastic beaker, helps him into a sitting position and tips it into his mouth. The cool liquid feels like heaven. It's barely slipped down his gullet when he gulps some more.

'Careful,' the nurse says. 'Not too much. We don't want you to make yourself sick.'

'How long?' he replies, looking at the clock. It shows the time as 9.45 in the morning.

'You've been out for a little under two days,' she says. 'You were suffering with severe concussion, blood loss and dehydration. The doctor decided to put you into an induced coma to give your body a chance to recover.'

Two days? *Two days?* He thinks about Chapman, the smug look on her face, the chaos outside the interview room and

Kipruto's dour expression. He thinks about the latest murder and the fact there was no way Chapman could have done it.

It doesn't matter anymore. He's off the case which means it's somebody else's problem, but even that thought doesn't give him any relief. The killer is still out there.

'You've had plenty of visitors,' the nurse says, arranging a bouquet of flowers on the windowsill. 'Firstly, there was your partner, Detective Bailey, who was very worried about you; then there was the DCS and his pretty wife who brought you some grapes; and finally, of course, there was your own wife and son. That boy is the image of you, by the way. You must be very proud.'

Her words jolt Raven back to life. The nurse doesn't know that he and Lisa aren't married. He forgives her for the mistake, because the big news is Lisa has been to see him, and what's more, she brought Harry. His son was here. Harry knows he's still alive.

'How were they?' he asks, his painfully dry throat now lubricated to the point of being useful.

'They were fine. Your wife was a little tearful, but your son was in good spirits.'

'Where are they now?'

She shrugs. 'I have no idea. They left when visiting hours ended last night. Your colleagues were here interviewing her just before she went home.'

'Interviewing her?' Raven asks. 'Why would they interview Lisa?'

The nurse averts her eyes. 'Maybe I've said too much.'

'No, tell me,' Luke says. 'Whatever it is, I need to know.'

'I hear she was left a package a couple of days ago,' she replies, anxiously eyeing the door. 'Apparently, it was quite nasty.'

'What kind of package?'

The nurse leans forward and cups her hand to her mouth. Raven smells the scent of cleaning fluid on her fingers and clothes.

'From what I hear, somebody left a human liver on her doorstep.'

Raven sits up, tugging furiously at the tubes in his arm. He throws off the blankets and swings his legs out of bed.

'Detective Raven, where do you think you're going?'

'To see them.'

'But you've just come round from a coma. You're in no fit state to leave the hospital.'

'And you've just told me the people I care about most in the whole world have been paid a visit by the serial killer I failed to put behind bars. Forgive me if I'm not in the mood for sitting here on my arse while that lunatic's got his sights on my family.'

He scans the room for his clothes, finds a holdall by the side of his bed and pulls out his bloodied shirt, creased trousers and tightly balled underwear. He's halfway to getting fully dressed when Bailey appears at the window. He hastily pulls the belt around his trousers as she enters the room.

'I see somebody's awake,' she grins. 'How you feeling, boss?'

'Like I've had enough of lying down on the job.'

'Will you tell him he should stay in bed?' the nurse exclaims. 'At least until the doctor's done his rounds.'

'I could,' Bailey replies. 'But I don't think he'll listen.'

Raven eyes the nurse. 'Can we just—'

'Sorry?' she replies, seemingly unsure which way to turn.

'Can you give us a moment, please?'

The nurse shoots him a disapproving glare. 'I'll have to place a call to the doctor about this.'

'I understand,' Raven says and ushers her out the door. 'Where's Chapman?' he asks Bailey.

'We had to let her go, pending further evidence.'

'And the last murder? Any intel?'

'Mason Ackhurst, thirty-two year old dentist. Found naked and face down in the mud by All Hallows playing field. Heart and liver removed.'

'I assume the killer kept the heart and took the liver.'

'He did.'

'Which he then left on the doorstep of Lisa's new house.'

Bailey's mouth falls open. 'How do you know about that?'

'That nurse may be good at her job, but it seems she's an even better gossip.'

He glances through the window and sees the nurse returning with a doctor in tow.

'Who has Kipruto put on the case?' he asks.

'Dawes,' she replies. 'Roger feels really bad about picking this up from you.'

'Good,' Raven says, collecting his things. 'Because then he won't mind me doing a bit of work on the side.'

'Kipruto won't like it,' Bailey says. 'Fitzwilliam's been all over him. There's a sweepstake going round about how long the DCS will keep his job. I'm in for a fiver on two weeks.'

'Randall will keep his job,' Raven says. 'Because we won't let him lose it. We're cracking this thing today.'

'But we don't even know who the killer is.'

Raven watches as the doctor heads towards the ward, clipboard in hand, pen clicking furiously.

'It's Chapman,' he replies. 'It's always been her.'

'But how could she have killed Ackhurst when she was in a cell with us?'

Raven pulls Bailey's handcuffs from the inside pocket of her jacket, slips him on his hands and gestures for her to open the door.

'That's what we need to find out,' he says. 'But I can't do that from inside this room.'

'What's going on here?' the doctor asks, looking down at the cuffs around Raven's wrists.

'I'm sorry sir,' Bailey says, catching on fast. 'But we have reason to believe that Detective Raven has been involved in some illegal activities. Unfortunately, that means we require him down at the station for questioning.'

'Can it wait?' the doctor exclaims. 'This man has been in a coma for the past two days, hasn't eaten anything since he came round, and has had just two glasses of water to rehydrate him.'

'Don't worry,' Bailey says, mock pushing Raven down the corridor. 'We'll make sure he eats and drinks plenty.'

*

They're in the car, heading back to the station, when Bailey's phone rings. She taps the display on the dashboard.

'This is Bailey,' she says.

'Crusher,' Dawes says, using Bailey's old PC monicker. 'We've had a bit of an incident.'

Bailey shoots Raven a sideways glance. 'What kind of incident?'

'You know the tank full of hearts we discovered at Chapman's place?'

'What about it?'

There's a pregnant pause. 'It's gone.'

Bailey pulls the car into a layby. 'Gone? What do you mean it's gone?'

'Gone as in disappeared.'

'But it was in the evidence room.'

'No, it wasn't,' Dawes says. 'The labs sent one of their drivers to collect it for forensic testing, but the guy never made it back.'

Bailey slams her hand on the steering wheel. 'Do you have the guy's name.'

'We do,' Dawes says. 'David Tarrow, driver for Lymington Security. We've been using them to ferry stuff back and forth for years.'

'But nobody thought to check up on Tarrow.'

'Why would we?' Dawes says, sounding offended. 'The security firm does that for us, and as far as they're concerned, Tarrow is a good egg.'

'Except he's vanished with police evidence.'

Raven leans across the car. 'Are you able to trace the car at all?' he asks.

'Raven?' Dawes replies. 'I had no idea you were there. How are you feeling? Boss says you took a funny turn.'

'Wasn't that funny, as it turns out,' Raven replies. 'Now, about the car.'

'Tracker on the car blinked out less than a mile from the station,' Dawes says. 'Phone went off grid about the same time.'

'Which means whatever Chapman's up to, Tarrow's in on it.'

'But why would anybody want a tank full of hearts?' Bailey asks.

Dawes offers an answer, but Raven is no longer listening. He's thinking; thinking about the extended network that now seems to be involved in what he'd initially thought was just another case of a rampaging psychopath. This is bigger than that. Much bigger.

'The Legion,' he says, almost without thinking.

'What?' Bailey answers, her head snapping towards him. 'You mean the organisation that went out of business as soon as Molly Staker put a bullet in her father's skull?'

'I couldn't see it at first, but what with Kuznecova being taken out, the second killer showing up while we had Chapman safely in custody, and now Tarrow stealing the victims' hearts, it's the only conclusion that makes sense.'

'What conclusion?' Bailey asks. 'Raven, what are you trying to say?'

He turns to her, barely able to comprehend what he's now thinking. 'That The Legion are back in business,' he says. 'And they're planning something big.'

CHAPTER 51: MAN-WOLF

The sky is a glorious blue, the sea as calm as a sheet of glass and the air thick with the smell of fried fish, pickled cockles, and cold lager. It's the kind of day that Kaden Chapman usually cherishes, but right now, the time for cherishing is long gone. The people she reports to, the people that really matter, are pissed with her, so pissed they've demanded she show up at their secret little hideout. She knows that's bad. She also thinks it's unfair. Sure, she's slipped up a couple of times and done things that weren't exactly in the plan, but what did they expect? She isn't exactly trained in her profession. It's a learn on the job type of deal, and as with any skill that requires precision, sometimes things go wrong. She's rolled with the punches and come up short, but she'll get back on the horse and keep riding. She's never been one to give up, even when things are looking as bleak as a family day out in Chernobyl.

She rides the bus inland, looking out the window at the docile little people going about their mundane lives. She feels sorry for them. They have no idea what exists just beneath the thin veneer they call normality, or the dark entities that lurk behind every door.

She had been as surprised as anybody when the black detective, Bailey, had told her she was free to go. She was even more surprised to learn from her lawyer that the reason they couldn't hold her any more was that another body had been found. That little snippet of news had left her feeling torn. The role of The Heart Breaker was her thing. If somebody out there was copying what she was doing, then they were just a knock off imitation, no better than the counterfeit Rolex watches you could get from the market stores by the seafront. But then she realised she was being churlish. What if there was a copycat killer? What did it matter to her? It had gotten her out of the police station, hadn't it? And her mission was still her mission, wasn't it?

She traces her finger in the condensation on the window and draws a seahorse, similar to the one tattooed on her shoulder. She's always loved these tiny little creatures. Beautiful, unashamed of what they are, full of a kaleidoscope of colours and as sexually fluid as the sea is wet. She's always thought the human race could learn a lot from seahorses, not least that you are special and unique, however you choose to be, and that public opinion is like water in a river. One day it's fresh, the next it's contaminated with so much shit.

The bus worms its way through the countryside, and pretty soon they're heading up into the hills. Little Gull is a tiny village just north of Annie's Cove. It has a church, a pub and a post box. That's it. It doesn't even have a village shop to speak of; just an old lady who sells fresh eggs and warm bread from inside her kitchen.

She gets off the bus at the bus-stop (buses only run here twice a day, once in the morning, and once just before sunset), and heads up the hill, turning right down a lane that's just wide enough to get a small car through. The people who run The Legion don't appear to be bothered about access. Hiding away has been top of their list of priorities ever since the world and their wife came down hard on them following The Hawk murders.

Kaden checks herself. She looks feminine today, which isn't the way she's feeling, but she thinks it might work for her in the current situation. Her boss is a man after all, and in her experience, men are softer around the opposite sex. She has a lot of arse kissing to do, and kissing a man's anal region always tastes better with lipstick.

She tries to remember which lane Legion Manor is located down, but after a few minutes of second guessing herself, she realises it's the one with the faded image of Jesus painted on the trunk of a dead sycamore tree. Irony isn't lost on the people that run the place, it seems.

She's feeling anxious now. She had been so close to completing her task. Just two more hearts and she would have had enough to complete the charm. She wonders if her boss will let her carry on, or if the presence of the copycat killer will be the thing to shut the whole operation down. She hopes not. She wants to see this through.

The gravel pathway passes through a series of dead sycamores before a canopy of ivy takes hold, creating a dark-green tunnel filled with ominous shadows and dark whispers. She's been here before, but she can't remember it being so creepy. It's like a clichéd backdrop for some shitty horror pic. She's not worried. It's just a bunch of plants and a bit of darkness. The Cardinal has already shown her he won't let anything happen to her. She's his prized jewel, the only one fucked up enough to do what he wants.

There's a sound to her right like something feral scratching around in the earth. Her eyes dart to it. There are deep gouges in one of the dead sycamores and a sticky black liquid oozing from the dry, flaking flesh. She steps closer to take a look, but there's another sound from behind her, and she whirls towards it, just catching a glimpse of something grey and hairy retreating into the shadows.

'Fuck this,' she says, and walks swiftly along the path. She hears something in the gravel behind her and starts to run, but she's never been that athletic and the thing gains on her.

'Get away from me!' she screams, flapping a hand behind her in an attempt to beat whatever the creature is away. She can't turn to face it because she's sure it will be so terrifyingly grotesque that she'll pass out from shock. She pictures some undead monster ripping her throat out, gorging on her blood as she lies there, grasping onto consciousness.

She runs faster, pounding her feet and breathing hard, but the house is so far away and the tunnel of ivy goes on for fucking ever. She can't get away. She's got no chance. She can hear gravel crunching, thick snarls, hot breath on her neck. She's seconds from death. She won't get the chance to finish what she started, not because The Cardinal is pissed with her, but because some undead monster in the woods is about to pull her apart like a slab of pulled pork.

'Kaden!' a voice yells, from up ahead. 'What are you doing?'

She looks up, losing her focus for a split second as she trips over her own feet, her legs becoming tangled together as she tumbles face first onto the gravel, smashing her elbow on the floor and grazing her knee. As she lies there, winded and in pain, she remembers the thing behind her and spins onto her back. There's no monster, no zombified, man-wolf type beast thing. Instead, The Cardinal peers down at her, eyes narrow, a wry smile on his lips.

'Have you lost your mind, love?'

'Something was chasing me,' she replies, peering into the gloom.

'I don't think so. The dogs are inside asleep, and the horses are in the stables.'

'I heard it. It took a chunk out of one of your trees.'

The Cardinal holds out a hand and pulls her up. 'I think you've been spending too much time smoking the devil's leaf, my dear.'

'It was there. I swear,' she says, but now she's not so sure.

'Come inside,' The Cardinal replies. 'I'll make you a cuppa and one of the lads will fetch you something for your scrapes. We've got a lot to discuss.'

Kaden follows him, glancing over her shoulder, eyes scouring the darkness for signs of the snarling thing with grey hair and long claws.

*

The Cardinal sits back in his chair and eyes Kaden Chapman across the table. He's disappointed in her. She's done some stupid things, despite him telling her not to. He's not used to people disobeying him. Since he'd been promoted to the esteemed position of Cardinal of The Legion most people just did as they were fucking told. Not Kaden. She's got a mind of her own, which is what had drawn him to her in the first place, but right now, that pig-headedness has caused a speed bump so big, he's had to buy the world's tallest ladder to get his people over it.

'You shouldn't have killed your uncle,' he says.

'I know, and I'm sorry. It won't happen again.'

'Hardly likely as the old boy is as dead as a T-Rex.'

Kaden shuffles anxiously in her seat. The Cardinal eyes Conor Byrne and his unhinged cousin, Shane. They're standing either side of the door, hands folded in front of them as if they're extras from a gangster movie.

'What was with the fingernail?' he asks Chapman. 'When you've killed before you've been… the other version of you.'

'You mean the manly version?' Kaden asks.

'Your words, not mine,' The Cardinal replies. 'But, yeah, now that you mention it.'

'I guess I felt feminine that day.'

'Feminine enough to kill somebody while wearing acrylics you clearly hadn't glued on properly?'

'Things got a little rough with Winston. I had to improvise.'

'And now Raven and his little band of Keystone Cops have your DNA linked to the DNA of one of the victims. You don't think that's just a little bloody—'

'—stupid,' Conor Byrne says, tone flat and menacing.

'Amateur is what it is,' Shane Byrne adds.

The Cardinal raises an eyebrow. 'I think the lads have a point, don't you agree, Kaden?'

'I realised my mistake as soon as it happened, but by then it was too late. I'm sorry.'

The Cardinal stands. 'There's a lot of fucking apologies coming out of that mouth of yours today, sweetheart. Maybe in the future you'll think before you do something stupid. That way, there'll be no need for all this nonsense.'

Kaden takes a sip of the shot of whiskey Shane had handed her to calm her nerves.

'So, there'll be another time?'

The Cardinal smiles. 'Do you think I plan to give up on our little endeavour?'

'I didn't know if you'd had… second thoughts.'

'Second thoughts are for the unconvinced, Kaden my dear, and the one thing you need to know about me and this little mission of ours is that I'm as convinced as a rabbi reciting the Torah.'

'That's good,' she says. 'Because I'm convinced, too. I'm totally convinced. I can't wait to meet *Him*.'

A shadow descends upon the room. The Cardinal takes a blade from the mahogany cabinet beside the fireplace and touches its tip. A drop of blood appears from a small wound on his finger.

'I'm sure *He* can't wait to meet you, either,' The Cardinal says, nodding to the cousins. Shane takes the hint and disappears through the doorway. 'You see, Kaden, He has big plans for us. For all of us, you included.'

'He can count on my dedication,' Kaden replies, looking relieved. 'I've never been more dedicated to anything in my life.'

'Dedication is just part of what *He* expects. *He* also expects complete servitude, a total willingness to give yourself to the cause.'

'I'm willing,' Kaden replies, running a hand down her neck which is now slick with sweat. 'I'm completely willing.'

The Cardinal moves behind her and draws the flat of the blade across her cheek. 'There cannot be one part of you that you hold back from *Him*: not one drop of blood; not an ounce of flesh; not one errant thought.'

'I understand, and I swear I will give everything.'

He slides the blade towards her throat and runs the cool metal across her chest. 'Eight vessels of blood to sate the thirst,' he says, just as Byrne returns, carrying a large box-shaped object covered with a black drape. 'Eight pounds of tissue to feed the beast.' Byne places the box on the table and slides it towards The Cardinal. 'Eight examples of humanity's lust, greed, envy and hatred to fuel the eternal flame.'

Byrne removes the drape, revealing six human hearts.

'The collection is good,' he says. 'But it's incomplete, even with the addition of the last heart which we gathered while you were in custody.'

Kaden's eyes flicker just a little.

'Oh,' he says. 'You thought we had nothing to do with that, didn't you?'

'I thought it might be a copycat.'

'That would have to be some serious wannabe, wouldn't it boys?' he says, laughing. 'Some kid who's prepared to go out, kill a guy, then cut out his heart, just to copy something he's read on the internet.'

'It happens sometimes,' Kaden says, but The Cardinal can see she doesn't really believe it.

'Hurts your pride, doesn't it? Knowing that somebody in our organisation has the guts and audacity to do exactly what you do. Makes you feel just a little less — how can I put it? — special.'

Kaden jerks away from the knife, but The Cardinal holds her shoulders, refusing to let her stand.

'I thought you said you wanted me to complete the mission,' she spits.

'I do.'

'Then stop goading me like a bitch and let me get the last two hearts.'

The Cardinal laughs. He finds Chapman funny, he always has. She has a coarse way about her, an attitude that reminds him of himself when he was a kid, never taking shit from anybody, never letting anybody see when they'd gotten to him. She's afraid, he can feel it in the sweat on her skin and the slight tremble in her throat, but she'll never let him truly see that, because to do so would be to admit her own insecurities, insecurities she's barely come to terms with herself.

He sets the knife aside, runs his fingers through her hair and pulls her head back. She gasps, but her eyes are steadfast. She hates him, he can see that now, but hate is good. Hate is exactly what *He* expects.

'Do you feel *Him* inside you?' he asks.

'*He* wouldn't want to be inside me. There's too much anger. It would rip *Him* apart.'

'You'd be surprised. *He* feeds on anger. *He* gorges on pain. *He* devours anguish. Everything you're experiencing is just a fraction of what *He* needs, but *He'll* eat it up just the same. *He's* in you, just as *He's* me, in the Byrne boys over there, and in every single person that lives and breathes on this big blue rock of ours.'

'People who aren't like us don't deserve *Him*,' Kaden replies. 'People who haven't suffered shouldn't be allowed to witness *Him*.'

'Have you suffered, Kaden?'

'Yes,' she says, looking up at him through glassy eyes.

'How badly have you suffered?'

'Worse than most.'

'Do you feel that suffering now?'

She draws back her lips, teeth like fangs. 'I feel it every second of every fucking day.'

He lets go of her hair, causing Kaden's head to fall forward, spittle dribbling down her chin. He clasps his hands together behind her, forming a strong ball of knuckles and skin.

'I need those other two hearts, Kaden.'

'I'll get them for you,' she says, barely loud enough for him to hear.

'The last one has to be his.'

'I know.'

'His is the only black heart that can complete the circle.'

'I understand.'

His pulse is racing now. The excitement has kicked in. They are so close to fulfilling the one job he was tasked with achieving by the invisible faces in charge, and in doing so, he completes the thing he swore to do four years ago when he was betrayed by the one person who should have known better.

'But it begs the question,' he says, looking up at Shane who has already started to edge closer. 'Who is deserving enough to be number seven?'

Kaden's head snaps up as Byrne pulls the garotte from his jacket pocket.

'Wait!' she says, but it's too late. The Cardinal holds her hands on the table as Byrne moves behind her. She thrashes around, tries to throw him off, but he's too strong and Byrne is too agile.

'Sorry, my love,' The Cardinal says. 'But *He* has spoken.'

Byrne pulls the garotte tight around her throat, and Kaden's eyeballs bulge out of their sockets, her tongue jutting from snarling lips.

'Look at it this way, dear. At least you get to help finish the job.'

CHAPTER 52: BACON

Lisa arrives at the West's house a little after 11 a.m. She's furious. Raven has discharged himself from the hospital, even though he's barely come round from injuries that could have killed him. The guy's a fucking imbecile. Worse than that, he's reckless, and he's showing that he doesn't give two shits about her or their son. Despite that, she has to find him. He needs to be saved from himself.

The house is cordoned off, but she ducks beneath the tape and knocks on the door. Billy answers, but it isn't the Billy she knows. The fake bravado has slipped from his face like melted ice cream. He looks anxious, worried.

'I need your help,' she says.

'I don't know,' Billy replies. 'Sally's still really shaken up.'

'If I don't find him, Bill, he'll end up getting himself killed.'

'He almost got us killed.'

'That wasn't his fault, and you know it.'

Billy glances over his shoulder. 'If I come,' he says. 'Sally comes too.'

'I don't know,' Lisa replies. 'I don't know what Luke's up to, but I'm guessing there's bad people involved.'

'And some of those bad people turned up at our house last night and nearly killed my wife, Lis. Either we both come, or neither of us do.'

Lisa wants to argue, but she doesn't have the energy or the time.

'I'll drive,' she says. 'And you can tell me everything you know about The Medics.'

*

They head to the snooker hall where Billy tells her The Medics hang out. He's dead against the idea, but Lisa won't be swayed. She's done messing around. She's seen Luke once since he's been back, and in that time, he's been beaten up, threatened with a chainsaw and collapsed into a coma. If she doesn't help him to see what a reckless idiot he's being, nobody will.

'You know, these people don't mess about, Lis,' he offers.

'Neither do I,' she says, lighting a cigarette as she lowers the window, not bothering to ask if either Billy or Sally mind.

They drive for a few miles, hardly speaking. Lisa thinks about her next move, exhaling slowly as she runs over her options.

While Raven was in a coma, she'd had some time to quiz Randall about the case. Although the DCS was coy about the details, it was obvious the person they had in custody couldn't possibly have been the same person who'd dropped the human liver on her doorstep. That meant somebody else was involved, and if Lisa had to take a guess, she'd put the blame squarely on the people who'd tried to have Raven rubbed out the day before. The same people who, if the rumours around the hospital were to be believed, had covered their tracks by erasing the chainsaw wielding hitman Billy had put a bullet in. Randall hadn't given her any intel on the culprits, but Ruby had let it slip, mainly because she'd seemed worried Lisa might do exactly the kind of thing she was planning right now.

'The Medics are bad people,' she'd said. 'Luke made a real mistake poking around in their shit.'

Cue her drive round to the West's, because if there was one thing Lisa knew about the chubby electrician who'd saved Luke's bacon more than once now, it was that he knew the kind of people most people would do everything they could to stay well clear of.

'Tell me about these guys,' she said, flicking her cigarette through the open window and lighting another.

'I went to school with Shane,' Billy replies. 'We were in the same class. Everybody knew the Byrnes, even my old man who'd spent some time inside with Shane's dad, Cian. Shane wasn't particularly bad at school, you just knew he had it in him. One time, one of the other kids said something to Shane about him being a "thick Paddy", and that was enough to get the kid a black eye and a broken nose. Three teachers had to pull Shane off the boy.' Billy pauses and then says, 'That's the thing about the Byrnes — it's not how good at fighting they are, exactly. It's how far they're willing to go.'

'So this Shane is the boss of The Medics?' Lisa asks.

'No, he's the nice one of the two,' Sally replies, still looking a little shaken. 'Tell her about Conor, Billy.'

Billy nods. 'Conor is a whole other level,' he says. 'I said Shane wasn't that bad in school. I can't say the same about Conor. He got kicked out in year nine for stamping on some boy's face repeatedly, just because he accidentally spilt juice over Conor's books. The boy had to go to a London hospital for reconstructive surgery.'

Lisa sneers. 'Sounds like a vicious fuck.'

'That's not even the worst of it. Conor spent three years in juvenile detention where he met some of the guys he eventually recruited into his gang, but while he was there, it's rumoured he strangled a kid to death for going up against him.'

'Did he get sentenced for that, too?'

Billy shakes his head. 'From what I hear, Conor got one of the other kids to take the rap for it.'

'How did he do that?'

'He cut off the boy's finger with a set of garden secateurs, told him if he didn't admit to the murder, he'd come back and cut off his dick.'

Lisa exhales through her teeth. 'And how long as he been running The Medics?'

'Eight or nine years, I'd say,' Billy replies. 'Maybe longer. They run the drug dealing network in town, have an illegal importing and exporting business, and they also offer "protection" to local businesses for a sizable cut of their profits.'

'Have they ever come after you, love?' Sally asks, gripping her husband's arm.

Billy shakes his head. 'That's one good thing about having an old man who spent most of his adult life inside. He made friends, important ones. Conor wouldn't touch me out of respect for his uncle Cian and my dad.' He points out the window. 'Take a right here, Lis,' he says, 'and pull over by the bookies. That way, if anything happens, we've got a quick exit up East Street.'

Lisa swings the car down the narrow lane and parks outside the betting shop. She steps out of the car, crushes her butt beneath the heel of her boot and opens the passenger door.

'You want me to come with you?' Billy asks, looking like that's the last thing he wants to do.

'What are you worried about?' Lisa replies. 'Like you said, Conor won't hurt you.'

'Not unless I do something stupid,' Billy says. 'And this? This is stupid.'

'Rubbish. I just want to talk to the guy.'

'Conor Byrne isn't really the type of bloke who enjoys chatting.'

Lisa pops a stick of gum in her mouth and half smiles. 'Funny, because I'm not the type of woman who enjoys hearing about the father of her only child being almost chopped to pieces.'

*

She bangs on the door hard enough to rattle the frame, and after almost a minute, some guy with a squashed nose, bald head and set of gold teeth appears.

'What the fuck is all the noise about?' he asks in a thick Irish accent.

'I want to talk to Conor,' Lisa replies.

'Who the fuck are ya?'

'Somebody Conor will want to speak to.'

'Well Conor ain't here, so you're out of luck.'

He goes to close the door, but Lisa isn't in the mood for being shut down so she kicks it open. The edge of the thick wood catches the bald guy on the side of his face, slicing his eyebrow.

'Bitch!' he cries, clenching a large fist.

Lisa doesn't hesitate. She brings up a knee, striking the bloke in his testes. There's a satisfying crunch and the guy collapses, air hissing like a burst balloon through his lips.

'Come on Bill,' she says, passing through the foyer and climbing the stairs leading to the bar. Billy follows behind, his mouth opening and closing.

Inside, there's another two guys, one with a face like a crushed squash ball, the other with thick eyebrows and the hint of a dark beard.

'Conor Byrne?' she asks, chewing gum furiously.

'Did you just knee Darragh in the nut sack?' Dark Beard asks.

'He had it coming.'

He bursts into laughter, clapping the other guy on the back.

'Did you hear that, Tadhg? Old Darragh took one in the crown jewels.'

'The little girlie was lucky to find 'em, Killian,' Tadhg says. 'From what I hear, they're smaller than a couple of M and Ms.'

That causes another volley of laughter that Billy mistakenly joins in with.

'Who the fuck are you?' Killian asks, no longer finding the joke amusing.

'Billy. Billy West.'

Tadhg retrieves something from his jacket and slips it into the palm of his hand. 'And what the fuck are you doing here, Billy West?'

'He's with me,' Lisa says. 'We're here to talk about Luke Raven.'

'The copper?' Killian asks. 'Why would we want to talk to a little woman like you and a fat fuck like him about a piece of sticky dog shit like that?'

'Because Conor tried to have him killed,' Lisa replies, realising this is the moment she crosses the line.

'That's some accusation, lady,' Tadhg says, stepping closer, eyes as dark as liquorice. 'I assume you have something to back it up.'

'Just this,' she says, and pulls a P365 handgun from her pocket.

'Lisa, what the fuck?' Billy exclaims.

'That's a powerful gun for someone like you to be carrying around,' Killian says, eyes twitching to his partner. 'You pull a gun like that, lady, and you want to make sure you're prepared to use it.'

Lisa pulls the trigger and a bottle of Jack Daniels explodes, showering Killian with glass and bourbon.

'Is that proof enough?'

Tadgh halts his advance and moves his hand slowly to the inside of his jacket.

'I wouldn't do that if I were you,' Lisa says. 'Unless you want to find out if I'm willing to shoot a little splat of shit like you.'

Tadgh holds up his hands, exposing the knuckleduster he'd pulled from his pocket earlier. 'No, no,' he replies. 'I believe you mean exactly what you say.'

'Conor's not here,' Killian says. 'He hasn't been here since very early this morning.'

'And Shane?' Billy asks, suddenly emboldened. 'Is he here?'

'He's with Conor as far as I know,' Killian replies. 'They had some business to attend to.'

'What kind of business?' Lisa asks.

Killian shrugs nonchalantly so Lisa shoots again, this time taking out a bottle of Chivaz Regal.

'He's talking with the boss,' Killian says, his calm exterior fracturing just a little.

'I thought Conor was the boss.'

'Of The Medics, yes, but this guy, he's a boss of something much bigger.'

His words hit home. She recalls her run-in with the kind of people who make The Medics look like the Chuckle Brothers; the people who snatched Harry, killed Luke's father, Sam, and had senior plants inside West Hampshire Constabulary.

'You're talking about The Legion,' she says, sneering as the name slips through her lips.

Killian doesn't answer, but the twitch in his eyes tells her she's right.

'Where?' she asks.

This time Killian's expression really does break, and she sees something she knows well, because it's the same emotion she's been feeling ever since setting foot inside the snooker hall. It's fear.

'I can't tell you,' he says.

'I don't really think you have an option in this matter, do you?' Lisa replies, wagging the gun.

'If I tell you, I'm dead.'

'If you don't tell me, you're dead too, so it seems like you have a choice to make.'

She hasn't spotted Tadgh edging closer, so when he goes for Billy with the knuckle duster, she's caught blindsided. Billy is light on his feet and moves instinctively, ducking out of the way, leaving the guy with the squashed face swinging wildly. In the melee, Lisa reacts, squeezing the trigger and putting a bullet in Tadgh's thigh.

'Shit!' he yells. 'You shot me! Bitch, you shot me!'

She fights to control the trembling in her arm long enough to turn the gun back on Killian and push out her words, her voice like a theremin.

'I'm not joking here! I need to know where they went!'

Killian looks at his pal who's bleeding out on the floor and then turns his attention back to her. His expression is far more uncertain, like a card player who's lost three hands in a row. He makes a choice. Luckily for him, it's the right one.

CHAPTER 53: 10 MG

Raven and Bailey arrive back at the station. Fitzwilliam's car is in the car park: a Lexus ES, 25 plate. He's out of the car, almost before Bailey shuts down the engine, and heads for the entrance.

'Let me in,' he says to the PC manning the desk, his warrant card thrust at his face. The young guy's eyes widen at the sight of him and does as he asks.

Raven can see Kipruto sitting in his office, Fitzwilliam standing, lecturing him. Detective Dawes sinks into the back wall, an uncomfortable spectator.

'Luke?' Kipruto says as Raven storms in. 'We're kind of in the middle of something here.'

'Detective Raven,' Fitzwilliam adds. 'I see you've still not learned how to knock.'

'You never told me The Legion were back in business,' Raven says, causing Dawes's head to swivel like a weathervane. 'You didn't think that was something I should have been told?'

Kipruto goes to speak but Fitzwilliam chimes in. 'What does the killing spree of some crazed maniac have to do with the resurrection of some long neutered criminal network?'

'Tell that to the people killed by Molly Staker and Anthony Richards,' Raven spits. 'Both of those serial killers were influenced by senior members of The Legion, so I would say it has a lot to do with it.'

Kipruto tries to intervene. 'Both Clarence and I thought it might be a distraction, given your history.'

'So you're blaming me.'

'Not blaming. Just explaining.'

Raven slams his hand on the table. 'We had the killer right here, and the only reason we let her go is because some other nutjob took up where she'd left off.'

'Which meant your case was flawed,' Fitzwilliam says, folding his arms.

'No!' Raven yells. 'It means whoever's in charge of The Legion just sent some other crazy to pick up the pieces.'

'Oh, come now Detective Inspector,' Fitzwilliam replies. 'Even you must see you're clutching at straws.'

'He's got a point, Luke,' Dawes said. 'There's no evidence to suggest somebody different was involved in the latest murder.'

'But there is evidence linking Chapman to both the murder of her uncle and her boss,' Raven replies. 'Which has to be enough to get the CPS to sign off on a conviction.'

Fitzwilliam shakes his head. 'I'm afraid not. I already had the conversation with Chief Prosecutor Warnock, and he's of the same opinion as me. Namely, an errant fingernail and the presence of a body in Chapman's home is not enough to convince a jury.'

Raven turns to Kipruto. 'When did we start allowing MPs to talk to the CPS on our behalf?'

'Since I was given responsibility for the safe operation of this place,' Fitzwilliam spits back. 'You may not think I'm up to the job, Detective Inspector Raven, but I'm afraid the people who actually matter do. That means Kipruto works for me, which de-facto means you all do.'

Raven tries to hide his disgust, but it's like a birthmark on his face. He can barely look at Fitzwilliam, let alone speak to him.

'Chapman did it,' he hisses. 'And The Legion are involved. If you can't see that, then I'm afraid I have to disagree with your superiors. You haven't got a *fucking clue!*'

He storms out, kicking a chair across the office as he goes. He's so angry he can barely breathe. His head is pounding again.

He can hear Fitzwilliam yelling at him from the office and Kipruto telling him to calm down, but he's too far gone for that. He heads outside, looks up at the looming clouds, and lets out an almighty yell.

'*Fuck!*'

He punches a metal sign that points to the electric car charging stations, putting a sizable dent in in the centre of it while simultaneously hurting his right hand. A couple of young PCs look up at him as they exit their car but hastily retreat when he shoots them a vicious glare.

Bailey appears by his side, but she knows better than to try to calm him down.'

'Kipruto is better than this,' he says, pointing to the station door. 'He knows The Legion are involved, but he's allowing his career to get in the way of logic.'

'He can only do what Fitzwilliam lets him,' Bailey replies. 'It's been that way ever since you left.'

'I didn't leave.'

'Okay, disappeared then. Either way, the DCS has had his hands tied this whole time.'

Raven pulls a hip flask from his pocket and takes a swig. He doesn't care that he's drinking in plain view of the station. The time for abiding by the rules has long gone, and in any case, he needs something, *anything*, to calm him down.

'That isn't going to help,' Bailey says.

Raven takes another pull, and this time he glugs, letting the whiskey slide down his gullet and set fire to his insides.

'On the contrary,' he replies. 'It helps a lot.'

Bailey places her hands on her hips and lets out a long breath. 'You know, working alongside you is even harder than they said it would be.'

'Funny,' he replies. 'Working with you has been an absolute joy.'

Bailey's stern expression breaks into a smile, and then she laughs. Raven laughs back, causing another PC walking past to look at them as if they've gone mad.

'Ignore us,' Bailey says, taking the hip flask from Raven's hand and raising it to her lips. 'We're just drinking to keep ourselves sane.'

'It'll take more than this, believe me,' Raven replies, eyes streaming.

They stand that way for a little while, laughing and drinking until the hilarity goes out of the situation. Raven realises he's probably out of a job, which also puts Bailey in a difficult situation.

'Go back inside,' he says. 'Make sure the bosses know you don't agree with the way I behaved. You need this job more than I do.'

'Where will you go?' Bailey asks.

Raven pulls a set of keys from his pocket. 'I'm going to drive myself back into town, see if I can't shake a few of my old contacts and find out where The Legion are operating.'

Bailey slips a hand into the pocket of her jacket and pulls out a folded sheet of A4 paper which she hands to him.

'Good job I printed this out, then,' she says. 'It'll save us the trouble of looking for a needle in a haystack.'

Raven eyes the neatly typed address on the printout, and the picture of the large, thatched cottage nestled between a clutch of green pines.

'Is this—'

Bailey grins and nods. 'We'll take my car,' she says. 'Because you look like you're at least 10 mg over the limit.'

CHAPTER 54: TALONS

Lisa steers the car through the narrow Westhampton streets, takes the first exit off the Palisades roundabout and accelerates through the country lanes that lead to Annie's Cove. Billy sits beside her, Sally in back.

'So what exactly happened in there?' Sally asks, hanging onto the grab handle for dear life.

'Let's just say it escalated quickly,' Lisa replies.

'Lisa shot a bloke,' Billy says, looking like he's just swallowed something nasty.

'She shot somebody? With what?'

'Simon owns a gun,' Lisa says, giving Billy a nasty side-eye. 'He bought one as soon as we got together. I guess he knew what he was letting himself in for when he met me.'

'It was probably just to protect you and Harry,' Billy says.

Lisa doesn't dignify that with an answer.

'Who the hell did you shoot?' Sally asks.

'Only a member of the most dangerous criminal gang this side of London,' Billy says. 'You know they're going to come after us, right?'

'They won't need to,' Lisa says. 'Because we're going straight to them.'

She rounds another bend, swerving wildly, narrowly avoiding an oncoming tractor.

'Not if you get us killed on the way,' Billy says, gripping the dashboard.

'If you want to drive, just say so,' Lisa replies.

'I don't mind your driving, just slow down a bit.'

They pass the exit towards the coast and continue following the road that leads to Little Gull, a place that Lisa has visited only once, and that was only to take a piss on the way back home from Lymington while pregnant with Harry.

'What are we actually going to do when we get there?' Sally asks.

'We're going to find out who paid The Medics to have Luke killed.'

Sally leans forward. 'Do you really think whoever lives at that cottage is going to just volunteer that information to you?'

Lisa doesn't answer. She hasn't thought that far in front. As usual, she's letting her heart rule her head, and right now it's telling her she has to follow the breadcrumbs. If she does, everything will be all right.

'You think Luke will go there, too, don't you?' Billy asks. 'You think he'll follow the same leads and end up in the same place.'

Lisa nods. She does. She and Luke Raven have always been sympatico, as if they were carved from the same rotting piece of wood. She knows that all roads lead to this place, even if she has no idea what this place really is.

'If Conor Byrne has given control of The Medics to somebody else,' Billy adds, 'then that has to mean the person in charge is some seriously nasty piece of work.'

'All the more reason to go after him.'

Billy huffs loudly. She can sense his discomfort.

'We need to drop Sally off,' he says.

'What?' Sally exclaims. 'I'm not going anywhere.'

Billy turns in his seat. 'I can't let Lisa go in there alone, Sal, but I won't let you put yourself in danger.'

Sally's eyebrows fold in the middle like two arcing wings. 'You don't get to tell me what I can and can't do, Billy West,' she says. 'I've got just as much right to see this through as you have.

I was in that house when those two goons showed up, remember? And it was me who ran to get help when Luke was in there getting three shades of crap kicked out of him.'

Billy shrinks like a wallflower.

'Looks like you've been put back in your box,' Lisa says, winking at Sally in the rearview.

'I don't mean anything by it,' Billy protests. 'I just worry about you.'

'And as much as that's sweet,' Sally says. 'Let me worry about myself.'

Up ahead, Lisa sees the lane she's looking for and indicates. She's about four minutes behind the person she really wants to be with, but she doesn't know it. Other than her trip to the hospital with Harry, she's as close to Luke Raven now as she has been since he came back from his enforced absence. What she also doesn't know is that they're both heading towards a darkness they can hardly fathom, and a shadowy abomination that lies in wait, its hot breath souring the air and its hooked talons cleaving great canyons in the sodden earth.

CHAPTER 55: BEEF TARTARE

They turn into the lane marked by a faded image of Jesus. The road becomes a dirt track, but Bailey persists, steering the car along a gravel path with deep potholes and clambering roots. Raven attempts to direct her, but it's no use. The suspension takes a beating and the wheel bearings scream out in anguish. Raven thinks if Bailey pushes the car any harder, the axle might break in two.

'Seems like whoever lives here doesn't have a lot of money,' Bailey says above the racket.

'Why do you say that?' Raven asks.

'Can't afford a new driveway.'

'It's probably in the owner's best interest to keep it like this. Makes smarter coppers than us less likely to bring a car down here.'

'That's assuming this guy is who we think he is.'

He is. Raven knows he is. He doesn't have an identity, has no idea who would take up the reins left by a guy so despicable even his own daughter hated him, but he knows The Legion are here. He can feel them.

'Do you think this will work?' Bailey asks. 'Running straight at them like this?'

'What option do we have?'

'We could try getting a warrant?'

'Fitzwilliam wouldn't allow it. He's been blocking this from the start.'

'But why would he do that?'

Raven has his suspicions, but no clear evidence. He knows The Legion have far reaching influences, but do they really have a fully-fledged member of the King's parliament in their grasp? It seems far-fetched, like something out of a conspiracy nut's Facebook page, but that doesn't mean it isn't possible.

'Either he's an idiot or—'

'—or he's corrupt,' Bailey says, completing what he's already thinking.

'I never said that.'

'You didn't need to.'

Something crashes into the windscreen hard. Bailey slams her foot on the brake, causing the car to slide sideways as gravel and dirt spray the paintwork. Raven's body bashes into the side panelling as she spins the wheel, but eventually the car comes to a screeching halt.

'What the hell was that?' she asks.

Raven opens the door but the car's facing the wrong way. He gets out, scanning the dark tunnel of ivy that envelopes them. There's blood on the windscreen and bonnet, crimson streaks that stretch from the roof to the front grill. He glances inside at Bailey who's still looking pretty shocked.

'Wait here,' he says, walking around the rear of the vehicle, following the deep grooves caused by the spinning tires. He sees the shoes before he sees the face, but he knows who the body belongs to straight away. He's suspected it ever since he heard about the last victim, the one that Chapman couldn't have killed. The shop worker had made a mistake, and because of that, The Legion had to cover their tracks. She was unnecessary collateral, just like Kuznecova.

'Oh Kaden,' he says, taking in the sight of her body. She's not naked like the others, but her chest is exposed and there's a gaping cavity where her heart had once been. Her eyes are peering up at him, sightless and innocent, one fake eyelash lying lopsided against her cheek. There's blood on her chin, but apart from that, she could still be the same angry young person he'd first met at the surf shop. There's a rope around her neck that's tied around a thick branch, which in turn is attached to a wire stretched taut across the driveway. He figures it must have been snapped by the approaching car. The whole thing has been staged for their arrival, just another show of strength from somebody who thinks they're above any repercussions.

Raven whirls round, suddenly realising they're completely exposed. If somebody is going to take them out, it will be now. He stands there scanning their surroundings, looking for any signs of movement, but after a moment, he relaxes. Killing them here isn't what this is about. It's just an introduction, a beaten and bloodied beef tartare before the main course, something designed to throw them off kilter.

'Jesus Christ,' Bailey says, opening her door.

'Let's move her,' Raven says, gesturing to Chapman. 'She doesn't deserve to be left out in the open like this.'

Together they move the body to the side of the road and cover Chapman's upper torso and face with a blanket from the boot of the car. Only her lower legs and heavy boots remain visible. It's not perfect, but it will have to do.

'Who the hell would do something like that?' Bailey asks, her voice wavering.

'I guess we're about to find out.'

'We should call for back up.'

'Do you think Fitzwilliam will send anybody?'

Bailey glares at the floor. 'Call Dawes then. Or Davis.'

'And risk their jobs too? Look, Alli, I know I'm asking a lot here, but if we don't see this through, this won't end. You must see that. Ever since I came back, everything has been leading to this: the killings; the attempt on my life; the human remains on Lisa's doorstep.'

'Seems like it's personal,' she says.

'Seems that way to me, too.'

'You've obviously pissed off some pretty nasty people.'

'I've pretty much made a career out of it.' He forces a grim smile. 'I'll completely understand if you want to head back. If I was in your position, I'd probably do the same.'

Bailey looks down at Chapman's lifeless body, and then back along the driveway towards the exit. For a minute, Raven thinks she might actually leave, but then her expression hardens and she turns back to him.

'You see, the thing is, Luke,' she says. 'People like Fitzwilliam piss me off, and that means anybody linked to him pisses me off too.'

She reaches into the car and pulls out the only gun they have. A Glock17 with one clip.

'So, what are you saying?' he asks, watching as she slips the gun into its holster.

'I'm saying we head up to that cottage and arrest anybody who looks like they might want to cut out our hearts.'

Raven takes a deep breath, knowing that they're walking straight into a trap, but also knowing that he has no choice but to face it head on. The past six years have been leading up to this one moment of grim finality. Whatever happens next, it will be over. The whole sorry mess will end.

'Then let's do it,' he says, eyes scanning the shadows for a creature lurking in the darkness, its lips drawn back across bared teeth, mouth spitting and snarling.

CHAPTER 56: TOILET CLEANER

DCS Randall Kipruto is having a crisis of conviction. He no longer knows who he is or what he stands for. Did he really think that by keeping the truth about the Legion from Raven that the returning DI would stand a greater chance of solving the murders? Did he actually believe giving Raven a deadline would make things better, not worse?

He eyes the phone, thinks of his wife and kids and lets out a long breath.

'Are you going to let him speak to me like that?' Fitzwilliam asks.

Randall doesn't answer.

'DCS Kipruto, I'm talking to you.'

He looks out into the office. Just over twenty people are out there, doing the jobs of more than fifty, working longer hours than is healthy. He thinks of Fitzwilliam, of the unnecessary bullshit he's had to put up with ever since agreeing to take the job.

He thinks about his career, the dreams he'd had when he'd first signed up to the force. His parents had been so proud of him, so happy that he'd chosen a noble profession, one that would make a difference — but what difference has he really made? Aside from helping Luke Raven bring down the Hawk and her father, he's been stuck behind a desk, juggling numbers and cutting costs to meet ever decreasing budgets.

Then he thinks about his two daughters and the universities they might attend. He thinks about the costs, about how he doesn't want them burdened with a £60,000 debt before they've even got jobs. He thinks about his wife, Ruby, and her completely understandable desire to come back to work after the maternity pay dries up. How can they make that work if he's out of a job? The cost of childcare alone would cripple them. He thinks about the house, the beautiful home they've built together. It's modest — just a three up, three down — but it's theirs, or at least, some of it is. The rest belongs to the bank until the mortgage is repaid, and even on the decent salary he now takes home, that could take up to three more decades.

Then he thinks about his moral integrity or what's left of it. He's already let Fitzwilliam and the others corral him into cutting back the taskforce assigned to finding Luke Raven, only to learn his old partner and friend was being held against his will in the Scottish Highlands, and now he's been bullied into keeping things from the one guy he owes his life to and told to forcefully remove him from the case.

He's torn in so many directions he can barely hold it together. He loves his family, would do anything for them, but does that include losing what remains of his sense of right and wrong? Is he so far gone that he can put everything he believes aside, just to stroke some misguided bureaucrat's ego so that he looks kindly on him during the end of year assessment?

'Kipruto!' Fitzwilliam yells. 'Have you lost your hearing, man? Your DI, the man you convinced me to bring on board despite my better judgement, has just insulted me, ignored your orders, and walked out of here like he owns the place! Are you going to do something about it, or do I need to recruit somebody in your place who will do just that?'

'Fuck this,' Randall half-whispers.

'Sorry?' Fitzwilliam asks.

Randall pauses, looks out the window again, and reaches for his badge. He takes a long hard look at it, thinks about his next words very carefully, and then slides it across the desk.

'I said fuck this, *sir*.'

Fitzwilliam's mouth opens and closes. 'Are you handing in your resignation, Detective Chief Superintendent?'

Randall collects his jacket, turns slowly and nods. 'I think I am, yes.'

'What… what the hell for, man?'

'I figured out what I stand for,' Randall replies, walking out the door. 'And it turns out I'm a better person than I thought I was.'

'You'll regret this!' Fitzwilliam calls after him. 'You'll never get another job in the force, Kipruto. I'll see to that. By the time I've finished with you, you'll barely be fit to clean the toilets.'

Randall hears his words, but he lets them slip past like dirty water. He's already feeling the burden lifting from his shoulders, as if everything that's been weighing him down has just been hitched to a slowly rising zeppelin.

He collects his keys and heads out the door, quickening his pace because he already knows where Raven is going. It's the place he should have sent a team to as soon as the news dropped about The Legion's growing influence, but for some reason he allowed himself to be convinced that the time wasn't right for an intervention. Now he suspects that if he'd gone against his superiors, much of what has happened over the past few weeks could have been avoided. That's a dark shadow on his conscience he'll have to come to terms with, but right now he has other priorities. He has to put things right, not just for himself, but for the victims. One of which is the person he's failed more than anybody else.

CHAPTER 57: PHOSPHUR

They dump the car out of sight behind a rusted metal container and approach the cottage from the south. Raven creeps round to the rear window, Bailey just behind. He doesn't like the feel of the place, the smell of it. It reeks of stagnant pond water and bins left unemptied. The sensation of something lurking just out of sight is still with him. He pictures Champan's body, the neat way her chest was cleaved open, and the surgical way her heart was extracted. Whoever killed her had taken great care. The question was, why? Why steal the hearts from the evidence room, why continue to kill and maim when the original killer was in police custody? Why then murder Chapman and leave her out there on the driveway for someone to discover? He can't make sense of it. All he knows is that the Legion are involved, and Kipruto and Fitzwilliam should have told him about their resurgence sooner.

'Next steps?' Bailey asks, but her question is answered by Raven taking a three-inch blade from his pocket and popping a window open. 'I'm not sure I'm comfortable with this,' she adds, but Raven already has one leg through the opening.

'The time for objecting was about an hour ago,' he says.

'I wasn't expecting to be breaking the law so soon.'

'Then get used to it. This is how I do things.'

He clambers inside, helps Bailey over the ledge and turns to take in their surroundings. The inside of the cottage is only marginally better than the exterior. It looks like the place hasn't been decorated for at least half a century. The brown and beige wallpaper is peeling from plaster peppered with dark spots of mould, and the dark brown carpet is frayed around the edges and threadbare in patches. The bookcase to their right is stacked with classic novels — Shelley, Wolff, Bronte — and coated in a thin layer of grey dust. The armchair that rests by the window has one fractured armrest and a dark stain on the spine. The smell of brown water is thicker in here, too, like the cottage has been doused in it.

'Reading room,' Raven whispers.

'Doesn't look like much reading has been going on in here for quite a while,' Bailey replies.

Raven keeps moving, heading towards the hallway. He's careful with his feet because the wooden floor is hardly stable. He peeps through the crack in the door. The hallway is long, which is odd, because from outside, the cottage looks much smaller. He pushes the tip of the knife through the crack and opens the door a little further. There's a creak from one of the hinges and a shower of dust from above.

He eyes Bailey over his shoulder and nods to the hallway. They slip through the gap. The place is eerily silent, like they've somehow entered a vacuum. A narrow beam of light slips through a gap between the front door and the frame, splitting the hallway in two. Everything else is dark. There's a set of stairs that lead to the first floor, framed by a banister with splintered wooden struts. The stairs are warped and uneven and turn a corner halfway up. Raven takes a look but decides against climbing them. They look like they'll be as noisy as a room full of frogs.

He cocks his head towards the rear of the house. The kitchen door is half open, but the room beyond looks as black as pitch. He inches along the hallway, passing a door beneath the stairs. It looks like it's locked, but he tries the knob anyway. It turns smoothly in his hand, and he feels the latch disengage. The door swings outward just a little, and there's a gust of warm air like a baby's breath. He turns his head to look at Bailey, but she nods towards the kitchen. She's right, they should check there first.

He leaves the cellar door open and pushes himself up against the kitchen wall, listening out for any sounds. There's none, not even the growl of a boiler or the hum of a refrigerator. He places a hand against the door and slowly eases it inward.

There's only a small amount of light leeching through the rear window which seems to be entirely covered by creeping ivy. A series of beige cabinets with crooked doors line the far wall and a rectangular table sits on a stone tiled floor, many of them cracked and badly stained. On top of the table is an ashtray with the stub of a cigar perched at an angle, the ash long since cooled. Beside it is a single cup of half consumed coffee and a chocolate digestive eaten down to a thumbnail sized morsel. Crumbs litter the table like light-brown ants. The back door is closed, a single key protruding from a badly tarnished deadbolt. Besides the obvious signs that somebody has been there, the only other thing that stands out is a copy of a leatherbound book, opened at a page depicting a horned creature with sabre-like teeth, a long mane, unfurled wings and hooked talons engaged in hand-to-hand combat with a bearded man dressed in a long robe.

An image flashes across his eyes, causing the pain in his head to flare like hot magnesium. He turns away, hand pressed against his right temple. He sees a red and black eye, cat-like and dilated. He smells the sulphur, feels the heat of a splintering crack in the earth. He staggers and is only vaguely aware of Bailey's hands on his shoulders.

'Luke,' she says. 'Luke, are you okay?'

He isn't. He's far from it. He knows what's waiting for him, just like he's known all along.

'Come on,' he whispers, feeling his way back along the wall. 'There's nothing in the kitchen.'

He reaches for the cellar door and pulls it further open. It's down there, the thing that's orchestrated everything. This can only end if he faces it. He realises that now.

'Go back to the car,' he says. 'Wait for me there. If I'm not back within thirty minutes, go find Kipruto, tell him that he needs to search this place. He'll find everything he needs here.'

Bailey shakes her head and begins to speak, but Raven doesn't wait for her answer. He steps inside, closes the door and locks it. Beneath him, something stirs.

CHAPTER 58: TUDOR

Lisa slams her foot on the brake. She's seen something, something she can't unsee. Billy has seen it too because he's already out of the car, tugging at the thick blanket covering the shape of a body.

'Oh my God,' Sally says, hand over her mouth.

'She's dead,' Billy replies. 'Whoever that is, she's dead.'

'How?' Lisa asks, suspecting she already knows the answer.

Billy peels the blanket back a little further and gets his answer. 'Jesus bloody Christ,' he cries, recoiling, dropping the blanket and backing away. 'She's got a great big hole in her chest.'

Lisa gets out of the car and starts walking.

'Where are you going?' Sally asks.

'We're sitting ducks in that thing,' she replies, her hand resting on the butt of her gun. 'If Luke's here, he'll be in the house, so I say we go there.'

She hears Sally getting out of the car and her and Billy pacing after her, but right now, all she can think about is getting to Luke. As usual, he's running headlong into a shit show, and just like last time, she's getting dragged along for the ride. She'd gotten used to the idea of bringing up Harry without his biological dad in the picture, but since she'd found out Luke was still a living, breathing thing that could once more be a part of their lives, she's had this image of them sitting round the table, eating pizza and laughing together like a real, no shit family. She won't let anybody take that possibility away from her, even if Luke is doing everything he can to rip her idealistic vision to shreds.

Up ahead, through the narrow aperture of the natural tunnel that blots out most of the sunlight, the cottage comes into view.

It's old, maybe two hundred years plus. The front is white plaster and black Tudor beams. The roof is red tile but not in a good way. Several of them are loose or missing entirely, making the whole thing look like a toothless smile. The chimney sits at an unnatural angle as if it's about to topple, and the gables are misshapen and sunken. The open driveway out front is infested with weeds, dandelions and nettles rising from the discoloured gravel like corpses dragging themselves from unmarked graves. The windows are lead paned and so dark. Even the door is black, painted in a thick pitch that seems to ooze from the ancient wooden slats.

She stops at the end of the entrance road and watches, waiting to see if anybody appears. There's nothing. No noise, no movement. The sky overhead is thick with grey clouds, and the air is damp as the thin mist of drizzling rain begins to contaminate the air.

'What next?' Billy asks, sounding out of breath.

Lisa thinks about that. What is next? Knock on the door? Go round the back? Sit somewhere out of sight and see if anybody makes a move?

'I've heard about this place,' Sally says, breaking the silence. 'It used to belong to a rich landowner back in the day.'

'Used to?' Billy asks.

'Yeah, the guy's dead now.'

'What happened to him?' Lisa asks.

Sally shrugs. 'From what I heard, he hung himself, but that might just be a rumour cooked up by the local gossip hounds.'

'Why would he hang himself if he was rich and had a place like this?' Billy says.

Sally gives the cottage the once over. 'Because this place is evil,' she says.

The words sound crazy spilling from the usually conservative woman's lips, but Lisa can't deny the odd atmosphere, like a thousand eyes are on them, watching their every move. If Luke is here, where is he?

'Fuck this,' she says, and heads straight for the front door.

She hears Billy call out behind her. 'Lis, what are you doing?'

'I'm cutting through the crap.'

She stomps across the gravel, swerves around a patch of brambles that have overtaken a muddy puddle that she assumes used to be some sort of water feature, and slams her hand on the door.

'Hello?' she calls out. 'Anybody home?'

Billy and Sally appear behind her. 'This is not a good idea,' Billy says.

'And your alternative suggestion is?'

'I don't know. Call the police?'

'And tell them what?'

'That there's a corpse on the driveway back there, one that's missing quite an important body part.'

'Luke is the police,' she says, whirling on him. 'And he's here.'

'Or so you think!'

'No, I don't think. I know!'

There's a scrape and a rattle, and the door opens revealing a tall man, a beaming smile shining through thin lips surrounded by a medium length grey beard. He's broad across the shoulders and thick set, but Lisa figures he's in his seventies because of the liver spots on his large hands and heavily lined forehead. The man is dressed in a grey sweatshirt, white collar protruding from a shallow V-neck, and dark blue jeans.

'Hello there,' he says, looking down at her. 'You must be Lisa.'

The familiarity shocks her. How could this stranger possibly know her name? Billy jerks beside her, and she turns to see his face has gone pale and his eyes are as round as teabags.

'Ron?' he says. 'Ronnie Valentine? Is that really you?'

'That's right, Billy old son,' Ronnie replies, reaching out a hand and clapping Billy hard on the shoulder. 'I bet you'd thought you'd seen the last of me.'

CHAPTER 59: DISEASE

The wooden stairs creak beneath Raven's feet. He's not as heavy as when he used to drink every afternoon and through the night, but he's still a big enough unit to cause a disturbance, and the centuries old timber is barely man enough to handle his size ten trainers. He fishes out his phone and flicks on the torch. Beneath him, a dusty, narrow space beckons. He descends one step at a time, taking care not to slip. He has no idea what he's about to face, but he knows that remaining upright is paramount.

The musty, fetid smell is even worse in the cellar. The brick wall is slick with damp. He reaches the floor and turns to face another door, this one smaller and with a single deadbolt holding it in place. He rubs his hands against his trousers, reaches up and attempts to release the lock. The deadbolt won't budge. It's rusted against the cavity. He reaches for his knife and attempts to scrape away some of the persistent corrosion, but it stubbornly clings to what remains of the steel.

'Fuck,' he cries out in frustration, but then spies the hinges which look loose against the frame. He uses his knife, slips it between the flaking wood and metal plate and levers the hinge away, rocking the knife back and forth until the screws fall to the floor. He does the same with the other hinge, and pretty soon the only thing holding the door in place is the rusted deadbolt.

He suppresses a cry of joy, instead choosing to jam his fingertips into the gap around the door, and pulls, leveraging it towards him until there's an opening big enough to slip his fingers through. The other side of the door is warm to the touch and completely dry. The damp hasn't made it all the way through, which is odd. He has no idea what's on the other side of the opening, and the thought causes him to draw his hands away, leaving the door to clatter back against the frame.

'Don't be such a dick,' he says to himself, annoyed by his own jitters, and takes a deep breath before pulling the door towards him once more. With a little jimmying and a lot of heavy breathing, he manages to drag it far enough to create an opening just the right size for his whole body to fit through, even though he has to stoop to allow his head and shoulders to make it through to the other side.

Once there, he finds himself standing in another narrow passageway, this one leading towards the front of the house. The walls are red brick, the floor a mixture of grey dust and fractured concrete. There are no lights so he uses his phone torch again, realising that he only has eighteen percent battery life left. On a phone as old as his, that will probably last him less than ten minutes. If he's going to find whatever it is he's looking for, he'll have to hurry.

He quickens his pace, but there's something about this narrow passage that sets his teeth on edge. It seems to stretch too far into the distance, way beyond the boundary of the house. He guesses he's now standing somewhere beneath the front driveway. He reaches a sharp right-hand turn which leads to a set of stone steps that in turn stretch into a deep, impenetrable blackness. More heat rises from this second stairway where the air is so thick with the putrid smell that he can barely breathe.

He looks down into the darkness. He gets the feeling that something is lying in wait. He can sense it, the toxicity of it. If he goes down there, there's every chance he might never come back. If he turns around, he'll never escape the thing that has been pursuing him, clinging to his skin like a tumour. The Legion has set this trap, and he's walked straight into it, knowing it's the only way, but also knowing there's every chance it will completely consume him.

Lisa's out there somewhere. His son too. Everything inside him yearns for them. The feeling's so strong it makes his insides flip. It's been crushing him ever since his memory came back. If he can just overcome this one, mind-enveloping thing; if he can do something to guarantee their safety. They don't deserve to be infected with his disease.

The cure is down that hole. It has to be. Why stage all of this if it isn't to lure him here?

He checks his phone battery. Ten percent. He has a few minutes left before everything goes dark.

He descends.

CHAPTER 60: BY A WHISKER

'Come on in,' Ronnie says, leading the three of them down a dark hallway before turning left into a large sitting room. The room is sparse. There's a three-seater sofa that's seen better days, a reading chair beside which rests a glass of whiskey, and an old analogue radio playing hits from the sixties.

'Sorry about the décor,' Ronnie adds, eyeing the room. 'Haven't had time to get the decorators in just yet, what with everything that's been going on. My wife keeps on at me to get it done, but you know what it's like, Billy. It's always one thing after another.'

'I didn't know you were married, Ron.' Billy says.

'She's a new bride,' Ronnie replies. 'Brazilian. A right little Latino minx, let me tell you. She's gone back to her mother's house in Sao Paulo for a few weeks, which suits me just fine. This old body can only keep up with someone like that for so long.'

Lisa is trying to hold it together while assessing the situation. She's never met the infamous Ronnie Valentine before, but she's heard all about him. He's the guy that convinced Luke and Billy to join his attempted robbery of the Goldbaum's jewellery shop when they'd both been down on their luck. The only reason the three of them weren't in prison together right now was because Luke had had a change of heart at the last minute and secretly tipped off DCS Christy Devereax, not realising she would send a gang of cronies into the bank to silence them. Luckily, Luke and Billy had escaped along the smuggler's tunnel that eventually led them straight to Molly Staker's underground lair, while Ronnie had cracked the heads of their would-be assassins and disappeared. Now here he is in all his grotesque glory. The only question is, why?

'About what happened,' Billy says. 'It was a mistake, all of it. Raven and me, we didn't know Devereaux was bent.'

'Water under the bridge, Billy my old son,' Ronnie replies, holding up a decanter. 'Best not to dwell on it. Now, can I get any of you lovely people a drink?'

'No thanks,' Lisa replies, lips thin, teeth bared.

'How about you, pretty lady?' Ronnie says, eyeing Sally.

'I'll take a little,' she says, voice trembling.

'Where's Luke?' Lisa asks as Ronnie pours the Scotch.

'You mean your boyfriend, Raven?' he replies, setting the tumbler down beside them.

'The father of my son, yes.'

Ronnie slaps his head. 'Ah, yes, that's right. Raven has a kid, doesn't he. A little boy. Harry, isn't it?'

Lisa doesn't answer. She just glares.

'You seem a little tense, if you don't mind me saying, love,' Ronnie adds, eyes flicking towards Billy. 'Is there something you want to get off your chest?'

'We're just worried about Raven,' Billy says, voice wavering.

'Don't worry about that old bent copper,' Ronnie replies. 'That bloke's got more lives than a Buddhist's cat. I'm sure he'll turn up eventually.'

'Why's there a dead body on your driveway?' Lisa asks, causing Sally to spill her drink.

'A dead body?' Ronnie replies. 'I'm sure you're mistaken Mrs… Draper isn't it?'

Lisa's hands clench into white knuckled fists. 'I'm not fucking mistaken. I saw her. We all did. Somebody cut out her bloody heart.'

Ronnie sets down his own glass and folds his hands in front of him.

'I heard you didn't like small talk, Mrs. Draper, and I can see now that you're the kind of woman who likes to get straight to the point.'

'Why did you send the Medics to kill Luke, and why won't you tell me where he is?'

Ronnie shoots Billy a smirk. 'She likes to ask a lot of questions doesn't she, Billy my boy? I bet she's a nightmare to spend an evening with. "Why" this and "why" that. Sometimes, Lisa, love, you have to accept you might never find the answers you're looking for.'

'Don't call me love,' she spits.

Ronnie stands so suddenly the three of them jolt. He heads to a bookshelf and extracts a dusty brown volume thick enough to prop open a door.

'When your boyfriend threw me to the lions, Mrs. Draper, I found myself on the lam, which isn't exactly a nice way to live your life, right Billy?'

Billy shifts uncomfortably. 'I wouldn't know, Ron.'

'No, but your old man would, and don't try to tell me he wouldn't because I did time in stir with him, didn't I? And I looked after him when he was dying.'

'I know, Ron, and I appreciate that, you know I do.'

'Not enough to tell me what Raven was planning though, was it?' Ronnie replies, slamming the book down on the table, knocking his glass on the floor and spilling whiskey over the rug. 'Now look what you've made me do.'

Ronnie looks down at the toppled glass and slowly spreading brown stain and glares at Billy. 'Clean it up.'

'Wh… what?' Billy asks, glancing at Sally.

'It's a simple request, Billy. You made me spill my drink, now clean it up before it stains my carpet.'

'But… I don't have anything to clean it with.'

'You don't actually have to do it, Bill,' Sally says, eyes flitting back and forth like tennis balls. 'You're joking, right?'

Ronnie turns to her. 'Do I look like I'm joking?'

'It was… an accident,' she says. 'Surely you can see that.'

Ronnie glares at her, eyes like glass. The thick veins in his neck tense. Lisa slowly reaches into her pocket for her gun. She doesn't want to use it, but this guy is something else. The grip feels warm, the trigger sharp and barbed. She thinks about what it might feel like, killing someone. Will it hurt? Will her heart be punctured with remorse? For a moment, she thinks that Ronnie is going to go for Billy's throat with those huge hands of his, but then he makes a gargling noise, his mouth widens, and he starts to laugh, actually full-on giggling.

'You always were easy to wind up, Billy my old son,' he says, slapping a hand on his thick thigh, spittle flying from his lips. Billy seems to shrink like a kid who's been humiliated by his parents. 'Now, where were we. Ah, yes, that's right. We were talking about Luke Raven shopping me to the old bill, weren't we.'

'We haven't got time for this,' Lisa says. 'I know Luke's here, and I know you know where he is.'

'All in good time,' Ronnie replies. 'You see, the point is, Lisa, I was in hiding for a long time. I was bored shitless, to tell you the truth. I couldn't go out for a drink, couldn't head to an Indian restaurant for my favourite meal — a lamb Jalfrezi, extra spicy — couldn't even walk down the street in case somebody recognised me. The Goldbaums were making a big fuss over nothing to that DCS of yours, and because of that, I was a wanted man.'

'You robbed their shop,' Lisa hisses. 'They had every right to want you behind bars.'

'I didn't rob anything thanks to that boyfriend of yours. Didn't walk away with a single penny. As soon as those fellas walked in — waving their guns around like it was some sort of Spaghetti

Western — I knew I had to get out of there. I was on the run from a crime I didn't actually commit.'

'Except you were out on parole, right, Ron?' Billy says, once more finding his voice. 'And getting caught breaking and entering would have been enough to put you back inside.'

'The prize goes to Billy West for being the smartest bloke in the room!' Ronnie cries. 'That's right. Breaching my parole meant I would be looking at another long stretch, possibly long enough to see me through to my grave. You see how that might have pissed me off, Lisa? Do you see now what your fella did to me?'

'Sounds to me like you were the architect of your own downfall,' she replies. 'If you didn't want to go back to prison, you should have stayed clean.'

Ronnie laughs and rolls his eyes at Billy. 'She's a good one, isn't she? Have you ever heard of a career criminal who went completely clean, Bill?'

Billy looks increasingly uncomfortable, but he offers a reply. 'Not that I can think of, Ron.'

'Not even your old man could stay on the outside for long, could he? Got himself nicked for holding up a corner shop if my memory serves me correctly.'

'He didn't hurt anybody, though. He was a good man,' Billy replies, but Lisa can see Ronnie's recollections have left an indelible mark.

Ronnie reaches down and picks up the thick book. He slaps a hand on the cover.

'Do you ever read the bible, Lisa?'

The question catches her off guard, but she spits out an answer. 'I don't read bullshit.'

'My thoughts exactly. A load of fairytale claptrap cooked up by a bunch of kiddie-fiddling nonces with nothing better to do than spout off their holier than thou proverbs to distract us from what they were really doing. If you ask me, the whole lot of them should be tied to an inverted crucifix and burned to death.'

'Is this going anywhere?' she asks. 'Because it seems to me you're stalling.'

'Not in the slightest, although I understand why you might think that. You see, my dear, what I'm trying to explain is how I managed to get myself out of that dark, cavernous pit your boyfriend left me in.'

'By talking your way out of it, I assume.'

'Almost!' he cries. 'You very nearly hit the nail on the proverbial head there, love, but you missed by a whisker. You see, when Raven and Billy here chased that young woman back to her father's place, and then that poor girl blew her daddy's head off, he inadvertently put an indefinite pause in the operations of an organisation designed to keep the whole world in balance. You… you've heard of them, right?'

'The Legion,' Lisa says, feeling her heart blacken.

'The Legion!' Ronnie replies. 'You've got it.'

'A bunch of sado-masochistic murderers,' she spits back. 'What have they got to do with any of this?'

'Not *they*,' Ronnie replies, looking up as a man with a neat crop of blonde hair appears in the doorway. '*Us*.'

Ronnie's bodyguard enters the room, hands thrust deep in his pockets, piercing blues eyes scanning the group.

'Hi, Conor,' Billy says.

'How you doing, Billy?' Conor Byrne asks. 'See you still haven't lost the weight.'

'Oh, you know,' Billy replies. 'Every day's a struggle.'

'Jesus,' Sally says. 'Billy, do you know every criminal in Westhampton?'

Billy shrugs. 'It's the job. I meet a lot of people.'

'Billy did the rewiring at the club,' Byrne says. 'Gave me a nice discount, too.'

Sally exhales, glaring at her husband like she's caught him in the next-door-neighbour's bed.

'You sent someone to kill Luke Raven,' Lisa growls at Byrne, hand still resting against the gun's grip.

'Guy's a bunch of unnecessary trouble,' Byrne replies. 'For everybody.'

'He's the father of my son.'

'Your boy would be better off without him if you ask me.'

'What gives you the right to make that decision?'

Byrne studies her, eyes lifeless and cold. 'I get to make any decision I fucking want, lady.'

'Now, now, Conor,' Ronnie interjects. 'Let's not let this little chat descend into unnecessary obscenities.'

'Let me spare your blushes,' Lisa hisses. 'I don't care if you're part of The Legion, Ronnie, or if your little lapdog here uses every swear word in the English language. I want you to tell me where Luke is, and I want you to tell me now!'

She pulls the gun, thrusting it in front of her, hands trembling. Sally gasps, Billy looks at her like she's lost her mind, and Ronnie laughs.

'She's got a little pea shooter, Conor!' he says. 'The woman thinks she's Calamity Jane.'

'I'll blow your fucking head off if you don't answer my question,' Lisa says, voice quivering.

'Not with that thing,' Conor says, steely eyes penetrating her soul. 'You'll barely break the skin.'

'Just fucking try me,' Lisa replies, trying to hold it together. 'Go on, I dare you.'

'What do you think, Conor?' Ronnie asks. 'Do you think she means it?'

'I think she's standing there defecating in her own knickers right at this second, Ron. I doubt if she even knows which way round that thing works.'

Lisa shoots the wall behind them, sending a cloud of damp plaster and brick dust raining down on them.

'Is that enough to convince you?' she says.

'Doesn't mean you've got the guts to shoot a real person,' Byrne replies.

'Then I suggest you call your little boy, Tadhg,' she says. 'Ask him how that hole in his leg's doing.'

That remark hits home, and Byrne's hardened expression cracks just a little. It gives Lisa the confidence she needs.

'Now, how about you lead me to where Luke is,' she says. 'Or one of you is taking one for the team.'

Ronnie doesn't blink or move. He's mulling it over. She doesn't know if she's achieved what she set out to do, or whether she's just poked a very nasty, ugly looking bear, but before she has a chance to press home her advantage, the big guy's expression changes.

'Right-o,' Ronnie says. 'As you've put it so succinctly, why don't we do exactly as you ask and take you to your fella. I'm sure he'll be just as pleased to see you as we are.'

Lisa watches as Ronnie gestures to Byrne. The crime boss-cum-bodyguard heads out into the hallway. She glances at Billy who's been glaring at her the whole time, and Sally, who seems to be on the verge of a panic attack, and cocks her head towards the door.

'This is a really bad idea,' Billy whispers.

'Maybe, but what choice do we have?'

She turns and follows the Irishman, but when Billy and Sally go after her, Ronnie shakes his head.

'Not you two,' he says. 'This offer is for the pretty redhead only.'

'You want me to go on my own?' she asks, her resolve wavering.

'I'm afraid so.'

'But—'

'What have you got to worry about, my dear?' Ronnie says. 'You're the one holding the gun.'

She considers her choices. It's pretty clear she's being tricked, but even if she is, what do the two men have to gain? The old guy's right. She does have the gun, which gives her an advantage. If the Irishman tries anything, she shoots him and then comes back to finish the job. Whichever way she looks at it, she's got the upper hand.

She gives Billy a knowing glance and offers a nervous smile. 'I'll be okay.'

Billy shakes his head, but her mind's made up.

'That's a good girl,' Ronnie says, winking at her as she departs. 'Conor will take you to Raven, and then this whole silly situation can be put to bed.'

She tries to shut out the crippling fear that claws at her with grasping fingers, and she steps out into the darkened hallway. She knows Byrne's going to try something at some point, and she'll have to be ready. She reconciles herself to that, because she's got the bit between her teeth and her snarling anger will keep her sharp. She's going to find Luke, and for the sake of her son, she's going to bring him home.

CHAPTER 61: MICKEY

Allison Bailey sits in the car, furious at Raven for locking her out like that. What was he thinking? She didn't even want to go into the cottage, and yet she found herself alone in the hallway, wondering how long it would take before the owner turned up and caught her with her knickers around her ankles, metaphorically speaking. After five minutes of weighing up her options, she decided that the only way forward was to go out the way they came in and do exactly what Raven said, despite her pride not wanting to give him the satisfaction. She'll vent her anger at him when he returns to the car though, because there's nothing in that basement, just like there's nothing in that cottage. Whoever killed Chapman is long gone.

She considers calling Kipruto and letting him know what Raven's up to, but she decides against it because she still has some loyalty to her partner. She's been a part of his team since she was a lowly junior PC, and even though he's dragged her and everybody else he's ever worked with through a swamp filled with faeces and human detritus on more occasions than she can count, there's something about him that makes her want to stand by him. Raven is more sincere than anybody she's ever met. She knows where she stands with him. There's no bullshit, no flannel. He doesn't even hide his flaws. It's endearing, but it's also extremely annoying.

She thinks about her boyfriend, Rory. He's different to Raven in so many ways. She never knows where she stands with him. One day he's buying her flowers and chocolates, the next he's off on yet another work's trip and she doesn't hear from him for days. In one moment, he's kissing her tenderly, telling her how he can't get enough of her, how she makes him so horny it hurts, and the next he's on his phone, scrolling for hours through Tik-Tok videos and barely paying her any attention. If Raven is an open book, Rory is as impenetrable as a bullet-proof vest. Perhaps that's why she likes Luke. He's the perfect counterpoint to her apathetic home life.

She likes her job. No, she loves it. There was a time when black coppers — especially black female coppers — had to fight tooth and nail to even hope to compete with their white male colleagues, but those times have changed. She despises government attempts at levelling-up by introducing ill-advised diversity quotas and forcing their white compatriots to employ 'people of colour' (another phrase she hates), but at least things are moving in the right direction. It's opened up an opportunity for her, and she's seized it with both hands, rising to the rank of detective through hard work, dedication, and above all, capability. She was always a good PC, and she's an even better detective. Raven can see that and so can Kipruto. She knows that by giving Raven the address and postcode of The Legion's supposed HQ she's taken a risk — possibly one that will backfire badly — but she's made it this far by following her nose. As far as she's concerned, Raven's been on the money ever since he came back, and Kipruto and the others have been putting obstacles in the way. Sure, there was nobody in the cottage, but that doesn't mean they're in the wrong place. There's no denying the body on the driveway, and there's no ignoring the coffee cup and half-smoked cigar on the kitchen table. Somebody's been here, and as far as she's concerned, that somebody is inexorably linked to The Heart Breaker murders. They just have to be patient.

Raven going into the cellar was a curveball that dented her resolve, but even the best coppers make mistakes. The guy's nothing if not persistent. He'll scan the downstairs area and come back with his tail between his legs. In the meantime, she'll wait for him to return and then give him a piece of her mind. She's an open book too.

She doesn't see the man standing behind the car or hear him as he approaches. When he opens the door and slips in beside her, she almost has a heart attack.

'Hello Detective,' the man says.

'What the fuck are you doing here?' she replies, reaching for her gun.

'I wouldn't,' he says, shoving the muzzle of his own Glock at her face. 'Blood tends to stain the upholstery.'

She runs his image through her jumbled memory and lands on the recent altercation at the snooker hall.

'Shane Byrne,' she says.

'One and the same.'

'Conor's cousin.'

'You're smarter than you look.'

'Raven was right. You're all on the payroll of whoever owns this place.'

'We have a mutually beneficial collaboration, yes,' Byrne says. 'We look after The Legion's interests, and they see to it that we can run our operation uninterrupted.'

'I thought you'd have more self-respect than that. Tell me, do you bend over for everyone who strokes your ego.'

His cheek twitches, and for a second, she thinks he's going to pull the trigger. When he doesn't, she lets out a breath.

'I'll let you have that one, copper,' he says. 'I warn you, though, one more and you'll be kissing goodbye to that pretty face of yours.'

She feigns arrogance. 'Aw, I bet you say that to all the girls.'

He ignores the sarcasm. 'Tell me, what's Raven up to in there?'

'He's looking for the killer.'

'Then he's in the wrong place. She's out there in the bushes.'

'There's two problems with that,' she replies, taking her time, trying to stall. 'One, when the last victim was killed, she was with us, and two, murderers don't usually cut out their own hearts.'

'Who's to say she didn't pay someone to kill that queer and then take her heart as one final act of contrition?'

'Did you meet Kaden Chapman?' she replies. 'She didn't have an ounce of contrition, not one.' She lets out a strangled laugh. 'I think your theory can be put on the shelf along with aliens crashing in Texas and some remote-controlled drone taking down the World Trade Centre.'

Byrne gives her a toothless smile, raising one eyebrow as he looks her up and down.

'You know, you're not bad on the eye for a black copper.'

'Just copper will do, but I appreciate the racist complement.'

'I might just fuck you before I kill you.'

Bailey's confidence falters. Hearing the 'K' word out loud is like injecting neat caffeine into her bloodstream.

'Not a smart move. That's not the kind of crime you can walk away from,' she says.

'Oh, you'd be surprised.' He winks, running a coarse finger down her cheek. 'I have friends in high places now.'

She tries to pull herself away, but Byrne grips her wrist with his free hand, dragging her towards him like a dog.

'How about we have ourselves a little fun, and then maybe I'll let you go, assuming you do yourself justice, if you know what I mean.'

She's so close to him now, she can smell the whiskey on his breath. The pulse in her neck is thrumming so fast, her head is spinning.

'How about you go fuck yourself.'

He punches her in the face, splitting her lip and filling her mouth with coppery stickiness. She raises her hands to protect herself, but he punches her again, this time in the nose, sending her vision swimming.

'I'm the one making the demands around here!' Byrne yells, spittle flying from his mouth. 'You're just a dumb black bitch who can't keep her nose out of other people's business.'

'Shane Byrne,' she says, spitting blood in her lap. 'I'm arresting you on suspicion of the murder of—'

He hits her in the throat, crushing her larynx. She tries to draw in oxygen, but she can barely manage it. She blindly reaches for the door handle, grasps at it and misses, but she gets there at the second attempt, pushing the door open with her shoulder and spilling out onto the patchy grass and dry earth. She vaguely hears another door opening and closing as she lies there, cheek pressed against the ground, gasping and wheezing.

'I was gonna give you a chance,' Byrne says, sounding out of breath. 'But you've been so fucking rude, I hardly think you deserve it.'

She remembers she has a gun, but as she lifts a hand to reach for it, Byrne stamps on her fingers, breaking two of them. She cries out, but it's just a hoarse, crackling exhale.

'Look at you, copper,' he says. 'Lying there in the dirt like a fucking tramp. If I hadn't just been to the toilet, I might have whipped out my mickey and pissed all over yers.'

She tries to crawl away, but her right hand is useless and her body is so starved of oxygen, it's barely mobile. She flips onto her back instead and looks up at her attacker, the oily black of his eyes, the palpable excitement building in his temples. He's smiling down at her, willing for her to do something stupid. She wouldn't, even if she could. She's been in the presence of death before when her mother passed, and she's looking right at it now.

She thinks about Rory, about what he might do when they break the news to him. Maybe he'll be happy. Their relationship was balancing on a thin wire anyway. Then she thinks about

Raven down there in the cellar, searching for something that's been eluding him ever since the two of them met. She hopes he finds it. She hopes he makes it out alive.

Panic grips her. She's so desperately scared of death. She doesn't want the lights to go out. She can't bear the thought of not being able to see her family again.

When Byrne stoops down, pulls her gun from her holster and turns it on her, she fights back the tears. She doesn't want that to be the last the world sees of her, the bloodied, battered mess of a woman who's only act of self-defence is to turn on the waterworks. She sneers instead, a hateful, spiteful act of defiance she hopes this bastard will never forget.

'Do it,' she says. 'Pull the fucking trigger. Put a bullet in my head, but don't think you're getting rid of me, because I'll come back and haunt the shit out of you. When I'm done, you'll be too afraid to look at yourself in the mirror because I'll be standing right there behind you.'

'I don't think so, Detective,' Byrne says, his tongue tracing the line of his lips. 'I don't believe in ghosts.'

There's a loud, ear-splitting retort, and then everything blinks out. There's just darkness. Utter, world-destroying nothingness.

CHAPTER 62: TORTURED

Darkness is a strange thing. It robs you of your sight but heightens a whole bunch of other senses you didn't know you had. Try to whisper an insult at a blind person and you'll find out just how good their hearing is. Try the smell test on somebody who's hard of hearing, and you'll be amazed at how keen their noses are.

Raven's phone battery doesn't last ten minutes. It barely lasts ten seconds. He's halfway down the stone staircase when it blinks out, and then he's floundering in the black with no idea how to get back. He holds out his hands and traces his fingers along the warm surface of the uneven wall, tentatively putting one foot in front of the other, making sure he doesn't slip and fall. He doesn't know how far the staircase goes, but he suspects it's far enough for him to break his neck if he's careless enough.

He stands there, thinking about what his next move is. He's come this far. He doesn't know what's down here in the deep, but he's pretty sure it's what he's been searching for. The identity of the people who manipulated Kaden Chapman into doing what she did and, perhaps, answers — answers that might tell him why he's this strange, fucked up, self-destructive, nihilistic, car-crash of a human who destroys everything and anything he's ever cared about. He doesn't deserve Lisa, and he definitely doesn't deserve a son like Harry. Their lives have been good while he's been gone, and he intends for them to stay that way. All he wants now is closure, and if floundering around in some underground network of passages and staircases until he eventually suffocates or dies of thirst is the way to get it, then that's fine by him.

He presses on, taking step after step, feeling for the indentations in the stone and the uneven width of each little ledge.

It's so hot down here, as if someone has deliberately switched on the heating. He unfastens a button of his shirt and hitches his collar away from his skin. Sweat drips from one throbbing temple down his left cheek. He's burning up from the inside out. He needs to find the bottom, has to locate a breeze, a shaft of cool air, anything.

His foot touches a covering of dust, and his hand finds the edge of the wall. He chances his other foot, and that finds the same grimy path. He reaches out a hand and finds a wall to his right and straight ahead. The staircase disappears behind him, and he's in a narrow passage that heads left. He follows it, both hands on the walls, eyes frantically scouring the oily nothingness for any sign of movement.

His mind plays tricks on him. There are bats flapping leathery wings in front of his face, moths flittering beside his ear, their dark heads tattooed with images of human skulls. There's a mischief of giant black rats running away from him, long tails weaving tapestries in the dust, and huge spiders covered in thick black hairs abseiling from the ceiling on dark grey threads, their sticky, silken webs clinging to his hair and skin.

He knows he's seeing things, that his consciousness is now as fragmented as his nightmarish premonitions, but he can't toss the images away. He throws out an arm, trying to swat a giant dragonfly that incessantly circles his head, but he overreaches and trips over his own feet, sent sprawling onto the dirt and stone, grainy fragments of decades old dust showering his eyes and mouth.

He hasn't made it far, barely thirty feet, but he hears a sound. He sits up, brushing the filth away. There's somebody up ahead. He can feel them, can hear their footsteps as they approach. He's suddenly afraid of the dark, as if his adult sensibilities have drifted from him like vapour. He rises to his feet, narrows his eyes, peering into an impenetrable emptiness. Then he sees him, the man he knows well.

'Hello, Dad.'

'Hello, Son.'

Sam Raven is dressed in a checked shirt and smart jeans, his grey hair cut short, his beard well-trimmed. He looks healthy. Something about that makes Raven mad.

'I thought you were dead,' he hisses.

'Don't believe everything you read, Luke. Didn't I teach you anything?'

Raven shakes his head, trying to toss out the insanity. This can't be his dad because his dad was killed by Bernie Staker and Robert Charon in a beach-house not far from where they're now standing. He's a ghost, he has to be, even though Raven doesn't believe in such crazy notions.

'Why are you here?'

His dad cocks his head to one side. 'Haven't you heard? This is where it ends.'

'I guessed as much. I assume you've come to watch me fail.'

'I've come to make sure it gets done, if that's what you mean.'

Raven feels bile rise in his throat like bitter lemon. 'You always enjoyed watching me stumble, as if you were afraid I would one day beat you at your own game.'

'And what game is that?'

'Fucking up people's lives.'

Raven is so angry now, his voice trembles around the edges.

'I saved people's lives,' his dad says. 'Just ask Lisa. She would never have got away from Staker if I hadn't intervened.'

'She would never have been there in the first place if it wasn't for you. Me and Mum, we didn't want you back. We'd already buried you.'

Sam Raven throws back a head and laughs. 'If there's one thing The Legion got right, it's that the dead never stay dead for long. Everybody has a second coming.'

The words hit home. Raven dwells on them like some unsolvable puzzle. Is this his second coming? Maybe everything that's happened since he escaped from the cottage is his second chance? If so, he's making a mess of everything. He could have gone to see Lisa; he could have spent time with his son. Instead, his been wallowing in self-pity, chasing ghosts, trying to solve a case that he's fabricated some connection to just so he can avoid confronting the terrible truth: he's lost Lisa and he's lost his son. Those two facts are as inescapable as death.

'I don't need you,' he grunts, pushing past his father, leaving him in his wake.

'We knew you were special, even before you were born,' his dad calls after him, but Raven can't focus on words or thoughts. He just has to keep moving, keep going forward. If this really is his final act, he plans to see it through. There's too much at stake to falter now.

With his father's ghost now just a fractious memory, he sees a light, the flickering orange of a candle up ahead through a narrow doorway. He races to it, his heart like a dead weight in his chest. Somebody steps across the candle's meagre light, a darkness that infiltrates the gloom, and then it's gone.

He reaches the opening and tentatively looks inside. There's a room. No, a space, a large, circular rotunda with inscriptions on the walls and paintings on the ceiling. He looks up at them, the depictions of winged creatures, barbed talons, rancid claws, blood-red eyes peering out from within hideous, ill-defined faces; bodies strewn like litter across vast open spaces, buildings burning like roman candles, mothers shrieking as children in swaddling are tossed from open windows high up in tower blocks made from matchsticks and straw.

The writing on the wall is indecipherable, a jumbled, hand-etched collection of strange runes and swirling lines moving from right to left. Raven runs a hand over them and feels the sharp, jaggedness of the carved stone. He feels something else too, a strange sort of incoherent familiarity that triggers anger and a sickening dread.

'You found the place, then,' somebody says in a thick Dublin accent.

Raven turns to the voice. Conor Byrne is crouching in the corner, blood dripping from one wilting hand, fingers hanging like willow leaves.

'What are you doing here, Conor?'

'The same reason you are. To find answers.'

'I'm here to solve a case. You and whoever runs this place have been up to no good.'

Conor lets out a wheezing laugh, ending with a wet, rattling cough. He leans over and hocks a thick wad of phlegm onto the floor. It's laced with red, too.

'You're hurt,' Raven says.

'Nothing I won't recover from,' Conor replies. 'A little blood here and there, it comes with the job, right?'

'My job and your job hardly compare. I try to save lives. You do whatever you can to ruin them.'

'Bollocks,' Conor grunts, standing upright, walking slowly across the open space. There's a blood stain on his shirt and a hole just beneath his ribs. He shuffles, pulling one leg behind him as if it's broken. He glances towards a dark place just out of the candle's reach. 'I give people what they want. You think this country gives a shit about the bottom feeders, the people who can barely keep a roof over their heads or put food in their cupboards. What I provide them is a release.'

'A release they can't afford, but one they can't ignore,' Raven says. 'And it's not just the drugs, is it? You intimidate people, break their bones if they dare go against what you and your gang demand. You're a bully, Conor, always have been. That half-wit cousin of yours, too. You think you're bigger than the average working person, better than them, but you're not. You're just some wet shit on the boot of a society that's fed up with low-life, wannabe crims like you. You're becoming extinct, mate, and I bet that hurts. It's probably why you signed up to go along with this load of horseshit, too.'

Conor laughs again, but this time the pain is etched into his face like a disease. He shoots another glance into the darkness before turning his attention to Raven 'You think this is horseshit? You're the bloke that's at the centre of it all?'

Raven rocks back on his heels. 'At the centre of it? I've been trying to stop it ever since that nutter Richards began cutting people up.'

'I was told you'd say that,' Conor says, hand pressed hard against his oozing wound. 'I said, "Nah, he'd never try that one on someone like me. He knows me too well." And yet here you are, doing exactly what the boss said you'd do.'

'And who is this boss?' Raven asks. 'Who's the big bad who's been pulling your strings?'

'You'll find out when he's ready,' Conor replies, a line of blood running from his open mouth. 'Until then, I've been told to keep you here.'

'Why here? Why drag me down into this room when all of this could have been settled back at the snooker hall?'

'Because you don't die easily, Raven. We keep knocking you down, and you keep getting that stubborn ass of yours back up again. This would have been so much easier if the Staker girl had killed you back at the cottage.'

'And rob us of all this fun?' Raven sneers. 'You're going down for this, Conor. You and your boss. There's no getting away from it. You're getting sloppy. You left a body on the driveway, for God's sake.'

'Doesn't matter,' Conor replies. 'We left her there for a reason. To draw you in. Now you're here, we won't let you walk away.'

Conor stands beside the large candlestick holding the gradually diminishing flame and turns back to the darkness. He pulls another, longer candle from his pocket, just as the first flame begins to flicker out, and he lights it, cupping his hands around the tip until the fire has gotten its hooks into the wick. He slowly bends down to a dark groove in the ground, touches the flame to the indentation, and steps back as the groove catches with a long line of flame that runs from his boot, racing across the floor, illuminating everything around it, before it encircles the darkest recess of the rotunda, flickering fire six inches tall surrounding a crumpled huddle in the dust.

Raven turns to Byrne, the candle in his hand illuminating his sickly grin, red lips painted in his own lifeblood.

'Recognise her?' Byrne asks, cocking his head to the faceless mass.

The dread in Raven's stomach is heavy, like a lump of dried cement. He crosses the room, not wanting to look, but unable to tear his gaze away. The slim body, well-worn T-shirt, tattoo on the side of a petite hand, red nails, red hair.

'Lisa?' he asks, but the body doesn't move. There are bloodstains drenched into the stone all around her. She's face down with her head turned away from him, her body motionless, no sign of breathing. No sign of anything.

Raven whirls on Byrne. 'What have you done?'

Byrne's expression is unmoved, not even the hint of a flicker in his dark eyes. He simply stares at the body, as if Lisa is a memory he's forced to hide. 'She fucking shot me,' he says.

Raven doesn't think. He runs headlong at the crime boss, slamming his fist into his face, knocking him to the ground, raining blow after blow on him, splitting his cheek, fracturing his eye socket, knocking out teeth. Byrne holds up his hands and tries to defend himself, but blood is still pouring from the bullet wound in his side and his body is weak. Raven hears himself grunting, spitting, cursing like a wild animal. He feels the crunch of bone beneath his fists, the tenderising of flesh under his heavy blows, the warm slick of blood as his knuckles split and tear. All he can see is Lisa's face the last time he saw her. She had been so determined then, so steadfastly brave. She'd stood up to a vicious gang of murderers and rapists and defied them to harm her child. Now she's lying in an underground hideout, brutalised, her life-force extinguished, her body slowly turning cold. He can't bear the thought of it. He can't even begin to believe it.

His arms ache, his fists hurt, but he keeps lashing out, keeps raining down the blows, smashing and hammering and clawing until Conor Byrne is nothing more than mashed meat and splintered bone.

He rolls off the body, unable to look at what he's done, and throws up. His vomit fills the shallow, flame filled trough, extinguishing some of the fire in a pool of bile and stomach contents. A long line of drool hangs from his lips. His breath catches in his throat. He sees Lisa's bare foot, her casual trainer lying next to her exposed calf. She's dead. He should have been there for her. He should have gone to her straight away rather than standing in the street like some scorned lover. He should have protected them. He should never have led The Legion back to her. She'd had nothing to do with this.

Blood runs towards him like a tide he can't escape. He knows it belongs to Byrne, but it feels like his own. He's no better than them now, as guilty as Kaden Chapman or Molly Staker, or even Anthony Richards. The bodies that have been mounting up in

Westhampton since those goddam dreams began to haunt his tortured mind are all on him, because he brought the rain of blood to the town.

He wants to go to Lisa but he can't bring himself to. If he sees her face, if he sees that she's no longer there, there'll be no turning back. There'll be no denying it, no trying to forget, no hope that this has all been some kind of ridiculous, soul crushing mistake.

The light falters as the flames fade. Raven is surrounded by death. He sits there, head between his knees, breath ragged, waiting for the darkness to return. It doesn't matter anymore, nothing does. He's lost it all, everything he ever thought he had. Maybe it was all just a lie, a sweet apple laced with bitter arsenic. Shadows creep in from the edges of the room like a black tide, drifting over Byrne's bloodied torso, slithering towards Raven's feet, his legs, his buttocks. His eyes are fixed on Lisa as the flames flicker to almost nothing. She's so close to him, less than a dozen feet, but she may as well be in another dimension. He's let her go. He's failed her.

He lowers his eyes, no longer able to take in the sight of her lying there. He doesn't see the runes on the wall glow with an otherworldly luminance, the mural on the ceiling start to blur and shift, or the body among the flames move slowly, hands pressed to the floor, arms tensing, back arching, torso shifting and twisting until she's sitting upright, facing him, black eyes peering out through a hanging mop of dark, obsidian curls.

CHAPTER 63: SYLLABLES

Billy sits on the sofa, gripping his wife's hand, wondering where the hell Lisa is. He doesn't know what Ronnie has planned for them, but he's pretty sure that Lisa's P365 will be about as effective as a spud gun. He should never have agreed to go with Raven's ex, and he definitely shouldn't have insisted Sally come with them. They're in a world of trouble, and unless Ronnie has some sort of crisis of conscience, he's pretty sure the guy who spent almost ten years inside with his dad is planning on killing all three of them.

'Maybe we should be on our way,' Billy says, puffing out his cheeks. 'It's getting late, and I've got an early start in the morning. You know what old people are like. One minute late and you're basically written off as unreliable.'

'But if you go, you'll be leaving your little friend with the attitude behind,' Ronnie replies. 'I don't think she'd like that, do you?'

Billy shrugs. 'Lisa's a big girl. She can look after herself. You probably noticed she likes to get her own way.'

Ronnie gets up and looks out the window, as if something's caught his attention. Sally grips Billy's hand a little harder and he shoots her a sideways glance. Her pupils are flicking to the right at something on the coffee table. Billy doesn't see it at first. He's too distracted by everything going on around him. Somebody's walking across the gravel driveway from the direction of the metal storage unit on the other side of the unkempt lawn. Because of the distance, he doesn't recognise him at first, but then the realisation dawns on him. It's Shane Byrne with blood on his shirt and hands.

'I wonder what's keeping them,' Ronnie says, cracking his knuckles, eyes fixed on the approaching visitor. 'Raven is only downstairs, after all. Shouldn't have taken them more than ten minutes to go fetch him.'

'What's he doing down there?' Billy asks, trying to force moisture into his cotton-wool mouth.

'Playing silly buggers, I expect,' Ronnie replies. 'The guy doesn't know when he's beaten, Billy. A bit like you, I suppose.'

Sally tugs at her husband's hand a little harder, and this time he spots it. A corkscrew. Gleaming, twisting metal jutting from a dark, cylindrical handle. Does she want him to kill Ronnie? Could he even do that?

'You see, we had this whole thing figured out all along. It was just a matter of time, of getting all the pieces in place, making the right sacrifices, and then making the bait so enticing, so downright unignorable, that Raven just couldn't resist.'

Shane is getting closer and he's carrying a gun. He's got that look in his eyes, the one that says he's in for a penny already so why not go the whole hog. Billy suspects that he's the hog and Sally's the collateral damage. He knew leaving Ronnie in the vault was a bad idea, but he never realised it would come back and bite him on the arse so terminally.

'We won't say anything, Ron,' he says. 'That thing with the girl on the driveway, it didn't happen. We didn't see it. We didn't see anything. Sal, tell him we didn't see it.'

Sally doesn't answer because she's too busy looking at the corkscrew, but it's too far away from Billy for him to do anything with it. If he makes a move, Ronnie will see, and he'll be no match against the big guy. Ronnie was heavyweight boxing champ on the inside, and his hands are bigger than Billy's head.

'There's no rowing back from this, I'm afraid,' Ronnie says. 'You picked your side the moment you left me down the hole, and ever since then, your card's been marked. Your dad would have been so disappointed with you.' Ronnie's back is to them, but Billy can see the anger tensing in the tendons of his neck. 'Unluckily for you, I've now got the resources and the influence to do something about it.'

Billy swallows empty air. It's one thing suspecting you're in it up to your ears, but it's another thing hearing it out loud. Sally's stopped tugging his hand which he reasons is a sign she knows it's hopeless, too. Lisa's dead, Raven's nowhere to be seen, and the two of them are backed into a corner with no means of escape.

'I'm sorry, Ron,' Billy pleads. 'I'm sorry for what we did. I know it was a shitty thing to do, and I understand if you want to take it out on me. But please, please, let Sally go. She had nothing to do with what went on at the Greenbaums', and she's a really good person. Like, really good. The best.' Sally manoeuvres against him. He wants to hold her, to tell her it'll be okay, but he can't, because it won't. Shane's standing in the doorway looking like he wants to butcher anything he sees.

'Is it done?' Ronnie asks.

'Easy as killing a pig,' Byrne replies, wiping the back of a crimson-soaked hand across his mouth. 'You want me to do these two, too?'

Ronnie turns to face them. 'I don't know yet. What do you think Bill? Shall I get Shane to show the pair of you a good time?'

Billy shakes his head. 'With all due respect, Ron, I was hoping you wouldn't.'

Ronnie runs his fingers through his beard, cigar shaped digits caressing his lips, his dark eyes like thin recesses.

'You see, you weren't supposed to come here,' he says. 'Raven, yes; the girl, Lisa, perhaps; but you two? I thought you had more sense.'

'You sent someone round our house to kill Luke and kill us too,' Sally hisses, causing Billy to whirl towards her.

'Sal!' he exclaims.

'No, Billy. He has to hear this. He's trying to spin us a line, telling us we're just collateral, but those two men who showed up at our house were going to kill me. You, too, if you hadn't shot one of them.' She snarls at Ronnie. 'You think you're the big guy, threatening two unarmed people just to get what you want. Well I'm not standing for it. If you want to kill us, just go ahead and do it, but I won't give you the satisfaction of hearing me beg for my life, because as far as I'm concerned, you're not worth the syllables.'

At first, Billy thinks the big guy's going to give Shane Byrne the nod, but Ronnie's hardened expression cracks and he starts to laugh.

'Two firecrackers for the price of one,' Ronnie says, slapping a hand on his thigh. 'I have to give it to you, Billy. You surround yourself with the kind of women I could get used to.'

Billy smiles half-heartedly, but it's Sally who fires back.

'We're also independent, free-spirited women who deserve to be spoken to directly, not the kind that jumped-up, flaccid dicked bullies like you get to refer to in the third person.'

Billy's heart freezes, a block of solid ice that turns every blood cell in his body cold.

'She doesn't mean that, Ron. She's just emotional.'

'The fuck I am!' Sally replies, her voice shrill. 'These people are going to kill us, Billy. Can't you see that. It doesn't matter what we say or do, your so-called mate is going to get his Irish Whitey Bulger wannabe to cut our throats and leave our bodies out on that driveway along with that poor girl they also butchered, and there's nothing we can do about it.'

'She's right, Bill,' Ronnie says, nodding. 'I know I'm acting like I'm thinking it over, but the thing is, you've seen and heard too much.'

Billy's stomach flips and his eyes glass over. 'But not Sally,' he says. 'Not my Sal.'

'I'm afraid so, mate. You've left me with no option.'

He turns to Byrne who responds by pulling a knife from his jacket and wiping it on his trouser leg. He approaches, his expression stoic, eyes laser focussed.

'Let's talk about this, Shane,' Billy says, hands held out defensively.

'Talking's over,' Byrne replies and plunges the knife through Billy's palm, driving him to the ground. Billy cries out in pain, Sally screams, and Byrne lifts the knife again. This time Billy knows his hands won't protect him, and the knife comes down like the executioner's axe. Outside, the birds chirp, the wind howls, and a car screeches across the driveway, siren blaring.

CHAPTER 64: DEATH MASK

Randall Kipruto has always been an observant man. That's part of the reason he was a good detective. The ability to take in every detail in a microsecond. He spies the body covered in a blanket at the side of the gravel track and realises that there's really nothing he can do for whoever the poor victim is beneath the white spotted, beige covering. He also spots Allison Bailey's car parked behind the metal container and the detective's body beside it, blood caked around the deep gash in her throat, eyes staring skyward, mouth open. He sees these horrors but reacts dispassionately, because that's what his years of training and experience in the field ingrained into him. His lack of emotion isn't callousness or a lack of remorse; it's a mask his mind deploys in moments of high stress and intense strain. His brain calculates that if there are two bodies on the property, there are likely more, but it's also equally likely that Luke Raven needs his help, and his slate with the DI already contains more debt than his performance to date has been able to pay back.

He spies the cottage, sees the dilapidated state of the exterior, and then clocks the large front-room window and the four people standing behind it. He recognises Billy West instantly, guesses the woman standing beside him is his wife, and then spies Ronnie Valentine, the man he realised several weeks ago is now the head of the local Legion faction. When he sees The Medic's main enforcer, Shane Byrne, lunge at Billy with a knife, he slams on the brakes, causing the rear of the car to spin out, spraying gravel and dust like confetti.

He throws open the door, hand moving towards his gun automatically, and runs towards the building. Everything thereafter seems to happen in super-slow-time. He sees the knife come down and pierce Billy's hand, he sees Billy's wife screaming and trying to push Byrne away, and then he sees Byrne raise the knife again and drive it into Billy's shoulder. Billy's wife claws at Byrne's face, but the Irishman tosses her aside. Ronnie's just standing there like a statue, a silent observer, taking in the carnage. Billy's on his knees, his face a death mask of pain, but he turns to his wife, chest bathed in blood, and he calls to her. She rises to her knees and screams at her husband to move, but Byrne's too fast and he lunges for the terrified woman. Despite Billy's injuries, he dives in the way, preventing Byrne from plunging the blade into his wife's head, but the edge of the weapon catches his throat and blood spurts from the wound. Byrne has the bit between his teeth now and looms over Billy, mouth snarling, muscles tensed. He takes a breath and raises the weapon once more, but Kipruto doesn't hesitate. He opens fire, shattering the window and catching the enforcer in the chest and stomach.

'Everybody on the ground,' he yells as he runs towards the window, but Ronnie is already on his heels and heads out into the hallway.

Kipruto clambers through the remains of the window and runs to Billy. His wife is with him, cradling his head in her lap, hand pressed to the gash in his neck.

'Call an ambulance,' she says, looking up at him. 'Please, my husband needs help.'

Kipruto tosses her his phone. 'Here,' he says. 'Call 999. Tell them you need urgent medical help and police support.'

He looks down at Billy. His shirt is soaked through and blood bubbles at his lips. He turns and grabs a tablecloth from the coffee table and hands it to Billy's wife.

'Press this to the neck wound,' he says. 'Try to stop the bleeding.'

Billy tries to speak but he's in too much pain.

'It'll be okay,' Kipruto says. 'You're a tough guy, Billy. You'll be okay.'

As he turns and races to the hallway, he hopes he's right. He hopes with every fibre of his being that for once, things will turn out okay.

CHAPTER 65: GREY AS ASH

Raven senses the presence in the room way before he sees the woman sitting there. He snaps his head up, expecting to see Byrne coming for him, fists clenched, teeth bared, but instead he sees someone else entirely. She's sitting on her haunches, hands folded in front of her, red wig in her lap and fake tattoo now just a smear on her hand. It takes him a moment to piece together what's happened. He had been so sure Lisa was lying within the flames, her body broken, blood seeping like wine all around her. This isn't Lisa at all. Relief hits him like a sledgehammer, but then the dread sets in.

'Hello, Luke,' Molly says. 'Long time, no see.'

'You're supposed to be dead,' he replies. 'Didn't you get the memo?'

'I would have been if somebody had taught my mother how to shoot straight.'

'She wanted to save you.'

'That moment passed when she walked out on me,' Molly hisses. 'As far as I'm concerned, the woman I killed was a stranger.'

Raven realises the room is glowing. It's like somebody turned on a switch. The letters in the walls are emanating a dull orange and the paintings on the ceiling are flitting in and out of focus. One of the demons glares at him, a vicious, sadistic malevolence oozing from its repulsive features. There's a sense of impending violence, a grim odour of despicable hatred.

'Why are you here?' Raven asks. 'What does any of this have to do with you?'

'The Legion had a problem that needed solving,' Molly replies. 'And what better person to call than the woman who killed their last Cardinal?'

'That was your father.'

'That bastard lied to me all my life. He didn't deserve to breathe air.'

'You're sick, Molly. You have to see that. What person in their right mind kills both their parents?'

'One who had to endure the kind of upbringing I had to go through. One who's own dad sliced off her mother's legs, just to teach her a lesson.'

The room is spinning, the atmosphere septic. Raven feels like he's being judged and weighed, as if every molecule in this strange, circular space is angled towards him. A breeze like a hot jet wafts over him, its acidic tang tinged with sourness.

'You said you solved a problem,' he says, trying to unpick the phantom. 'What problem did the Legion have?'

Molly smirks. 'You, Luke. You've always been the problem.'

Her words jab at him like hard body blows. It's the second time he's heard them today.

'You incarcerated their puppet,' Molly continues. 'You stopped her from doing the one thing they asked for.'

'The hearts,' Raven says. 'That's why she was taking them. Not because she had some sort of fetish for them, but because The Legion demanded them.'

Molly nods. 'Don't get me wrong, I'm sure Kaden got off on it, but they promised her redemption if she gathered them for them. Eight of them in total.'

Raven mentally calculates how many dead bodies there have been with their chests carved open. At first, he forgets to include Chapman's own brutalised body. With her, the total is seven.

'So you came to harvest the last.'

'I took the gay man's first, then Chapman's. I enjoyed it. Would have liked to have tasted them, actually, but of course, that wasn't allowed.'

'Must have been hard for you.'

'You mean not eating them? Yeah, tougher than you can imagine.'

'I mean killing a young woman like that. A young woman like *you.*'

'Chapman was nothing like me,' Molly spits. 'She was an amateur, a patsy pandering to middle aged men who can't get it up. As far as I was concerned, her heart wasn't dark enough to be included in the collection, but they saw some sort of sad, pathetic pathos in it: the heart of the woman who carved out the first six. She couldn't even cover her tracks properly. What was the point of her?'

Raven allows the pieces to click together. At the same time he'd been released from hospital and made his way back to Westhampton, Molly had been doing the exact same thing, heading back to the town that had destroyed both of them, as if the place had some sort of magnetic, subconscious hold on the pair of them. Then, while he was chasing down the killer, she was re-connecting with the same organisation she'd once been a subversive child of, and as soon as he'd laid hands on Chapman, she was brought into the fold to finish off what Chapman had started. The only question was, who was in charge of The Legion now? Who was pulling the strings of this whole charade?

'So what next?' he asks. 'I mean, what happens now? You're here, I'm here.'

'Exactly,' she replies. 'That's exactly the point.'

'The point?'

'This whole thing has been about this moment, Luke, just like the whole thing with Richards, just like the whole thing with me. Maybe it hasn't played out the way my father or that sycophant,

Charon, wanted it — not exactly — but what does it matter when the end result pans out the exact same way?'

'I'm not following you,' Raven says, but perhaps he is. Hasn't he had the feeling that something else is at play, that every move he's been taking is some pre-planned routine like a choreographed dance sequence? What if his premonitions have been pointers, pre-scripted advisory notes to get him heading in the right direction? What if he's never really been in control at all?

Molly doesn't reply. She gets up, steps over the remains of the dying flames and walks towards the darkness at the other side of the room. She pulls a zippo lighter from her pocket, reaches up and lights a series of candles that reveal what's been hidden from Raven ever since he stepped into the rotunda. There's a deep depression in the ground that his eyes can't perceive. He walks towards it, his feet like heavy slabs of granite tied to his ankles. Molly is smiling back at him, but the hint of humour never reaches her eyes. They're grey as ash, her lips too. She's like a cadaver with a beating heart, a body on a mortician's slab that breathes and feels.

'Take a look,' she says, eyes lowering towards the shallow hole.

He's scared to peer into that darkness because he senses the beast that lurks there. The demon with fetid breath, red blazing eyes, coarse hair on thick, scaly skin, a plume of black feathers erupting from a gargantuan skull within which a wide mouth brims with teeth dripping with torn skin and shredded flesh. Molly reaches up and places her hand on his scalp, and gradually she moves his head. The worst thing is, he lets her. It's like he can't help himself. He's being manipulated now, just like he's been manipulated all along.

Lisa is lying at the bottom of the well, hands tied with thick wire around iron clasps that are stained red. Her feet are similarly bound, and her slim waist is restrained by a wide strap that's pulled taut across the hole's diameter. She's gagged with what looks like a strip of gauze, and there's blood on her forehead and cheek. She peers up at him, the fear like a red smear across her face.

'Lisa,' he says, his throat clogged with sand and dust. 'What have you done to Lisa?'

'Nothing,' Molly replies. 'Not yet, and maybe I won't. That, my friend, is entirely up to you.'

Raven wants to grab the woman and throw her across the room, smash her head into the stone wall, show her what he does to people who hurt his family, but for some reason he just stands there, mute and breathless.

'What do you want from me?' he asks.

Molly moves her hand from his skull, tracing a finger across his face, a long nail carving an indentation into his skin that runs down his neck, across his collar bone and onto his chest.

'That,' she says.

'My body?'

'Your heart.'

Molly walks to the other side of the rotunda and lights another series of candles. A vast area of the room is now bathed in a yellow glow, and Raven sees what's lurking there. It sends his mind reeling. He's read about Aztec rituals before, about the carving out of human hearts from prisoners of war to feed deities that demanded the provision of human flesh, but he's never seen anything like this. There's an image on the wall, a depiction drawn in blood of a creature he recognises. Richards had called it Angra Mainyu, the Zoroastrian evil spirit. Others call it Iblis, Krampus, Lucifer, Mara, Pazazu, Mogui. Whatever its name, it has been trailing Raven ever since the premonitions started, and perhaps even before, when his dad had been the Curator of the Legion, and evil had wafted through their house like the noxious stench of a blocked sewer. He'd been just a kid then, haunted by nightmares that seemed to continue long after his eyes had opened. His mother had helped him shake them, cradling him in her arms while he sobbed, his body trembling with every whooping breath. His dad had just watched him in silence, arms folded, eyes cast downward as his only son remained gripped in some sort of crippling state of catatonia. He had never questioned the nightmares, never thought they were unusual, because having them was all he ever knew. But now, standing here, staring at that bloodied depiction with preserved hearts pinned to it with large obsidian stakes that penetrate the hard stone at the base of the throat, its clawed hands, hooved feet, callous eyes, and snake-like penis, he remembers. He recalls this horrific thing looming over him like an impenetrable cloud, breath like spoiled meat, blood dripping from its open lips, coagulating on his chest and spattering his cheeks, and he knows. This demon has been watching him from the moment he was born.

'There's just one piece missing,' Molly says, tracing the blade of a blackened knife across his throat. She walks over to the mural and jabs the blade at the demon's chest. 'And it goes right there.'

'And if I don't give it to you?' Raven asks.

'Then I use hers,' Molly replies, pointing to the hole. 'Her heart isn't as pure, but your seed is inside her and she's given birth to your child, so we're thinking it should work.'

'And if it doesn't?'

Molly's eyes darken for a split second. 'Then we'll take Harry's.'

The sweat beads on his brow. He has no choice. He can't let anything happen to Lisa. He can't let anybody hurt his son.

'How do I know you'll release her?' he asks. 'What's stopping you from taking my heart, killing Lisa, and then going after my son?'

'Because you have my word,' a man replies. Raven's head snaps to him, wondering who the hell has managed to creep up on them.

'Ronnie?' Raven says, wondering whether he's hallucinating. 'Ronnie Valentine?'

'The one and the same.'

'I don't under—'

'You don't need to understand,' Ronnie interjects, standing in the centre of the circular room, hands thrust deep in his pockets, blood on the collar of his shirt and the right-hand pocket of his jacket. 'You just have to do as she asks.'

'You're the Cardinal, aren't you,' Raven says, still unable to fathom what's happening.

'I am.'

'You came back after the thing at the jewellery shop.'

'Like my old man used to say, if opportunity comes knocking, only a fool would let it pass by.'

'But this wasn't you. This devil worshipping, sado-masochistic bullshit. This wasn't what you were about.'

Ronnie shrugs. 'What can I say? It seems an old tiger really can change its stripes.'

Molly steps towards Raven and presses the knife to his chest.

'So what do you say, Luke?' she asks. 'Are we taking this thing out of you, or are you going to do the dishonourable thing and make us cut it out of your girlfriend?'

Raven's eyes are glued on Ronnie's face. He can see the hatred in there, the unabated loathing. The Legion have played a blinder, getting the one guy who despises him more than anybody else to help them. Valentine would have taken this job on for free if it meant he got to watch him suffer.

'You're enjoying this, aren't you?' he spits.

'More than you'll ever fucking know, mate.'

Raven turns and grabs Molly's hand, but rather than pushing her away, he pulls the knife towards him, splitting his skin just above his left nipple.

'If you want it, take it,' he says. 'But not until you let Lisa go.'

CHAPTER 66: SHADOW DANCE

Kipruto runs down the hallway and into the kitchen, scouring the darkness for signs of Ronnie Valentine. He's not there. Nobody's there. He heads to the dining room, pressing his body against the wall before he kicks the door open, gun gripped in two hands, eyes flitting from left to right. It's empty in here too. He eyes the staircase, but he suspects he would have heard a guy as big and unwieldy as Ronnie charging to the first floor like a bull at the Festival of San Fermín.

He stands in the hallway, hands on hips, but then he sees it: the crack beneath the stairs; the little sliver of darkness that penetrates the painted wood of the frame. He goes to it, pushes a finger into the slim gap and pulls. The cellar door opens, letting out a warm jet of air that wafts over his face. There's a smell like decades old mould and a dirty refrigerator, but he doesn't let it stop him. As the wail of an ambulance penetrates the silence, he places one foot on the first step and descends.

*

They pull Lisa out of the hole. She's barely conscious. Raven goes to her, but Ronnie holds him at arm's length, telling him to back off before somebody gets hurt.

'Luke?' Lisa says but her voice is so reedy, it sounds like wind whistling through broken guttering.

'It's me, Lis. It's Luke. I'm here.'

She tries to stand but her legs buckle, and Molly watches her fall. He tries to go to her again, but this time Ronnie aims a punch at his abdomen, knocking every ounce of air out of his body. He crumples in half, one knee going to the ground. He lifts his gaze, glares at Valentine, drool spilling from his open mouth.

'I'll fucking kill you,' he hisses.

'Not likely, mate. In about five minutes, the main organ keeping your pathetic little body alive will be pinned up on that wall.'

'I'll come back and haunt you then, terrorise every second you breathe air.'

'Haven't you heard?' Ronnie replies, a dark smile carving his face in two. 'A person that sacrifices their heart can never come back. They're damned for all eternity, thrown into the fiery pit and left to burn forever. You get that, Luke? The enormity of it. You'll die infinite deaths, and there's not one thing you can do about it.' He laughs, pulling a thick cigar from his pocket. 'Shall we get on with it?' he says, blowing smoke.

There's a raised platform to the left of the blood and gore-soaked artwork and Molly gestures to it with the knife.

'Just lie down over there, Luke,' she says. 'Make yourself comfortable. This shouldn't take long.'

Raven shoots Lisa a glance. She's managed to pull herself up to a sitting position, but she's still heavily concussed. She can barely keep her eyes open.

'What are… you doing?' she says.

'I'm doing what they ask,' he replies. 'But don't worry. You and Harry are going to be okay.'

'Don't… let them hurt… you. Luke, listen… to me. Don't let… these fucking people… hurt you.'

Raven approaches the stone platform and hoists himself onto it, unbuttoning his shirt as Molly stands beside him. He can't take his eyes off Lisa. She's been the one thing that's been keeping him going this whole time, and even though they're in the same room, he can't touch her, can't sit with her. After tonight, he'll never see her again, but that's okay. She'll be okay. Harry will be okay.

'Nice tits, Luke,' Molly says, watching as he lies back on the cold stone. 'I've seen them before though, haven't I?' She winks at Lisa. 'Me and Luke, we spent a lot of time together up in those hills. You know what it's like when boredom sets in. You get up to things you might not normally do, what with Luke being so old and everything.' She traces the knife down his stomach, across his belt and slowly drags it towards his groin. 'Not bad, though, for an old timer. I've had worse.'

'You're a… psychopath,' Lisa says. 'You took… Luke away from me when we were—'

'When you were what? About to make a go of it? Are you kidding? Don't forget I've known your boyfriend since I was a kid, and back then, when he was a bit younger, he'd fuck anything that had a pulse. There was that woman, wasn't there? The blonde. Worked behind the bar at the pub. What was her name again? Help me out here, Luke. Oh yeah. Daisy. That was it. You really had a thing for her back then, didn't you? You were all over her like bad aftershave from what I can remember. Even got yourself in a bit of trouble with your boss over it. You must remember, Lisa. Daisy, right? He must have come home smelling of her, you know the sex smell, because he was constantly rubbing his skin up against her—'

'Shut your mouth,' Raven says. 'You don't get to talk about Daisy like that, not after—'

'Not after what?' Molly interjects. 'You mean after she got murdered because of her connection to you? Pff, that must sting, like, so much. You fucked a barmaid multiple times behind your pregnant girlfriend's back, and because of that, the guy you were trying to put behind bars stabbed her to death. That guilt's got to leave a stain, right? A really dirty, bloody stain that not even the best detergent can get out.'

'I said don't talk about her like that!'

'You hear that?' Molly says, smirking as she turns to Lisa. 'I think lover boy still has a thing for the barmaid. I heard he was a bit kinky, but fucking a corpse? That really is a step too far.'

Raven leaps up and grabs Molly around the throat.

'There, there, Raven,' Ronnie replies. 'Don't forget our deal. You give us your heart, and we let Lisa and Harry live.'

'I pity you,' he spits at Molly, his mouth inches from her upturned face. 'I pity you for everything that happened to you. Your mother didn't want you and your dad was a sick sadomasochist, but that doesn't excuse what you've become. It doesn't justify what you're doing.'

Molly's eyes flit with defiance, and she jabs the knife home without hesitation, penetrating the flesh between Raven's ribs. He cries out, clinging to the platform to stop himself falling. The room shakes and the runes glow with a fierce intensity.

'Exciting isn't it?' Ronnie says, clapping his hands together. 'Pretty soon *He'll* be here, and then everything we've done, everything we've gone through, it'll all be worth it.'

Blood bubbles on Raven's lips. He suspects the knife has nicked a lung. He glances at Lisa who's trying to stand. He desperately fights to get to her, but Molly twists the knife and another sharp bolt of agony blazes through his body.

'Lie back,' she says. 'Don't worry. If you play nice, I'll make it quick.'

Ronnie stands beside her, mouth twitching, knuckles cracking. 'I'd do as she asks if I were you, Raven. She really can be a sadistic little fucker when she wants to be.'

'It's my forté,' Molly replies, sneering.

'You let Lisa go,' Raven says. 'I'll only do this once you let her leave.'

'No Luke!' Lisa cries, but she's on unsteady legs and her body swims back and forth like a pendulum.

'She can go whenever she wants,' Ronnie replies. 'We're not holding her back.'

'I'm not going,' Lisa says. 'I'm not leaving you.'

'You have to,' Raven says, blood spilling from his mouth.

'I can't.'

'You have to. For Harry.'

He lies back on the table, grimacing as sharp needles of pain dance across his skin. Molly moves with him, the knife still jutting from his ribcage like a creature tearing itself from his bloodied torso. Ronnie approaches and chains his wrists and ankles to the stone platform.

'That's a good boy,' Ronnie says. 'This will all be over soon enough.'

The image on the wall starts to shift. The outline drawn in blood starts to smear and run, rivulets of crimson that drip down the coarse stone. One of the hearts appears to move, as if something is inside it, desperate to get out.

'Stop hurting him,' Lisa says. She claws at Molly's hair and neck. The younger woman turns, and without blinking, punches Lisa in the face, sending her staggering.

'Get out of here!' Raven yells. 'Just go. Go now!'

Lisa turns and wipes blood from beneath her nose. She looks every bit the woman he remembers. Blazing red hair, tattoos down one arm, silver hoops through both nostrils and lip. She spits blood on the floor and clenches her fists. She's never listened to a word he says, and she won't now. He has to find a way to make her leave.

'Molly's right!' he yells. 'I don't love you. I never did.'

Her eyes dart towards him. 'What?'

'Daisy. It was always Daisy. You were just a hobby, something to pass the time with. I never meant for you to get pregnant. If I'd had my way, we would have had an abortion.' The words are killing him. The pain is worse than the knife in his side.

He fights to control his emotions, to make everything believable. Lisa has to buy this. For her sake and for the sake of his son, she has to believe he's being real.

'You don't mean that.'

'I've never meant anything more in my life.'

Molly's laughing, a belly laugh that doubles her over. 'This is better than watching Gogglebox.'

'I looked for you, Luke,' Lisa says, tears glistening in her eyes. 'I looked everywhere night and day for months, *years*. I was the one chasing down the leads. I was the one on the phone to Randall every single day. If it wasn't for me, the police would have shut the case down after the first year, but they kept it open, just because I believed. I really did. I knew we'd find you.'

The next sentence sticks in Raven's throat like nettles. He can barely push it out. 'Didn't stop you meeting someone else, though, did it? Didn't stop you getting married.'

Lisa makes a sound as if she's going to vomit. 'It was four years. Four years of waking up thinking you were still sleeping beside me. Four years of not knowing whether you were alive or dead. Four years of re-living that horrific day over and over, not sleeping, barely eating, feeling like my whole life had been put on pause.'

'If you loved me like you said you did, you would have waited.'

'I did wait! I waited so, so long!'

'Not long enough.'

'I was lonely.'

'I was on my own, too, trapped in that house, not knowing who or where I was, slowly dying from a brain injury that would have eventually killed me.'

Molly offers a wry smile. 'That was me. I did that.'

'I wanted you to come home,' Lisa says, tears sliding down her cheeks, hot and salty. 'Harry wanted his dad.'

'I didn't want to come home,' he says, every syllable killing him slowly. 'I didn't want to face up to my problems. I never wanted to be a husband. I never wanted to be a father. I wanted anything but you, Lisa. I didn't want what you had to offer. Not the dinners for two, not the endlessly long days out at the park, not the mind-numbing, paint-by-numbers sex. I just wanted my old life, the one I liked, the one where I didn't have to be or do anything.'

'You bastard,' Lisa grunts, her arms clasped around her chest. 'You bastard.'

Luke feigns contempt. It hurts like nothing he's ever felt before. Lisa weeps, but she's angry, too. The pain is like a mask of confusion, a two-sided coin.

'He's said his piece, so off you pop,' Molly says, waggling her fingers. 'Raven and I have some catching up to do of our own, and the last thing we need is you lurking around like a bad smell.'

Lisa staggers back, stumbling in reverse towards the exit as she wipes snot from her lips and tears from her cheeks. Raven watches her go, his emotions like a tornado in his guts. He could have said anything to her, could have said that every day he wakes up thinking about her, that the only reason he didn't go to see her is because he couldn't face losing her, but right here, right now, she just has to be gone. He knows he'll never see her again, but he has to come to terms with that because she has to be safe. He can't be selfish anymore. He has to put her and Harry before everything else.

'Are you going to let her walk out like that?' Molly asks Ronnie.

The big guy shrugs. 'It won't matter much once this is all done,' he replies.

'I'll kill you,' Raven growls. 'Both of you. Whatever happens here, this isn't the end.'

'Oh, but it is,' Ronnie says, gripping Raven's shoulder in one giant hand. 'Because you're the one we needed. Now we've got you, nothing can stop what we've got planned.'

Molly rips open Raven's shirt and draws a circle on his chest. The moisture evaporates from his mouth. This is it.

'I just have to ask,' he says. 'Why me? If you wanted me so badly, why not just kill me up there in Scotland.'

'Because I didn't know,' Molly replies. 'Wished I had. Once we disappeared, we were gone. No contact, no Legion.'

'Bernie always knew there was something about you,' Ronnie replies. 'But he wasn't sure. It was only when your old man came back on the scene that he started to piece it together.'

'Piece what together?' Raven asks. 'That I'm a pain in the arse?'

'That Sam kept a secret from us.'

'My father was all about secrets.'

'Not like this.'

The room shook, the engraving glowed, and the paintings on the ceiling began to slip and move.

'Your dad committed himself to a cause a long time ago.'

'I know,' Raven replies. 'The Legion. He was delusional, thinking that a fucked-up institution like that could somehow make him happier.'

'It wasn't The Legion,' Ronnie says. 'Bernie didn't even know about the kind of guy he was recruiting until it came out years later, long after your dad had done his little disappearing act.'

Molly is getting impatient and starts to trace the line of the obsidian blade around the arc of the circle.

'It seems your dad was quite the satanist when he was a kid, and he did something pretty stupid.'

'He did a lot of stupid things, like treating my mum like she was worthless.'

'This was… far worse than that.'

Raven thinks about his dad, about the moment he'd walked back into his life, long after the family had gathered around his grave and mourned his loss. He'd barely been able to look at his father let alone speak to him. That hatred was always there, like a boil that needed lancing.

Molly pushes the knife beneath Raven's skin and begins to peel it away, and he grips the stone beneath him, feeling the hot sear of agony as it traces its way across his shoulders.

'Your father wanted power, Raven, that's all he ever wanted, and he thought the only way to get it quickly was to get the kind of help that could make anything possible.'

Raven can barely hear the words. The pain is unbearable. He's bleeding from the deep wound in his side and now the horrific gash in his chest. The only thing that makes it manageable is the fact that Lisa has made it out. He can get some comfort from that, at least.

'Your dad became obsessed with something he'd read in one of the ancient texts,' Ronnie says. 'He was convinced there was a way to get everything he wanted in life by committing himself to the one true deity. He even got people involved, witches and shamans, people who do this kind of thing for a living. They say he drained a pint of blood from his body and fed it to the shaman, and by doing this, the devil entered the shaman's body and spoke to your old man.'

'This is bullshit,' Raven growls as Molly makes slow, precise cuts across his skin. The mural on the wall is raining blood now. It pours from the outline, creating a red mirage, a hellish monster creeping from the depths of the grisly façade. The hearts begin to move in unison, pulsing and flexing, fluid seeping from the severed arteries. Somehow, they're alive. Raven tries to hold it together, even though the pain is so intense he can barely stay conscious.

'It's not bullshit!' Ronnie cries. 'That deal was made, and after that, your dad was recruited by The Legion, he befriended Bernie Staker, rose to the rank of Curator and became a very wealthy man. That's not a coincidence, Raven. That's cause and effect.'

The hearts pound, the blood jets from the wall like oil, and the rock begins to stretch and fold. Raven watches it through the thick veil of agony that semi-blinds him. Molly is leaning over him, the sweat glistening from her taut features. Her dark curls tumble over her face as she strains to put more pressure onto the dagger, driving it further and further into his flesh. She's laughing as if the whole thing is some contest-winning joke. She places one hand on his cheek and offers a dispassionate sad-face.

'Oh baby,' she says. 'Does it hurt.'

'Fuck you,' Raven spits. 'And fuck you too, Valentine. You want to believe that my dad was some devil worshipping crackpot, that's fine by me. I hated the guy anyway.'

'You're missing the point, Raven old son,' Ronnie replies. 'This isn't about how crazy your dad was — and believe me, for a while there your old man was off his fucking rocker — this is about what he was willing to give up to get what he wanted.'

A hand emerges from the rock, hooked nails like talons, fingers as thick as branches. It grasps at the air, flexing and raking, trying to find purchase. Meanwhile Molly keeps slicing and cutting, and the pain is so intense now, Raven's mind dances with insanity. He feels the blood that coats his body, but in his mind it's a dark grey cloak that he's wrapped inside, the thin tendrils that emerge from the velvet material slipping into his skin and injecting him with an oily black substance that mummifies his festering corpse.

'You want to know what he gave up?' Ronnie asks.

Raven doesn't answer. He can't. He can't feel his face anymore, can't even feel the knife. It's like a vital nerve has been severed and everything has become a numb, vacuous space that he merely exists within.

'Tell him,' Molly says, eyes flitting, lips sneering. 'Tell him, Ron. He needs to know.'

'He needs to ask me,' Ronnie says. 'I'm not giving this to him unless he asks me himself.'

Raven watches the wall sever down the middle as something enormous shifts. He wonders why the ceiling isn't collapsing in on them or why the walls aren't breaking apart. There's a face in the granite, barely discernible but he knows it's there. He can see the shallow depressions where its eyes would be. He can make out the ragged line of a snarling mouth, the broken collection of serrated teeth. It snarls and spits, desperately frustrated by the densely compacted stone's unwelcome embrace.

'Ask him, Luke,' Molly says, licking his face with a moist tongue as she slides the knife ever deeper. 'Ask him. He wants to tell you.'

Raven tries to turn his head away, but she stays with him, her cheek pressed against his, eyes wide and rampant. Their bodies are slick with blood. She breaks away from him momentarily, leaning down to lap up the gore from his chest. Her tongue flicks at the wound, causing a fresh bout of agony to race through his torso. When she looks up, her lips and chin are dripping with him.

'Get… away from me,' he manages to grunt, but she laps him up some more, drinking him like his essence is nothing more than a glass of warm Burgundy.

'Ask him,' she spits through blood and tissue. 'Ask him or I'll chew my way through you until I hit an artery.'

He's barely alive, his body now just a departing vessel. He doesn't need to know what his father did — it will all be immaterial anyway — but there's a curious part of him, a little tic inside that wants to hear it. He wants this to end, but knowing is better than not knowing. It just is.

'Tell me,' he snarls, his voice fuelled by agony and hatred. 'Just fucking tell me.'

Molly giggles and blood sprays from her open lips like juice from a ripe apple. 'Do it,' she says. 'Tell him what Sam did.'

'He sold you, Raven' Ronnie replies, his ashen complexion bathed in shadows. 'He sold his unborn son.'

'Sold me? To who?'

Ronnie eyes the creature in the wall, the unnamed thing that's straining to be unleashed. 'You've belonged to *Him* all along. Ever since your dad made that deal. That's why *He's* been coming for you all this time. That's why Staker was so fucking desperate to get his hands on your son. He knew that if you belonged to *Him*, then your son did too, but I'm not like that. I don't fuck with kids, never have. As far as I'm concerned, it's the adults that need to be taught a lesson, not the children, and you and I have a history longer than the Great Wall of China.'

'People can't just sell their kids to the devil,' Raven says. 'That's just make believe.'

'Is *He* make believe?' Ronnie replies, watching as the creature inches further from its rocky confines. 'Is that thing made up, because it looks fucking real to me.'

At that moment, Raven realises Ronnie is scared. Whatever he's signed up for, he didn't expect it to end like this. Maybe he thought he'd settle a score, watch as the crazy Staker girl ripped his heart from his lifeless body, but at no point did he actually believe that the ritual would work.

'*He* wants your heart, Luke,' Molly says, blood running from her chin in one snotty strand. 'It's the last piece of the jigsaw. *He* wants what he owns, and when *He* gets it, everybody in the whole world will see what *He's* capable of.'

'You're… fucking insane,' Raven replies.

'Oh, baby, of course I'm insane!' she roars. 'I've got good genes. I'm as crazy as my mum and as evil as my dad. Why do you think I'm trying to eat you? I find you delectable. If I could, I'd devour every last piece of you!'

'Just get on with it,' Ronnie says, now so anxious that his usually confident demeanour is as flaky as pastry. 'If we're going to do this, let's get it done.'

Molly wipes the blood from her face with the back of her hand, spits a bloody chunk of phlegm onto the floor, and raises the knife.

'You heard him?' she says to Raven. 'He wants this finished.'

Raven thrusts his head forward in defiance. 'Then… do it! Kill me, you cunt! Cut out my heart. I don't care. You've already taken the only two things I care about. There's nothing left to give.'

Molly's eyes flicker with the orange of a thousand candles. The muscles in her neck flex. She grips the hilt of the blade, looks down at Raven, and licks blood from her lips.

'It's been fun, Luke,' she says. 'Whatever happens now, I'll always have the moments we shared.'

Raven lies back, closes his eyes, and waits for the inevitable abyss to swallow him whole.

*

Lisa flees from the rotunda, the milky sheen of her mobile phone torch lighting the way. She's barely regained consciousness. She had been hit pretty hard by the cannibal bitch just after she'd put a bullet in the Irish bastard, Conor Byrne. Everything else was just a hazy blur until she'd seen Luke lying there, bloodied knife protruding from his ribcage.

Tears stream down her cheeks. She hates that. She never cries. She hates Luke for making her feel this way; she hates him for what he said; she hates him for the way he always treated her; she hates him for putting her in this hellish situation. He's risked everything, *everyone* — Harry, Billy, Sally, her — just because of his stubborn drive to solve a case. If he'd have just come straight back home when he'd arrived back in Westhampton, none of this would have happened. Sure, they'd have had to deal with the whole marriage situation, but that was just an adult issue they would have somehow figured it. This, however? This isn't a normal adult issue. This isn't even a normal human issue. It's madness. Insane, occult craziness on a whole other spectrum.

She keeps running, knowing she needs to get back to her son, but although her feet are moving and her heart is hammering, something slows her down. She can't shake Luke from her mind. He's still back there, bleeding out on a stone slab. That bitch and her cockney wide-boy are going to kill him. She's torn. Torn because she wants to cradle her son in her arms and keep him safe, but confused because she still has feelings for a man she should despise.

She stops, grabs the wall, glances over her shoulder. She turns back to the way ahead, knowing there's safety that way. Safety and security. Her husband is waiting for her, a man who asks for nothing, has given her a happy home, and above all, never lets her down. She turns back to the darkness, imagines Luke being butchered, sees the pain carved into his features like the dark caress of the reaper's calloused fingers. Then she thinks of Harry, her son, her boy. Is what Luke can give him worth saving? Isn't Simon the man who can help her give Harry the life he truly deserves?

The exit beckons. It's warm out there. There's light, hope, a future. The other way is black, nihilistic, terrifying. The problem is, she's never been comfortable with safety. She's never enjoyed normalcy, maybe because normalcy has never been her friend. She's as self-destructive as the man she's left behind, as brutally tragic as the guy who right now is being carved up like a Christmas turkey. She can't let that happen, can she? If she does, what does that make her? A conspirator to murder? A denialist?

A cold, dispassionate bitch? The truth is, for all his faults, she loves Luke Raven more than she's ever loved any man, including her husband. There's passion in their relationship, volatility, excitement. She knows it's pathetic. She knows she's courting chaos as some kind of mutated catharsis. She knows that right now he might be beyond saving, but save him she must, because without him, she's incomplete, like a jigsaw puzzle without edges, a key without teeth.

She whispers Simon's name, but her broken voice is almost apologetic. The decision has been made for her because she doesn't have the will to make a conscious choice. She turns back toward the darkness and braces herself. The fires of hell await her, and somehow, she has to find the strength to douse the inferno. She takes a breath.

She's too preoccupied by her own thoughts to realise there's somebody else in the tunnel with her. Something touches her shoulder, a hand from an unseen assailant, and she steels herself for death. This will be her final mistake, another moment where her lust for the man who has tormented her for most of her adult life steers her into unparallelled trouble. Her voice catches in her throat as she turns, and she pictures the monster from the wall, the demonic presence that still lurks in her lungs like oxygen aflame.

'Lisa,' Kipruto says, looming at her from the shadows. 'Are you okay? Have you seen Valentine? Did he come this way?'

For a moment she doesn't recognise the DCS — the image of the creature stills clings to her with old, withered bones — but then familiarity clicks. She grabs her friend's shoulders and pulls him close, hugging him as if he's a life raft collecting lost souls.

'Luke's back there,' she whispers, her voice as unfamiliar as a stranger's. 'They're going to kill him.'

'Show me,' Kipruto replies. 'Show me where he is.'

And so she does. She musters every ounce of determination she has left and walks them down that shadowy corridor to an end that has no beginning.

*

The pain is like nothing he's ever experienced. It rips through his innards like an aggressive contagion. He's soaked in his own essence, his sweat and blood drenching his shirt, his hair, his jeans. Molly's grin forms an upturned dome that splits her face, an unhinged door with gleaming teeth and lapping tongue. Her eyes glisten with damp flames. Her hair creates a tangled drape that separates them. Above him, the thing from within the rock strains and pushes as it tries to release its mountainous form from the earth that contains it.

'This isn't what I signed up for,' Ronnie says, his voice like a squeaking gear. 'This can't be real.'

'Shut your mouth,' Molly spits, her grin fixed in place. 'You knew exactly what you were getting into.'

'I only knew what they told me, but I didn't actually believe it. Who would? This stuff is crazy.'

Raven tries to use the blood on his arms to slip his hands from the manacles, but he's so weak, he can barely twitch his fingers.

'I'm leaving,' Ronnie says.

'Suit yourself,' Molly replies. 'But don't think I won't come and find you when all this is done.'

'I can't breathe,' Ronnie replies. 'I feel like I'm suffocating down here.'

'Then fucking die already,' Molly growls. 'You're no use to me anyway.'

Something in the rock splits, releasing the creature's right forearm. Raven watches as a claw-like appendage slices the air above him. The blackened flesh hangs from ash-grey bones, pink sinew and tissue oozing with long lines of dark red that spatter on the floor and walls. Elephantine fingers tipped with short-sword talons grasp at Raven's hair, barely missing his exposed forehead as the sharpened edges cut his sweat-soaked locks down to the follicles. From deep in the rock, the creature's maw opens, spraying stone and dust from within a limestone throat and granite jaws. There's a deafening scream like the earth opening from the depths of its core, and the monster's upper torso comes into view, revealing a chest squirming with faceless slug-like leeches that cling to thick hair coated with oily sputum. The breast plate is split at the centre, and from within the chest, a dozen human faces sprout, their grotesque, undulating lips uttering silent, agonised screams of endless torment.

There's a rattling breath from behind Raven, and he strains his neck to see Valentine holding the wall, sweat streaming from his forehead and neck. The older man fumbles with the collar of his shirt, initially missing the top button but then tugging at the fragile material, tearing it like skin as he attempts to ease the pressure on his constricted windpipe. His other hand goes to his chest, his fingers seemingly tugging at an invisible boa constrictor.

'Need... air,' he says before stumbling forward, pinwheeling his arms like a tightrope walker. One foot catches the other and he falls, dropping to his knees, his hands slamming against the stone floor. His face turns the colour of ripe aubergine. His breath becomes a dry wheeze. He utters a choking, snarling sound, one hand on his face, his bloodied palm leaving a red velvet smear.

'Looks like he's on his way out,' Molly says, lip curling, eyes grinning. 'The old boy's heart's about to explode.'

The creature turns to the old man slowly dying on the rotunda's floor. Valentine's old body is of no interest to it. It's come to collect a debt, and only Raven's soul will do.

'Raven...' Valentine manages in a thick rasp. 'Raven...'

Luke looks the old man in the eye, and what he sees terrifies him. There's nothing but black in Valentine's gaze, a swimming sea of emptiness. If the creature from the rock represents hell, then Valentine's soul is purgatory, and it's as vacuous as the deepest trenches of the ocean. The old man cocks his head at the creature that's slowly forming from the granite, and he sneers, hate oozing from his dripping lips like acid.

'I'll...see you there... Raven,' he scowls. 'I'll...see you...'

Valentine's eyes roll into his skull as he topples forward, face slamming into the dusty stone, splitting his nose and cracking his cheekbone. The beast's shadow slips over him like a shapeless death cowl as Valentine's hands claw at the earth. His body jerks and spasms, and with one final heave of his useless lungs, a final, coarse breath escapes from his bloodied lips. As he dies, his body slumps like a deflated balloon, and the thick mass of who he was is dragged, lifeless and bedraggled towards the earth.

'See you Ron,' Molly laughs. 'It was fun while it lasted.'

She twitches, as if restarting her internal computer, and looks down at the black knife in her hands as though she'd forgotten it was there.

'Looks like this is it, Luke,' she says. 'The big finale. It's what our one true deity came all this way for, after all, and who are we to keep *Him* waiting, right?'

The skin across Raven's chest has been peeled away, revealing blood-soaked muscle and tissue. His heart lies beneath, pumping faster than he ever thought possible. He knows now that this is how it has to end, his body opened like a can of beans, the organ inside extracted and pinned to the gore-soaked stone where the monster awaits. He fears for Lisa, he fears for Harry, but perhaps if he gives the beast what it wants, this will all be over. They can carry on the life they'd made for themselves. They can be happy, free from the tyranny he had forever brought upon them.

Molly grips the hilt of the dagger and raises it high above her head. Her hands tremble as an invisible energy courses through her body. Above them, the monster roars, a noise so loud and tremulous that the ground beneath them shakes as if it's about to split wide open.

'Here we go, Luke!' Molly cries. 'Time to see what you're made of!'

Raven braces himself, cries out for the two people in the world he cares for the most, and watches as the blade comes at him, Molly's face desperate and hungry as the knife slams into his chest plate. The pain is so terrible he almost blacks out, but for some reason, consciousness clings to him. He watches the bone separate, the muscle snap like elastic, and the veins sever. Molly carves and pulls, and he screams as if hell itself has opened up inside him. The beast cries out as the rock forms around it, creating an abdomen, a groin, the top half of an enormous calf.

Raven feels Molly's hands inside his body, searching, rummaging. His heart races, pushing the blood that remains around his broken body, sending his head spinning like a coin. He grinds teeth like gravestones as he tries to blot out the pain, but the darkness evades him. He can see everything, can feel everything.

Behind Molly a shadow forms, a shape without signature. Raven sees it, watches as it mutates and solidifies, and as Molly cuts an aortic valve, he sees his dad. He's alive but not alive. He's there with him but hardly there at all.

'Son,' he says. 'Don't worry. It will soon be done.'

'This is all your fault,' Luke replies without making a sound. 'You did this to me.'

Sam Raven nods, but the smoky haze that forms his head breaks off in little whisps of dancing vapour. 'I didn't know then what I was doing.'

'You could have told me. Maybe I could have done something.'

'There's no escaping this, Luke. Once the promise is made, it can't be broken.'

'So, I just go with him then? Forever?'

The shadow flickers as if it's about to disintegrate. 'You must have known this was how it would end. You've always been different. You've always seen things.'

'I've been tortured from the moment I was born. You should have aborted me in the womb.'

'Your mother would never have allowed that.'

'My mum has been cursed since the day she met you.'

'She didn't deserve it, neither did you, but know this. If I could do anything to make this all go away, I would.'

'Then do it.'

'It's impossible.'

The hatred pulses through Raven's body like poison.

'Then why are you here?'

The shadow breaks apart then reforms like oil rising to the surface of the ocean.

'I gave a promise. I have an obligation.'

'To watch your son die?'

His father shakes his translucent head. 'No, but I can't avoid it.'

'What then?'

The shadow fractures again, and this time only thin tendrils hold the fragments together. 'I have to watch as the darkness passes over.'

'I have it!' Molly cries, tugging and pulling, ripping muscle from tissue, blood vessels from elastic veins. Raven cries out but still his stubborn consciousness holds on. He should be dead. Why isn't he dead already?

More rock tumbles from the rapidly destabilising wall. The domed ceiling splits down the middle like a cracked egg. Plaster and earth spill through the narrow crevice. The monster lurches and snatches at Raven's chest. It wants the unseen thing that Molly has grasped between her narrow fingers. The room is filled with a cacophony of noise: of the beast's ear-splitting rasp; the rotunda slowly coming apart; of Molly gasping and groaning as if she's in the throes of an all-body climax; and of Raven screaming, his agony leeching from his soul like an unwanted spirit.

'I have it!' Molly repeats. 'It's beautiful!'

It comes away from Raven's chest with a snap and a gurgle. She lifts it up as Raven watches, eyes like saucers, his mouth twisted in a malformed sneer of revulsion. It's black, as dark as the universe; as utterly eternal as a ceaseless void. It moves. It pumps. It's as though it's breathing. Oily fluid leaks from the arteries. Ashen flesh leaches through Molly's fingers like spoiled meat. He knows now why he has tormented everybody he meets. He knows now why his father abandoned him and his mother has always been so distant. He knows now why his addictions have always felt tethered to him like splintered ships in a raging storm. He knows now why he can never be with Lisa, can never be a good father to his son. He's cancer. He's a contagion. He's death.

'*It's here!*' Molly screams at the undead creature now leering from the rock, its left leg now the only remaining part of it still fully encased in the limestone. 'Take it. Devour it. *It's yours!*'

The beast reaches with one extended arm as Molly holds up the dark heart, black blood spattering her face and chest. Raven watches with dread, knowing that once the unreal entity takes the thing it most desires, hell will be released from the molten depths of the Earth and there'll be no stopping its awesome, destructive force. He's failed. He's failed everybody. Nothing he's ever done to make things right has worked. He should have stayed dead. He should never have come back.

A slate claw touches the heart, and the flesh of the severed organ reaches towards it. It wants to be taken. The monster laughs. The debt is almost repaid. In the shadows, Sam Raven smiles. He can be free. An oath cast in a time when there was so much at stake will be fulfilled. The end is so close.

'Luke!' Lisa cries as she appears in the rotunda, phone gripped in one hand, torchlight slicing Sam in two. She doesn't pause, doesn't hesitate. She launches herself at Molly, fists raised, lips snarling, phone sent clattering across the ground.

'Get off of him you *bitch!*'

*

There's a noise from up ahead and Lisa races towards it, Kipruto in her wake. She knows Luke is there. She can hear his voice. It sounds like he's in the throes of some horrific pain. Her heart is ripped in two. She left him in there, left him to die. She can't let that happen. She won't

She rounds the corner, and in a split second she sees too much for her mind to comprehend. Luke is lying there, his prone body soaked in so much blood. The wall of the room has crumbled as if there's been some sort of earthquake. Ronnie Valentine is face down on the ground, blood seeping from a shattered face. Molly Staker has something in her hands that has her in its thrall, but Lisa can't quite make out what it is. Behind Luke's captor, a shadow dances and flitters like dust mites in a swirling eddy. Lisa thinks she sees a familiar face in the ashen haze, but she knows she's mistaken. That person died on the day The Legion crumbled.

Kipruto arrives behind her, gun drawn. He sounds out of breath, like a pair of bellows about to explode.

'Stop! Police!' he hollers. 'Molly Staker, I'm placing you under arrest for the murder of—'

'Oh, fuck off, pig!' Molly cries, eyes ablaze like tiny wildfires. 'You're late. You're way too late!' She reaches for the knife, but Kipruto reacts first, squeezing the trigger. There's a soft click as the gun jams, but Lisa's already moving. She won't let the murderous cow hurt Luke anymore.

'Get off of him you bitch!'

Molly laughs and looks up at something in the rock, something that Lisa only perceives in the farthest reaches of her vision. Flayed flesh, disembodied faces, dark blood oozing from broiled skin. An unseen force wills her to stop, but her anger is boiling over. She's an out-of-control train roaring down the tracks, a truck with no driver racing towards the edge of the cliff.

Molly sees her determination, and something shifts in her. She looks down, spies the dagger on the edge of the platform and reaches for it. Her fingers touch the hilt but Lisa won't be stopped. She grabs it too, her fingers wrapping around Molly's. There's a desperate tussle, a back and forth where both women will not let go.

'He's already dead!' Molly screams. 'The debt has to be repaid!'

'You're one sick, crazy fuckhead!' Lisa replies, and with her free hand claws at Molly's face, drawing blood.

Molly cries out and brings up a knee, striking her attacker in the abdomen. Lisa is winded but she forces the pain away. She punches Molly in the tit, pushes her back. Molly responds by kicking her in the shin. They're against the wall, writhing and scratching, clawing and hitting. The knife is still wedged between them, a dark mass of sharp rock and cold metal.

Lisa is vaguely aware of Luke beside her, of Kipruto trying to unjam his gun, and of the shadow creature that watches on. She grits her teeth, uses every muscle in her body, willing this to end, knowing it has to end for Luke, for her, for Harry. If they have any chance, she has to finish it now.

'You've lost him, Lisa,' Molly spits. 'You think you have his heart, you think it's yours to own, but you're wrong. I have it. I've taken it from you.'

The young woman's words rock Lisa like a blow to the temple, but she fights against her emotions, knowing that the Staker girl is an expert manipulator. Her soul is tied to Luke's, just as their DNA is connected through their son. Molly can never have Luke's heart, just like she can never have a piece of what they have.

'It's black,' Molly continues. 'Blacker than the darkest night. Blacker than hatred. Blacker than the most depraved evil.'

Lisa's fury erupts. Luke isn't that. He's never been that. She pulls at Molly's fingers, bends them back until the ring finger snaps. Molly screams and it's the only distraction Lisa needs. She feels the knife now, wraps her fingers around it, slips it from her opponent's grasp and raises it.

Molly looks up, and in that instant, she knows.

'Doesn't matter what you do,' Molly says, eyes filled with hatred as hard as diamonds. 'Just like it doesn't matter what Luke did. *He*'s coming, Lisa. There's no stopping *Him*.'

'You're a sick lunatic!' Lisa screams. 'You can take your Legion back with you to whatever shit stain you came out of!'

She lets out a hoarse scream and brings the knife down. When it splits Molly's face open from forehead to chin, carving her nose apart, mutilating her tongue and halving her frontal lobe, Lisa continues to push, driving Molly to the ground with her own body on top of her, spilling and tumbling until they are one conjoined entity, a mass of bones, skin and flesh, their forms joined together by blood, sweat and love indistinguishable from unimaginable fury.

EPILOGUE:

'Come on, it's time.'

He hears the voice through a crackle of static. Shuffling, slipping, a metallic scrape. There are images too, scrambled like a jigsaw. Hazy light and garbled interference turn everything into a kaleidoscope of faded colours and inky shadows. Somebody stands over him, and for a moment he remembers. The dagger. The monster. The debt was paid. He's dead. He's heart has been ripped from his gaping chest.

He struggles to breathe but wonders whether oxygen is important in hell. He's no longer human, after all. Does that make him evil? Is he being summoned to carry out some unthinkable act of destruction? Could he even bring himself to do that?

'Luke,' she says, and now he's thrown into confusion. Is that Molly? Is she dead too?

'Luke,' the woman repeats. 'We're here. We're all here.'

Her voice reaches down and pulls him out of the depths, and his eyes open a little, letting painful light spill into the suffocating darkness.

He sees her hair first. The light from the window glistens from it, creating a crimson halo that he can barely maintain focus on. Then she touches his hand and he sees the tattoo, the dragon that stretches from the wrist to the tip of the pinky.

'You're alive,' she says. 'You're back with us.'

He turns to the partition between this bright room and the corridor. There are three other people with him. A woman with dark hair, Sally, sits in a chair, damp tears glistening on her cheeks. A boy stands beside her. Blonde hair, round face, eyes as blue as sapphires. He sees his own face in the kid's features. Harry smiles at him and he attempts a smile back. Behind him, standing upright but with his arm strapped to his body, his neck in a thick bandage and his face looking a little drained of colour, is Billy. He gives Raven a knowing nod.

'You had us worried there, mate,' Billy says. 'You've been through the mill a few times, haven't you?'

'You're not looking so chipper yourself,' Raven says, his voice as ragged as dust.

Lisa grips Raven's hands tight and her fingers are warm. He relishes her touch. This is the moment he's been dreaming of. Lisa and Harry, both of them here with him. He has an awful sensation that perhaps this is a dream, but even if it is, he wants it to last forever.

'The doctor said you were coming round,' Lisa says. 'I wanted us all to be with you when you did.'

'You killed her, didn't you?' Raven asks, a fractured recollection rapidly forming in his mind. 'Molly. You saved me.'

'She had it coming,' Lisa says. In her eyes, he sees the angry determination that has always drawn him to her like ravens to roadkill.

'I'm sorry I brought this on you.' He turns to the others. 'On all of you.'

Sally takes Billy's hand. 'It's over now,' she says, her staccato syllables belying the trauma she still feels. 'We made it out alive and that's all that matters.'

Harry comes to him and stands there studying his face. 'I remember you, Dad,' he says. 'Even though I was only little when she took you, I never forgot you.'

'And I never forgot you,' Raven says. 'You were on my mind every second of every minute of every day.'

Harry places his hand over both Raven's and his mother's, and the three hands form a clenched fist, an impervious ball of Raven flesh and bone that can never be severed.

'I'll never leave you again,' Raven says. 'I'll be here whenever you need me.'

Lisa's eyes flit with an emotion Raven can't place. She looks up at Billy. 'Will… you and Sally take Harry to get something from the machine? He hasn't had any breakfast.'

'Sure,' Billy says. 'Come on, kiddo.'

'Wait,' Raven says. 'Now? We've hardly had any time together.'

Lisa moves to the side and he sees there's someone else in the room, somebody he's yet to be introduced to.

'Hello Luke,' Simon Draper says. 'I wish we could have met in better circumstances.'

Billy and Sally lead Harry out the door, and in that one moment, Raven realises this isn't going to be the happy ending he's been hoping for.

'I'm so glad you're okay,' Lisa says. 'And I'm so happy we're together again.'

'But not in the way I want,' Raven says, looking up at Draper. 'No offence.'

'None taken.'

'You know I'll always be connected to you,' Lisa says. 'Always, just as you'll always be connected to me.'

'By Harry,' Raven answers. 'He'll always be the bond between us.'

Lisa nods, eyes flitting to her husband. 'But you have to realise, things have changed since you went away.'

There are those words, the tragic confirmation that Lisa isn't leaving her husband. The two of them can't be together anymore. His endless fuck ups have finally put the last nail in that particular ash-filled coffin.

'Not for me,' he says. 'You've always been the one, Lis. You will always be the one.'

Tears appear in Lisa's eyes. Yellow sun glistens on the salty dampness. She squeezes his hand, but there's something empty in her grip. In that moment, she's joined to him, but the connection between her and Draper is much, much stronger. She turns to her husband.

'Maybe Luke and I can have a moment,' she says.

Draper's lips start to form an argument, but he pulls back. 'Okay. I'll just be out in the corridor.'

Raven watches him leave, but he knows he'll never be gone. Not completely.

'I'll always love you,' Lisa says, dabbing her face with a tissue. 'I'll always be there for you.'

'But you can never be with me.'

'We're bad for each other.'

'And that's what makes us good.'

She shakes her head. 'Those times have gone. We have Harry to think about now.'

Raven has no answer for that. He knows it's true. Harry is everything.

'I can see him?' he asks.

'Every day if you want to.'

'And your husband will be okay with that.'

'We've spoken about it,' she says, glancing at Draper who's sitting outside. 'He knows you'll be in our lives. He's not thrilled, but he also knows it's a deal breaker.'

A tiny laugh slips out of Raven's lips, causing the pain in his chest to flare up. 'You never did take any shit,' he winces.

She laughs back. 'And I never will.'

'I have changed,' he says. 'You might not believe it, but something happened to me down in that hole. Something weird. The bad part of me, the dark part, I think that's gone forever.'

Lisa shakes her head. 'All I saw was a crazy bitch about to kill you.'

Right then, he realises she hadn't witnessed any of it. Not the inhuman creature from the rock; not his father's ghost; not the black, pulsing heart.

Lisa peers into his eyes, studying him, looking for any sign of weakness. He lets her in, allows her to explore him, because he no longer has anything to hide. Just as he thinks she'll swim inside his psyche for eternity, her red lips break into a wide smile.

'I don't know,' she says, 'I think I can still see a hint of the dark half you've always had. The naughty half.'

'No,' he replies, desperately trying to close the hatch to his soul. 'It's gone. I swear.'

'I sincerely hope not,' she says, offering a lopsided grin. 'Because the darkness is what makes you *you,* Luke. Keep a little of it if you want, just for me. Just don't drown us all in it.'

He laughs again, but this time it's laced with irony. He can never tell Lisa that Molly ripped the darkness from him, because how would he ever explain it in a way that didn't sound like lunacy? He just knows it to be true, just like he knows that he and Lisa can only ever be lovers in his imagination.

'I'll always love you,' she says.

'I'll always love you, too.'

She bends down and kisses him on the lips, and for a moment, at least, it's like old times. He relishes the taste of her, the softness of her lips, the gentle flicker of her tongue. When it ends, he keeps hold of the memory. He'll never let it go.

'I'll see you tomorrow?' he asks.

'I'll be here,' she replies.

'Bring a cheeseburger.'

She smiles and her face is so bright, it drives the shadows from the room, sending them to a place from where, perhaps, they might never return.

*

Harry stands by the vending machine and studies the assortment of chocolate bars. He's angry with his mum for sending him away. He just wants to be with his dad. He's grown up not knowing him, but now he's back with them, he wants to spend every second with him. Even though they don't know each other, not really, he feels the connection, the bond that only blood can have. Real blood.

'What are you having, Haz?' Billy asks, fishing in his pocket with his good hand for change. 'Pick whatever you want. My treat.'

'You can't just give him whatever he wants,' Sally says. 'What about his teeth?'

'He's got plenty of 'em. What's one little molar gonna hurt?'

Harry's not paying attention to the chocolate bars. He's still thinking about his dad and what his mum's about to tell him. That's why she sent them away. That's why he's standing by a stupid vending machine looking at dumb chocolate bars. He doesn't even like chocolate.

'Billy? Billy West?'

Harry looks up to see a tall man in work clothes on the other side of the waiting room with a bloodied bandage around his head.

'Jonny?' Billy exclaims. 'Jonny Pinner, as I live and breathe. You remember Jonny, Sal? I rewired a few houses for him.'

'I remember,' Sally replies. 'Bought us all an Indian takeaway when the job was done.'

'Cost me an arm and a leg, too, if I remember rightly,' Jonny says, and before Harry knows it, he's standing on his own, wondering whether he could just slip off without the pair of them noticing.

'I'd go for the Snickers if I were you,' somebody says. 'Although in my day, they were called Marathons.'

Harry looks up. There's an older man standing beside him: grey hair, grey beard, checked shirt. He looks just like his dad, if his dad was a pensioner.

'Not hungry,' Harry replies.

'It's understandable,' the man says. 'You've had a trauma. A thing like that, it can make you lose your appetite.'

Harry's still thinking about what his mum is saying at that very moment, knowing in the pit of his stomach that she won't be getting back with his dad. There's only one reason she would choose not to. Simon.

'You know who I am?' the man asks.

'I think so. You're my granddad, although I thought you were dead.'

'Some things can't die,' Sam replies. 'Memories, for example. History books. Old photographs.'

'That's how I know who you are. I've seen some pictures of you with my dad.'

Sam smiles. 'You look just like him, you know?'

'My mum always says that,' Harry nods. 'Except I've got blonde hair, like my mum's when she forgets to dye it.'

Sam laughs. 'Isn't it strange how adults like to pretend they're something they're not?'

Like Mum and Simon, Harry thinks to himself. *She doesn't love Simon and neither do I.*

'I can help you, if you like,' Sam says. 'With that little problem of yours.'

Harry's brow creases into a tight little knot. 'Can you read my mind?'

'You're my grandson, Harry. I know everything about you.'

'Even what I'm thinking?'

'Even what you're thinking.'

Something about that comforts Harry. He likes the idea of having a conspirator to the dark thoughts that linger in his head. It gives him a kind of validation.

'How would you help me?' Harry asks.

'I can't share that just yet,' Sam replies. 'Let's just say you won't be disappointed.'

Harry's heart leaps. Is his granddad suggesting he could get his mum and dad back together?

'Yes, I am,' Sam says. 'That's exactly what I'm suggesting.'

'I don't know,' Harry replies. 'Mum would get angry.'

'What's new? Your mum's always angry.'

Harry laughs. His granddad really does know everything.

'There's just one catch, though,' Sam adds. 'Just one little detail we have to iron out.'

'You want money?' Harry asks, feeling despondent. 'Because I don't have any.'

Sam mocks disbelief. 'What kind of granddad would I be if I took money from my only grandson?'

Harry blushes. He shouldn't have said that. 'I'm sorry.'

'No need to apologise. Apologies are for the weak. There is something I want, however.'

Harry's curiosity peaks, so he asks, 'What is it?'

His granddad's eyes flit back and forth, as if a second pair of eyelids, milky like cataracts, have just closed and opened like a camera shutter.

'You have to commit yourself to me.'

'But I'm your grandson. Aren't I committed to you anyway? Isn't that what family is?'

'I guess so,' Sam says, laughing. 'You really are a smart boy.'

Harry laughs too.

'But this commitment is a little stronger, Harry,' his granddad continues. 'It would make us really close. Closer than you've ever been to anybody else.'

'You'd be like an older brother?' Harry asks. 'Like, much older?'

'I'll ignore the casual ageism, if you don't mind,' Sam replies. 'But yes, very much like that.'

Harry thinks about it. His mum and Simon had spoken about having more kids, a thought that makes him want to puke, but having an older brother? That's something he's never really thought about.

'I guess that would be pretty cool,' he says.

'Then you just have to say it,' Sam replies.

'Say what?'

'Just five little words.'

'What sort of words?'

'I commit myself to you.'

Harry thinks that's simple enough, even if it is a bit weird. The deal seems a little lop-sided, though. Firstly, his granddad will get rid of Simon, which is awesome. Secondly, he'll convince his mum and dad to get back together so they can be a family again. Thirdly, he'll become his older brother while still being his granddad. It seems like a no-lose situation.

'I'll do it,' he says.

'You'll do what?'

'I commit myself to you.'

Something happens then. His granddad's skin flickers grey and black, as if his body has become ash. Something appears in his chest, like a human face but without eyes. Then, even before Harry can comprehend what just happened, everything's back to normal again.

'Shall we go,' Sam asks, holding out his hand.

'Go where?'

'To do what you asked me to do.'

Excitement builds in Harry's belly, but then he remembers the two people who are supposed to be looking after him. 'What about Billy and Sally?'

'Do they look like they're worried about where you are?'

Harry glances at the two of them. They're still laughing and joking with the man with the bandage around his skull.

He shakes his head. 'I guess they'll find me soon enough.'

'That's right,' Sam replies, looking down at Harry's hand as he slips it into his own. 'Pretty soon, everybody gets found. Sometimes it just takes a little longer than we'd like.'

They walk along the corridor, a sea of dark scales trailing behind them as blackened hands reach through cracks in the walls, stretching and grasping like the fingers of starvation. In the waiting room, the world grows dark and the flames of a place once forgotten burn eternal. Somewhere in the distance, the black heart is beating, and its call is as powerful as the loudest scream.

A NOTE FROM THE AUTHOR

I started my first novel, Pale Face and The Raven, way back in 2018. Back then, when I was still a walking cadaver for the new corporate army, I could never have dreamed I would one day get to do this writing thing for a living. A lot of things have changed since those halcyon, pre-COVID days, but the one thing that has remained constant is my love for dark fiction.

The genre manifests itself in many forms, but for that first book, the thing that spoke to me the most was a horror-crime genre-mash. My protagonist, Luke Raven, was originally called Luke Regan — a nod to my decidedly British seventies upbringing (anybody remember The Sweeney?) — but as soon as the tone of the book became apparent, I figured my flawed hero needed a much darker moniker. What's darker than a raven, after all? A raven with a suntan, I hear you holler (groan).

I never intended for this horror-crime series to be a trilogy, at least not at first, but as the characters developed and I grew to like Lisa, Billy, Randall, Ronnie and the rest of Raven's motley crew more and more, I began to wonder if there really was more to this story than the slightly fever-dream plotline of Pale Face. Queue book two, the support of a growing collection of loyal readers, and the introduction of a little-known wannabe cannibal called Molly Staker.

I took some time off from Raven after The Hawk to write a couple of books I needed to get out there (The Faraway People and What Doesn't Cure You. Check them out if you haven't already), but Luke Raven was always in the back of my mind. I'd left him hanging by a thread at the end of The Hawk, and although I had an idea where the jump point of a possible third book might be, it didn't really take shape until I started typing. It might surprise you to know that I originally killed Molly off in that rather tragic prologue, but our loveable baddie refused to die.

Needless to say, I'm pleased she made a return in the dramatic final act, and I'm even more pleased that she and Lisa fought it out to the death. I think there's something poetic in that.

I need to give some thanks before I sign off, firstly to my wife, Jo, who acted as first editor for Black Heart; my children, Jayden and Harley, and their partners, James (who also happens to be my very talented cover artist) and Georgia, who give me moral support on a daily basis; my mum and dad, without whom I'd have never taken up writing in the first place; the many fellow indie authors I've met over the years; and my beta readers for this book (Niamh, Cressida, Jenny, and Michelle), all of whom picked up things I either hadn't spotted or hadn't paid enough attention to.

Lastly, to all my readers, whether you're on the mailing list, you follow my infrequently updated socials, or you just take a casual interest. All support counts, no matter how it's provided. Every writer will tell you the same thing — without it, the nagging doubts start to become a series of spiteful jabs in the temple, some of which can be quite bloody and painful.

I can unequivocably confirm that this is the end of the Raven series (said with almost believable sincerity), and while I'm sad to let Luke go (my wife even shed a few tears after that epilogue), I'm happy that it ends the way it does.

Anyway, as always, happy reading, and keep those pages turning. The sustainable energy created from your page flips (or eBook scrolls if that's your thing) is what keeps the lights burning bright.

Take care,

Stacey

ABOUT STACEY DIGHTON

Stacey Dighton is an author of horror and fantasy fiction. He lives with his wife in the south-east of England and has two adult children. He loves reading great fiction, listening to rock music, playing guitar and travelling — sometimes all at the same time.

ALSO BY STACEY DIGHTON:

Pale Face and The Raven (Raven Part 1)
The Hawk and The Raven (Raven Part 2)
The Maidens of Fey and Other Dark Matter
The Faraway People
What Doesn't Cure You

www.staceydightonstoryteller.com

Printed in Dunstable, United Kingdom

72319458R00221